"I should have given you something to sleep in," Linc said.

"No need." It was much too easy to imagine slipping one of Linc's T-shirts over her head. Of course, it had been a fantasy that had fueled her teenage self for a long time. "It's one night. I'm fine like this."

"Have you slept at all?"

She nodded and stood. The spacious nursery felt much too close. "I think I'll fix Layla a small bottle. Maybe she'll sleep afterward. You want to hold her?"

He immediately shoved his hands into his front pockets.

She averted her eyes from the fine line of dark hair running downward from the flat indent of his navel and headed toward the doorway. "I'll take that as a no."

"She's happy with you."

He flipped on lights as they made their way to the kitchen. Before Maddie could mix up more formula, Linc did.

She sat on one of the bar stools at the island and watched.

And wondered some more.

About him and Jax.

About the nursery.

About how the bare skin stretching over his shoulders would feel beneath her fingertips...

* * *

Return to the Double C:
Under the big blue Wyoming sky,
this family discovers true love

YULETIDE BABY
BARGAIN

BY
ALLISON LEIGH

First Published in Great Britain 2017
By Mills & Boon, an imprint of HarperCollins*Publishers*
1 London Bridge Street, London, SE1 9GF

© 2017 Allison Lee Johnson

ISBN: 978-0-263-92353-7

23-1217

MIX
Paper from
responsible sources
FSC™ C007454

This book is produced from independently certified FSC™ paper to ensure responsible forest management.

For more information visit: www.harpercollins.co.uk/green

Printed and bound in Spain
by CPI, Barcelona

A frequent name on bestseller lists, **Allison Leigh**'s high point as a writer is hearing from readers that they laughed, cried or lost sleep while reading her books. She credits her family with great patience for the time she's parked at her computer, and for blessing her with the kind of love she wants her readers to share with the characters living in the pages of her books. Contact her at www.allisonleigh.com.

For beautiful little Monroe Lea,
who has been born into a wonderful family.
Welcome to the world!

Chapter One

"Are you a social worker or not?"

Maddie Templeton's jaw tightened at the impatient words being spat at her through the phone line. She wished she could pretend she didn't recognize the owner of the voice.

This was the last thing she needed. She'd already spent the entire day dealing with tying up troublesome details at work before a forced two-week vacation. Then she'd rushed home to change into somewhat date-worthy clothing and driven the thirty miles over winding roads from Braden to Weaver, where she was supposed to meet a man named Morton for dinner.

Only Morton had stood her up.

Instead of having a date for the first time in months—which was a generous estimate, if she were truthful—she'd ended up spending the evening with her grandmother. Not that Vivian wasn't entertaining enough. She just wasn't the kind of company that Maddie had been hoping for.

Now, it was after ten o'clock, and after returning to the house she shared with her sisters—knowing *they* were probably out with guys who'd never dream of standing them up—she just didn't feel in the mood to deal with Lincoln Swift's phone call.

Because she couldn't stand Lincoln Swift.

If only she'd let the phone continue ringing as she'd walked in the door. Eventually, it would have gone to voice mail, and she'd be happily trespassing in Greer's bathroom by now, watching her sister's claw-foot tub fill with hot water while she decided what task to tackle first on her use-it-or-lose-it vacation time.

Instead, she leaned against the half-finished kitchen cabinets—the do-it-yourself refinishing job had been stalled for months—and fantasized about hanging up on him. After telling him just how little she thought of him.

After all these years, turnabout *would* be sweet.

But instead of letting every bit of her day's frustration out on the man, she swallowed it down. "Yes, Linc, I am a social worker," she said evenly. "What's the problem?" There would *have* to be a problem to make Linc ever reach out to the likes of her.

"I don't want to get into it on the phone. Just come to the house."

"I'm sorry." Even though her teeth clenched and her hand tightened around the receiver, she managed to channel the dulcet tone that Greer used in the courtroom before skewering someone. "What house?"

As if Maddie didn't know perfectly well that he'd moved into the grand old mansion once owned by his grandmother, Ernestine Swift, after her death. Maddie knew every corner of that mansion, too. But only because as a child, she'd accompanied her mother every week when Meredith cleaned the place for Ernestine.

That was how she'd met Linc and his brother, Jax, in the first place.

They'd chased each other all over that place.

Until Linc had decided he was too old for such nonsense and pretty much seemed to forget Maddie existed.

Then it had been just Jax and Maddie.

Until Linc had decided *that* was nonsense, too.

"My brother's gone and done it again." Linc's voice was tight. "Are you going to help me or not?"

When she and Jax had dated, they'd been in high school, but even then Maddie hadn't been serious about him. He was a lot of fun. But good boyfriend material? Definitely not.

Aside from her sisters, though, he'd been just about her best friend in the world. Until Linc made sure she knew she wasn't good enough for Jax in any way, shape or form.

That had been thirteen years ago, and it still held the record as the single most humiliating moment of her life—far outstripping being stood up by a computer programmer named Morton.

She dropped the dulcet tones for her usual frankness. "Jax is thirty years old, Linc. He's a grown man. Whatever he's gone and done, he can undo." Jax had had plenty of practice, after all. And it wouldn't be legal trouble. If it were, Linc definitely wouldn't have called her. Swift Oil, his family business, had a phalanx of lawyers on the payroll.

"He's not *here*. He's out of town." Linc sounded like he was talking through his teeth, too, and it took no effort at all to conjure an image of his face.

Which annoyed her to no end.

Even though she ran into Jax fairly often around town, she'd had only a few dealings with Linc since that long-ago mortifying day.

He ran an oil company.

She was a social worker.

Since he'd moved back to Braden when his grandmother died, they'd rarely run into each other. Which was saying something because, on a good day, the population there didn't break 5,000. The last time she'd seen him in person had been at Ernestine's funeral. Three years ago.

She'd offered her condolences and left the very second that she could.

She squared up the stack of paint chips sitting on the counter that her sisters had been squabbling over for a month, trying to block the memory of the grief that she'd seen in his face that day. "If Jax isn't there, then what are you even calling me for?"

"Because his kid *is* here," he said even more sharply. "Isn't that what you deal with? Kids left to fend for themselves because their parents can't be bothered?"

She straightened abruptly from her slouch, and felt her red sweater catch on a nail. He could have been describing his and Jax's parents, but she had the sense not to point that out. She carefully unhooked the threads of her sweater before they unraveled. "Jax has a child?" She knew she sounded shocked, even though it wasn't such a shocking thought.

Jax loved women, after all. He'd never been without at least one on his arm from the time he'd entered puberty. But he'd always claimed he'd never get caught by one the way his dad had been.

Linc made a sound that wasn't quite an oath. "Just

get over here, would you please? I didn't know who else to call."

She grimaced. "You must be desperate, indeed."

"I'll leave the gate open," he said flatly.

A moment later, all she heard was the dial tone.

He'd hung up on her.

"I'll leave the gate open," she muttered, hanging up harder than necessary. Typical Linc. Issuing edicts as if he had a divine right to do so.

It would serve him right if she ignored him. She *was* supposed to be on vacation, after all.

But what about the child?

Jax's child?

She huffed out a breath and left the kitchen, returning to the foyer where she'd left her boots. The artificial Christmas tree that her sister Ali bought was sitting in its enormous box, blocking half the room. None of them were thrilled with having an artificial tree instead of a fresh-cut one, but Ali's overdeveloped sense of safety had prevailed. She was a police officer and had just dealt with a family home burning down from a tree that went up in flames. Neither Greer nor Maddie had had the heart to argue with her. They'd both promised Ali they'd help put it up this weekend.

Maddie sat down on the box, pulled on her leather boots and zipped them up to her knees.

Despite the weatherman's dire predictions, it still hadn't snowed yet, but the temperatures were already cold and bitter. She wrapped a scarf around her neck on top of her coat before she let herself back out into the night. Her car was parked in the driveway; both engine and interior were still warm from the drive back from Weaver.

At least she wouldn't have to go so far to get to the

old Swift mansion. It used to sit on the eastern edge of Braden, but due to progress, the town limits had been creeping past it for years. Now it was more like a crown jewel in the center of town.

When she arrived, the ornate iron gate guarding the long drive to the house was open, just as Linc had promised.

She drove through it, and memories of climbing on the thing pulled at her. The first time, Maddie's mother had been horrified. But Ernestine—seeming old even then—had merely laughed and waved it off. How could Maddie be expected to not climb on it when her grandsons were doing the same thing?

Maddie rubbed her forehead, trying and failing to block out the images of her, Jax and Linc running around that first summer. She and Jax had been six, Linc a much older and wiser eleven.

By the time she and Jax were eleven, Meredith was no longer cleaning the mansion for Ernestine. But Maddie's friendship with Jax—and her fascination with Linc, who'd totally lost interest in them by that point—had lived on. For a few more years, anyway. Until he'd made so very plain what he thought of her.

Her headlights swept over the stone wall that ran alongside the narrow driveway as it curved its way to the mansion sitting atop the hill.

Her mouth felt dry.

Which was just plain stupid.

The drive swelled out into a circle in front of the house before narrowing again as it continued off into the darkness. She hadn't been out there in more than a decade, but she assumed there was still an enormous detached garage next to the gardener's shack.

She parked in the circle and took a deep breath before

getting out of the car and reluctantly climbing the brick steps. As soon as she reached the door, she could hear the wailing from inside and her gloved hand paused on the lion-shaped doorknocker.

It was the distinct wail of a baby.

She started when the door opened, the doorknocker yanked out of her lax fingers before she could even properly use it.

"Took you long enough," Linc greeted her as he shoved the infant car seat he was holding into her arms.

She rapidly adjusted her hold on it when he let go and backed away. Like he couldn't get away fast enough.

From the baby? Or from Maddie?

She averted her gaze, but not fast enough to keep from noticing that his disheveled blondish-brown hair showed a sprinkle of gray on the sides that hadn't been there three years ago, and the faint lines arrowing out from the corners of his hazel eyes weren't quite so faint anymore.

And he looked better than ever.

Dammit.

She channeled Greer's dulcet tones again. "Good to see you, too, Linc." She smiled insincerely and looked down at the wailing baby. A girl, if the pink blanket was anything to go by. "Where's her mom?"

"Who the hell knows?" He shoved his long fingers through his hair. "I came home and that—" he waved at the infant seat "—was sitting all alone on the doorstep."

She stepped inside and set the carrier on the old-fashioned table in the middle of the spacious foyer. After dumping her purse on the table, too, she delved beneath the pink blanket, relieved to feel warmth coming off the crying baby. "How long ago?"

"You're not shocked?"

She deftly released the harness strapping the baby into the seat and picked her up. "By a baby being left somewhere or by *you* calling *me* about it?" She didn't wait for his answer as she tried to soothe the baby. "Unfortunately, I can't say this is my first experience with an abandoned baby. How long ago did you get home?"

He was wearing a dark blazer over a white shirt and blue jeans. Date wear.

She hated the fact that she'd even noticed. Or that she cared.

The baby was still wailing, so hard that she was hiccupping. "It's okay, sweetheart." Maddie jiggled the baby and blindly swept her hand inside the car seat, finally finding a pacifier wedged under a corner of the fabric lining. She touched it to the baby's lips and she latched on to it greedily.

"Silence," Linc muttered. "Thank God."

Maddie refrained from telling him that he could have found the pacifier, too, if he'd tried. Through the fleecy polka-dotted sleeper the baby was wearing, she could feel the diaper was heavy. "So? How long ago?"

"Less than an hour ago." Linc raked his fingers through his hair again and paced on the other side of the foyer table. "A few minutes before I called you the first time. It took three tries before you bothered to answer."

"Don't make it sound like *I've* done something wrong," she said. "I was out, too. It is allowed, you know. Even for social workers."

And those too lowly to consort with the vaunted Swift family.

She pressed her lips against the child's temple, banishing the thought.

The baby's forehead felt sweaty, but that could have

just been from all her crying. "Is there a diaper bag or something?"

"Or something." He set a small plastic garbage bag on the table next to the car seat.

Maddie quickly reached for it and their hands accidentally brushed. She ignored the heat that immediately ran under her skin and tipped the bag over. A half-dozen diapers and a thin container of baby wipes scattered across the table. A small can of powdered baby formula and an empty, capped baby bottle rolled out.

She grabbed a diaper and the wipes and marched around the table, heading into the house. "Go make a bottle with the formula," she told him. "I'll get her diaper changed, and then I'll call my uncle."

Linc stared after Maddie's departing form. Her hair was as dark as it had always been, but it was longer now than she'd used to wear it, tumbling well past the bright red scarf wrapped around the collar of her short black coat. Below the coat, her hips—trim as ever— were outlined in black denim jeans tucked into her flat-heeled brown boots.

She always had liked wearing boots. Not the cowboy kind, either.

He grabbed the container of formula and the bottle. Not that he knew what to do with them. "Why do you want to call your uncle?"

"He's a pediatrician," she answered as if it should be obvious. She'd laid the baby on the antique bench situated against one wall of the living room. Even though the baby's legs and arms were waving around, Maddie competently peeled back the neck-to-toe outfit, revealing a tiny white T-shirt that didn't reach past the baby's rosy belly and a fat-looking disposable diaper. "Poor thing is soaked." She sent him a chastising look as she slipped a fresh diaper under the existing one.

"Save that look for the person who dumped off the kid on my front porch."

She pulled out a wet wipe from the plastic container. "How long do you think she'd been there before you got home?"

"God only knows." His first reaction when he'd realized what was on his porch had been to call the police. He'd had his phone in his hands when he'd spotted the note tucked next to the kid's head.

After reading it, he'd learned that the little girl's name was Layla and that she belonged to Jax. Supposedly. Which meant there was no way he could call the police.

And there was no way to reach Jax, either, since he'd found his brother's cell phone sitting dead in the kitchen where Jax had forgotten it.

He'd found the phone a week ago.

But his brother had been gone longer than that.

He focused on the top of Maddie's head while she undid the wet diaper.

He knew she still hated him. And why. But even if he'd had to do things over again, he would still choose the same path.

"I was busy all day at the office. Worked there until about seven, then went straight on to a dinner engagement." It was as good a way as any to describe the irritating evening spent with his parents. They'd thrown a party, celebrating their thirty-fifth wedding anniversary.

Linc might have celebrated it, too, if he didn't know what a joke their marriage really was. If Blake Swift wasn't cheating on Jolene, then Jolene was cheating on

Blake. Except for the delight they took in making each other miserable, Linc still couldn't understand why they remained together. He also would have accused Jax of making a getaway before the party, except Linc knew perfectly well that his brother couldn't care less what their parents did.

"There was nobody here at the house to notice anything?"

"No."

She'd finished diapering the baby. She kept her palm on the baby's chest as she glanced up at him. "No?"

He frowned. Her pretty eyes were as dark as chocolate and yet the doubt in them was as clear as a spotlight. Another thing that hadn't changed over the years. Everything going on inside Maddie's head was broadcast through those expressive eyes. Her two sisters had the exact same eyes—the exact same looks, in fact, since they were identical triplets—but he'd never thought their emotions were as transparent as Maddie's.

And he'd never looked at Greer or Ali and felt a slow burn inside.

"Who do you think *should* have been here?"

She looked back at the baby. "I figured you'd have a housekeeper or something." She slipped the baby's kicking legs back into her stretchy clothes. "At least she seems to have been warm enough. I don't see any signs of frostbite. She still needs an exam, though." She folded the used diaper and wipe into a ball, secured it with the sticky diaper tapes and held it out.

He was glad his hands were full. He lifted them—formula can in one, empty bottle in the other.

She rolled her eyes and picked up the baby, nestling her in one arm as she stood. "Kitchen still in the same place?" Not waiting for an answer, she walked past him and around the staircase.

He followed. "Where would it have gone?"

She ignored the question. When she reached the kitchen, she tossed the diaper into the trash bin located in the walk-in pantry, then returned to stop in front of him. She took the can from his fingers and set it on the wide soapstone-topped island. Then she took the bottle and before he knew it, she was holding out the baby.

Layla watched him with wide blue eyes. She was going at the pacifier as if it might actually produce milk.

"Oh for heaven's sake, Linc!" Maddie sounded exasperated. "Just take her. She won't break."

He wasn't so sure. He gingerly placed his hands near Maddie's, underneath the baby's arms. As soon as he did, Maddie moved hers away. She went to the sink and turned on the water to wash her hands.

The baby was a lot lighter than he expected, considering how heavy she'd been when strapped inside the car seat.

She opened her mouth, the pacifier dropped out and she let out an ear-piercing wail. For such a tiny thing, she made a helluva racket.

He wasn't a man who panicked easily, yet that was all he'd done since he'd realized there was a baby on his doorstep.

"Nope." He pushed the kid back at Maddie. "No way."

"Oh, for the love of Pete." She took the baby back. "Get me the pacifier."

It had rolled under the scrolled wooden edge of the island. He grabbed it, handing it to her.

"Wash it, would you please?" She handed him the bottle. "And this, too."

He joined her at the sink. "Aren't they supposed to be sterilized or something?"

"In a perfect world, probably. But who knows what other conditions this baby has endured. For now, hot water and a good wash with soap will have to do." Without waiting for him to finish washing the pacifier and bottle, she tucked one wet finger into the baby's mouth.

The crying stopped.

But that was the only bit of relief he got.

"Now that my hands are busy, you can make her a bottle," Maddie ordered. "Directions are on the side of the can."

He peered at the small print on the can. He'd left his reading glasses in his jacket and it was impossible to read.

Maddie was pacing around the island, bouncing the baby a little with each step. "How do you know for sure she's Jax's baby, anyway? Do you know her name?"

"Layla. And of course she's Jax's."

"He told you?"

"He didn't have to." Glad for the excuse, he left the can on the counter and went back out to the foyer. When he returned, he had his reading glasses as well as the note. He unfolded it and spread it on the counter so she could see. "This was stuck in the car seat with her."

Maddie pursed her lips as she studied the single line of looping handwriting. "Jaxie, please take care of Layla for me," she read. Her eyes lifted to his for a moment. "Jaxie?"

"You know how women are with Jax." Even Maddie had been susceptible to his brother, once. Until Linc set her straight.

"The note isn't signed."

He gave her a look. "Presumably, *Jaxie* knows who the mother of his own child is."

"But he obviously didn't tell you about her."

"Yeah, well, we don't really talk to each other a lot anymore."

"How long has he been out of town?"

He shrugged. "Little over a week."

"He still lives here, doesn't he?"

"Yes. So?"

"So how can you live in the same house and not talk to each other?"

He wished he hadn't said anything. "It's not germane."

Her eyebrows rose. "Oh. Well, if it's not *germane*." She gave him a wide-eyed stare and grabbed the washed pacifier, trading it for the tip of her index finger in the baby's mouth. Then she took the baby bottle and filled it part way with tap water, added a few scoops from the can of formula without so much as a glance at the tiny print, and screwed on the nipple. She shook the bottle vigorously and held it under running hot water. "While you're feeding her, I'll call my uncle and check in with my boss to let him know what's going on. I have enough autonomy to set up the emergency placement, but Ray's still going to want to know about it. He's a stickler that way. But no matter where the placement ends up being, Layla still needs an exam first, particularly considering the way she was left. Just because I didn't see any signs of injury, it's not a medical assessment. And Uncle David's qualified to make one, which means maybe we can avoid having to involve the hospital, too. Are you *sure* you don't know who her mother might be?"

"If I did, I wouldn't have needed to call you." He tossed his reading glasses onto the island alongside the note. "And what the hell is 'emergency placement' supposed to mean?"

Chapter Two

Ignoring Linc's annoyed tone, Maddie turned off the water and dried the bottle with a towel she pulled from the drawer next to the sink, all with one hand. The white cloth was clean and crisp, just like the towels that Ernestine had kept there when Maddie was a child. She wondered if Linc had changed anything at all around the house since his grandmother died.

The black-framed glasses were definitely a new addition for him, though—and an unwelcome, unexpectedly sexy one.

"Emergency placement," she repeated smoothly. "It's what it sounds like." Layla's eyes were fastened on the bottle and she wrapped her little starfish hands around it as soon as Maddie put the nipple near her lips.

The baby's eyes nearly rolled back in her head as she guzzled the lukewarm formula. "Poor baby. You're so hungry." Anger threatened to boil inside her over the baby's neglect, but she knew better than to let it get the best of her. She couldn't be effective in her job if she let herself be consumed by anger or horror over the situations she saw.

When she looked at Linc again, his brows were pulled even closer together above his long, narrow nose.

She definitely shouldn't take any pleasure in antagonizing him. Not under these circumstances.

"Emergency placement is a temporary measure while the authorities have a chance to investigate the whole situation," she explained calmly. "Once that's done, our office will make the report to the prosecutor's office. If there are criminal charges involved, he'll probably handle the case. If there aren't, he'll likely leave it in our department's hands to make a recommendation to the judge—"

"Judge! Who said anything about a judge?"

She watched him for a moment. Linc had always been much harder to read than Jax. But the fact that he was more alarmed than ever was obvious. She just wasn't entirely certain why. Despite the past, he'd called her to take care of the situation, and that was what she was doing. "No matter what led to Layla being left on your doorstep, this situation is going to involve the family court," she said a little more gently. "Judge Stokes is a good guy—"

"I don't care how good a guy he is. There's no need for a judge. No need for your boss, for that matter."

"If you didn't ask me here to do my *job*, then what is it that you expect me to do?"

He gestured, encompassing her and the baby in his short, impatient wave. "What you're doing. Taking care of the kid."

"I'm not a babysitter, Linc! And this *kid* is an infant.

Two, three months old, tops, if I had to guess." She flicked the fingers of her free hand against the note still lying on the island. "And assuming that can be trusted, she also has a name. Layla. Aside from that, we know nothing for certain."

"Jax—"

"Jax isn't here. So I'll tell you the same thing Judge Stokes is going to tell you. This child appears to have been abandoned and—"

"No." He crossed the room in two strides and took the baby out of her arms.

The bottle fell out of Maddie's grasp and rolled across the table. Layla's eyes rounded and she opened her mouth to protest loudly, but he caught it before it rolled onto the floor and shoved the nipple quickly back into her mouth. The baby subsided, blissfully guzzling once again, even though Linc was essentially holding her like a football under his arm. "You're not sticking her with a bunch of strangers."

"I don't even know how to respond to that." Layla was kicking her legs so enthusiastically, Maddie was afraid the infant would squirt out from Linc's grasp like a wet bar of soap. "She's going to spit up everything she drinks. Give her to me."

"No."

She lifted her eyebrows. She wasn't a seventeen-year-old girl who could be easily brushed off by him anymore. She'd cut her teeth in adult probation before transferring into family services. *"No?"*

"If you're not going to help, then just go home." He turned away from her, walking out of the room. Layla's legs bounced.

Maddie followed after him, skipping twice to dart around him and block his momentum. "You don't get it!"

He frowned down at her. "I get that you're in my way."

"You can't unring the bell here. I can't pretend you didn't call me." She tried to slide Layla out of his grip.

He caught one of her hands in his, holding it away.

"Linc! I have a legal obligation to rep—" She broke off when he squeezed her fingers. Not enough to hurt, but enough to express himself. His hazel eyes were hard and his jaw was so tight, it looked white.

"To do nothing," he ground out. "She's my *niece*."

Maddie exhaled, feeling a sudden wave of sympathy that she hoped was more from exhaustion and goodwill toward his brother than because of tender feelings for Linc himself. "You *think* she's your niece," she corrected in an even tone. Based on a note that said nothing of substance.

"She was left in my care."

"Jax's care, actually. And you're saying he's out of town. Have you tried calling him? To see what he has to say about the baby?"

"He'll be home soon." Linc's tone was flat.

She didn't believe him.

"Do you even know where he is?"

His expression turned darker, his jawline whiter. "No."

She sighed.

There was no earthly reason why she should want to help him. Yet that was exactly what she realized she was going to do. Or try to do. It would involve an end-run around her boss, but he was already going to be annoyed with her anyway, so she supposed she might as well be hung for a sheep as a lamb.

"I'll call Archer." Her brother, though personally exasperating, was a well-respected attorney practicing in Braden. "He used to clerk for Judge Stokes back in the day and they have a good relationship. Hopefully good enough to cut out some of the steps and get you appointed temporary custodian right from the start."

"Perfect."

"He can *try*. It's still a longshot," she warned. "You're a single man with no proof right now that this baby is your niece, so you don't have that relationship on your side. I'm on a first-name basis with all of the individuals around this region who are qualified foster care providers, and there's not a single, unmarried man among them. So—"

"I don't care who or what they are. I'm not some perfect stranger! Everyone in this town knows the Swift family."

Not necessarily a good thing. She kept the thought to herself. "Swift Oil pumps a lot of money into Wyoming," she allowed. "But—"

"But nothing. That should at least buy me enough time with the judge so that I can prove she's my niece!"

He wouldn't be able to buy anything else with the judge. She had plenty of experience with Horvald Stokes. The judge cared about one thing—the well-being of a child. Period. "Without the mother here to say anything, you'll need a DNA test to prove it."

"Then I'll get a freaking DNA test!" His voice rose. "How long can that take?" Layla's face crumpled and she started crying again.

And Linc looked like he was about to lose it.

Maddie decided not to tell him that Layla would need the test, as well. And that would require the judge's order, too. "I'll call Archer," she said again and this time, successfully lifted the baby out of Linc's arms. She offered Layla the bottle, but the baby turned her fussy face away. Maddie put her against her shoulder as she walked back out to the foyer, rubbing her back. "It's okay, sweetie. What a night you've had, huh?"

"That's one way of putting it."

She worked open her purse and started rummaging inside. "I wasn't talking to you."

As if she would ever call *him* sweetie.

Her fingers latched on to her cell phone and she dragged it out of her purse. "When did you start needing glasses?"

She didn't bother dialing her brother's home phone. There was no way he'd be home on a Friday night. Archer was the only person she knew who liked his women more than Jaxon Swift did. Instead, she dialed his cell phone and hoped that he would at least be somewhere that the signal reached. Around their area of the state, such a thing was never guaranteed.

"Why?"

She tucked the phone against her shoulder as she bounced the baby and started unwinding her winter scarf. "Just trying to make conversation."

"I don't need conversation. I need results." He left the foyer.

She made a face at his departing back and finally freed the scarf. She dropped it on top of her purse and started unbuttoning her coat.

"This better be good," Archer's voice suddenly came on the line. "I was in the middle of something."

"Middle of some*one* more like," she said. "I need a favor." She quickly told him the situation. "Do you mind calling the judge for me? See if he's willing to even consider it?"

"What's your boss say about it?"

She mentally crossed her fingers. "He said it's my call." As lies went, it wasn't the worst she could tell.

Under ordinary circumstances, Raymond Marx trusted Maddie's judgment.

But she had only had a few days off in the last three years. And he'd been adamant. The rules required a minimum of two continuous weeks off every year. She was well past that. Which meant that in this instance, her boss would say she was on vacation and should hand off anything even remotely approaching a case to one of her associates for the next two weeks. Period. She was supposed to be out living her life. Having a date or two. He'd even set her up with his buddy, Morton. Because, despite being a stickler for the rules, Ray really did care about his people.

"Are you going to help me or not?"

"Stay by the phone," her brother said in answer, and disconnected.

"Nothing like being surrounded by abrupt men," she murmured. She managed to shrug out of her coat and the baby finally gave up a hard little burp.

"Attagirl." Maddie shifted her hold on Layla and offered the bottle once more. "Pretty much my thinking, too, where they're concerned."

"Where who are concerned?"

Of course Linc would choose that moment to return.

She rounded the foyer table, for some reason wanting to keep it between them. "Nothing important. This looks like the same table that your grandmother had when my mother and I were here. My mom used to let me dust the base because I was always begging to help." Until she'd learned cleaning was really a chore and not a game.

"It is the same table. No reason to change it."

She chewed the inside of her cheek when silence fell and she had no brilliant ideas of how to fill it.

Fortunately, her cell phone rang just as she could feel a blush starting to rise in her cheeks. "It's Archer already." She didn't expect such a quick response to bode well, and considering the way Linc's lips thinned, she suspected he had the same feeling.

She managed to hold both Layla and the bottle with one hand as she pressed a key and held the phone to her ear. "Any luck?"

"Depends on who's asking," Archer said. She could hear music in the background. "Not surprisingly, Stokes isn't inclined to depart from usual procedure, kiddo. File a report with the sheriff and turn the baby over to the hospital until an emergency placement can be made."

She sighed, shaking her head slightly when Linc's eyes captured hers. "Well, thanks for trying. I'll get the ball rolling with the sheriff—"

"No." Linc's voice was adamant in her one ear, and Archer's "Hold on, kiddo," was cautionary in the other.

She ignored Linc for her brother. "What?"

"Being the weekend and all, Stokes suggested that *you* could personally take the child into protective custody until the hearing can be scheduled about Swift's petition. If you agree, that is."

Linc was standing still, watching her intently. She wished that he'd at least pace. Then he'd be doing something else with all that pent-up frustration besides shooting it all at her from his eyes. And maybe she'd be able to breathe more normally.

It was galling that even after all these years, just being near him made her...edgy.

Layla had drained the bottle, so Maddie set it on the table, repositioning the baby once more against her shoulder as she considered Archer's words. The hearing had to be scheduled within forty-eight hours, excluding the weekend. "At the latest, we're looking at midweek, then." At which time the judge would likely order the baby be placed into shelter care while the prosecutor's office investigated. They'd start by determining whether Layla was already reported as a missing child, and then try to locate her mother.

But to locate her, they'd need to identify her.

In the meantime, Linc would get a head start on reaching Jax. And maybe he could succeed before Ray even found out about Maddie's involvement.

"Stokes said to call his clerk Monday morning first thing," Archer told her. "The judge'll make room earlier in the schedule if it's humanly possible. It's that or emergency foster care for the next several days," he concluded.

"I'm aware of that." It wasn't as if Braden had an overabundance of qualified providers willing to take an infant on a moment's notice. The last baby she'd had to place in emergency care ended up more than fifty miles away. If a caregiver couldn't be found, the baby would be assigned to the hospital, which wasn't ideal, either. For now, Maddie did have time on her hands. And she was perfectly qualified to take care of Layla for a few days, so long as she didn't have Linc breathing down her neck the whole while.

"So? What'll it be, Maddie? He's waiting for me to call him back to confirm."

Layla burped again and then turned her head against Maddie's throat, letting out a shuddering sigh.

Maddie sighed, too. She'd always been able to keep an emotional distance when it came to children—at least professionally.

But none of the children who'd ever passed through her casework had been a relative of a friend.

Linc finally moved, but only to plant his hands flat on the foyer table while he bowed his head.

Or a former friend.

She looked away. When Ray did discover what she was doing, he would just have to understand. She might be on vacation because of him, but what she did on that vacation was entirely up to her. "Tell Judge Stokes that I agree."

"You don't sound too happy about it, kiddo."

She didn't look back at Linc. "It'll be fine." The trick would be to maintain her usual professionalism. Forget the past. Forget everything but the baby. "I appreciate the help. Sorry to interrupt your evening."

"No harm. I'll catch you Monday."

"Thanks, Archer." She ended the call.

"What hearing? What did you agree to?"

There was a mirror on one wall and she could see in it that Layla's eyes were at half-mast. She also could see that Linc had lifted his head and his eyes were dark and intense.

Professionalism. She took a quick breath and turned to him. "The judge is willing to let me take Layla into protective custody. There will be a hearing scheduled by the middle of the week, at the latest, when he'll probably order her into foster care."

"But he could leave her in my care."

"She's not in your care, Linc. She's in mine. Temporarily. What happens after that depends greatly on Judge Stokes. If he decides that placing Layla with you is in her best interests, then that's what he'll do."

"But if my DNA proves she's my niece—"

She lifted her hand. "That's going to take at least a week. Maybe more. Until then, I'm telling you not to put all your eggs in that particular basket. Because it's beyond unlikely that you'll be granted temporary custody as a foster-care provider. You're not qualified, and I know Judge Stokes. He's never done that before. He's not likely to do it now just because you *want* him to."

His lips twisted. "You're enjoying this."

She had enough experience under her belt dealing with families in turmoil to keep from losing her patience.

"There is nothing enjoyable about an abandoned child, I promise you. And maybe none of it will be necessary. Maybe you'll reach Jax. He'll come back and offer proof that he knew nothing about this situation at all. He'll claim her and everyone will be happy." Maddie turned the car seat around on the table and carefully lowered Layla into it.

Linc looked alarmed. "Where are you taking her?"

"Nowhere." Yet. "She's falling asleep and the seat is as good a place as any." She shook out the pink blanket and gently spread it over the baby before picking up her phone again.

"Now who are you calling?"

"My uncle." Because that was one thing she would not neglect.

"It's too late."

She shook her head, already finished dialing. "He's had late calls like this before. Uncle David! Hi." He'd answered on the first ring. "It's Maddie. Sorry for the late call but I have an abandoned baby—"

"She's not abandoned," Linc interjected.

She turned her back on him. "I don't know how long she was left alone outside, but I didn't see any signs of frostbite or other injury. I'm guessing somewhere between eight and twelve weeks old. But she's in my care at least through the weekend, and you know how we'll ultimately need a medical eval for her case—"

Unable to stand listening to Maddie's one-sided conversation, Linc picked up the baby—car seat and all—and carried her from the foyer.

He wasn't thrilled with the decisions being made around him. But he also knew that he didn't have much of a choice.

He bypassed the kitchen and carried the baby into his study, where he carefully set the car seat on the floor.

He sank wearily onto the couch, staring down at the baby's face. Her eyelids were closed, looking delicate and pink. Her lashes were soft feather fans of pale brown, much darker than the wisps of hair on her round little head.

He'd never been around babies. Never wanted to be, particularly after his wife got pregnant with someone else's. Dana had then become his *ex*-wife. That had been nearly six years ago.

Layla hitched in an audible breath, which made him hold his. She sucked at her bow-shaped lips and her pink eyelids fluttered.

But she didn't wake.

He exhaled slowly, and slid off the couch to sit on the floor next to the car seat.

"Linc?"

"In here." He didn't raise his voice. Maddie still must have heard, because a moment later she came into his study. She stopped when she saw him sitting on the floor.

The leather creaked as she slowly perched on the far cushion of the couch. "Are you all right?"

"They must pay you to ask." He was certain she hadn't asked out of friendly concern.

She didn't answer immediately, but slid down to sit next to him on the floor, her back against the couch. The car seat was between them. "Considering I'm on vacation, technically, I'm not really getting paid for this at all." She sounded carefully neutral.

He gave her a sideways look. "Vacation?"

"Another thing even social workers are allowed." She stretched out her legs and fiddled with the plain watch strapped around her narrow wrist. "My boss scheduled it. Told me he didn't want to see me in the office for the next two weeks."

"Big fan of yours?"

She shrugged, neither confirming nor denying.

"If you're on vacation, what are you doing here?"

"You didn't exactly give me a chance to tell you." She folded back the edge of the pink blanket with her slender fingers. Her fingernails were short, neat and unvarnished. "I work in family services, Linc. Vacation or not, this is what I do."

"You could have sent someone else."

"You called *me*. At my home. If I'd known any one of my associates would have done just as well, I'd have been more than happy to send someone else." Her fingertips grazed the downy blond hair on Layla's head. "You're stuck with me now. At least until the hearing next week." She drew her hands back and went onto her knees, wrapping her fingers around the carrier handle.

"What are you doing?"

"Right now, Layla is in my care. Which means where I go, she goes." She stood, picking up the carrier. "And I'm going home. It's been a very long day, and my uncle is going to meet me there."

"Why not here?"

"Because we're not staying here," she said with exaggerated patience.

He stood, closing his hand over hers on the handle.

She froze, her expression tightening. "Linc, don't even ask me to leave her with you."

"I wasn't going to."

Her gaze flicked up to his, then away.

"You could both stay here." He realized his hand was still on hers and let go. "You know how big this place is. There's lots of room."

"There's room at my house, too."

She lived in a worn-down Victorian that she shared with her sisters. He'd driven by it more than once. His brother's bar was nearby.

"Does it have a nursery?"

She waved her hand, taking in their surroundings. "The only thing that seems to have changed since the last time I was here is this room, and your grandmother didn't have a nursery, either."

"I've changed a few things. And she put in the nursery a few years before she died."

Maddie gave him a surprised look, but still shook her head. "A nursery isn't a necessity."

"Maybe not. And there's nothing in it but furniture, but it's better than that." He gestured at the car seat. "Better than that house of yours."

"What do you know about my house?"

"It was on the condemned list when you bought it."

"It *was* not!"

"Okay. Maybe not." He waited a beat. "If Jax asked, you'd agree."

Her lips compressed. "If Jax were here, presumably

he would know who the woman was who left Layla for him and the situation would be entirely different."

Linc's stomach burned, worse than it had when he'd called her for help in the first place. "Please."

She rested the car seat on the arm of the couch and her lashes swept down. She exhaled heavily. "Fine. But just because it's already so late." But then she sent him a skewering look. "And *just* for tonight."

If he could talk her into one night, he figured his chances were pretty good of talking her into another.

But all he did was nod. "I'll show you where the nursery is."

Chapter Three

Maddie jerked awake, staring into the dark for a second before she remembered where she was.

Under Lincoln Swift's roof.

And Layla was crying.

She pushed the button on her sensible watch and groaned a little when it lit up with the time. It hadn't even been two hours since her uncle had left.

Every muscle she possessed wanted her to roll over and curl up against the pillows.

But she shoved aside the blanket that she'd pulled over herself and climbed off the bed. Aside from removing her boots before lying down, she was still fully dressed.

The bedroom she was using connected directly to the nursery. Linc's warning about furniture being the only thing the room possessed had been accurate.

The mattress inside the spectacularly beautiful wooden

crib had no bedding. The drawers of the matching chest contained nothing but drawer liners. The changing table held no diapers.

She couldn't help but wonder if it ever had.

Only the toy box held anything of note—a stuffed bear easily as big as Layla. It was dressed in overalls and cowboy boots. Even all these years after Maddie had dusted the ornate base of the foyer table, she could remember Ernestine talking about her husband, Gus. He'd died when he was still a relatively young man. No matter what sort of success the wildcatter had found before his death, though, he'd always worn overalls and cowboy boots.

One thing Maddie was used to doing, though, was improvising. She'd folded a regular bedsheet tightly around the crib mattress and Linc had produced a woven throw to use as a blanket. The pink one Layla had been left with had fallen victim to what Maddie kindly termed a "poopsplosion" while her uncle had been examining Layla. Linc had promptly turned green and produced a trash bag, seeming horrified that Maddie had been prepared to just toss the blanket in the washing machine. Instead, he'd promised to replace the blanket with a half-dozen if need be.

As for diapers and such, they had only what remained of the meager supply that had been left with Layla—also strongly depleted after the poopsplosion. Which meant Maddie was going to have to resupply. Soon. Because when it came to disposable diapers and formula, there was only so much improvising she was willing to do.

The second she picked up Layla, the baby stopped crying.

Her diaper still felt dry when Maddie checked, and

she cuddled her close. "You just want a little company, or are you hungry?" She turned the light on in the empty closet, leaving the door nearly closed so a little light seeped through, then sat down on the upholstered rocking chair in the corner and stood Layla on her thighs. The baby pushed down on her feet, bouncing jerkily. "I think it *is* just company you want. Don't you know that it's two in the morning, sweetie?"

The baby babbled and grabbed two handfuls of Maddie's hair, yanking merrily.

Maddie winced. "You need better toys than my hair," she murmured ruefully as she tried to disentangle herself.

"I'll take care of that tomorrow."

Startled, she looked over at the open doorway where Linc stood.

She might have gone to bed fully dressed, but Linc clearly had not. He wore only a pair of jeans. The rest of him above the waist was bare.

Gloriously bare.

She was glad for the dim light, because she was pretty sure if there'd been more, she wouldn't have been able to hide her gawking.

It *really* had been too long since she'd had a decent date if she couldn't keep from drooling over Lincoln Swift.

He stepped into the room and she quickly shifted her focus to the baby's grip on her hair. "A few plastic things from your kitchen would do just fine."

"Babies need stimulation. Your uncle talked about that when he was here."

"Yes, they do. Doesn't mean they need a bunch of fancy toys, though." Finally freeing herself, she quickly twisted her hair behind her neck with one hand and grabbed the baby's hands. "Oh no you don't, missy." She patted their hands together and Layla chortled, bouncing on her legs again. "They need love and attention. They need a safe environment and to feel secure."

"And health care and college funds."

She looked up at him. He'd crossed the room and was facing the oversize teddy bear.

She turned Layla around so she was sitting on Maddie's lap. "So what's going on between you and Jax?"

Except for the way the sinewy muscles roping over his shoulders flexed, he gave little response. "Nothing new. How do I get a DNA test done?"

Layla leaned her head back against Maddie's chest, and she couldn't resist rubbing her cheek against the infant's silky hair. "The hospital in Weaver can facilitate it. I know they've got a sizeable backload, though." His determination wasn't exactly a surprise, even though it had been more than a decade since she'd come up against it. "You *do* expect Jax to come back, don't you?"

Linc turned around, folding his arms across his wide chest. It only seemed to make his jeans hang even more precariously below some serious washboard abs. Maddie might be feeling her age lately, but Linc was five years older and, on him, thirty-five sat *very* well.

"He always comes back. He does own Magic Jax. Sooner or later, he checks in on the bar."

"And you really have no idea where he could be?"

He shook his head, then rubbed his hand over his chin, and then down his chest.

She chewed the inside of her cheek, trying not to stare. "You're going to look for him anyway. Right?"

His lips thinned. "I should have given you something to sleep in," he said, rather than answering her question.

Which just made her wonder even more about the

state of their brotherly love. "No need." It was much too easy to imagine slipping a T-shirt of Linc's over her head. And it wasn't professional at all. "It's one night. I'm fine like this."

"Have you slept at all?"

She nodded and stood. The spacious nursery felt much too close. "I think I'll fix Layla a small bottle. Maybe she'll sleep afterward. You want to hold her?"

He immediately shoved his hands in his front pockets.

She averted her eyes from the fine line of dark hair running downward from the flat indent of his navel, and headed toward the doorway. "I'll take that as a no."

"She's happy with you."

She realized he was following her, and hoped that he would turn into whichever room leading off the wide hallway belonged to him.

But he didn't. Soon, she'd reached the staircase. He flipped on a light as she grabbed the bannister and started down.

Since Maddie had first promised that she would at least stay there for the night, he hadn't made a single attempt to hold the baby. "You realize that if you *do* get your way where Layla is concerned—no matter how temporary—you're going to have to hold her. You're going to have to change a diaper or two. And you're not going to want to throw away every blanket just because it gets a little soiled."

"I'll cross that bridge when I come to it. Jax and I had nannies when we were little. So can Layla."

Sure. A single, male foster father. Who hired nannies. Judge Stokes would *love* that.

Maddie pressed her lips together and continued down the stairs in silence.

He flipped on lights as they made their way to the kitchen. The lone baby bottle was still sitting on a clean towel next to the sink where Maddie had left it last. Before she could mix up more formula, Linc did.

She sat on one of the bar stools at the island and watched.

And wondered some more.

About Linc and Jax.

About the nursery.

About how the bare skin stretching over Linc's shoulders would feel beneath her fingertips…

She swallowed and looked down into Layla's wide-awake face. The baby's fingers were again wrapped in Maddie's hair. Linc was warming the formula by holding the bottle under the faucet and running hot water the same way she'd done it. "From what I've heard, Swift Oil is doing well."

He made a sound. Agreement, she guessed. Although if Swift Oil weren't doing well, he wouldn't admit it. Greer would know. Her sister kept her finger far more securely on the pulse of local businesses than Maddie did.

Layla continued tugging merrily on Maddie's hair.

She noticed a crock of cooking utensils sitting next to the enormous gas range, so she got up and pulled an oversize wooden spoon from the selection. Layla released Maddie's hair and grabbed for it. Maddie returned to the stool, holding Layla on her lap. The wooden spoon smacked the counter and Layla jerked, gurgling. "Fun stuff, huh?"

Her eyes strayed to Lincoln's back, roving up the long, bisecting line of his spine. She was vaguely mesmerized by the shift of muscles.

But then she realized he'd shut off the water and was turning toward her, and felt her face start to flush.

Fortunately, he didn't seem to notice as he handed the bottle to her. "Hope it's warm enough."

She shook a few drops onto her inner wrist. "It's fine." The sight of the bottle had tempted Layla away from her banging. She quickly abandoned the spoon to reach for the bottle. Soon, her head was tilted back against Maddie's chest as she sighed and drank.

Something ached inside Maddie. Unless she ever met a guy who didn't stand her up, there wasn't any likelihood of answering that particular biological tick-tock anytime soon.

"Surprised you're not married by now with kids of your own."

Had he always been a mind reader?

She didn't look at him. "Could say the same about you. I'm sure you could have found someone good enough to take the illustrious Swift name." She shifted the baby's weight a little, almost missing the twisted grimace that came and went on his face. "What?"

He just shook his head before opening the refrigerator. "You want something to eat? Drink? Maybe a bottle of one of Jax's precious Belgian beers?" Linc glanced over his shoulder at her, holding up a dark bottle. "Suppose not," he answered before she could, and stuck the beer back on the shelf. "Milk is probably still more your speed."

She assumed that wasn't a compliment. "I don't need anything, thank you. And what's wrong with milk, anyway?"

"Not a thing." He pulled out a bottle of mineral water and let the door swing closed as he twisted off the cap. "If you're ten years old."

She made a face at him.

He sat down on one of the other bar stools. "Or nursing an ulcer."

"Speaking from experience?"

"So I've heard."

No doubt. He was more the type to cause them in someone else.

Despite everything, the thought felt uncharitable.

Layla's warm little body was growing heavier as she relaxed.

The only sounds in the kitchen came from the soft ticking of the clock on the wall and Layla's faint sighs as she worked the nipple.

Maddie swallowed. Her lips felt dry. She stared at the white veins in the dark gray soapstone counter, trying not to be so aware of him sitting only a few feet away. "Hard to believe it's going to be Christmas soon," she said, feeling a little desperate to say something. "The year's gone by really fast."

"Tends to do that the older you get."

She snuck a glance at his solemn profile. "You sound like your grandmother."

His lips kicked up before he lifted the green bottle to his mouth again.

"I remember the way she always decorated this place for Christmas." When Layla's head lolled a little, Maddie set aside the nearly empty bottle and lifted the baby to her shoulder to rub her back. Layla promptly burped and snuggled her face against Maddie's neck. "She always had the tallest Christmas trees. Tallest I'd ever seen, at least. Up until my grandmother, Vivian, moved to Weaver a little while ago from back East."

"We've met."

Maddie blinked but then dismissed her surprise.

Why wouldn't Vivian Archer Templeton—who was Richie Rich-rich thanks to Pennsylvania steel and a bunch of wealthy dead husbands—have met the guy who ran Swift Oil? "Anyway," she went on, "Vivian's tree was crazy tall the same way Ernestine's used to be. My grandmother's was more like an untouchable art piece, though. All covered in crystal and gold. What I remember about the trees here is that they were much homier." Popcorn garlands. Popsicle-stick ornaments. Real candy canes that Jax would sneak to school and share with Maddie and her sisters. "Her trees were like the ones my mother had. Only more than twice the size."

"My grandmother did love Christmas," Linc agreed. "I also think she was trying to make up for what Jax and I didn't have at home."

Maddie slid him a glance, surprised by the personal admission. "I must have been in junior high before I realized that you and Jax didn't actually live here all the time with her."

"Would have been easier if we had." He rested his forearms on the island and slowly rotated the water bottle with his long, blunt-edged fingertips. "She always dragged us to church when we stayed here." His hazel gaze drifted her way. "Could have done without being forced into a necktie for that."

She couldn't help smiling. "Jax always complained about having to wear a tie, too."

"Only good thing about going was knowing that Ernestine's pew was across the aisle from your folks' pew. Could watch the lot of you crammed between Meredith and Carter, wriggling and whispering and wanting to be anywhere else just as bad as me and Jax."

For some reason, his observation unnerved her.

"Church wasn't so bad." She still went most every week, after all. The church pew that his grandmother had always occupied was typically filled now by the mayor and his family.

She turned so that Linc would be able to see Layla's face. "Is she still awake?"

"Her eyes are closed. Looks asleep to me."

"Success." She carefully slid off the barstool. "And back to bed for everyone." She started to leave the room, but Linc didn't make any move to follow. "G'night."

"Night, Maddie."

A shiver danced down her spine.

She blamed it on a draft and quickly left the kitchen.

Even when she'd reached the top of the stairs, the light was still on in the kitchen.

For all she knew, he was often awake at two in the morning.

Which didn't matter to her one bit. Because she couldn't stand him, after all.

She padded silently down the hall and back into the nursery. Moving at a snail's pace lest Layla awaken, she gingerly lowered the baby back into the crib. And then she didn't breathe for what seemed another few minutes while she waited for Layla to stir.

When the baby just continued lying there, breathing softly, arms raised next to her head, fingers lightly curled into fists, Maddie finally exhaled. She leaned over the edge of the crib and gently covered Layla with the woven throw.

"Shoot for daylight next time," she whispered, before straightening and crossing to the closet to turn off the light.

Then she returned to her bedroom. There, she stretched

out on the bed once more and pulled the blanket across herself.

As tired as she was, though, all she did was stare into the dark.

Not thinking about her old friend Jax, and where he might be, or when he might return. And whether or not he really was Layla's father.

No. All she could think about was Linc.

And that dang shiver she'd felt when he'd said her name.

Both the females under his roof were still sleeping.

Linc finished silently closing the wooden blinds hanging in the window of the nursery. When the morning light was no longer shining through, he crossed the room, hesitating at the doorway into the adjoining room, even though he'd been determined not to.

He'd already glanced through the opening once.

Just long enough to see Maddie's long dark hair strewn across a white pillow.

An image that was going to be hell on him until he could banish it from his memory.

If he could banish it.

It didn't even matter that beneath the blanket, Maddie was fully dressed. The sight was still more tempting than any he'd seen in too long a time.

And, if she woke up and turned over, seeing him standing in the doorway leering at her, she'd grab up Layla and be out of there in a flash.

It was only that very real possibility that finally made him move away and leave the nursery altogether.

He didn't return to his own suite at the far end of the hall. He'd already showered and dressed for the day. He'd done it in record time, half expecting to hear Layla wailing at any moment.

But all had been peaceful in the nursery.

It was just inside his own head that everything was turbulent.

He usually spent most of his time at the office, even on the weekends. Swift Oil hadn't been the three-man operation Gus Swift had founded for a very long time. The company Linc had been entrusted with was now one of the major employers in the state. Certainly the major employer in Braden. The only company in the region rivaling his in terms of employment was Cee-Vid, located in Weaver. But not even Cee-Vid had the history of Swift Oil. The tech company hadn't been so much as a glimmer of thought when Gus Swift had first started out wildcatting with *his* father in the early 1900s.

When Linc wasn't working at the office, he was out working in the field. There was always something that needed doing, and when there wasn't, it meant there was something that needed undoing.

Something almost always caused by his and Jax's father, Blake. Blake, who was either diving into yet another inappropriate relationship, or planning another scheme guaranteed to cause Linc's ulcer to flare.

But that morning, the last thing on Linc's mind was the company. For the moment, anyway, Swift Oil was safe enough.

So instead of heading there, he went downstairs and into his home office. He'd plugged in his brother's dead cell phone the night before and when he picked it up and turned it on, he was rewarded by the familiar buzz that he got from his own phone.

But that was as far as he could go.

Because he didn't know his brother's password.

Knowing Jax, it could be anything from the name of his first girlfriend to the stock number of his favorite beer.

He sat down behind his desk, studying the cell phone screen. It bore a picture of a sailboat with a leggy blonde sunbathing on its deck.

Linc didn't know if the photo was some stock thing or from one of Jax's frequent escapades. For all Linc knew, the blonde could be Layla's mother. Though, admittedly, she didn't look to be in the family way. Even in the small picture, the minuscule bikini left nothing to the imagination.

He drummed the side of the phone a few times with his thumb. Then he abruptly swiped the screen and typed in "Maddie."

"Incorrect Password" flashed back at him before the sailboat returned to view.

He almost wished the attempt had been correct. He figured he could deal with his brother still carrying a torch for his high school girlfriend if it meant that Linc gained access to whatever secrets the phone might hold about Jax's present whereabouts. It wasn't as if Maddie was still likely to fall for Jax's charms. She was an adult now. Not a teenager who'd been too pretty, too soft-hearted and way too innocent for her own good.

Once upon a time he'd thought the same of Dana. And look where that had ended.

He quickly typed in "Dana."

The sailboat remained.

He pinched the bridge of his nose.

It ought to be too early for a headache.

"Linc?"

He dropped his hand and looked over to see Maddie standing barefoot in the doorway. Her hair was messy around her shoulders and her chocolate-colored eyes were dark and drowsy.

He couldn't stop the heat streaking through him any more now than he'd been able to when she'd still been a teenager and too damn young for him.

And it annoyed the hell out of him.

Jax may have slept with Dana. But Linc wasn't going to return the favor by poaching Maddie, no matter how attractive he found her. She wasn't too young for him now, but he still considered her off-limits. Not because of Jax. But because she was a decent woman. And the last woman who'd gotten involved with the Swifts and remained decent had been his grandmother.

His "What?" was more a bark than a question and her soft, drowsy eyes went cool.

She tugged down her sleeves. "I wanted to let you know that we'll be leaving now."

If his *what* had been terse, his "No!" was a flat-out command.

She lifted her eyebrows, unperturbed. "I'll let you know when the hearing is scheduled with Judge Stokes." She turned on her heel and disappeared from view.

He shoved away from his desk and went after her.

For a woman short enough to fit in his pocket, she moved fast, marching halfway up the stairs before he caught her arm. "Wait."

She looked pointedly at his hand on her arm and he released her. The second he did, she went up two more steps.

He caught her arm again. And this time, ignored her pointed glare. "I said, wait."

"So?" She yanked her arm free. "I'm not one of your oil minions, Lincoln. Layla needs diapers and formula. And I have things to do." She started to turn again, but stopped. "And don't suggest that I leave her here while I go and do them."

That had been the last thing on his mind.

He didn't want to let Layla out of his sight, but he still didn't welcome any notion that he'd have to take care of her *himself*. Not when the only thing he knew about caring for her had so far been learned from watching Maddie during the past eight hours.

"I'll pay you."

Her expression went from annoyance to fury to disgust. All in the blink of an eye. "Stooping to bribery isn't going to win any points, Linc."

Bribery? He nearly choked on the word. "I'm not bribing. I'm just willing to pay for your time. Why not? I pay for everyone else's."

"Well, not mine!" Her voice rose and her arms went out. "Get it through your head, Linc. For the next few days at least, Layla is under *my* care, by order of Judge Stokes. You started all of this by calling me in the first place. Now I'm going to do my job, whether you like it or not. The only thing *you* need to focus on is finding Jax!"

"I don't want you taking her out of the house."

"You're not calling the shots this time, so that's just too darn bad." She stomped up the rest of the stairs.

He followed her into the nursery where she scooped a very awake Layla out of the crib. "If you take her, I'm afraid you won't bring her back."

The admission didn't even make her hesitate. "You still keep talking as if *I* have some choice in the matter. Layla's immediate future is going to be determined by Judge Stokes." She carried Layla into the adjoining room. The bed looked pristine, as if Maddie's long thick hair had never spread across the white pillows at all.

"Even if I find Jax?"

"Even if you find Layla's mom!" She seemed to realize she couldn't put on her boots and hold the baby at the same time, but rather than try to hand the infant to him, she just set her in the middle of the bed before yanking on her socks. "I knew from the get-go that this was no safe-haven situation. Layla isn't a newborn, but even if she were, there would still have been protocols to follow when surrendering her. Appropriate places authorized to take a baby under those circumstances." She zipped her boots over her narrow jeans, right up to her knees. "Layla's too old. You heard my uncle. Considering her motor control and size, she's more likely three months than two. Parents don't get to just abandon their children on doorsteps without having some sort of reprisal. Layla's mother could walk in your front door right this minute and she wouldn't be allowed to bundle her up and truck on home with her! Even if she weren't guilty of abandonment, she is certainly guilty of neglect!"

"I don't give a damn about Layla's mother. As you're so fond of reminding me, she left her own baby on a freaking doorstep!"

Layla, apparently tired of their raised voices, got into the act, too, adding her own high-pitched wail.

Maddie gave him a now-look-what-you-did glare and scooped up the infant. "Like I said. She needs diapers and formula. So if you wouldn't mind moving out of our way, I'll go take care of those little requirements."

"I'll get you all the diapers and the formula you need. Just stay."

She lifted her chin. "You're free to buy whatever the heck you want, Linc. But I'm not staying. And I'm taking Layla with me. If you don't find Jax before the hearing, I can tell Judge Stokes that you've been helpful and supportive where the baby's welfare is concerned." She gave him a chilly, steady stare. "Or not."

So much for soft-hearted.

"Is this your version of hardball, Maddie?"

"Call it whatever you want." She didn't seem the least bit fazed as she brushed past him, carrying the baby in one arm and the car seat in the other. "It's the truth. You'll learn what everyone else learns sooner or later—don't piss off a social worker. It doesn't matter who you are or what you've achieved. We can be your best friend. And we can be your worst enemy."

He followed her back to the stairs. "You walked in the door last night already thinking of me as the enemy. You're still holding a grudge because I told you to stay away from Jax all those years ago."

She didn't even hesitate. "Don't give yourself so much credit, Linc. I don't think of you as the enemy. In fact, I really don't think of *you* at all."

Chapter Four

"No." Ali was staring at her.

"You actually said that to him?" Greer was staring, too.

They were all sitting at the table in their eyesore of a kitchen. Layla—dressed in a diaper and nothing else—was lying on a blanket inside the portable play yard that Maddie had initially bought as a Christmas gift for her expectant sister and brother-in-law. The baby didn't need any clothes besides her diaper for the simple reason that the furnace in their house wouldn't shut off.

As a result, even though it was about thirty degrees outdoors, they were all dressed down to summer-weight clothes as befitted the overly toasty ninety degrees inside. Ali was even wearing a bikini top with her cutoff denim shorts.

"What else should I have said to him?" Maddie knew she sounded defensive, but couldn't help it. "Just because Lincoln Swift runs Swift Oil doesn't mean he runs everything else. He doesn't need to think he can run me."

"Don't you think you might be overreacting a little?"

Maddie glared at Greer. "Whose side are you on?"

Her sister lifted her hands peaceably. "Whose side are *you* on?"

"Layla's, obviously." She leaned over the side of the play yard and tickled the baby's tummy. Layla squealed and rolled partway onto her side, playing with her feet. "Who could leave such a darling like you that way?"

"Someone who was pretty desperate." Greer sipped her orange juice. She'd been working on case files when Maddie arrived, and a pencil was skewered through her hair, holding it off her perspiring neck.

"Maybe she had a furnace gone berserk, too," Ali said around the ice cube in her mouth. She was leaning back on two chair legs, her own bare feet propped on the corner of a sawhorse. "Lord knows it's making me feel pretty desperate. But I've gotta say, if a hot, manly-man like Lincoln Swift wanted me to stay a few nights under his roof, I'd be hard-pressed to say no." She raised a staying hand toward Maddie. "And I *know* he was supposedly awful to you back in the day, but the guy *is* hot."

"Supposedly?" Maddie made a face and refilled her own glass of juice from the pitcher Greer had set on the table.

"Even if Jax is Layla's daddy, she shouldn't have been left alone the way she was," Greer continued, as if Ali and Maddie hadn't spoken. "But it's all speculation until we learn more."

"I'm worried about Linc being able to find Jax any time soon," Maddie admitted.

"Did he say that?"

"He didn't have to. He doesn't know where Jax is. And he wants a DNA test to prove he's her uncle."

"Smart," Greer said. "In the absence of her parents, it would give him a positive legal stance. And you know it's a given that Judge Stokes will allow Layla to be tested considering the circumstances."

Layla let out a happy squawk when she managed to fit her toes into her mouth.

"On the up side in this whole thing, you *did* get to tell off Linc," Ali chimed in.

"I didn't tell him off." Not exactly. "He could have been a perfect stranger and I wouldn't have done anything differently."

Greer laughed softly. "So you'd have ignored your boss's vacation edict altogether *and* spent the night in a perfect stranger's house? Oh, Maude darling, I don't think so. You always did have a soft spot for both of those Swift boys."

Maddie gave Greer an annoyed look. "Don't call me *Maude*." She grabbed the paint chips from the table. "You two need to decide on paint, if we're going to get this room finished anytime soon."

Ali grabbed them back, shuffling them quickly. "I still want this one." She set the stack in the center of the table as if that decided the matter. "Too bad y'all were so careless handling the note left with the baby. I could have had it checked for fingerprints."

"Would only matter if Mommy Doe were already in the system. DNA's going to be the best bet." Greer picked up the chips and reshuffled. "And I still want this one. Where is the note, anyway?"

"Linc has it."

"The prosecutor's office is going to need it if they open an investigation."

"That's too dark. The kitchen'll feel like a cave." Ali quickly returned her paint choice to the top of the stack. "And we're all *assuming* that Mommy Doe was the one to dump Layla on the doorstep. What did the note say again?"

"Jaxie, please take care of Layla for me." The words felt tattooed in Maddie's mind. She took the paint chips and fanned through them. Greer wanted green. Ali wanted gray. There had to be a compromise they could all like. "I've dealt with a lot of strange situations, but this is one of the strangest." She flipped the paint chips around, leaving her choice on top. Svelte Sage.

"At least she's physically healthy," Greer murmured. She leaned over the edge of the play yard and offered Layla a finger. "You said Uncle David found no signs of malnourishment. No physical abuse."

"Thank God," Ali muttered.

"In fact, you're pretty perfect," Greer crooned, "aren't you, sweetheart?" Layla gurgled happily in response, which seemed to be all the prompting Maddie's sister needed to pick her up.

The second she did, though, she wrinkled her nose and handed the baby to Maddie. "Squishy diaper."

Maddie abandoned the paint chips for the baby. "Your fingers suddenly broken?"

"This is your job, hon. Not mine." Unperturbed, Greer sat back at the table. "Fun stuff like feeding her a bottle? Give me a call. Otherwise—" she waved her hand in a shooing motion "—she's all yours."

"Amen to that," Ali agreed.

Maddie grabbed a diaper from the package she'd picked up from the drugstore on the way home from

Linc's house, and took Layla into the living room where she could lay the baby on the couch. "What are the two of you going to do when Hayley's baby is born and you have to babysit?" Their half sister was five months pregnant with her first child. "It's just a wet diaper."

"Yeah, but you never know when a diaper is going to contain a surprise."

Maddie snorted, thinking of the massively messy diaper of the night before. "Trust me. This sweet girl gives you plenty of notice when that's the case."

She finished fastening the fresh diaper in place and balled up the wet one. A motion outside the window above the couch caught her eye and she watched a car pull up in front of the house. "Dad's here." She picked up the baby and carried her back into the kitchen, which—as hot as it was—was still the coolest spot in the house, thanks to the windows they'd opened.

"Thank God," Ali said fervently. "We can't afford a new furnace if Dad can't get this thing fixed for us. I'm tapped out for the next few months. I can't even afford to buy a new dress for Vivian's Christmas party this year. I wish she'd get over the black tie business. Got anything in your closets?"

"Don't look at me," Greer said. "Last thing you borrowed from me, you never returned. The only downside to asking Dad for help with the furnace is the number of times we're bound to hear 'I told you so.'"

None of them could argue that point. They all knew Carter considered the house his triplet daughters had purchased against his advice to be an absolute money pit.

Maddie threw away the wet diaper and put Layla back in the play yard, along with two brightly colored plastic cereal bowls from the cupboard. The baby immediately grabbed the red one and tried to fit it into her mouth. With the baby safely contained, Maddie washed her hands and went out to the living room where her sisters were already greeting their father.

"Hi, Daddy." She lifted her cheek for Carter Templeton's kiss when it was her turn. "Thanks for coming."

"Good thing you warned me," he returned, pulling off his jacket to reveal a short-sleeved T-shirt beneath. "Hot as a pistol in here."

"Which is why I'm hoping you brought your toolbox." Ali was looking pointedly at their father's empty hands.

"In the car. I know between the three of you, you can't seem to keep track of a hammer, much less a pipe wrench."

Ali whooped and immediately darted out the front door, not even stopping to get a sweater or shoes.

Carter just looked resigned. "How long's the furnace been running like this?"

Maddie led the way down the stairs to the basement. "It was running full blast when I got home this morning."

"This morning?" Carter's voice went tight with paternal overprotectiveness.

It didn't matter that she and her sisters were thirty years old. Carter took his fatherly duties very seriously.

"I had a case come up last night." Halfway down the stairs, she started feeling a little relief from the heat.

"A case." He sounded disbelieving. "Your mother told me you're on vacation for the next couple weeks."

She looked over her shoulder at him. "Some things interrupt a vacation, Dad. You know that better than anyone." He'd been an insurance agent and she couldn't recall a single time growing up when he hadn't dealt with one emergency call or another from one of his clients. "I'm taking care of an abandoned baby for a few days until we can get her situation resolved. Needless to say, it would be nice not to roast her out while she's staying with me."

"If I can't get this thing fixed, I'll have to get it cut off. Then you can start worrying about her freezing instead. What're you going to do for heat? You and your sisters will have to come home."

"This is home. I appreciate the offer—and I'm sure they would, too—but the fireplace is sound. We can manage if we need to." They may not be able to agree easily on paint color, but she knew her sisters would feel the same.

He made a grunting sound and moved past her when they reached the bottom of the stairs, heading toward the ancient furnace squatting like an antique behemoth in the middle of the room. "I warned you about buying a house with fifty-year-old plumbing and heating. But none of you would listen."

Ali had skipped down the stairs behind them. She set the toolbox on the cement floor, giving Maddie a wry look.

Carter bent down to open up his tools. "Go on," he said. "You know I hate someone watching over my shoulder."

It was a good enough excuse for both Maddie and Ali, and they retreated to the main floor, where they relocated the portable play yard to the living room. With Layla occupied with the colorful bowls, her fascinating toes and the monkey mobile hanging above the play yard, Maddie and Ali started unpacking the brand-new artificial Christmas tree.

More than an hour later, the furnace was still blasting

hot air. They'd opened up more windows, their father had gulped down a glass of tea and gone to the hardware store for a part, and she and Ali were still trying to decipher the instructions for the tree. Even Greer had taken a break from her case files to assess the situation.

Maddie was pretty sure the opportunity to feed Layla her bottle was the real draw, though. She'd had to use the last of the powdered formula to prepare it, which meant another trip to the store was imminent. She couldn't just swing by the corner drugstore where she'd gotten the diapers—the small spot on the shelf for formula had been cleaned out of product.

But at least the errand would give her a break from the hot house.

"I don't care what the diagrams look like." Ali tossed aside the single sheet of paper. "I'm telling you, we've got the whole bottom section upside down." She waved her hand with a flourish. "Just look at it!"

Maddie glanced toward their third sister. "What do *you* think?"

Greer barely looked up from Layla at the strangely box-shaped half tree. "I think this sweet girl is falling asleep on me." Her voice was soft. Crooning.

"I think someone's biological clock is ticking," Ali muttered sotto voce.

"Please," Greer said, obviously overhearing. "Speak for yourself."

"Trust me. I don't even own that clock," Ali assured her. She started dismantling the half-built tree. "Screw the directions. I'm starting over."

"We could have just had a live tree," Greer pointed out once Maddie took the sleeping baby and carefully transferred her back into the play yard. "It's a little more obvious whether they're upside down or not."

"Be glad we *don't* have a live tree," Ali retorted. She rebundled her hair in a messy knot and swiped her damp forehead with her arm. "It would be dried out in two days with the way the furnace is going full bore. You want to chance a fire—"

Greer lifted her hand. "Don't start. Sometimes you sound just like Dad."

Ali threw a tree branch at her head. Greer deflected it and propped her hands on her slender hips, studying the mess of tree branches tangled together with a rat's nest of tiny lights. "I thought these things were supposed to be easy to put together."

"All I know is that it was the one the sales guy recommended at Shop-World. And it was the best one of the few we could actually afford." Ali flipped over the base portion and managed to fit it back into the stand, but only by whacking it a few times with the heel of a boot. She straightened, stretching her back. "Okay." She waved at the branches littering the hardwood floor. "I've done my part. Rest is up to you."

"That means you," Greer told Maddie. "I've got to get those case files reviewed before Monday court. And it's just too hot to concentrate here. I'm going to head over to the office instead."

"You said you were going to help," Ali groused.

"And I will," Greer insisted. "*After* I get my work done."

"Well, *you* are going to decorate this sucker," Ali told her. "You got out of all the Christmas stuff last year, but if you try again, I'm going to hang wanted posters all over the branches."

"That'd be festive," Greer drawled. "I'll decorate, okay?"

"She better," Ali muttered as their sister left.

"She will," Maddie soothed. She would have accused Greer of shirking her Christmasy duty, too, if she weren't perfectly aware that their eldest triplet had a workload with the public defender's office that was completely insane. The fact that Greer had been home on a Saturday morning at all was unusual.

But Ali—as a police officer—was less tolerant of their third sister's career as a public defender.

So Maddie picked up a handful of the prickly branches without complaint and started fitting them in place under Ali's watchful eye.

They were still working on it when their father eventually returned, but neither paid him much attention as he came inside. "I suppose you're going to want me to fix that mess of a tree, too?"

"No," Ali drawled immediately. She was standing on a stepstool, fluffing out the upper tree branches. "And it's not a mess."

Maddie didn't look up. She was on her knees, her head wedged between the branches as she tried to locate the electrical plugs connecting all of the light strands together. She loved her dad. She really did. She didn't know what they would do without him. But sometimes, his attitude left a little to be desired.

Maybe their tree was a bit of a mess, but it was theirs.

"Thanks, though, Daddy," she added tactfully. "But you're already taking care of the sauna." She wrinkled her nose trying to alleviate a sudden itch. "That's a lot more important."

He made a "humph" sound full of doubt, but fortunately dropped it. All she could see of him through the tree were his shoes as he passed by. She finally felt the distinctive shape of the last plug and managed to thread the other cords through the branches until they met.

"I've finally got it, Ali." She stuck out her hand blindly. "Hand me the extension cord, will you?"

"Here."

The voice was deep. Definitely *not* her sister's, but recognizable anyway.

She let out a slow breath, taking the cord that Linc handed her and making the connection.

Then she extricated herself from the tree branches, giving Ali a withering look. Couldn't her sister at least have warned her?

But Ali had moved off the stepstool to sit on the couch. She was bouncing Layla on her lap, grinning like the Cheshire cat.

"I didn't know why your door would be open the way it was, so I came in to check." He took off his leather jacket. "Pretending you're in the tropics?"

Maddie swiped her tangled hair away from her cheek and scrambled to her feet, wishing like fury that she hadn't tied her ancient T-shirt in a knot under her breasts. With the paint-stained shorts she was wearing, she probably looked more like the seventeen-year-old he'd deemed unsuitable as a girlfriend for his brother than the responsible adult she really was.

"Furnace is on the fritz. What are you doing here? There was no need to check up on Layla." She gestured toward her sister and the baby. "As you can see, she's still with me. I haven't secreted her away to a foster family behind your back."

"I brought you supplies."

Only then did she realize the front door was still open and a pile of stuff was sitting right outside. A gigantic box of diapers. Three containers of formula powder. A case of ready-to-use formula bottles.

She didn't want to feel touched. Or concerned. But

she was—deeply. How was he going to react when things didn't go his way at the hearing? "You really didn't need to do all this." There was even a large box displaying a photo of an infant swing and a shopping bag bulging with heaven only knew what. "I hope you kept your receipts for when you end up returning most of it."

He just gave her a look.

Right. Lincoln Swift probably never returned anything.

"Your face is all red," he said.

"It's hot, as you've so tactfully observed." She folded her arms across her front, trying to hide the pale skin of her bare midriff. "My dad is working on getting the heat fixed."

"I ran into Carter outside. He told me."

She could just imagine. Her dad wasn't one to mince words, even in the best of circumstances.

Linc tossed his jacket aside. "And I meant your face is really red."

He was wearing the same gray pullover that he'd been wearing that morning. Cashmere, probably. With a thin line of white from his undershirt showing above the crew neck that had her thinking about what would be beneath *that*.

"Yeah." She rubbed her chin, hating the fact that he made her feel so self-conscious. And the fact that she knew what sort of body lurked beneath the cashmere. "I know. I'm a mess."

"No." Ali had unfolded her legs and stood. She stepped closer, carrying Layla. "Looks like you're getting a rash."

"Oh, for heaven's—" Maddie looked across the room toward the antique mirror hanging over the fireplace mantel. Her jaw dropped at her reflection, and she scrambled around the tree box and the play yard to get a closer look.

Her face was covered in red spots. And when she lifted her fingers to touch it, she realized the same splotches were springing out on her arms. And they were all suddenly itching as though a dozen ants were attacking.

In the mirror, she could see Linc lift Layla away from Ali. He held her awkwardly to one side, as if to shield her from whatever menace Maddie presented. The baby's legs dangled and she kicked them happily, as if it were some fun game. But it was a game that ended quickly when Linc laid her down inside her play yard. "What the hell have you exposed her to?"

"Nothing!" Maddie started rubbing her itching jaw and made herself stop. Her gaze fell on the tree. The damned prickly artificial Christmas tree that she'd been wrestling with for more than an hour. "It's that tree," she pointed accusingly.

"I don't know," Ali drawled. "Sure it's not mange?"

"Ali!"

Her sister laughed, spreading her hands. "I'm kidding!"

Maddie wanted to kick her. "Why aren't you breaking out in a rash?" They were identical sisters, for heaven's sake. If something about the tree was giving Maddie an allergic reaction, shouldn't it do the same with her sister?

Ali shrugged. "Clean living?" She tightened the messy knot on her head. If she felt the least self-conscious about her appearance around Linc, she hid it a lot better than Maddie did. "Go take a cool shower," she advised. "Maybe it'll help."

"Not if it's measles or something equally contagious," Linc said flatly.

"It's not measles!" Maddie could feel the situation escaping her control. "I've had all the shots I'm supposed to have. I am not sick, so stop hoping that I am."

"I'm not hoping anything." He stepped between Maddie and the baby, but he looked toward the front door as if measuring the distance. "I'm just being cautious."

"No, you're being ridiculous. And stop eyeing the door like that. I know what you're thinking, too. But you'd have to pick her up again to kidnap her."

His hazel eyes went hard. He looked incensed. "Kidnap. Do you always assume the worst, or is it just with me?"

Ali stepped between them. "Go take a shower," she said calmly to Maddie. "See if it helps. Linc isn't going anywhere. Are you, Linc?"

He looked like he wanted to argue. But maybe he had some respect for Ali's position as a cop, even though she was dressed like a sweaty beach bum. "For now," he said through his teeth.

Maddie met her sister's eyes. Linc had resources on top of resources at his disposal. And she'd seen desperate people do all sorts of desperate things they would never consider under ordinary circumstances. "I'll be just a few minutes," she warned.

"Take your time," Ali said easily. "It'll give Linc and me a chance to catch up." She sent Linc a winsome smile that made Maddie feel an unwarranted stab of jealousy. Ali had always been able to wrap men around her fingers with that smile. "Right, Linc?"

Chapter Five

"Good news." Her uncle David peeled off his sterile gloves and pitched them into the trash before flipping on the faucet to wash his hands. "Looks like a simple case of contact dermatitis." He turned back to Maddie where she was sitting on the examination table in his office.

After a shower had failed to bring her rash any relief, Linc had insisted she see a doctor. Then Carter had come up from the basement while she'd been arguing that Linc did *not* need to drive her to the hospital in Weaver, and had sided with him. Ali was the one to hurriedly suggest their uncle as an alternative.

Probably because she knew that Maddie had been about ready to lose her mind.

"Next time you touch your fake tree, wear long sleeves and gloves," her uncle advised, tilting her chin. "And try not to stick your face into it." He smiled. He was a few years older than her dad, and in general a much more easy-going guy. "Calamine and an anti-histamine ought to take care of it. I'll prescribe something stronger if that doesn't give you some relief by tomorrow."

She hopped off the child-size table and tugged the hem of her sweater down around the blue jeans that she'd changed into. Even beneath the denim, her legs felt itchy. "Thanks. I appreciate you taking time for me. I was afraid I was going to get dragged to the hospital in Weaver whether I wanted to or not."

"No problem. Had several patients today anyway. But a trip to the hospital seems a little extreme."

She was pretty sure nothing about her uncle's offices had changed since she'd been a child and he'd been her pediatrician. Even the painted cartoon characters circling the walls looked the same. "Would you do me a favor and tell Lincoln Swift that?" He was waiting for her in the waiting room. She hoped. "He's determined that I'm Typhoid Mary. Dad was almost as bad."

David chuckled as they walked back to the waiting room where his receptionist was cuddling Layla while Linc sat stiffly in one of the chairs. He was watching a trio of young children playing in the corner where a miniature table and chairs were situated. What he was thinking was anyone's guess. Maddie was just relieved to see that he hadn't bolted with the baby.

When she'd gone back to the examining room with her uncle, she'd tried to take the baby with her, but her uncle had intervened. She'd had no graceful way to get out of it, and had left the baby with Linc. Maddie doubted that he'd been the one to unbuckle Layla from her carrier. Which meant the receptionist had probably done it.

"I'm not contagious," she announced when he spotted her. "Sorry to disappoint you, but all I need is an antihistamine and a lot of calamine." She went to the receptionist to retrieve Layla, murmuring her thanks.

"She was fussing a little, so I took her out of the car seat," the woman said. "I hope you don't mind. I asked your husband, only he said he wasn't your husband." She was a young brunette Maddie didn't know, and she giggled a little as she went behind her desk. She was giving Linc an entirely appreciative look.

To his credit, he didn't seem to notice.

Maddie fit Layla back into the carrier that was sitting on the empty chair next to Linc. Before leaving the hot house, Maddie had dressed the baby once more in her polka-dotted sleeper. It was starting to look a little worse for wear. At the very least, Maddie would need to buy or borrow a change of clothes to get them through the next few days. But she wasn't going to say a word about it to Linc.

If she did, he'd show up with an entire winter wardrobe.

"Now that you know I'm not going to give some dreaded disease to Layla, you can drop us off at my house and head on your way." She hadn't wanted him to drive her, but she'd lost that argument, too.

"I spoke with Carter. He says your furnace is a lost cause. But he did get it disconnected. So the heat's off."

Her nerves tightened. Which was annoying in and of itself, because she was not usually the type to be so easily annoyed. "I would have found that out when I got home, but okay."

"He also said to tell you that your mom'll have your old beds made up for the night."

"And I'll tell him, again, the same thing I'll tell you. We'll be sleeping under my roof tonight, just like usual."

She yanked on the jacket she'd left in the waiting room and wrapped her fingers around Layla's seat handle, carrying it toward the door.

She tried hurrying ahead of Linc, but it was fruitless. He was at least a foot taller, and when his hand closed over the heavy carrier handle next to hers, she reluctantly let him take it from her.

She shoved her hands into her pockets. What was worse? Her skin tingling from that brief, disturbingly warm contact, or itching like fury?

While he set the car seat in the back of his enormous crew-cab pickup, he left it to her to buckle it in. She had to climb up inside the pickup to do it, and since she was already there, when she finished securing Layla she just buckled herself in beside her. "Home, James," she muttered under her breath while he rounded the pickup to get behind the wheel.

"Say something?" His eyes found hers in the rearview mirror as he started the engine.

She shook her head and tucked her itching hands beneath her thighs. If she bathed in a vat of calamine, perhaps she could avoid taking an antihistamine. They always made her feel exhausted.

"It's supposed to snow tonight."

She shifted, pressing her thighs a little harder against her hands. It wasn't as good as the forbidden scratching—but it was better than nothing. "Well. It's mid-December. Snow happens."

"Temperature's supposed to drop another twenty."

"I appreciate the weather report, Linc." She dragged her hands free and rubbed the back of them against her ribs. If he didn't get moving soon, she was afraid she'd beg him to make a stop so she could stock up on a gallon or two of calamine. Because she was pretty sure the bottle in her medicine cabinet wasn't going to cut it. "Could we, uh, get going please? Layla needs a diaper change." It was an outright lie, but she figured a forgivable one given the circumstances.

He stretched his arm across the seat as he looked back at her. "You're not going to have any heat," he said with the patience of one speaking to a nitwit. "Your furnace is disconnected."

She grimaced. "You and my father ought to form a club. The house was over ninety degrees when we left it. And we had windows open! It's not going to cool off that fast. We're not going to freeze in our sleep. Layla will be *fine*." Oblivious to being the topic of conversation, the baby's eyelids were beginning to droop. Layla was like nearly every baby ever: a running car engine inspired her to catnap.

Linc's lips compressed. He turned around to face the front and put the truck into gear. "You're more stubborn than you used to be."

"Yeah, well, I'm not seventeen anymore."

He made a sound. "Trust me. I've noticed."

She flushed. He didn't make it sound like a compliment.

"What I'm getting at is obvious," he continued. "*I* have a furnace that operates properly."

"And I have firewood and a fireplace. I'm not bringing Layla back to your house."

"Until the judge says so."

She pressed her knuckles against her ribs, rubbing in circles, and sighed. "I don't know how many times I need to warn you how unlikely that is. At least until we know more about Layla."

"Everyone thought it was unlikely my grandfather would strike oil, too."

She looked out the windshield. In the distance, she could see the oil derrick that stood like a metal monolith on the horizon. Every school kid in Braden grew up hearing the story of Swift Oil's first successful oil strike. That discovery well was no longer active, but only because it didn't need to be. The home office of Swift Oil was still located in Braden—a tribute to its humble beginnings, or so the advertising went—but there were three other offices spread around the state, dealing in everything from crude oil to natural gas to alternative energy.

Yet for all of Gus Swift's early success in the oil business, it had never seemed to Maddie that the man's family had ever benefitted all that much. Ernestine had been widowed when her only son, Blake, was still young. She'd never married again, and Blake turned out a jerk. She'd done more to raise her grandsons when they'd come along than their parents had.

"Does your dad still have a hand in running Swift Oil?"

"Why?" The single word held a wealth of suspicion.

She let out a huff. "I don't know! Do you have to be so touchy? I'm just making conversation and trying not to scratch! I've never had poison ivy, but I bet this is worse."

He braked at a stop sign and looked over his shoulder at her again. "It's not worse than poison ivy. I had it when I was a kid. Your face isn't even all that red anymore. And I'm not touchy."

She raised her eyebrows. "O…kay."

His jaw canted to one side. But then he turned to face the wheel once more and continued driving. "I contacted one of my lawyers while you were in with the doc."

"And?"

"He specializes in mineral rights. He referred me to someone else who deals in family law."

She knew all the attorneys in the area who handled anything remotely regarding family law. There were only a few, including her brother. "That's good. Who?"

"Tom Hook. Over in Weaver. He's setting up the DNA testing. So it will all be official, in case I need to use the results in court."

"Tom's a good guy." A rancher as well as a lawyer, the older man had a sensible approach to things that Maddie generally appreciated. "He handled a custody case I was involved with a few years ago."

"You're not going to argue about it with me?"

She couldn't help groaning as she wriggled in the seat, rubbing her itching back against the leather upholstery behind her. "Just because I'm following the rules about Layla's immediate status doesn't mean I'm hoping you're *not* her uncle. For her sake, I mean. Get that established and things are much simpler. Until Jax returns or we find Layla's mother or another close family member, you'll have every right to request she be placed in your care. Until then, or if the test is negative—"

"It won't be."

She ignored that. "Then shelter care is still necessary. Did Tom give you any idea when the test would be scheduled?" If genetic testing was conducted for legal reasons, there were certain stipulations that had to be followed. The entire process was witnessed. Strictly controlled and documented.

"He's getting back to me on it."

He turned down another street and they passed Magic Jax, the bar his brother owned. "Have you talked to any of Jax's workers at the bar? Seen if anyone there knows how to reach him?"

"The manager."

"And?"

"He's new. Didn't even know Jax had left town. But then the guy doesn't strike me as the sharpest crayon in the box."

"What about the servers?" The last time she was in the bar—admittedly quite some time ago—all of the servers had been female. Comely ones. Jax liked comely women.

He shook his head. "I just spoke with the manager this morning. Bar doesn't open until later this afternoon."

She studied the back of Linc's head. His thick hair was a little long at the neck. A little wavy at the ends. At his grandmother's funeral, it had been rigidly short.

"Is that scratching I hear?"

She immediately flattened her fingers against her thighs, holding them still. Beneath the denim, her skin felt on fire. "No."

"You always were a bad liar."

She made a face at the back of his head. Childish? Yes. But also satisfying. "Unlike you, who *always* spoke the truth. As you saw it, anyway."

He made another turn. "We're back to that? Are you ever going to get over it? It was a decade ago."

"Thirteen years." The words escaped before she could stop them.

"Fine. *Thirteen* years ago. You and Jax weren't suited. I'm sure your parents thought the same thing."

Her dad had been full of dire warnings about Jax's reputation. Her mother had been less concerned; she'd understood that Maddie and Jax were just buddies. Of course, Meredith had once caught Maddie doodling *Mrs. Lincoln Swift* all over her notebook, too.

His eyes caught hers in the rearview mirror again. "Are you going to sit there and say you've been nursing a broken heart for Jax ever since? What's been stopping you? I've been gone for more than half that time."

"That's not the point."

He gave a disbelieving snort. "He'd have broken your heart long before now if I hadn't stopped things before they went too far. And you have to know it, too, by now."

It was her turn to snort. "As if that was your concern. You just didn't want Jax being serious about *me*. My mother had cleaned house for your grandmother. We weren't country club folk."

"Country club folk!" They'd reached her house and he pulled up to the curb, stopping so hard that she jerked forward. He looked back at her again. "What the hell is that supposed to mean? Braden doesn't even have a country club. Not then. Not now."

"No, but there were still differences between your family and mine. You got back from graduating college and decided I wasn't good enough for your family and that was that!"

"It wasn't you who wasn't good enough. Even as a teenager, Jax was a chip off our old man. I didn't want him putting *you* through the wringer."

Layla whimpered and Maddie automatically stroked her soft little arm, soothing her. "Please. You'd been off to college for four years. At that point, I bet I knew Jax better than you did. He wasn't going to put me through any wringer!"

"Well, if you thought he'd put a *ring* on your finger, you were going to be disappointed. Jax still doesn't know how to commit to anyone. And he doesn't give a damn who gets hurt in the process."

"Oh, for Pete's sake! I was seventeen. I didn't want a ring. Pretty much all I wanted was a date to prom!" She shoved open her door and hopped out, intending to go around and unbuckle Layla from the other side, but Linc beat her to it.

"Just go inside and take care of yourself," he said when she hovered near his side while he struggled to release the car seat. "I'm not going to steal her, for Christ's sake."

She supposed she deserved that.

She turned and headed toward the house, scrubbing her palms down her legs as she went. The front door was closed, which she took as a good sign. When she went inside, though, it was only marginally cooler.

All of the supplies that Linc had brought earlier had been moved inside and stacked on the couch, covering nearly every inch.

The Christmas tree had been pushed into one corner of the living room. Even though Maddie had to admit that it was a nicely shaped tree—now that it was put together properly—she had no desire to go near it ever again. If it were going to have more decoration on the green branches than a few hundred tiny white lights, Greer would have to hold up her end of things.

Beyond that, there was no sign of Ali or her dad.

Linc came in, holding the carrier in front of him as if it was a bomb in danger of going off. "She's still asleep," he whispered.

"Congratulations. Set her carrier in that chair." She pointed to one of the armchairs near the couch. "She'll be fine there for a while."

He did as she asked, then stood back, hands on his hips as he studied the room.

She looked at it through his eyes. The furniture was straight out of the eighties. A shag rug equally mismatched to the Victorian architecture partially covered the parquet wood floor, not even remotely hiding all of the boards needing repair. "What's wrong, now?"

He just shook his head and silently moved the armchair until it was butted up against the other chair, effectively walling in the car carrier. "Now there's no way she can fall out." He was still whispering, even though Maddie hadn't.

She bit the inside of her cheek. The car seat harness still buckled around Layla would have done the trick, but oddly, Maddie didn't have the heart to point it out to him. Or address the fact that the play yard that was pushed against the wall doubled quite well as a crib.

Instead, she waved at the couch. "You really overdid it with the supplies. But thank you. It was very generous." She pressed her fingertips against her chin, trying not to scratch.

He pulled off his jacket and tossed it on top of the gigantic box of diapers. "Where do you want the swing?"

She raised her eyebrows. "To stay in the box?"

In answer, he pulled a folding knife from his pocket and silently began slicing open the tape holding the box closed.

She exhaled. He clearly had no intention of leaving yet. "You are way too used to getting your way."

"Shh. You'll wake her up." Finished with the tape, he pocketed the knife again and folded open the box flaps. "And when I can get what I want, why not?" He began extracting the swing parts. "So, where do you want it?"

Since the coffee table was the only place left in the

room to sit, she sat down on the edge of it and tucked her hands under her thighs again. "I guess where the chair used to be before you fashioned it into a crib."

He set the white-painted metal legs on the marks left in the rug by the chair and reached back into the box. "Find me a screwdriver, and then go take something before you scratch holes through your jeans."

"I'm not scratching."

He just gave her a look.

She got up and went into the kitchen where she hoped she would find a screwdriver lurking in one of the drawers. Her father hadn't been exaggerating when he'd complained about their ability to keep hold of simple tools. For whatever reason, they kept disappearing, only to turn up in the strangest places.

Maddie blamed it on Greer. Greer blamed it on Ali. Ali blamed it on ghosts.

There was no screwdriver. Not in the drawers. Not on top of the refrigerator. Not inside the old-fashioned metal breadbox, even though Maddie had found a hammer there once.

She went back into the living room.

Layla was stirring, making sounds, but not yet opening her eyes. Linc was sitting on the floor, surrounded by infant swing parts. The directions—looking considerably more detailed than the Christmas tree instructions—were lying on the floor, but he didn't seem to be giving them any attention. "I can't find a screwdriver," she admitted.

"You can't be a homeowner without basic tools."

"You sound like you went to the school of Carter Templeton." She spread her hands. "What can I say? Blame the ghosts. Ali does."

He pulled out his pocketknife again. "Ghosts?"

"It's just something she says." Heaven forbid he take

that seriously. She could just imagine him in front of the judge. *Your honor, she thinks her house has ghosts...*

"We don't have ghosts."

"Glad to hear it. Did you at least take something for your rash while you were crashing around in the kitchen?"

"I wasn't crashing around."

"Enough to wake up Layla."

Maddie glanced again at the baby. Still no opened eyes. "I didn't wake her up." But she hadn't gotten to the medicine cabinet yet, so she left the room again, heading upstairs.

She found the bottle of calamine lotion without a problem. But the contents were separating and when she checked the expiration date, she could see why. She dropped the bottle in the trash and grabbed the box of antihistamine tablets, reluctantly swallowing a dose before going back downstairs.

This time, Layla's eyes were open.

Maddie stepped around Linc, who was impersonating MacGyver by using his pocketknife as a screwdriver, and unfastened the harness straps so she could lift the baby out of the car seat. "Hello, sweet pea."

Layla screwed up her face and let out a lusty wail.

Linc frowned accusingly. "What are you doing to her?"

"Pinching her, of course," Maddie deadpanned. "I'm sure she's hungry." She plucked one of the ready-to-use bottles from the case he'd brought and went into the kitchen. They still had only the one nipple. She quickly prepared the bottle and laughed softly when Layla grabbed for it, her wailing ceasing the second she got her mouth around the nipple.

With Layla happily gorging herself, they returned

to the living room once more. Maddie nudged one of the chairs away from its "crib" mate enough so that she could sit down with the baby in her lap.

She watched Linc for a moment. He had the legs of the swing assembled and was working on putting together the seat. The direction sheet was now shoved halfway beneath the coffee table.

"You seem pretty adept at that."

He didn't look up. "Putting a few parts together—it's not rocket science."

"Or a Christmas tree," she murmured. She watched Layla's blissful face for a few moments. "Why did your grandmother put in a nursery?"

Chapter Six

Why did your grandmother put in a nursery?

Maddie's question circled inside Linc's head while he popped the seat into the motor assembly. He wondered if she already knew the answer. Or at least suspected. But if she did, she was better at hiding her thoughts than he'd given her credit for.

Either way, he might as well tell her. There were plenty of other people who knew.

Jax, for one. Not only had Dana cheated on Linc with him, it turned out she'd been cheating on Jax, as well.

"Because my wife was pregnant." Using the dinky screwdriver attachment on his knife, he tightened the seat.

He finally glanced at Maddie when her silence lasted longer than usual.

She was staring at him, her soft lips parted. "You have a child?"

"No." He connected the swing legs and tightened a few more screws. Nor did his wife, since she had chosen to end the pregnancy.

Maddie was still staring. "I've never heard you're married. You don't wear a ring."

"That's because I took it off when I stopped being married. It was a long time ago."

"How long?"

He wished he'd kept his mouth shut. "Six years." He flipped the swing right-side up and eyed the last part. It was a mobile meant to be hung from the housing above the seat. He unfurled the tightly wound purple and pink horses and threaded it into place. "I thought babies liked bunnies and bears and little baby stuff."

"Sorry?"

He flipped his hand across the mobile, making it swing. "These are horses."

"Unicorns." Still holding Layla, Maddie slid off the chair onto her knees and came closer. With her free hand, she stilled one of the dangling unicorns. "There's the silver horn. It's just a little bent, but the fabric will straighten out in time." She stilled another. "This is a Pegasus. You'll have to know these things with a little girl around. It's all unicorns and a flying Pegasus at first. Until she gets a little older and then, like with me, it *is* all horses. Real ones. I always wanted one, but the closest I ever got to any was at your grandmother's."

Her lashes lifted and he got a blast of her warm, chocolate eyes.

She blinked once and looked back at the mobile. "She had three. Laughy, Taffy and Daffy. Taffy was always the first one to get to the apples we'd feed her." She gave him a self-deprecating smile. "You don't need me to tell you about *your* grandmother's horses."

Nor about Maddie and her sisters feeding them apples. Carrots. Whatever they could get their enthusiastic little hands on.

He remembered all right.

But he made a face and pushed to his feet. He'd do what was right where his brother's child was concerned. But he didn't want to sit there feeling this churning inside. He already had one barely healed ulcer. He didn't want another.

"Call me when you come to your senses and are ready to stay at my house," he said abruptly. "I'll send someone to pick up all the gear so you don't have to drag it along with you and the baby."

The soft look that had been in her eyes disappeared. She focused on the baby in her arms as she moved back to the chair. "I'll call you when I know when the hearing is scheduled," she corrected.

He made himself shrug. As a little girl, she'd been shy and eager to please. As a teen, she'd been wide-eyed and innocent, no matter what she claimed about his brother and the prom. As a woman, he was quickly learning there was no point in arguing with her. He'd have to trust that she'd come to her senses soon enough. "Call me if you need anything else."

She gave a pointed look at the swing and the supplies covering the couch. "I think Layla is set for quite some time."

"And you?" Instead of heading to the door the way he should have, he crossed to her and lightly caught her chin, nudging it upward. She still had a splotch of red on her right cheek and a slightly smaller patch on her chest, right above the scooped neckline of her ivory sweater. Layla's head was lolling against Maddie's chest as she ate, causing the sweater to dip even more, giving

Linc an excellent view of smooth, pale skin cupped by creamy white lace.

Not that he looked.

Layla's big blue eyes were staring up at him, looking almost glazed. She didn't even blink as she drank.

Ernestine had never blinked when she was ferreting some truth out of him, either.

So maybe he looked. For a second.

Shoot him. He wasn't dead.

He let go of Maddie's chin. "Are you set, too?"

Her pupils seemed to dilate. The splotch on her cheek became less noticeable because the rest of her face turned pink. "For what?" Her voice sounded a little faint. Then her lashes lowered. She gave a quick cough. "I mean, I'm fine, too. I think the, um, the antihistamine is starting to kick in already."

"The itching better?"

She shook her head and a lock of long brown hair slid over her shoulder. "Starting to want a nap. Stuff always makes me sleepy. That's why I hate taking it."

Layla had one little dimpled hand spread against the side of the bottle, looking as if nothing else on earth existed but that bottle. But the second she spotted Maddie's hair, she wound her other hand around it. Her eyelids finally drooped to half-mast.

"You're not the only one wanting a nap."

Maddie looked down at the baby. The pink was fading from her face and her expression turned tender. She tugged the bottle away and dabbed a drop of formula from the baby's chin. "Looks like milk coma to me." She set aside the bottle before pushing to her feet. Then she carried Layla over to the play area and gingerly lowered her down into it. Layla gurgled a few times and threw her hands out wide, then gave a soft snore.

Maddie straightened and pressed her hands to the small of her back, arching.

"That's why you need to use a crib," Linc pointed out. "Saves your back. You don't have to reach so far down for the baby."

Her lips twitched. "Nice try." She started to scratch her chest, but curled her fingers into a fist and headed toward the door instead. She yawned before she even got it open.

"Who's going to watch the baby while you sleep? You're the only one here."

"You're joking, right? Moms have been sneaking naps along with their babies since the dawn of time. I may not be a mom, but I figure it's still a good plan."

She swung the door open even wider and the cold air was almost a relief. Because it was still way too warm in the house.

"I'd better stay."

She handed him his jacket, then shoved at his shoulders. "You'd be a lot more useful tracking down Jax." She seemed to realize that he hadn't progressed an inch out the door, and snatched her hands back. "Go to Magic Jax. Talk to Jax's waitresses in person. See if they know anything."

She was right. He'd planned to do all of that. But plans seemed to have a way of changing whenever Maddie was around. "Don't forget to put some of that pink stuff on your rash."

She pressed her palm against her belly and dropped it immediately.

Considering how she'd had her T-shirt tied up underneath her breasts when she'd been hanging half in, half out of the Christmas tree, he could only imagine how irritated the rest of her torso was. "I'd offer to help with the hard-to-reach spots, but you'd probably take it the wrong way. Wouldn't want to be accused of bribery again."

"Wouldn't matter anyway, since we're out of calamine. And you can joke if you want about bribery, but there have been attempts. More than once and not just with me." She leaned against the door. Her eyes were looking drowsier by the second. "Generally the situations that land families in my office are the kind of situations that cause desperation. And desperation is a powerful motivator for people to do the kind of unreasonable things they'd never ordinarily consider."

"I'm not desperate enough to do anything stupid."

Her smooth brow wrinkled. "You were desperate enough to call me last night for help."

"Yes, but that wasn't stupid." Not for any of the reasons she seemed to think, at least. "Go take your nap with Layla. I'll be in touch."

She nodded, but stood in the open doorway watching him until he got in his truck. Only then did she finally close the door, and he drove away.

Since he was in the area, he stopped first at Magic Jax. It wasn't quite time for the bar to open but there were a few cars parked in the lot, so he went around back and pounded on the locked service door until it opened.

Even though it had been years since Linc stepped foot in the place, he still recognized Sal Romano's face. The bouncer had been with Jax longer than anyone else his brother had ever hired. Maybe because they were friends from way back.

The burly man grinned, showing off his two front teeth capped in gold. His long hair had more gray than red and was held back in a scraggly ponytail. "Damn!

Hell must have frozen over." He stuck out a beefy hand. "How you doing, Linc?"

Linc's palm was swallowed in the other man's handshake. "It's been a while."

Sal chuckled. "Long enough for both of us to be looking grayer, anyway." He stepped back so Linc could enter the building. "What brings you by? Finally checking up on your investment?"

There weren't too many people who knew that Linc had staked his brother enough to start up the bar nearly seven years ago. And nobody but Linc knew that he'd stupidly done so at the behest of his then-wife. The only solace to that was knowing that Dana had been faithless to Jax, too.

"Checking up on my brother, more like." He followed the bouncer around the crates waiting to be unpacked in the stockroom and into the small business office. "Don't suppose you've heard from him lately?"

"Nah." Sal sat on the edge of a scarred, metal desk. "But you know Jax. He gets a wild hair about something and off he goes. Chasing snow. Chasing waves." Sal scratched the rattlesnake tattoo climbing up his forearm. "You're not worried about him, are you?"

Worried? No. Furious? Yes. Still, Linc shook his head. "Just have some stuff we need to deal with."

"Swifty stuff." Sal nodded sagely. "I'll bet."

Linc didn't bother to correct him. Aside from Jax's shares in the family business, his brother had little interest in the running of it. And that was fine, until recently, when Linc needed Jax to vote with him against their father's proposal to sell the company outright to an outfit based in Oklahoma.

But Jax had left town first, leaving Linc on his own to try to talk reason into his dad. Typically, Blake was more concerned with lining his own pockets than he was with the fact that selling their company to OKF meant they'd also be selling out their employees.

As a result, Linc had been forced to go straight to OKF to kill the deal.

He still wasn't entirely sure he'd succeeded.

"Jax talk to you a lot about the company?"

Sal laughed again and shook his head. He picked up a clipboard that was thick with papers curling up at the edges and flipped through them. "Just enough so that I know he enjoys the perks that come with it. Telling the ladies he owns a bar is one thing. Telling them he's one of the owners of an independent oil company? Well, you know how that is. Tends to net him a whole different class of lady."

"Any ladies in particular?"

Sal stopped flipping pages and signed the top sheet, then dropped the clipboard back onto the desk. His smile faded. "You wanting to know if he had a particular woman when he went off this time?"

If Jax did have a woman with him, it wouldn't have been Layla's mother. What would have been the point of leaving Layla the way she had? Why would the note be meant for him, when he wasn't even there? Still, any information was better than no information. "Did he?"

Sal's expression turned sober. "I don't know for sure. But I know who was coming around before he left. You're not going to like who it was."

Linc exhaled, knowing instinctively what the other man was going to say. He'd successfully escaped his ex-wife. But Jax had never seemed able to do the same. "Dana, I suppose."

He nodded. "Sorry, man. Gotta suck knowing your own brother's—uh, seeing your ex-wife."

All things being relative, Linc could name a few other things that ranked just as high on the suck-o-meter. "Any women come in here yesterday specifically looking for him?"

"Hell, Linc." The bouncer's expression turned wry. "Half o' Jax's customers are women coming in here specifically trying to meet him. Think it's one of the reasons why he's hardly ever here anymore. There's such a thing as too much of a good thing."

"What about the last year? Anyone seem particularly involved with him besides Dana?" He knew his ex-wife couldn't be Layla's mother. He'd have recognized her handwriting on the note, for one thing. And for another, he'd run into her about six months ago when he'd been in Cheyenne on business. She definitely had not been pregnant.

"No more than usual." Sal's eyes narrowed. "What're you really trying to find out?"

Linc sighed. Word was going to get out soon enough about the baby, he supposed. "Someone left a baby with me last night."

The bouncer looked stunned. "Jax's baby?"

Even though he had a sudden image of Maddie shaking her head and cautioning him about his conclusion, Linc nodded. "That's my thinking, anyway."

"Well, damn." The other man spread his palms. "Sorry I'm not more help."

"Don't worry about it." At least Sal had been more enlightening about Jax than the bar manager. "You need to be the one managing this place."

Sal just shook his head. "Then I'd have to do all that hiring and firing. Those cocktail waitresses we've got? Constantly coming and going. Don't have a single one who has been here more than half a year. But look. If

I hear anything about your brother, I'll let you know."
He shrugged. "He never stays gone more than two or
three weeks at a stretch. Christmas coming? He'll be
back in time for that. Always busy here at the bar during the holidays."

"Thanks, Sal."

"You bet. A couple of the girls ought to be coming
on shift by now. Maybe they know more than I do."

Linc wasn't going to hold his breath. Still, he went
out through the front where a skinny girl was twin-
ing silver and red garland around a Christmas tree that
looked very similar to the one Maddie and her sisters
had put up. Not surprisingly, neither she nor her co-
worker gave him any useful information and he left.

Before finally heading to his office, though, he
stopped at a drugstore and bought a couple large bottles of calamine lotion. Then he drove back to Maddie's
house. The front door wasn't propped open this time,
but it was nevertheless unlocked.

Annoyed, he silently pushed it open.

In the living room, Layla was still sleeping flat on
her back. Maddie had moved all the stuff off the couch
and was sprawled on it, also flat on her back. It was a
toss-up as to who was sleeping more soundly.

He stood there, watching both of them.

After a few minutes, though, he made himself move.

He carried the containers of formula into the kitchen,
shaking his head over its deplorable state. It was obvious that she and her sisters were trying to renovate
the room, but equally obvious that they were nowhere
near completion.

He was tempted to explore the rest of the house and
see if it was in an equally unfinished state. The living room hadn't been so bad. Besides the serviceable

furniture that he'd bet they'd gotten secondhand, the wood floor had shown signs of its age. But the fireplace looked sound enough. At least from the outside.

If she was going to insist on staying there—and needing to use the thing—he'd make sure the chimney was cleaned.

The packing materials from the infant swing were still on the floor, so he gathered it all up, stuffing it back in the oversize box and leaving it in the screened-in porch at the back of the house. He'd haul it away later if she wanted.

He set the bottles of calamine lotion on the coffee table where Maddie was sure to see them when she woke and, on the back of the swing's instructions, wrote a note that he propped against the bottles.

Then he crouched next to the net siding of the play yard. He watched the baby's little chest rise and fall. "See you soon, Layla," he whispered.

She slept on.

He pushed to his feet and left.

Stop leaving your doors unlocked.

Maddie sighed and folded the paper until Linc's note no longer showed. She ran her fingers along the edges as she looked at the bottles of calamine.

It was entirely unnerving to know that he'd come into the house while she slept.

"He could have been anyone coming inside," she said to Greer. It was only her sister returning to the house that had woken up Maddie. Layla had already been awake, gurgling nonsense to herself as she played with her plastic cereal bowls.

"In Braden?" Greer raised her eyebrows. "I sort of doubt it."

"Crime happens here, too. If it didn't, you wouldn't have a job as a public defender. Ali wouldn't have a job as a police officer."

"Point taken. But we don't have home invasions," Greer amended.

"What if he'd taken Layla?"

"He didn't." Her sister gestured toward the calamine. "He didn't take away. He delivered. I think it was pretty sweet of him, actually."

Maddie made a humming sound. She wanted to disagree. But couldn't.

"In fact, I'm definitely getting the sense that Lincoln Swift doesn't disapprove of you quite as much as you always said."

Maddie pushed her disheveled hair behind her ears. "I never said he disapproved of me. He just didn't think I was good enough to date Jax."

"Well." Greer still didn't look convinced. "Linc definitely has a protective streak. I mean, look around."

Maddie chewed the inside of her cheek. "He *says* he only warned me away from Jax for my own protection."

"Hmm." Greer nodded slowly. "I could see that, considering the family history. Blake Swift is notorious for cheating on his wife."

"Jax and I were kids! We weren't destined for marriage. We weren't destined for anything. He was just fun to be around."

"True. Although, I always thought Linc was more interesting than Jax."

He was.

He is.

Maddie rubbed her finger against the dull throb behind her forehead. Darned antihistamines. "Really? I never thought about it," she lied. Then she ruined it all. "Did you know that he'd been married?"

Greer looked surprised. "Should I have? You're the one who had a crush on him."

"I did not!"

"How'd you find out?" Greer leaned forward, her eyes sly. "Tender confidences?"

"You read too many romance novels."

Her sister snorted. "I read legal briefs and professional journals. And I think you're being evasive."

"It's no big deal," Maddie said defensively. "It just came up in conversation."

Greer gave her a knowing look. "Must have been some conversation."

She wished she'd kept her mouth shut and changed the subject entirely. "Did you finish all your lawyerly homework?"

"Almost. A few hours tomorrow and I should be set for court on Monday."

"Good. The tree still needs decorating. And *I'm* not going to do it."

"Since you still have a rash on your face, I suppose that's fair." Greer nudged one of the calamine bottles closer to Maddie. "He clearly bought it for you to use."

Maddie hesitated. She didn't know why she was so reluctant. But she'd spent so many years thinking the worst about Lincoln Swift. Seeing him this way—so intent on Layla, who may or may not be his niece—was messing with her mind.

Obviously.

"Come on, Maude," Greer chided. "No time like the present."

"I should check Layla's diaper." The baby was trying to fit her entire fist into her mouth. The fact that she was also holding on to one of the plastic cereal bowls at the same time only added to the challenge.

"Yeah, she looks positively miserable." Greer handed Maddie one of the bottles of lotion.

"Oh, fine." Maddie snatched it out of her sister's hand. "But only if *you* change Layla's diaper."

"I don't do diapers and all that baby stuff, remember?"

Maddie made a face at her. But since that face still felt distinctly itchy—along with half of the rest of her body—she took the calamine lotion upstairs to her room and happily threw off her clothes. She didn't bathe in the soothing lotion, but by the time she was done dabbing it all over her rashy parts, she almost looked like she had.

Once the liquid was dry, she pulled on loose pajama pants and a camisole and went back downstairs.

Greer was holding Layla, singing softly.

Greer always claimed to be "all about" her career. After watching her with the baby, though, Maddie considered the claim laughable.

Leaving her sister with Layla, she went to the hall closet and dragged out the storage tub containing their Christmas decorations. She set it on the coffee table and worked off the lid. "Don't do all that baby stuff, huh?"

Greer wasn't fazed. "Look, Layla. It's the pink-painted lady."

Maddie spread her arms and twirled once. "Ever fashionable. If Martin could only see me now."

"Who?"

"The guy who stood me up last night."

"I thought his name was Morton."

"Oh. Right." She lifted the baby out of her sister's arms and gestured at the storage bin. "Get to work."

"I will." Greer rubbed her arms. "Do we still have

a window open somewhere? It's finally starting to get a little cool in here."

"I don't know. I'll check in a minute." She grabbed a diaper from the box and laid Layla out on the couch. She peeled her out of the sleeper and changed her. "Then I'm taking this little girl upstairs for a bath."

"In other words, you're using my bathroom."

"It's the only one with a decent tub." When she and her sisters had purchased the house, they'd agreed to be responsible for the renovations of their own bedrooms, but to pool their efforts for the rest of the house. This meant that they could work at their own speed for their own space as they saw fit.

Greer had immediately remodeled her bedroom and en suite. Maddie's was a work in progress. She had an operable shower, but barely. And Ali's was mostly a plan in her mind, which meant she was usually borrowing Maddie's shower.

"True," Greer was saying. "But I'd rather help with Layla's bath than decorate the tree."

"Fine. And when Ali comes home and finds it still undecorated, we'll end up with a tree full of God knows what from the police station." She'd threatened them with Wanted posters, but knowing Ali, the tree would be accessorized by handcuffs and billy clubs.

Greer rolled her eyes and reached into the box. She pulled out a bundle of red and green garland. "Where is our baby sister, anyway?"

A whopping total of thirty minutes had separated their three births. Ali appreciated being called the baby about as much as Maddie appreciated being called by her given name, Maude.

"She probably got called in to work again. You know how her sergeant has been riding her lately."

"Yeah, well, baby sister should have thought about the ramifications before she decided to date then dump her sergeant's son."

"Come on, Greer. That's a little harsh."

"Sorry! But we all know it's never a good idea to be too female in our respective workplaces. It only ends up biting us in the butt."

More so with Ali than either one of them, Maddie thought.

She waited long enough to see that Greer really was putting the garland on the tree, then carried Layla out of the room. She stopped in the laundry room to toss the sleeper into the wash and patrolled the house for open windows before proceeding upstairs to Greer's bathroom.

It was a little chilly, so she turned on the heat lamp before pulling out a clean towel that she spread over the white and black hexagon tiled floor. She settled Layla on the towel while she started the bathwater. Once there were a few inches of warm water and she had soap and towels at the ready, she reached for the baby, who'd managed to get a foot away, simply by virtue of her churning legs. "Not so fast there, speedy." She pulled off the diaper and swung the baby over the edge of the claw-foot tub. Layla squealed, obviously delighted, when her toes hit the water.

"So you like baths." Kneeling next to the tub, Maddie lowered the baby until she was seated, keeping a secure hold of her. "That'll make this nice and easy. I bet your mommy gave you lots and lots of baths." She dunked the washcloth in the water and squeezed it over Layla's shoulders. The baby laughed and Maddie's heart melted. "Oh, sweet pea. I don't know how anyone could leave you." She sluiced more water over her and ran the wet washcloth over her head, turning the soft blond tufts dark. "But we're going to get it all figured out," she murmured. "You're going to have a happy ending. That, I can promise you." She reached for the bar of soap.

The pink lotion she'd spread over her arms was beginning to wash away from the bathwater.

She sighed a little.

She could promise Layla a happy ending.

But she couldn't promise the same thing to Linc.

And she was uncomfortably aware that she was beginning to wish she could.

Chapter Seven

Maddie awkwardly maneuvered the stroller she'd borrowed from one of her most reliable foster moms through the front office door of Swift Oil.

It was Monday morning. There were two inches of snow on the ground outside.

And Maddie had spoken with Judge Stokes's clerk.

A middle-aged woman was sitting behind the modern-looking reception desk and she quickly hopped up when she spotted Maddie and came over to hold open the door for her. "Let me help you."

"Thanks. I think—" she edged the stroller slightly to the left and felt it clear the threshold "—I've got it." She looked over the top of the stroller at Layla, bundled in her fleecy sleeper and the puppy-patterned blanket that had been in the bag of stuff Linc had brought to the house on Saturday. The baby's eyes were bright and blue above the squeaky giraffe she was chewing. The toy had also been in the bag. Along with a rattling ball well-designed for infant hands and a purple, plastic horse.

"Isn't she a sweetheart?" The woman's expression was openly longing as she let the door close and moved around the stroller to admire Layla. "I keep waiting for a grandchild, but so far neither of my sons is cooperating." She finally looked up at Maddie and introduced herself. "I'm Terry. Receptionist and—"

"—gatekeeper."

Maddie's heart jumped in her chest. They both looked over to see Linc. He was standing in one of the hallways that extended from both sides of the reception area.

Terry was much less surprised. "And gatekeeper," she said with a chuckle as she straightened and tugged at the hem of her bulky Christmas sweater. "I was just getting ready to ask this pretty mama what I could do for her."

Maddie flushed. "I'm not Layla's mother. I'm only her care provider," she corrected. "And—"

"—she's here to see me," Linc told Terry. "Layla's my niece."

Terry looked delighted.

Maddie felt dismayed.

"I didn't know your brother had children," Terry said. "Your mother never mentions grandchildren when she comes by the office."

Linc's expression turned sardonic. "You know Jolene. She'd pretend that Jax and I were still in short pants if she could. Otherwise, it's getting harder for her to pretend to still be thirty-nine."

Terry just laughed and swatted her hand at him, as if he were joking. Maddie was fairly certain that he hadn't been. "Go on with the both of you, then. Someone has to work around here."

"Come on back to my office." Linc turned on his heel, disappearing beyond the stylized black wall that bordered Terry's work area. Maddie quickly pushed the stroller forward to follow him.

"Nice meeting you," she told Terry as she passed her.

"You too, honey." The phone on Terry's desk beeped and she reached out to answer it. With her other hand, she waved bye-bye to Layla.

Maddie caught up to Linc only because he was waiting at the point where the hallway turned left in front of a glass wall.

"In here." He stepped aside so she could push the stroller through the door that was propped open.

Why had she ever thought it was such a good idea to tell him about the hearing in person? A phone call would have done just as well. And she could have put off being anywhere near him for another twenty-four hours.

But she was there.

Bing Crosby was softly crooning "Have Yourself a Merry Little Christmas" on the sound system.

She entered the office.

Linc lifted his arm, nearly brushing her shoulder, and she drew in a quick breath.

He merely pushed the door so that it swung shut. It was a glass door. Entirely transparent. It shouldn't feel like he'd just closed out the rest of the world.

But it did.

She slowly exhaled. He was dressed in jeans and heavy work boots, with a dark gray shirt hanging open over a white T-shirt. And though he looked like he'd be more comfortable around an oil rig, he smelled like a guy gracing the cover of *GQ*.

Or how she imagined such a guy would smell.

One part of her wondered how quickly she could get

that seductively woodsy scent out of her head and one part of her wondered how long she could hold on to it.

She watched him move behind a massive wood desk that wasn't the list bit modern. He sat in his chair and leaned back, propping one boot on the corner of his desk as he gestured to the chairs in front of it. "Sit. Otherwise, you look like you're ready to make a run for it."

Great. She felt her face flush and rolled the stroller closer to sit in one of the chairs. She pulled the front of the stroller around so that Layla could still see her, and moved aside the blanket so the baby wouldn't swelter in the warmth of the office.

"Sleeping in your parkas yet?"

She ignored him. Mostly because he wasn't far from the mark and her face was already feeling flushed enough. His and her father's dire predictions about the house getting too cold without the furnace had been pretty accurate. Maddie had kept Layla in bed with her, just to make sure the baby stayed warm enough, and Greer had gone around town borrowing space heaters from their friends. "Judge Stokes scheduled the hearing for tomorrow," she told him baldly. It *was* supposed to be the reason she was there. "Nine a.m. sharp. I was in the area, so I figured I'd save a phone call."

Liar, liar, pants on fire.

She ignored the taunting voice inside her head.

He dropped his boot to the floor and leaned his arms on the papers strewn across the desk. His long fingers closed together. "Sooner than you expected. That's good though?"

"It's not bad," she allowed. She hadn't spoken with him since Saturday. "I should have called to thank you for the calamine."

He lifted a few fingers dismissively. "Doesn't look like you need it so much now."

"Not so much." She made herself lower the hand she'd lifted self-consciously to her cheek. "I don't suppose you've heard from Jax?" She knew it was a long shot and when he shook his head, she wasn't surprised. "And your DNA test? Is it scheduled?"

"I'm heading over to the hospital in Weaver this afternoon about two. Hook's going to meet me there."

"That's good." She leaned over to pick up the giraffe when Layla threw it.

"Want to go with me?"

She nearly dropped the giraffe herself. She handed it back to the baby, trying not to stare at Linc. "I, uh, I—" She broke off and cleared her throat.

"Never mind," Linc said before she could think of what to say. "It was just a thought."

"No, I just—" She broke off when there was a noise behind her, and looked over her shoulder to see Blake Swift pushing through the glass door.

"Linc, what's this bullsh—" Blake abruptly stopped speaking, whether because he realized he had more of an audience than he expected or because of the glacial look that his son was giving him, Maddie couldn't tell.

"Well, well." Blake's expression shifted from annoyance to something else that Maddie couldn't quite put a name to. He strode across the gleaming wood floor to take her hand. "And who is this pretty little thing? I'm sure we've never met." His thumb moved across the back of her hand. "I would certainly have remembered *you*."

Wolfish.

That was what it was.

There could never be any doubt that Blake was Linc's

father. Or any doubt that Linc would be just as handsome in another twenty-some years.

But for all of her opinions about Linc, that expression was one she had never seen on his face. She sincerely hoped that looks were the only thing he'd inherited from his father.

She slid her hand free from Blake's, resisting the urge to wipe it against her jeans as she leaned down to retrieve the giraffe from the floor once again. "Maude Templeton," she said crisply. "And we have met, actually. A long time ago." She'd been eleven.

She looked at Linc. "This afternoon sounds fine." She handed the giraffe to Layla and stood. "I'll leave you to your business."

"Templeton," Blake was murmuring. "The name sounds familiar."

"Maddie," Linc spoke over his father. "You don't have to go."

"I do. I, uh, I have a meeting—"

Blake suddenly snapped his fingers, interrupting her lie. "Maddie. Your mama's Meredith Templeton." His lips curved. "Well, no wonder. You're as pretty as she was. You've got a sister, too, don't you? Twins?"

"Triplets." Like it or not, there were no other sets of triplets in Braden that she was aware of. The locals tended to know who she and her sisters were even if their paths had never specifically crossed, which wasn't the case where Blake was concerned.

She edged around the stroller, keeping her eyes on Linc. "Shall I meet you there?" She felt reluctant to mention exactly *where* they were going in front of his father.

Linc had leaned back in his chair again. "I'll pick you up. No need for us both to drive."

She nodded. "Okay, then." She started forward with the stroller. She couldn't pass Linc's father without saying *something*, but she was darned if she'd tell him it had been nice to see him again. Not when he was the reason her mother had felt forced to stop cleaning for Ernestine all those years ago.

Nevertheless, Maddie managed a polite smile as she steered Layla around him. Because her mother would have her hide if she ever learned Maddie was rude to anyone. Even Blake Swift. "Have a nice afternoon." She pushed the stroller through the still-open door.

Linc thoughtfully watched Maddie's hasty exit.

When she was no longer in sight, he slid his attention to his father.

Blake had thrown himself down in the chair that Maddie had vacated.

"What do you know about Meredith Templeton?" Linc kept his tone mild, but inside he felt anything but.

"She was a sweet piece of—" Blake frowned a little when Linc glared. "Work," he finished. "She used to clean house for Mother, until—" He broke off.

"Until?"

Blake shrugged. "Until she quit."

Linc had never once given any thought to why Maddie's mom had stopped cleaning for Ernestine all those years ago. His grandmother had gone to the same church as Carter and Meredith Templeton. She'd always liked Meredith. Used to say that she had "pluck."

But now, he knew there was a reason.

And that it involved his own father.

"What'd you do? Sleep with her, too?"

Blake huffed, assuming a wounded expression. "No!"

Understanding hit. "She turned you down." Good for Meredith.

Blake's lips twisted. "Don't know why. It's not like she was such a saint. Her reputation—"

"Don't." Linc lifted his hand. "Don't even go there." He couldn't stomach hearing his dad badmouth Maddie's mother. "What'd you barge in here for, anyway?"

"My contact at OKF tells me you're backing out of the deal."

"There was never a deal."

Blake's eyes hardened. "My mother may have left you in charge here, but I still own just as much of an interest in the company as you and Jax do. We've all got a third, sonny boy."

"And without one of the thirds here to side one way or the other, you and I are at a stalemate. Which means no deal." Linc stood. "And the reason why *your* mother left me in charge was because she knew I actually cared about this company. And, because I do care, I've got work to do."

He grabbed his jacket off the coat tree that had belonged to his grandfather. It, along with the desk, were the only things Linc had managed to save when his father had decided it was time to remodel the home office.

Just bringing it into the twenty-first century, Blake had said.

Since Linc had been busy negotiating drilling rights at the time, he'd been happy enough to keep Blake distracted with the remodel…and the pretty architect who'd been the latest to catch Blake's eye.

"That's not work you're thinking about," Blake said now. "It's that pretty little Maddie. You responsible for that baby she's got?"

"What if I am?" He knew what his unsubtle father

was implying and didn't care that his answer would be misconstrued.

Blake just laughed. "Then you're more a chip off this old block than I gave you credit for. Just be careful, boy. You'll marry her, like I married your mama when she got knocked up with you, but she'll end up turning on you the same way Jolene turned on me."

"It's amazing that you still believe you're innocent where Mom is concerned." His mother's infidelities were generally in retaliation for his father's.

Not surprisingly, his father didn't turn a hair. "When Jax gets back, I'll talk him around on the OKF deal," he warned.

"The deal is dead. Period."

"Then I'll find another. Only good thing about Swift Oil is the money it's worth. Money that I can spend a lot better somewhere else besides this bustling metropolis."

"I'm sure you'll try." Blake always did. For as long as he'd lived in Braden, he'd claimed he'd wanted to be elsewhere. Linc pushed his father's shoulder until Blake preceded him out of the office. "And nobody's forcing you to stay here. There's a perfectly good house waiting in Cheyenne that you insisted you had to have. Remember it?" As far as Linc knew, Blake hadn't been there in several years.

"Your mother's there. Drove over yesterday."

"So that's yesterday. What's your excuse been for the last year?" He pulled the door shut. "Don't answer that. I'm not interested in who she is."

"A shame. She has a sister—"

Inured to his father's ways, Linc simply walked away. His dad would either go into his own corner office and try cooking up another headache for Linc to deal with, or not.

He returned to the lobby. "I'm going out to check on Number Five, and then I've got to take care of some business in Weaver," he told Terry. "Anyone calls, I'll get back to them tomorrow."

"Sure thing, Linc." Terry pushed a button on the fancy telephone switchboard. "Merry Christmas," she said cheerfully into her headset. "This is Swift Oil. How can I help you?"

Outside, the ever-present wind was blowing a few snowflakes around and he turned up the collar of his jacket as he walked to his truck. Someone had stuck a circular under his windshield wiper. He pulled it loose, tossing it on his passenger seat as he got inside.

Ordinarily, it took about an hour to drive out to Number Five, which was not the name of a particular well, but the name of an entire oil field. Halfway there, the line of brake lights on the highway warned him it wasn't going to be so quick that day.

He sighed, joining the string of stopped vehicles. He'd wait for a while, but if it took too long, he'd have to turn around and head back to Braden.

He wasn't going to miss the appointment in Weaver no matter what. Not the least because Maddie had agreed to accompany him, though that had been pretty damn surprising.

Almost as surprising as his invitation had been in the first place.

He still didn't know what had gotten into him.

After about ten minutes, the traffic hadn't progressed so much as an inch.

He picked up the flyer from his windshield. There was an advertisement for Christmas Eve church services on one side and a schedule of local holiday events on the other.

The only thing he knew about any of them was that Swift was sponsoring Glitter and Glow that weekend, the same way it had always done. The annual parade had been going on since he'd been a kid. No matter how bad things were between Linc's parents, Ernestine had always made certain that Linc and Jax went to the parade.

He'd have to make sure Layla got to see it, too.

The traffic finally started moving. Linc crumpled the flyer into a ball and tossed it aside.

Maddie paced the length of the living room. It was nearly two o'clock. Linc could be there at any moment.

"Why did I say I'd go?"

She looked over at Layla, who was squirming around on the activity floor mat that Linc had bought. Layla, however, provided no answer. She was more interested in the crinkling, squeaking and vibrating zoo animals that hung from the padded frame arching above the mat from each corner.

Maddie exhaled. She tugged down the sleeves of her sweater. She needed to relax. Get a grip on herself before Linc got there.

She reached the fireplace where the banked fire was doing a good job of keeping the living room toasty, turned and paced back to the staircase. "It's just a trip to the hospital. No big deal." She shoved her sleeves up and made her way toward the fireplace once more.

The oversize flower-patterned purse that she was using as a diaper bag was on the coffee table. She stopped in front of it, checking the provisions she'd packed inside for about the tenth time. It was so full that there was no hope whatsoever of getting the zipper on it closed.

Twelve diapers was probably a little excessive. They wouldn't be gone all day. Just a few hours at the most.

She pulled out half of them and left them on the coffee table, and paced back toward the fireplace. "If we hadn't gone to his office this morning, we wouldn't be in this fix," she told Layla. "I'd have called him about the hearing, and he probably would have mentioned the DNA test." Layla's eyes followed Maddie as she passed her again. "But even if he'd asked us to go, I'd have been able to say no. On the phone. Easy-peasy." She stopped in front of the improvised diaper bag. Shoved three of the ones she'd just taken out back inside. "Maybe another bottle of formula," she said. "Just in case there's a delay."

Layla managed to bat the vibrating monkey with her waving hands and then let out a toothless smile and a laugh.

"Right." Maddie exhaled again and went into the kitchen. She'd unpacked the case of ready-to-use formula and stacked the bottles in one of the doorless wall cabinets. She pulled one down, then muttered an oath when it caused an avalanche of the others. She tried catching them before they all rolled right out of the cabinet, but managed to save only a few. "Swift, Maddie." She crouched down to corral the escapees. One had rolled all the way to the refrigerator and she crawled after it.

"Still not locking your door, I see."

She jerked back, knocking her head against the frame of a base cabinet. "*Must* you keep sneaking up on me?" She rubbed the back of her stinging head and glared at Linc. And immediately wished that he didn't look so darned good when she was always feeling so darned...not.

"Lock your doors like you should." He extended his hand.

He meant to help her up. She knew that. Instead of taking his hand, she plunked the bottle of formula into his palm and pushed to her feet all by herself. She still had a rashy patch on her right forearm and she yanked her sleeves back down where they belonged. "Stop going through doors whether they're locked or not."

His lips twitched. It was the closest thing to an actual smile that she'd seen on his face in more than a decade.

And darned if her heart didn't go all aflutter.

Far more annoyed with herself than him, she plucked the formula out of his hand and went back into the living room where she tucked the bottle into the already-stuffed purse, alongside the one she'd already prepped with the nipple and cap. "We're ready to go. I just need to buckle her into her carrier."

"No need."

Something inside her nosedived. "Oh." She didn't look at him as she went to the fireplace and picked up the poker. "You didn't need to come by. You could have just called." She moved the screen a few inches so she could jab the burning wood. A flurry of sparks exploded, dancing up the flue.

"To notify you that I had a car seat installed in the truck?"

She looked over her shoulder at him. She'd thought he was canceling. "What?"

He crossed to her and took the poker out of her hand. "I feel better around you when you're not armed." He hung it back on the hook and replaced the fireplace screen. "You need a permanent screen."

"Um." She curled her fingers against her palm and tried not to sound as bemused as she was. "Why?"

He lifted the three-panel screen. "Hardly baby-proof. I'll make sure you get one." He set the screen back in place.

"That's not—" She broke off at the look he gave her. She'd been about to say *necessary*. But what was the point? He was going to do what he wanted to do no matter what she said. And she didn't have the heart to remind him again how small the chances were of Layla staying for any length of time with either one of them. "We should get moving," she said instead. She pulled on her coat. "I've heard the highway's been a mess today with the ice." She picked up the baby and the bulging purse.

"It has. Almost didn't make it out to Number Five at all." He took the purse from her, his gaze lingering on the contents. "You packing for the night?"

"No. So don't go getting any ideas that I've changed my mind about staying with you." She felt more flushed than ever. "I mean staying at your house."

He looked amused as he pulled open the door for her, gesturing for her to precede him. "Take notes. I'm turning the lock, such as it is." He flipped the knob lock with exaggerated care. "I assume you do have a key?"

"I have a key."

He pulled the door closed, then took her elbow. "Watch the steps."

She had been going up and down the front steps of the house ever since she and her sisters purchased it. Two years of step navigating. Summers and winters and everything in between. But she didn't pull her elbow away.

When they reached his truck, he opened the back door, displaying the expensive-looking car seat. She couldn't even imagine where he got such a fancy one around Braden at all, much less on such short notice. She fit Layla into the seat and fastened the harness. Then she handed her the giraffe and stepped back down to the ground.

"You're not sitting back there with her this time?"

Great. "I, uh, I tend to get carsick in the back seat on long rides." She'd never been carsick in her entire life.

He shut the door for her without responding and crossed around the front to get behind the wheel.

She'd already buckled herself in and tucked her oddly nervous hands between her knees. "I've never known why the Number Five field has that name," she said once he pulled away from the house. "I mean, there aren't fields named Numbers One through Four."

He gave her a sideways look. "You've never been out to the oil field?"

She shook her head. "Should I have?"

"Schools send students out there on field trips at least once a year these days."

Despite herself, she chuckled. "I haven't been a schoolkid for quite some time now."

"I noticed."

A quiver slid down her spine. She blamed it on the truck tires rumbling over a rough spot in the road. "So why is it named Number Five?"

"That's how many times my grandfather proposed to my grandmother before she accepted."

"You're joking."

He shrugged. "Look it up."

"I will. So you better not be pulling my leg."

His lips twitched. "What're you going to do if I am? Report me to the police?"

"Now I know you're joking."

"Suit yourself. But if you'd ever been out there, you'd see there's a plaque about it and everything."

"No man in his right mind would propose *five* times. He'd give up!"

Linc's hazel gaze slid over her. "Maybe Gus considered Ernestine worth the effort."

For some stupid reason, she felt that quiver again and now she had no rough road to blame it on.

She gave him a cross look. "Keep your eyes on the road. The last thing we need is to get in an accident."

He smiled outright.

Maddie swallowed hard and looked out the window. *It's just a trip to the hospital. No big deal.*

Yeah. Right.

Chapter Eight

"All right." Justin Clay slid the last cheek swab into a vial, capped it and affixed a label preprinted with Linc's information over it. "My lab's pretty backed up right now, but we should have the results in a week." He glanced at Tom Hook. "You'll want a copy, I assume?"

The older man nodded. "I'd appreciate it." Since his part was done, he shook Linc's hand and left.

Justin looked at Linc. "You realize we're going to need something to compare your results against, right? Otherwise, it's simply an interesting genetic study."

Maddie held her breath. She hadn't specifically addressed the issue with Linc, but when he glanced at her, she knew it didn't matter.

"I know," he said. "I want it ready, though, when we *can* compare it against Layla's. I don't want any time wasted. At least on the things I can control."

"Good enough. DNA typing is all a puzzle of percentages. So it would help if we had more profiles than just you and Layla to compare—Jax, her mother, other possible fathers—but I guess if they were available, you wouldn't be here like this." Justin spun around on his metal stool and placed the vials on a tray on the metal table behind him. Then he turned to face Linc again as he pulled off his sterile gloves. "I've been meaning to call your office," he said. "Set up a meeting to talk about some equipment we're hoping to upgrade."

Justin not only ran the hospital lab, he was also Maddie's cousin, a fact that had only been discovered after her grandmother had moved to Wyoming. "I thought you just finished expanding the lab," she said. Thanks in no small part to Vivian's significant financial contribution.

"We did." He gestured with one arm and grinned. "Now we want to fill it with some more cool stuff. I know Swift Oil has been a big supporter of the hospital in the past."

"I'm sure we can work something out," Linc assured him. "Thanks for helping me with the test. I didn't expect personal attention from the lab director himself."

"Glad to help." Justin wiggled Layla's foot. "Seems like yesterday when Gracie was this little. Now, she's already a year old and running circles around Tabby and me."

"They do grow fast," Maddie agreed. "Are you two going to Vivian's Christmas party?"

Justin smiled ruefully. "Don't think there is any way of getting out of it since my wife already has her dress. Although, if Gloria has her way and actually manages to get Squire to go, there are sure to be some entertaining fireworks."

Maddie laughed. Squire was Justin's grandfather.

To say there was no love lost between him and Vivian was an understatement. The two seniors had even run against each other earlier that year for a seat on the Weaver Town Council.

Vivian had lost, but not by much. And considering she was a relative newcomer to the area—whereas Squire Clay had been ranching there since the dawn of time—that was a feat in itself.

"I really can't see your grandfather crossing my grandmother's doorstep no matter how persuasive Squire's wife can be," she said. "But that would probably be entertaining."

Justin glanced at the clock on the wall then back at Linc. "I don't mean to swab and run, but I've got another appointment. I'll have one of my techs show you the way out." The lab didn't have a complicated layout, but it was secured behind locked doors.

"Thanks." Linc shook his hand, and then Justin hurried off, his white coat flapping around his long legs. A moment later, one of Justin's staff escorted them out of the area.

Maddie chewed the inside of her cheek as the security door swung closed with a soft click, leaving them in an antiseptically austere tiled hallway. Their footsteps echoed as they headed down it toward the elevator. "I know what you're thinking." She had to hurry a little to keep up with Linc's long-legged stride.

"That your grandmother's Christmas party sounds like the hot ticket in town?"

"No. Well," she allowed quickly, "I suppose it sounds like it."

"At least your family does something together, even if it is full of fireworks." Along with his jacket and Maddie's coat, he was also still carrying the overstuffed flowered purse. It ought to have looked silly hanging off his broad shoulder.

Instead, Maddie was well aware of the number of appreciative female glances he'd garnered when they'd entered the hospital. She could only imagine how much more appreciative they'd have been had he also been carrying the baby.

There was just something about a man tending a baby.

About *him* tending a baby.

She swallowed down the disturbing notion. "I meant about Layla also needing a DNA test."

They'd reached the elevator and Linc's shoulder brushed against hers when he reached out to press the call button. The doors immediately slid open. "I can manage to figure out a few things on my own." His voice was dry.

"Then you understand why I couldn't just have Layla's test done today, too?"

He put one hand on the doors to make sure they stayed open. "Yes. You going to get on the elevator? Or do you want to just stand here in the hall for a while?"

She carried Layla onto the empty elevator, moving to the rear corner. When he took the opposite corner, she wondered if it was simply habit, or if he too felt the need to keep some space between them. "I wasn't trying to keep you in the dark about it."

"I know."

"It's a matter of privacy," she added doggedly, because she wanted him to be really clear on the matter. "Even though she's an infant, Layla has rights we have to protect—"

"I *get* it, Maddie."

She pressed her lips together.

They both focused on the elevator display. The car seemed to take forever moving from one floor to the next, and there were only three. She didn't even realize that she'd been holding her breath, until the doors slid open again and she hurried through them.

The main floor of the hospital was considerably busier than the third floor had been. They'd barely gotten out of the elevator before people were quickly stepping into it.

She didn't pay them any attention until one of them said her name. "Maddie?"

She glanced back at the man. She'd only met him once, when he'd been with her boss. But she still recognized him. "Mar—Morton." She was painfully aware that Linc had stopped to look, too. "What a surprise."

Morton smiled genially, as if he hadn't just stood her up a few days earlier. "I'm the one who works here. I think that makes your presence more a surprise than mine." His eyes were frankly curious as he took in Layla and Linc. "I was sorry that things didn't work out last Friday. We can try again this week, if you're available."

She just stared at him, not sure at all how to respond. He was about Linc's age, had half the hair, and none of the washboard abs. Not that she'd ever seen Morton without his shirt. She hadn't needed to. But when she'd met him the one time with her boss, he'd seemed nice enough.

Until he'd left her sitting for an hour at the restaurant where they'd agreed to meet before she'd finally given up on him and left.

"I...don't think so," she told him.

Linc's hand suddenly closed over Maddie's shoulder and she nearly jumped out of her skin. "Aren't you going to introduce us?"

She hesitated.

That was all Linc needed, evidently, and she watched with some horrified bemusement when he extended his other hand toward Martin. *Morton!*

"Lincoln Swift," he said.

Morton's expression grew even more curious as he shook Linc's hand. "Morton Meadows."

"So, Morton. How do you know our Maddie?"

Maddie shuffled her feet, but Linc's hand didn't drop away from her shoulder. "He's a friend of my boss," she said abruptly. It was bad enough to have been stood up. She didn't particularly want Linc knowing about it, too.

"Well, a friend of yours, too," Morton said with a chuckle.

She felt her jaw loosen a little. "Uh, sure. Whatev—"

Mercifully, Layla decided to take center stage at that moment, opening her mouth and letting out a loud wail.

Maddie jiggled the baby, who'd been an angel up to that point. "She's sleepy and probably hungry by now." She pulled the pacifier out of the purse Linc was holding and looked up at him. The baby turned her face away from the pacifier and wailed louder. "We should—"

"Go," he finished. "Good idea." He gave Morton a dismissive smile that Maddie couldn't help but enjoy as they turned and headed toward the hospital exit again. Only when they reached it did Linc's hand finally move away from her shoulder.

He held up her coat. "You'll want this. It's started snowing again."

She looked through the glass entrance. Sure enough, the snow was falling again. She knew there was no point in trying to hand Layla to him, particularly with the way she was crying, which meant Maddie had to suffer through him helping her on with her coat while she shifted the fussing baby from one arm to the other.

But when he started to button her in, she couldn't take anymore and she quickly stepped away. "I'm good. Thanks." She tried offering the pacifier to Layla again, but the baby still wanted nothing to do with it.

"Hold on." Linc gestured at the arrangement of chairs near the doors. He set the purse on one of them, pulled out the premixed bottle and uncapped it.

Maddie exchanged the pacifier for the bottle, and Layla went to town on it, her cries immediately ceasing. Maddie swirled the puppy blanket up and around the baby. "Okay," she said, feeling a little breathless. "We're good now."

"We can sit here if you want."

She already felt like they'd been drawing more than enough attention. "She'll be fine finishing in the truck."

He looped the long strap of the flowery purse over his shoulder again and they headed out.

The snow danced around them, but Maddie didn't mind. She felt overheated to her bones, courtesy of the hand that he lightly pressed against the small of her back as they walked through the parking lot.

When they reached the truck, she passed him Layla's bottle long enough to get the baby latched into her seat, then hurriedly climbed up beside her again.

"Not worried about getting carsick?"

Their fingers brushed when she quickly took the bottle back from him and offered it once more to Layla. "She can't hold the bottle by herself yet."

That was true, at least.

He reached in and set the purse near her feet. Then

he straightened and his eyes met hers, probably not even intentionally.

But she still felt something in her chest squeeze.

His eyebrows drew together. "What?"

She shook her head and made herself push some words out through her tightening throat. "You have a snowflake on your nose." And on his hair. On his shoulders. Like nature had decided to sprinkle him with glistening sugar.

He brushed his hand over his perfect nose and closed the truck door.

She let out a shaky breath and managed to somehow fasten her own seatbelt one-handed since Layla was adamantly opposed to having the bottle nipple move even an inch away from her.

Then Linc was getting in behind the wheel, and starting up the truck. He flipped on the wipers and they brushed easily through the snow accumulating on the windshield. Maddie imagined she could feel his gaze on her through the rearview mirror, but kept her own strictly on the baby. He steered the truck out of the hospital parking lot and within minutes, they were leaving the town behind.

The only sounds were the engine, the thrum of tires on the snowy highway and the sweet, soft noises Layla made as she guzzled.

Maddie leaned her head against her seat and unfastened her coat. She started to relax.

"So what's the story with Meadows?"

So much for relaxing.

She focused on Layla. "There's no story."

"Two of you sleep together or something?"

She looked up, gaping at him in the rearview mirror. "No!"

"Yeah. Figured. No chemistry between the two of you at all."

She huffed. "Then why even say such a thing!"

"Because it's pretty entertaining seeing the way you react."

She rolled her eyes. If her cheeks were as red as they felt, she would look in need of calamine lotion again. "You're annoying."

He actually chuckled.

She would have been even more annoyed at that, if she weren't flabbergasted to hear him laugh.

"He stood me up for dinner," she admitted severely. "No meal together, much less anything else."

"So he's an idiot. What about Jax?"

The baby bottle almost slid out of her hand. She quickly adjusted it before Layla could get riled up. "What about him?"

"Sleep with him?"

She opened her mouth. Closed it again. Shook her head. "This is not a conversation we are having," she muttered as much for her own benefit as his.

"So you did."

"No, I did not sleep with Jax!"

"Ever?"

She kicked the back of his seat. She'd rather have kicked him, but since she was not a violent person, it had to do. "I was seventeen when you told me I needed to stay far, *far* away from Jax."

"Which isn't an answer."

She kicked his seat again. "I wasn't sleeping with him at seventeen! Or eighteen, or any other time. And none of it's your business anyway! Not Martin or Jax or—"

"Who's Martin?"

"Morton!" She thumped her head against her seat-back. "Just…just be quiet. My sex life—" *or lack of it*, she amended quietly to herself "—is none of your business. I'm not asking *you* about the women you've slept with." Just the thought of them was enough to make her feel jealous, and she hated that fact.

"Been a while, has it?"

She closed her eyes and threw her free arm over her face for good measure. She'd choke before she told him just how long a while. The last date she'd had was almost a year ago. As for sex, that was even longer ago. "Whatever this game is, I'm not playing."

He chuckled again. "You're pretty cute when you're pissed off."

"I must be cute around you all the time, then," she muttered.

"So when is your grandmother's party supposed to be?"

"Night before Christmas Eve." She dropped her arm and watched his forehead in the rearview mirror. "And why are you being so chatty, anyway?"

"It's better than thinking about those cheek swabs or what that judge of yours is going to say tomorrow morning."

He couldn't have said anything more effective.

All of her annoyance drizzled out of her.

Layla hadn't quite finished the bottle, but her eyes were closed, so Maddie fit the cap back on the bottle and dropped it inside the purse. "Linc, even if the judge doesn't rule in your favor tomorrow morning, it doesn't mean that Layla's going to disappear somewhere terrible. I promise you, she would be with very qualified caregivers. I would see to it personally."

"That doesn't make this any better."

She leaned forward as far as her seatbelt allowed, and touched her fingers to his shoulder. "I know. But you're doing everything right here. If you're her uncle—"

"What if I'm not?"

She hesitated. "You've been adamant that you are." She hadn't considered that he'd allowed any room for doubt, no matter what her opinions might have been. "And you know, Jax will come back. Like you said. He always comes back. He's just off somewhere skiing or... or something. Chances are, he'll show up and explain all of this. Who Layla's mother is. Why she would have left Layla the way she did. And he'll do what's right."

"If he even recognizes what's right," Linc murmured. "He's with Dana. My ex-wife."

Maddie blinked. She wasn't sure if her "Oh," escaped her lips or if it was just sounding inside her head. "I'm sorry," she finally managed. She didn't know what else to say.

"Me, too." The tires hummed in the silence. "For him. He should have learned his lesson where she's concerned by now." He was silent for another moment. "He's too much like our parents. Maybe he never will learn."

She sincerely hoped he would learn. His mom and dad had never been any sort of parents. She'd recognized that even as a kid. It had been Ernestine who'd provided her grandsons with love and attention and boundaries. Was it going to be left to Linc to do the same with Layla? "If he's with your, uh, with Dana, then do you know how to reach them?"

"I know who he's with. Doesn't mean that I know where."

She chewed the inside of her lip. "You don't think that Dana is Layla's—"

"No." Linc's voice was flat.

She let it drop even though her head was about to explode with unasked questions. "Right now, let's just take it one step at a time. The first step is the hearing tomorrow morning."

He made a sound. Of agreement, she supposed.

She looked over at Layla. The baby's sleeping face was angelic, and she lightly grazed her fingertip over her soft, soft hair.

Then she had to close her eyes, because they were suddenly burning with tears.

The next morning, Maddie beat Linc to the courthouse.

In fact, she and Layla seemed to beat everyone.

When Maddie pushed the stroller through Judge Stokes' courtroom door, the room was empty.

She didn't worry, though. She knew she was a few minutes early. But it had just been easier to come to the courthouse than keep huddling around the space heaters and the fireplace at home, because the temperature had dropped another ten degrees since the day before.

There were three rows of wooden bench seats on either side of the center aisle behind the bar, and she maneuvered the stroller into the front row.

She unwrapped the blanket tucked around Layla and smiled into her face, squeezing the squeaking giraffe until the baby chortled and grabbed the giraffe for herself. Layla squeezed it, too, and jumped when it squeaked, then laughed all over again.

Maddie cupped her hand tenderly over the baby's head. "Sweet girl."

"What the *hell* are you doing here, Templeton?"

Maddie jumped, dropping her hand. She looked

around to see Raymond Marx standing in the doorway of the courtroom. To say her forty-year-old boss looked displeased was putting it mildly. His bald head was red, his wrinkled tie was more askew than usual, and he was sweating. As if he'd run all the way to the courtroom from their office down the street.

He approached her and jabbed a finger in the air. "I warned you. No cases for two weeks."

"Ray—"

"Don't *Ray* me. You do this all the time, and I told you it had to stop. You're going to burn out and quit, and I'm going to lose my best worker." He reached her row and put his hands over the stroller handle.

Panic shot through her and she grabbed the side of the stroller. She wasn't sure what she could do if he decided to take Layla from her, but she knew she couldn't let it happen.

"Best worker or not, you had no right approaching the judge the way you did. This is an agency matter and you know it."

She opened her mouth to defend herself, but he raised his palm, silencing her. "You're off this case as of right now."

"But—"

"And while I decide what to do with you, instead of vacationing for the next two weeks, consider yourself suspended instead. Without pay. Maybe then you'll take me seriously."

She shoved off the bench. "That is *not* fair."

"What's not fair is you thinking you don't have to follow the rules."

"I have followed the rules," she said hotly. "Every single one. Except the vacation guideline. Guideline! You forced my vacation, and you know it. And while *on vacation*, I assessed Layla's situation when I became aware of it. I saw to the safety of this child, and I reported it!"

"To the court," he said through his teeth. "What about to your boss?"

"Good morning, Ray." Judge Horvald Stokes ambled into the courtroom from the door behind the bench, carrying his coffee and a doughnut. He was at least twenty years older than Ray, and had all of the hair that Ray did not. It was just bright white. As was his beard. Which tended to make Judge Stokes look a little like Santa Claus, particularly when he wore a red sweater, as he was now. "You're sounding in rare form this morning." He lifted his doughnut in cheer. "Morning, Miss Maddie."

She swallowed, reminding herself that what she had done was nothing illegal, but just outside of protocol where her stickler of a boss was concerned. "Good morning, Your Honor."

The judge approached to peer over the stroller at Layla. "Aren't you the cute one?" Then he headed back to the ramp that led up to his bench. He set down his coffee and swallowed half of his doughnut. "Ray, your knickers tighter than usual this morning for some reason?"

"No, Your Honor."

"So you look like you're gonna have a stroke every morning?"

Ray gave her a fulminating look, as if this were all her fault. Which she supposed it was. "No, Your Honor," he said grimly. "Just an internal matter that's causing me some...concern."

The judge smiled. "Well. I'm not one to get into

your internal matters. So what say you settle it outside of my courtroom?"

"With pleasure." Ray started to pull the stroller away from Maddie.

She held fast. "Don't do this, Ray. You can suspend me if you want. Fire me for that matter. But this child is in *my* protective custody right now. Not the department's."

"If it weren't for the department—"

"I'd have still called Maddie."

They both turned to see Linc entering. His intense eyes lingered on her face as he approached. Tom Hook was with him. "What's going on here?"

"Internal matters," Judge Stokes said dryly. He swallowed down the other half of his doughnut and pulled on his black robe, though he didn't bother with zipping it up. "Morning, Tom. Good to see you. Been a while." The side door swung open, and the court reporter came in, carrying his steno writer, followed by the clerk and the court officer. As usual, the judge greeted them all by name. Typically, Judge Stokes liked to keep everyone comfortable.

Until he didn't. Then he'd zip up his robe, and it would be all business. Period.

Maddie was following the proceedings with one ear. The rest of her was focused on Linc, her boss and Layla. The baby's face was scrunching up as if she sensed the tension around her and Maddie made herself relax. She sat down on the long wooden seat and squeezed the giraffe a few times. "Everything's fine, sweet pea."

"This isn't going to be the last of it," Ray warned her. But even he didn't have the nerve to interrupt when the court was called into session.

Tom and Linc sat at the table in front of her, Ray at the other.

She should have called Archer to come and represent her. She just honestly hadn't thought she'd need him.

The court clerk read off the details of the hearing, then handed Judge Stokes a sheaf of papers.

"Thank you, Sue." The judge folded his arms in front of him atop the papers he set on his desk. He looked at them all in turn. "So," he said. "We've got what appears to be an abandoned infant. That still the case?" He glanced up with an arched brow. Receiving no correction, he continued. "All right. That leaves us with the question of what to do about that."

Ray popped out of his seat like an overwound jack-in-the-box toy. "Your Honor, my department is fully prepared to handle the matter and I apologize that you were called in prematurely—"

The judge lifted his palm, silencing Ray the same way that Ray had silenced Maddie. "Let's just focus on the child for the moment. Aside from the note you referenced in the filing, is there anyone in this room who can tell me for certain who she is?"

Tom Hook stood.

Judge Stokes looked at him. "For *certain*, Tom?"

"No, Your Honor. But my client is working to that end."

"Good for your client." The judge focused on Linc. "What is it that you hope to prove, Mr. Swift?"

Linc stood. He was wearing a black suit and was easily the most formally dressed one there. And Maddie could see just how tight his broad shoulders were. "That Layla is my niece. My brother's child. Though I don't believe he was aware of that fact."

"And your brother?" The judge glanced through the papers. "Jaxon Swift. Why isn't he here today?"

"Mr. Swift's brother is out of town," Tom interjected. "My client is making every effort to reach him. I can't emphasize enough that he is very certain his brother is unaware that any of this has occurred."

The judge looked from Linc's table to Ray's, then back again. "I knew your grandmother, Mr. Swift," he said suddenly. "A good woman."

"Yes," Linc agreed quietly. "She was."

"Mmm." The judge flipped through the papers again. "This is a problem. Suppositions aside, we have an unknown mother. Unknown father. Going to involve a heck of an investigation."

Maddie swallowed. She reached into the stroller and plucked Layla out of it, holding her close. Not because Layla needed it.

But because she did.

Particularly when the judge sat back and suddenly zipped his robe.

Chapter Nine

The judge looked at his clerk. "You awake there, Sue?"

Sue gave him a look.

"Just checking." Judge Stokes looked out at them again. "All right then. I want a thorough investigation where Layla's parents are concerned. To that end, I'm ordering genetic testing of Layla." His expression was solemn. "Let's get it ruled out that someone somewhere else isn't frantically searching for their child. And—" he eyed Linc "—I'll allow the comparison to the results you're submitting. If anything comes of that, then we'll be meeting here again sooner rather than later."

"Thank you, Your Honor," Tom said.

The judge nodded briefly. He looked toward Ray. "Meanwhile, baby Layla will require suitable shelter care until a custodian—whether Mr. Swift or another party—is named."

Maddie sucked in a quick breath and stood. "I'm suitable."

Even across the room she could hear her boss groan. "Maddie Templeton is presently on suspension."

The judge sighed a little. "That internal matter, I suppose."

"Yes."

"If my suspension is an issue, then I'll quit." Her voice was husky but it was still clear.

Linc turned around and looked at her.

She kept her eyes on the judge. "I'm a qualified foster-care provider, Judge." A fact that he knew perfectly well. "Whether I'm employed by the department or not."

The judge tapped his thumbs together a few times. "What's the basis for Miss Maddie's suspension, Ray? She's always seemed very capable to me."

"Ignoring departmental rules."

"With regard to what?"

"Vacation," Maddie inserted quickly.

The judge looked pained. "Is that true, Ray?"

"Well, yes."

"Not abuse of power. Not dereliction of duties. Not even using the office copier for her own personal use. Which is something we have all done anyway."

"No." Ray straightened his wrinkled tie. "If anything, Maddie is too far the opposite. She's determined that every family finds a happy ending and you know how impossible that is. She takes cases to the extreme."

"Sort of like taking vacation rules to the extreme?" The judge's voice turned dry.

"She took on a case when she shouldn't have," Ray maintained doggedly.

"Your Honor," Tom interrupted. "Considering my client's desire to care for this child he believes to be his niece, he could have chosen not to notify anyone at all and none of us would be the wiser. But knowing of her expertise, he chose to reach out to Miss Templeton for assistance."

The judge pursed his lips as he looked at Linc, who'd faced forward once again. "Why Maddie?" He lifted his hand. "Cool your jets, Tom. Let your client answer. I just want to know."

"She's an old friend," Linc said evenly.

"So you didn't contact her in an official capacity."

"No." He waited a beat. "She very quickly advised me of her legal obligations, though."

The judge smiled slightly. "I'll bet she did." He tapped his thumbs together a few more times. "You married, Mr. Swift?"

"Not anymore."

"Too bad. Kids?"

"No."

"Dogs? Cats?" The judge lifted his hand. "Don't answer that." He looked toward Ray. "I can't tell you what to do about your sacred vacation rule, Ray. But seems to me that you're wound up over a whole lot of nothing." Then he looked at Maddie. "You're willing to provide a safe and stable environment for baby Layla? See to all of her needs, physically and otherwise?"

"Yes, Your Honor."

He nodded once. "Good enough. Look sharp, everyone," he said. "I'm ordering that Layla temporarily remain in the care of Maddie Templeton. And I want an update on the investigation and the baby's care in one week's time when I will reassess the matter. Got that, Sue?"

"Got it, Judge."

He slammed his gavel once. "Adjourned."

Then he stood up, unzipped his black judge's robe and disappeared through the back door to his chambers.

"Congratulations." Tom shook Linc's hand. "Stay of execution, as it were."

"For a week." Linc looked at Maddie where she was sitting on the bench behind them, hugging Layla to her. Maddie was pale. His chest felt tight. "Only because of her," he said gruffly.

Tom shrugged. "It's still a win in your column for today. Meanwhile, my advice is to find your brother before the authorities do. Get him back here. And stay in touch with me."

Linc nodded. "Thanks, Tom." He shook the lawyer's hand. "I will."

The lawyer moved away. He leaned over, murmuring something to Maddie on his way out of the courtroom.

Maddie smiled a little, then sobered when her eyes met Linc's.

"You wouldn't really quit your job over this," he said.

She rubbed her cheek against Layla's blond hair. "Fortunately, we don't have to find out." She stood.

The rumpled guy who was obviously her boss stopped next to them. "Maybe suspension is a bit much."

She lifted an eyebrow. "You think?"

"Don't push it, Templeton." He studied the baby in her arms. Layla had tucked her thumb in her mouth and was looking drowsy and very comfortable nestled against Maddie's chest. "Prosecutor's going to want the note."

Maddie looked quickly at Linc. "You still have it, right?"

He reached in his lapel pocket and withdrew the

small piece of paper. "I kept a copy of it for myself." His lips twisted slightly. "Used the office copier."

Maddie bit her lip, looking down at her toes.

Ray took the note and unfolded it. He shook his head. "I hope for everyone's sake this doesn't get messier before it gets better." He patted the baby's back gently. "See you here next week." Then he strode away, too.

Maddie's chocolate gaze lifted to Linc's once more. "My house is freezing," she said baldly. "And that swing you got for her won't fit in my car. You'll have to pick it up."

He squelched the leaping sensation inside him. "You've come to your senses."

"No. I'm pretty sure I've lost them." She started to lower Layla into the stroller but the baby squawked out a protest. "My parents' house is perfectly well-heated, too." She dropped her too-full flowered purse into the stroller and grabbed the handle with her free hand, steering it clear of the bench seat. "And my mother *loves* babies."

He covered her hand with his and she went still. "Then why?"

"Because it's the right thing to do."

"For Layla."

Her gaze slid away. Her voice went husky. "And for you."

Then she shifted, pulling away from him. She pushed the stroller toward the courtroom doors, but stopped just shy of them. She looked back at him where he still stood, feeling rooted to the ground. "I'll need a key to your house." She was back to her usual briskness.

"I'll get you whatever you need."

Something came and went in her eyes. "Let's just start with the key."

Then she turned and pushed the stroller through the courtroom door.

Linc slowly sank back down onto the chair. He wasn't used to feeling like the stuffing had been pulled right out of him. He stared at the courtroom around him. It had emptied entirely after the judge exited.

She'd been willing to quit her job.

He rubbed his hand down his face but he couldn't rub away the shock he'd felt when she'd said it to the judge. Or the way her expression has been so certain.

The side door opened and Sue, the court clerk, entered. She stopped in surprise when she spotted him. "Mr. Swift. I'm sorry. I didn't realize you were still here. Was there something else you needed?"

He knew she was married to one of his engineers and wondered how often she had to clerk for some case involving a Swift Oil employee. "No, I was just thinking if these courtroom walls could talk."

"They'd know better than to try." She seemed cheerful enough as she set a stack of files on her desk, clearly getting ready for the next case.

He pushed to his feet. "I guess I'll be seeing you next week."

She smiled. "Jerry's always telling me what a decent man you are, Mr. Swift. I wish you good luck with all of this."

"Thanks, Sue."

"Merry Christmas."

He smiled faintly. For the first time in a long time, he actually felt a little anticipation where the holiday was concerned. "Merry Christmas to you, too."

A loud thump vibrated through the walls, making Maddie jump nervously.

She looked at Layla, lying on the changing table inside the nursery at Linc's home. "Sounds like Uncle Linc is back," she said. Rather than leave the nursery to go and see, though, she finished fastening Layla's diaper and then tucked her into one of the stretchy knit sleepers that Ali had produced when she'd come home after her shift to find Maddie packing her suitcase. "He's going to think you're pretty as a picture in your new clothes."

Layla kicked her legs enthusiastically. Her eyes danced as she looked up at Maddie.

The adoration in the baby's eyes was almost too much to bear.

She picked up the baby, cuddling her close. Maddie had given Layla her bath and she smelled like everything that could possibly be right in this world. "Of course," she whispered, "even without all your new things you're pretty as a picture."

"It's a picture all right," Linc said, walking into the nursery. He was still wearing the suit from that morning, but the tie was gone and the top two buttons of his white shirt were undone. "Where do you want this?"

She quickly looked from the strong column of his throat to the infant swing he was carrying. "That's a good question." She glanced around the nursery. It had been perfectly spacious the first time she'd seen it. Now there were boxes of baby items everywhere. While she'd been packing clothes to last her for the coming week, she felt certain he'd sent someone to Shop-World in Weaver to buy out the entire baby department. "Wherever you can find room."

He smiled slightly. "It is a little crowded in here now."

He had enough gear to outfit half a dozen nurseries.

And they didn't even know what would happen with Layla once the next week passed.

"A little," she agreed. With her foot, she nudged a tricycle into the corner. It would be two years before Layla would be ready for the thing. "Here." Moving the trike had freed up a few spare feet of floor space.

He deposited the swing in the spot and glanced through the doorway to the adjoining room. "You get yourself settled all right?"

"Yes. You didn't have to send over Terry with keys this afternoon, though. We could have just waited until this evening to come here."

"She had some other errands to take care of for me, so she was already out and about." He picked up one of the sleepers from Ali that Maddie had yet to put away in the chest of drawers. "Fitting for the season," he drawled. The sleeper was fashioned like something Santa's elves would wear. The one that Layla currently had on was dark blue and covered in white snowflakes. "Looks like someone else has been doing some shopping, too."

"Blame Ali. I haven't had time to take care of anything except the necessities, much less go shopping. It's a good thing you bought so many diapers the other day. We're going through them like nobody's business." Maddie settled Layla into the seat of the swing. It was surprising how heavy a fifteen-pound baby could be. "The only things we're still missing are extra bottles and nipples. Pretty much the most basic of basic." She snapped the safety harness together and turned on the swing. Fortunately, it also ran on batteries, because there was no way the power cord could have reached its spot in virtually the center of the nursery.

The unicorns, no longer looking scrunched up from

being packaged in a box, began slowly revolving above Layla's head as the seat of the swing started swaying.

Linc was watching Layla so intently that Maddie felt a stab somewhere in the vicinity of her heart. "Listen." She snatched up the damp bath towels from the rocker where she'd dumped them. "I left a bit of a mess in the bathroom. If you wouldn't mind sitting with her for a few, I'll just get it cleaned up." There was no earthly reason why she couldn't have nipped into the adjoining bathroom for a few minutes to take care of tidying up when Layla was so securely contained in the swing, but she didn't figure he needed to know that. "Here." She patted the upholstered chair in invitation, and carried the towels out of the room.

She didn't wait to see what he would do. Because she knew if she did, he wouldn't do anything.

The bathroom was a Jack and Jill, opening to both the nursery and Maddie's bedroom. She went through the door and turned on the water, making as much noise as she could to prove how necessary her task was. She pushed the door to the nursery partially closed and used one of the towels to mop up the water that she and Layla had splashed onto the cream-colored tile. While she was crawling around on the floor, she peeked around the door to see if any progress had been made in the nursery.

Linc was sitting on the rocker. He'd discovered the video baby monitor box that she'd yet to unpack. His eyes, however, were trained on the bathroom doorway.

She flushed and backed out of view.

"I still see you," he said.

She sat up on her knees and caught her reflection in the mirror over the sink. "Still see me what?" she asked innocently. But her cheeks were red. She climbed to her feet and spread the wet towels over the side of the tub and the separate glass shower enclosure. She figured with a little practice, she'd be able to bathe Layla without creating a swamp on the floor, but for now, she was still adjusting.

The front of her sweater felt damp, but at least it didn't show. And the damp patches on the front of her jeans that did show would disappear soon enough. She briskly tightened the ponytail at the back of her head and went back into the nursery, propping her hands on her hips. "What were you saying?"

"What's going to happen next week in court?"

She exhaled. She understood his concern, but she hadn't expected the question quite so soon. "Hasn't Tom Hook explained everything to you?"

Linc inclined his head and set aside the plastic-covered box. "I want to hear it in your words."

She didn't know whether to be touched or not.

She turned around one of the child-size chairs that went with a matching craft table and perched on it. "What happens next week depends on a lot of things. If Layla's mother returns in the meantime, for one."

He snorted softly. "Pardon me if I don't hold my breath. Not even *my* mother would have done what she did."

Maddie wasn't touching that with a ten-foot pole. "Also, if the investigation about her yields anything," she continued. "If you reach Jax or if he returns. If we have the results of both your and Layla's DNA profiles. I'll pick up the court order tomorrow for her test and take her back to the hospital to get that done. You've seen for yourself that it's not going to traumatize her for life or anything." She reached out to slow the swing down a notch.

"A lot of ifs. I don't like a lot of ifs."

"You're in the oil business. Aren't you surrounded by ifs? If this well keeps producing. If it doesn't."

"If I can keep the wolves at bay," he murmured. "All the more reason not to like them."

"What wolves?"

He shook his head. "Judge Stokes said it was too bad I wasn't married. Why? It's not going to even matter when I'm proven to be her uncle."

"Okay. Let's say you are her uncle. That means Jax is her father." Maddie spread her hands. "If he can satisfy Judge Stokes that he wasn't a party to the way she was left with you, then there's no reason I can think of why Layla wouldn't be awarded to him. If he can't prove it, then he'll probably be charged with child endangerment. Neglect at the very least. So will Layla's mother. Whoever she turns out to be."

"Jax wouldn't endanger a child. Not his or anyone else's."

"Well, I don't think so, either." She could see that Layla was nodding off and she turned the setting on the swing even lower. If the baby didn't have a full bottle before she fell asleep, Maddie was going to be in for a long night. She'd learned that in just the past few days. But she was also loath to interrupt the moment with Linc.

So she continued. "But, for the sake of argument, let's suppose that for whatever reason, the judge terminates Jax and Layla's parent-child relationship. That means someone else—you, for instance as her closest responsible relative—could be made her guardian. But nothing is automatic. Not when Layla is already under the protection of the court."

"So even if I'm her uncle, I would have to pass muster."

"Essentially."

"And even if I'm her uncle, I'd pass muster better if I had a wife."

She spread her hands again. "I know it sounds ridiculous, and it *shouldn't* matter. But it does. The court is going to want to place Layla in whatever family situation will best provide for her health and her safety. In a contest between a married couple and a single person, particularly a man—sorry, but that *is* what you are— the married couple usually wins."

"Then I need a wife."

Maddie couldn't stop the short laugh that escaped. "I never pegged you for being dramatic."

"I'm not being dramatic."

Alarm niggled at her insides. "Well, you surely can't be serious!"

His gaze was steady on her face. Uncomfortably so.

She swallowed and strove for reason. "Linc. The only thing you need to be shopping for this week are baby bottles. Certainly not a wife."

"I don't think I'd have to shop far."

Of course, he'd have some female in mind. A man like Linc would naturally have a woman around. Women around.

The alarm spread, running through her veins like some rampant drug, bent on destruction.

"I'm sure you wouldn't," she managed more or less evenly. "Whoever you were out with last Friday night, for instance. But trust me. You don't need to jump that particular gun quite so fast. I mean, what if you're *not* Layla's uncle? Then this is all moot."

"If I'm not, then obviously, I'll need a wife even more."

Her stomach churned. "Why?"

He looked at her, as if it should be obvious. "You said yourself that there weren't any unmarried male foster parents. How else can I make sure Layla could stay here? With me."

"You don't really want a baby." She gestured at Layla. The infant's eyes were closed; she was blissfully unaware of being at the center of so much turmoil. "I can count on one hand the number of times you've actually held her. If she's not your niece, then—"

"You don't know what I want or don't want."

It was like being punched.

Maddie exhaled carefully, knowing that he was right. Aside from what he believed his responsibilities were to Layla, she didn't know anything at all about what he did or didn't want. His ex-wife had been pregnant. This nursery had obviously been built for that child. A child he'd denied having in front of the judge.

If his words were true, was he really simply trying to fill that void?

"Okay," she finally said. "You're saying you want to *keep* Layla?"

"Don't you?"

"Well, yes." The admission came automatically. "But—"

"Then the solution is simple. *You* can marry me."

Her stomach fell away completely. "What?"

"Marry me," he said with inordinate patience.

She scrambled to her feet and the child-size chair tipped over, making a huge racket.

He remained silent. His eyes followed her as she backed away. Though where she thought she would go, she didn't know. Layla was now sound asleep in the swing. She hadn't even started at the chair noise. If Maddie snatched her and took off, the only decent place to go would be her parents' house. And she was too old to be running home to Mom and Dad just because her job was too uncomfortable.

The job's *uncomfortable?*

She stiffened her shoulders, propping her hands on her hips. She'd keep her wits about her if it killed her. "Don't joke. This is too serious."

"Layla's already bonding to you."

"What do *you* know about babies bonding?"

"I know enough. Forget I asked. I made the mistake of thinking you were as interested in her welfare as I am."

She clenched her teeth, feeling dizzy inside from her seesawing emotions. "Up until now, the worst thing you've ever said to me was that Jax and I were bad for each other." She jabbed a finger through the air. "You're the bad one. Suggesting you and I get married? We don't even like each other. Much less feel any of—" she broke off, waving her hand and feeling her face getting hotter by the second "—*that.*"

"I'm not suggesting a real marriage," he said evenly. The more uptight she got, the more reasonable he seemed to sound. And it was infuriating. "Just a mutually beneficial arrangement where Layla is concerned. Although you're living in la-la land if you really think there is no—" he waved his hand mockingly "—*that* between us."

The top of her head ought to be smoking, considering the fire burning inside her face. "Go find some other nitwit to fill the bill."

He watched her through narrowed eyes for a long moment. Then—as if her answer really didn't matter all that much, anyway—he shrugged and stood. "That may be some of your best advice yet."

He stepped around the swing and she quickly moved even farther aside.

"Don't worry, Maddie. I'm not my grandfather. I won't ask five times."

Her hands curled into fists. She lifted her chin and made herself meet his eyes. Why would he, when there was no love at all in the asking? All he needed—thought he needed—was a wife for the sake of appearances only. "And I'm not your grandmother. So at least we've got that clear!"

Chapter Ten

By Friday, Maddie didn't need to turn on the lights anymore when she headed downstairs to fix Layla's middle-of-the-night bottles. She'd gotten plenty of practice memorizing the stairs by then.

And fortunately, aside from the night of the marriage "discussion," she hadn't run into Linc during any of her nighttime foraging.

Truthfully, she hadn't run into Linc much at all.

On one hand, it gave her much-needed breathing room.

On the other hand, his absence just made everything worse.

Because if she'd been concerned about his lack of physical interaction with Layla before, it was even more worrying now, the longer it went on.

He left the house at dawn each day. And then he didn't return until Layla was already in bed for the night.

Working a lot? Keeping wolves at bay?

Avoiding the very baby he claimed to want?

Avoiding you?

Out trying to find a nitwit wife?

The noise inside her head was deafening.

Maddie looked down at Layla in the dim light from the pantry while they waited for the bottle to heat.

"He sure hasn't stinted on stuff for you, though," she murmured to the infant. The bottle warmer was state-of-the-art. So was the set of bottles and nipples that went with it. Linc may have been intentionally absent, but he was making certain that Layla had every material thing she could possibly need.

There'd been the warmer and the bottles. A wardrobe fit for a princess. A potty chair that looked like an actual miniature toilet that wasn't necessary, considering how far-off potty training would be. The fancy multi-strapped baby carrier, though?

Maddie bent over the top of Layla's head and dropped a kiss on her sweet-smelling blond hair.

The carrier was definitely spot on the money even though it had taken her several tries and watching a few online videos to get the hang of using it.

Now, instead of having to hold Layla in her arms, she simply strapped her into the soft carrier. Layla got to look out at the world, whether they were the inside the Swift mansion or out in the yard. And Maddie's back didn't get quite so tired as she hefted around a baby that was gaining weight by the day.

She pulled the bottle from the warmer and tested the formula. It was as perfect as the price tag promised and she offered it to the baby. For herself, she broke off half a brownie from the batch she'd made earlier that evening and stuffed it into her mouth. Then she flipped off the pantry light and padded barefoot through the dark kitchen. They went into the living room, but instead of heading straight for the staircase, she lingered in front of the unadorned picture window. It overlooked the long, sloping yard that glimmered whitely beneath the moonlight.

She leaned her head closer to the baby's as they stood by the window. "Your Uncle Linc used to pull me and my sisters on a sled down that hill," she murmured. "Back then, I thought this was the perfect house with the perfect yard." She shifted slightly from side to side, rocking Layla as she drank the bottle. "When you're a little older, maybe he'll take you sledding, too."

She heard a sound and quickly looked over her shoulder.

But she saw nothing except the same dark shapes of furniture. As usual.

"Old houses settle," she told Layla. "That's what I have to remind Ali all the time about our house. It's not ghosts moving things around. It's just the bones of an old house creaking." She rocked her some more. "Maybe we'll go over there tomorrow. See if Auntie Ali and Auntie Greer have agreed on a paint color for the kitchen yet. Shall we make a bet that they haven't?"

"What're the odds?"

She whirled, and Layla protested when she momentarily lost the bottle. Maddie blinked, peering harder into the darkness.

"You don't need to sneak around in your own house," Maddie told Linc, finally making him out sitting in one of the leather wing chairs near the cold fireplace.

"I've been here since you came downstairs." She only realized he had a glass in his hand when he moved his arm and she heard the soft clink of ice. "When you started talking to yourself, I figured I'd better warn you I was here."

"I was talking to Layla." She looked back out the window. The view from the bedroom and nursery upstairs was entirely different—from there, you could see the rear of the house and the stable that, sadly, sat empty these days.

"You make the brownies?"

She wiped her lips, as if he'd caught her with her mouth full. "Yes. Sorry. I kind of made myself at home." Because she'd been going stir-crazy inside his home between endless diapers and bottles and sleepless nights not entirely due to Layla.

"I ate half the pan when I got in a little while ago."

"Kind of late, even for you." She tucked her tongue between her teeth, intending to leave it at that. But of course, to her shame, she couldn't. "Hot date?"

"And if I said yes?"

She made herself shrug, though he probably couldn't make her out any more clearly than she could him. "More power to you," she said blithely. She kept looking out the window. "She know you're in the market for a missus to your mister?"

The ice clinked softly. She heard a faint rustle and felt herself tense as he moved to also stand at the wide window. "You always wanted to sit in the middle of the sled," he said. "Greer in the front. Ali in the back."

"Greer liked to think she was steering. Ali liked to think the back was a wilder ride." She pressed her cheek against Layla's hair, finding that the contact steadied her. "Surprised you remember."

"I remember everything." He lifted his glass and took a sip. Now that he was closer, she could make out the short tumbler and smell the whiskey. "The only happy days we had back then were when we were here with my grandmother."

"I'm glad you were here a lot, then." She chewed the inside of her cheek. "Your grandmother was a really nice woman. My mom always said how much she loved you. You and Jax."

"I know what my dad did. Or tried to do." He took another drink. "Where your mom was concerned. I didn't know back then, but—"

"It doesn't matter," she said quickly. "It was a long time ago."

"If my grandmother knew, she would never have let your mom quit."

"That's why my mother never said anything to Ernestine."

"Instead, she told you?"

"She didn't have to. I used to dust under the foyer table, remember? Not very noticeable to someone who isn't looking."

He absorbed that and swore softly. "Another reason to apologize."

"You're not responsible for what your father did." She sighed faintly. "I didn't even really understand what was happening until later when my mom explained why we weren't coming here so regularly anymore. I don't think your dad ever actually touched her. He just made it too uncomfortable for her with his comments."

"You started coming around again later with Jax."

And by then, Linc had gone away to college. But getting into that period of history was probably not the most sensible thing to do. They'd hashed it over enough, but the results were still the same.

So she changed the subject entirely. "How'd you meet your wife?"

She felt him go still. "Dana?"

"Have you already gotten yourself another one?"

"*Ex*-wife." His voice sounded clipped. "College."

That was what she'd figured. "Love at first sight?"

He lifted his drink again. She could tell his glass was nearly empty just from the sound of the ice. "More like sex at first sight."

She was hardly a prude, but her cheeks turned hot. She pressed one against Layla's head. That's what she got for asking such a question. Being aggravated by the answer was her bad luck. "Sixty-two percent of relationships that start out as sex end up failing."

"You're making that up."

"Entirely."

He let out a short breath. Not a laugh. But more amused than not. "I didn't know your name was really Maude."

It was lobbed from the same left field as her question about his wife. Ex-wife.

"Yes, well, I don't much care for it. It is my legal name. I use it when I need to, but otherwise..." She shrugged. "All my friends know me as Maddie. Greer's got a great name. Ali is really Alicia. Perfectly good name, too."

"Ali fits her better. And you do seem more like a Maddie than a Maude, too."

"I'll take that as a compliment. Our parents named us after some old relatives."

"And Archer?"

"Family name, too. On my dad's side. Archer and Hayley had a different mom. She died when they were little. Then my dad met Meredith, who already had Rosalind."

"Another sister? I don't remember—"

"She grew up in Cheyenne with her father. It was not an easy divorce between my mom and Rosalind's dad. We only got to see her for holidays and a week during summers. She's a lawyer too, though."

"Three lawyers, a cop and a social worker."

"And a psychologist," she reminded. "Don't forget Hayley. I studied psychology, too. Just didn't take it in quite the same direction as she did." Maddie realized that Layla had sucked the bottle dry, so she gently tugged it away. Then she stuffed it in the loose side pocket of her flannel pajama pants and unzipped the fabric carrier to slip Layla out of it.

"What are you doing?"

"I learned the hard way about her burping in this thing." She lifted the baby to her shoulder and firmly patted her back. "Also learned how nicely the carrier turns out after a spin in your washing machine, though." She didn't need to see his face to imagine the grimace he was probably making. "This was a really good purchase," she told him.

"Terry picked it out."

"Ah." She smiled faintly. "I wondered if you'd just opened a website and clicked a buy button or something." Layla burped loudly. "Hurray, sweet pea. And no spit-up. Double hurray."

"She's throwing up?"

"Spitting up," Maddie corrected. "She's not sick. Just getting air with the formula and developing her digestive system. It's normal." She watched him from the corner of her eye. "Would you like to put her back down? She might not sleep as long as I keep hoping, but she does at least fall right back to sleep after her night bottles."

She held her breath when he actually hesitated.

But then he swirled the ice in his glass and took a step away. "She's used to you."

She exhaled. "Linc, she won't get used to *you* unless you give her an opportunity. She's had her poopsplosion for the day and she's not spitting up. You've managed to avoid holding her except for a few occasions. What's the problem?"

"There's no problem."

Layla sighed hugely and curled against Maddie's chest. And oh, how she wished that Linc could experience just how wonderful it felt.

"Does it have something to do with the baby Dana had?"

He didn't answer for a moment. "She didn't have it."

She sighed. "I was afraid it was something like that. You know, sweetie, miscarriages are—"

"She had an abortion. By choice. Her choice."

Maddie's words stopped up in her throat. It wasn't that she was opposed to abortion per se. In fact, she considered herself to be squarely in the pro choice camp. As long as that choice was a responsible one. But Dana had been his *wife*. "I'm sorry," she finally managed.

"It wasn't my child," he said bluntly. "And you don't have to make some big deal about that being why I don't hold Layla."

There were some who thought the history between her parents was a little scandalous. But Meredith and Carter's affair that ultimately produced Maddie and her sisters was nothing in comparison to the stories that just kept coming where Linc's family was concerned.

"Did you know all along that the baby wasn't yours?"

He turned and plunked the glass down on a side table. She thought he wasn't going to answer, particularly when he moved away from the window and headed across the room toward the staircase. "No."

She winced.

And he expected her to believe that his behavior now was unrelated?

She deftly zipped Layla back into the pack—facing toward her this time—and pulled the bottle out of her pocket to leave next to his abandoned glass.

Then she followed him, going up the stairs as quickly as she could without jiggling Layla too much. "When *did* you find out?"

He stopped on the landing and it was a miracle that she didn't bump right into him because of the dark. "I knew it was a mistake to tell you."

"Linc—"

"I found out the baby wasn't mine when I told my brother that Dana was pregnant."

She inhaled sharply. "*Jax* was the baby's father?"

He let out a short, unamused laugh. "That's the irony. When he learned there was going to be a baby, he admitted they'd been sleeping together."

Her shoulders sagged. She couldn't imagine how painful that had to have been.

He was on a roll, though. "But then when we confronted Dana about which one of us *was* the baby's father, it turned out that neither of us was. She was cheating on me with him. And cheating on him with someone else. Just one, big damn sick soap opera with my twisted ex-wife at the center."

Maddie didn't even realize she'd reached for his hand until her fingertips grazed him. "Now I understand why you said you and Jax don't talk much. You probably never forgave—"

Linc turned his hand and squeezed hers briefly, then

let go. "Don't. Don't make so much of this. Jax was as much a sap as I was. More, because he still lets her suck him in whenever she gets bored. He's no saint. He's pulling stunts all the time that cause problems. But he's still my little brother." She felt more than saw him spread his hands. "So. There you have it. The sordid tale of the brothers Swift. We are the logical by-product of Jolene and Blake Swift. Cheaters, one and all."

Maybe Jax was. As friendly as they'd remained over the years, he'd never divulged a word about any of this to Maddie.

What would *she* do if one of her sisters betrayed her so deeply?

The question didn't have an answer. Because she knew that they would never do such a thing.

"So who have you cheated on, Linc?"

His silence felt stoic.

Her heart was pounding so hard it was a wonder that it didn't wake up Layla. Or maybe it was the reason why she was already asleep. The comfort of heavy vibration. Like a truck engine.

"You aren't answering, because there is no answer. You haven't cheated on anyone," she concluded huskily. "It's not in your nature."

"What do you know about my nature?"

"I know more than you think."

"Really?" He suddenly stepped closer.

Every one of Maddie's nerve endings seemed to ripple. And there was still a baby positioned squarely between them.

He lowered his head toward hers.

Her heart beat even faster. She swallowed hard. If he kissed her, she wasn't sure what she would do. Slap him? Ignore him?

Kiss him back?

She moistened her lips.

His head was inches away from hers. His voice seemed to drop an octave. "Am I going to end up having to fight you for Layla?"

"Wha—" She frowned, actually feeling a little dizzy. She took a step back and would have tipped right down the stairs if not for the way he grabbed her arms.

Her heart lodged inside her chest even more tightly as she clutched him in return. "God." Falling on the stairs would be bad enough. With the baby strapped to her chest, it would have been devastating.

"You need a light when you use the stairs."

She felt shaky, but she still managed to shrug off his hold as she moved farther away from the steps.

Kiss him?

As if.

"It's not the lack of light. What do you mean *fight* me for Layla?"

"You said you wanted her, too. The other night."

It had been a thoughtless admission. He hadn't said anything at the time, and she'd hoped he'd forgotten. Or that he hadn't taken any notice.

So much for that idea.

The backs of her eyes burned.

She turned along the hallway and headed toward the nursery. "I would never fight you like that," she said huskily.

"Even if I find the nitwit wife I need?"

She exhaled heavily, annoyance immediately swelling inside her. "For God's sake, Linc. Wasn't one bad marriage enough? You really want to have another? No woman in her right mind would seriously entertain the idea of a marriage of convenience with you! It would never work."

"Why the hell not?"

"Because you're—" She broke off and hurried through the nursery doorway. With the tiny plug-in nightlight, the room felt blindingly bright after the deep darkness in the hallway.

Linc was hard on her heels. He was dressed in dark jeans and an equally dark long-sleeved pullover. Definitely not worn-out pajamas like she was wearing. He looked as dreamy as ever, while she looked like a woman getting three hours of sleep at a stretch because the baby she was caring for wouldn't sleep past that yet.

"I'm what?" He sounded just as annoyed as she felt. "In relatively good health if you don't count the ulcer? Basically house trained?"

She turned on him. "Ulcer?"

"It's an exaggeration." He snatched up the overall-dressed stuffed bear and shook it at her. "I run an oil company for God's sake. Some people actually consider me to be a decent catch."

"It wouldn't matter if you shoveled horse stalls for a living," she said impatiently. "You're still—" she waved her hand expressively at him *"—you."*

He tossed the bear aside. "What the hell is *that* supposed to mean?"

"Shh! You know very well what that means. I hardly need to bolster your tender ego." She quickly unzipped the pack and slid Layla free, depositing her gently into the crib. The baby was wearing one of her new, footed sleepers that kept her perfectly warm without a blanket.

When Layla didn't stir, Maddie turned away from the crib, peeling herself out of the buckles and straps of the fancy baby carrier. She dropped it on top of the changing table and walked into her bedroom.

She wasn't surprised that Linc followed.

She was surprised, however, when he pushed the door closed between the bedroom and the nursery.

She swallowed, abruptly dry-mouthed. The bed behind her was rumpled from her sleeping in it. The clothes she'd worn that day were tossed in a heap on the side chair next to the door. Her lacy bra dangled off the top.

And it was all visible, since she'd left her reading lamp turned on.

She crossed her arms, painfully aware that without the baby carrier strapped all around her torso, the ancient white cami she wore was very thin. Very clinging. And her breasts felt so tight they ached.

"It's late," she said in her best listen-to-me-or-else tone. The one she'd used back in her adult probation days. "We should both be in bed."

His hooded gaze slid toward the bed. He lifted an eyebrow. "Is that an invitation?"

She flushed so hard her face hurt. "No!"

"Pity."

"Do not toy with me, Linc. I'm in no mood."

"You're the last person I'd toy with," he assured her. "You're pretty much holding what I want right in your pretty little hands."

She closed her eyes and raked her fingers through her hair, wanting to pull it right out. "How many times do I have to tell you that *I* am not the one who'll decide anything where Layla is concerned?" She released her hair and it tumbled around her face, the ponytail holder failing completely. "All I can do is make sure she's taken care of and still keep her accessible to you while I can!"

"*That's* why you put yourself out on the chopping block the way you did?"

Why, oh why couldn't she have just heated up Layla's bottle and brought her back upstairs to feed her?

Why did she have to go into the living room? Why did he have to be in there the way he had been?

He didn't like so many what ifs.

She didn't like so many whys.

She pushed the hair out of her eyes, not looking at him. Just once, she'd like to feel like she was at her very best around him. That she was at the top of her game. "If I tell you yes, will you leave me alone?"

"Is it the truth?"

She sighed. "Yes, it's the truth. In case you never noticed, I'm a terrible liar."

"I noticed."

Of course he had.

She walked over to the door that led into the hallway and opened it. Even he wouldn't be able to ignore the message. "Good night, Linc."

His jaw flexed. He moved to the doorway, towering over her the way he always did.

When he lifted his hand and touched her chin, pushing it upward, she froze. Kept her lashes lowered.

"What am I going to do with you?"

Something inside her ached. "You could try to make me go away like you did before. But that would mean Layla goes with me."

"Not everything is about Layla."

At that, she did lift her lashes. She looked up at him. "Now who's a bad liar?"

His lips thinned.

She lifted her chin away from his fingers. She pulled the door open even wider, clinging to the knob because she honestly wasn't sure that her shaking knees would hold her up. "Right now, everything is about Layla. There is not one single thing you could do or say to make me believe otherwise."

His gaze roved over her face. Looking for what, she couldn't say. But it left her feeling almost as raw as that damned artificial tree of Ali's had.

"Then I guess there's nothing else to say but good-night," he finally said.

He stepped through the doorway, leaving the small circle of light cast from her reading lamp. She still kept watch until he wasn't even a shadowy shape in the dark hall.

Only then did she finally close the bedroom door and lean back weakly against it.

Chapter Eleven

"Svelte Sage." Looking triumphant, Ali waved the paint chip in front of Maddie. "Greer and I both love it. She gave her vote of approval before she went into work, not even thirty minutes ago."

Maddie blearily eyed the color sample. It was vaguely green. Vaguely gray. Vaguely brown. It was also the one she'd chosen a week ago. "Looks fine."

"It's better than fine. When the cabinets are done in off-white, it'll look spectacular." Ali peered into Maddie's face. "I thought you'd be more enthusiastic."

Ali had greeted her with the sample practically the second she'd walked into the house.

Maddie sank down on the couch, one arm around Layla, who was once more strapped in the fabric carrier. "I'm thrilled," she assured her sister. "Maybe when we actually have the kitchen finished—" in the next millennium, hopefully "—I'll be even more thrilled." She hooked the toe of her boot around the coffee table and dragged it a little closer so that she could prop her feet on it. Once Linc had left her bedroom the night before, it had been hours before she'd finally fallen asleep. Only to be awakened a short while later by Layla, yet again.

"You're exhausted is what you are," Ali said tartly. She nudged Maddie's legs to one side and sat on the coffee table. "You look like death warmed over."

"Thank you *so* much." Then she promptly yawned.

"How much partying are you doing over there with our resident oilman?"

She closed her eyes and leaned her head back against the couch. Layla wasn't asleep, but she was perfectly content sitting the way she was in front of Maddie. "I've, uh, actually hardly seen him." She mentally crossed her fingers. "It doesn't feel as cold here as I expected it to be."

"There was frost on the *inside* of the windows last night. Just in case you're considering leaving the swell Swift digs." Ali wiggled Maddie's shin. "Sit up. Take off that contraption you're wearing. I'll watch Layla for an hour and *you* can take a nap. Or a shower. Either one would be an improvement."

Maddie peeled open her gritty eyes. "It's so nice to be able to count on such sisterly support."

"I said I'd watch Layla," Ali countered. "That's pretty supportive if you ask me."

"Only if you change her diaper when she actually needs it." Maddie sat up with an effort and undid the carrier, working the infant out of it. "You ought to try it," she told Ali. "Makes carrying her a lot easier."

"Well, for now, I'll pass on the straitjacket." Ali lifted Layla onto her lap, kissing her cheek and neck so noisily that the baby chortled. "God, I love that sound." She shoved Maddie's shoulder. "Now, for the love of God, *go*."

"I had a shower yesterday," Maddie groused as she headed toward the stairs.

"Did you actually turn on the water?"

She rolled her eyes, ignoring Ali. The truth was, though, that her shower had probably lasted all of three minutes. Because that was about how much time Layla had allowed her.

She passed Greer's open bedroom door and was momentarily tempted to use her bathtub. But if she actually laid down in a soaking tub filled with hot, bubbly water, she wasn't sure she'd ever want to get out.

So the shower it was.

Maddie's barebones bathroom was colder than a witch's glare. But she turned on the space heater she dragged in there and let the shower steam fill the air. It got so cozy that when she stepped under the hot spray and let it sluice over her, she might actually have nodded off and napped right there, still standing up.

How did mothers everywhere manage to care for infants day in and day out without help? Even though Maddie was a qualified foster-care provider, she'd never had a three-month-old. She'd had a three-week-old once. The baby had slept and ate and pooped. But mostly slept. She'd had a three-year-old, too, who slept solidly through the night, thirteen hours straight. There'd been others over the years, but never for more than a few days at a time.

She and Layla were now on day eight.

Only the fear of running out of hot water made her lethargic limbs finally move. She washed her hair. Twice. Shaved her legs. Twice. When she finally shut off the water and climbed out into the steam-shrouded bathroom, she felt cleaner than she had in a week. Most of her toiletries were at Linc's, but she found an old comb and managed to work out the tangles in her hair before twisting it into a braid.

Then, still wrapped in the bath towel, she went into the bedroom and crawled under the covers.

An hour. One entire blissful hour, she told herself. With no thoughts of Linc allowed.

She closed her eyes. In seconds she was asleep.

And dreaming about Linc.

"Well, there's Sleeping Beauty finally."

Maddie smiled ruefully and padded into the kitchen wearing her one pair of flannel-lined jeans and a thick red sweater. "You let me sleep too long," she told Ali. "But I see you discovered the miracle that is the baby carrier."

Ali grinned. She was standing at the sink washing dishes, wearing Layla in front of her. The baby was obviously happy to be up close and personal with the occasional soapsud that found its way to her. "This thing is great," she agreed. "Once I figured out how all the straps and buckles worked. I could carry this little girl all day long, I think."

"She'd let you." Maddie found a mug and filled it with the cold coffee that was still in the coffeemaker. She stuck it in the microwave to heat it up. "She *much* prefers to be held than not. She has made that perfectly clear to me." She leaned over and kissed the baby on her head. "Haven't you, sweet pea?"

Layla gave her a smile that made Maddie feel good all the way to her toes.

Ali wasn't smiling, though. She was watching her

with narrowed eyes. "She's not going to be so easy to give up, is she?"

"She's not mine to give up. Remember?" The microwave dinged and she took out the mug. The liquid was lukewarm, but she routinely drank worse at the office, so it would do just fine.

"Do *you* remember?" Ali's gaze was steady. "Really?"

Maddie swallowed.

"Oh, Maddie," Ali sighed. "This is what you do. You get too involved."

"This is different."

Her sister lifted an eyebrow. But she withheld comment and rinsed another dish and placed it in the plastic drainer. Then she pulled the plug and watched the sink drain from below where the pipes were visible thanks to the unfinished, doorless cabinetry.

"What are you doing?"

"It's been leaking this week." Ali snatched a soup pot, quickly stuck it under the pipes, and then covered Layla's ears. "Another damn thing to fix." She shot Maddie a look. "Do *not* tell Dad."

"If you could keep your ghosts from moving the tools, I can probably change out the pipes. Ray and I did it once for a family we were helping."

"Didn't know that plumbing was part of the job description in family services."

Maddie carried her coffee over to the table and sat. "When it comes to family services, a varied skill-set is the name of the game. And sometimes you have to get involved."

You can marry me.

She pinched the bridge of her nose, willing away

Linc's voice. She was not considering it. "Not that involved," she muttered.

"What?" Ali was looking at her.

"Nothing." Maybe sleeping three hours had been too long. Maybe it had turned her brain to mush. "Did you feed Layla?"

"Yup. She sucked down all eight ounces of one of those bottles you had in the diaper bag. Fancy bag, too. Quite the step up from that purse you were using."

"Linc got it. What about her diaper? You have checked it, haven't you?"

"No, I took her to the neighbor to do it." Ali rolled her eyes. "Yes. She peed twice. Fortunately, just pee, else your nap would have been shortened to deal with it. Relax, would you?"

"Sorry." Maddie propped her chin on her hand. Her sister was dressed similarly to her, though she'd pinned her hair on top of her head. most likely to keep it away from Layla's grasping hands. "How've things been at work this week?"

"Pretty much the same. Sarge remains pissed off at me. So he's still assigning me every crap detail he can." Her sister shrugged. "It'll blow over eventually. Fortunately, he hasn't blocked me out from everything concerning Layla. I know there haven't been any recent reports of a missing baby at least."

"What about the note? Do you know if anything's being done about it?"

"I know it's written on paper that can be bought in nearly any store. How's life with Linc?"

Despite her best efforts, Maddie could feel her face warm. "I told you earlier, we rarely see him. He works a lot."

"So why do you look like you've been caught with your hand down his cookie jar?"

"Ali!"

"That's what this is really about. Not just a sweet little baby. You're falling for him, aren't you?"

"I'm not falling for Lincoln Swift!"

The back door opened just then and their mother hurried inside, slowing only long enough to make sure that Vivian, who was following her, made it in safely, too.

"Don't coddle me," Vivian said a little testily as she shrugged off Meredith's hand. She was almost as petite as Meredith, who was only five feet tall. "I'm old. Not dead. At least not yet."

"Don't joke," Meredith chided. Because it wasn't a joke. Vivian Archer Templeton, on the high side of her eighties, had an inoperable brain tumor. So far, it was just "squatting" as Vivian liked to say. But they all knew that anything was possible. Nothing could happen with it. Or everything could happen with it.

Needless to say, they all hoped for the nothing end of that particular spectrum.

Vivian made an impatient sound. But there was still a gleam of affection in her dark brown eyes as she looked at her daughter-in-law. "Better to joke than to run around morose all the time." She patted her stylish silver hair as she surveyed the deplorable state of the kitchen. "Would you *please* let me get this place finished for you?"

Meredith had spotted Layla and was greedily slipping the baby out from the carrier. "Watch your hair, Mom," Maddie warned. Then she looked back at her grandmother. "We are not letting you pay for our refurbishing." It was an old argument. "Want me to take your coat?" It was a fancy fur. Real, no doubt.

"No thank you, dear." Vivian sat at the table, giving Maddie's mug of coffee an appraising look. "We've just come from lunch and won't be long. Here." She pulled a bundle of red yarn from her pocket. "Your mother told me about the baby."

Maddie shook out the bundle. It was a baby-size knitted cap. "Did *you* knit it?"

"Good Lord, no." Vivian looked appalled at the very idea. "You should put it on her head, though. It's very chilly in here. I suppose you've noticed."

Maddie and Ali shared a look. "You could say that."

"Meredith, your daughters are as stubborn as that son of mine you married."

"Yes they are, Vivian," Meredith returned equably. She was cuddling the baby, who had, despite the warning, wrapped her little hands in Meredith's long dark ringlets. She might be in her fifties now, but their mom had more hair than all three of the triplets combined. She also got along a lot better with her mother-in-law than Carter did. "I can't believe this is Ernestine's great-granddaughter."

"*Possibly* her great-granddaughter," Maddie corrected. "We still don't have proof."

"All I've heard about it is bits and pieces. How is Linc?"

Maddie didn't dare look at her mother. "Fine." She buried her nose in the dreadful coffee.

Vivian toyed with the rings on her fingers. "He's a handsome one, that Lincoln Swift."

"He mentioned you've met," Maddie mumbled.

"If I were thirty years younger—"

"You'd still be too old for him," Meredith said, laughing.

"True. And handsome or not, I could never do better than my dear Arthur." He'd been the last of her four husbands, and to hear her tell it, the great love of her life, even though she still used the name she'd gotten when she'd married Carter's father. She looked at Ali and Maddie. "I expect both of you to bring suitable escorts to my party next week."

"You'll be lucky if I arrive wearing a suitable dress," Ali warned, not in the least bit cowed.

"What about you?" Vivian caught Maddie's eye.

"I, uh, I'll borrow something from Hayley again." She would need to remember to call her about it.

"And an escort?"

"Archer will do."

Vivian sniffed derisively. "He's your brother. He should be bringing a woman of his own."

Ali grinned. "He'd have to throw dice to choose just one."

"Is that why you dropped by?" Maddie had become very fond of her grandmother over the past year. But she wasn't oblivious to Vivian's attitudes. Admittedly, she'd made a lot of progress since moving from Pennsylvania, but she was nevertheless a duck out of water. Caviar and diamonds among cowboy beans and boots. "To make sure we don't embarrass you at your party?"

"What would a good party be without someone getting a little embarrassed by something? You'll bring Lincoln Swift."

"I will?"

"You like him, don't you? I hear you're staying under his roof."

"That's temporary. And strictly because of the baby."

Vivian waved her hand, looking unsettlingly crafty. "Bring him anyway. He'll be an interesting addition to our evening."

"I can't just drag him to a party, Vivian."

"Maybe you can ask Morton," Ali suggested slyly.

Meredith glanced up from Layla. "Who's Morton?"

"Nobody," Maddie assured her. "Nobody at all."

"I knew a Morton once," Vivian reflected. "Pillar of salt, he was."

Despite herself, Maddie laughed. She glanced at her mother, and wished she hadn't. Meredith was watching her with a knowing look.

Mrs. Lincoln Swift.

She quickly looked back at her coffee. She wasn't seventeen anymore, doodling dreamily on a school notebook. "So, anyone going to the Glitter and Glow parade tonight?"

"I tried talking your father into it. So far, he's refusing," Meredith replied. "Says he's already put in his time sitting out in the cold watching crazies wearing Christmas lights when you girls were growing up."

"He'll give in. He always does when it comes to you. Which is why he's there, every year, watching the crazies. As for me, I'll be working, keeping the peace among them." Ali plucked the pencil out of her hair and fluffed it out around her shoulders. "What do you all think of me trying to go blond?"

"I think you should concentrate your efforts on this house and let your hair alone," Meredith said dryly. She handed the baby to Maddie. "Vivian, I'd better get you back to Weaver before they start closing off streets for the parade and make it impossible to reach the highway."

"You didn't drive yourself to Braden?" Maddie asked. Vivian had an ostentatious Rolls Royce that she tended to drive like a maniac. "Are you feeling all right?"

"I'm fine," Vivian assured her blithely. "The Rolls is simply having a tune-up."

In Vivian-speak, Maddie knew that could mean anything from an oil change to dent removal.

"Maybe we'll see you at the parade," Meredith said as they left. "Bring Linc. Ernestine used to take him and Jax every year." She closed the door after Vivian.

Maddie exhaled. She worked the cap over Layla's head. The baby immediately began trying to pull it back off.

"Remember when life used to be uncomplicated?"

She looked at Ali.

"Yeah," Ali said wryly. "Me, either."

The Glitter and Glow parade ran through the center of Braden every year. From his upstairs bedroom, Linc could probably see the lights of it if he'd wanted to.

Maddie and Layla had been gone all day. She'd left the house early that morning and still been gone when he came home after spending the day on conference calls with his lawyers and the folks at OKF.

If it weren't for the clothes that were still lying in a pile in the bedroom, he would have been certain that she didn't intend to bring the baby back. That *she* didn't intend to come back.

But what were a few pairs of jeans and a hank of lace, anyway? She'd told him that first night that Layla's needs were basic. Maybe Maddie's were equally basic. Maybe she didn't care about leaving the clothes behind, if it meant she didn't have to put up with Linc anymore.

He exhaled heavily and turned away from the window.

Jax's phone was sitting on his dresser. He'd kept it charged, even though he still hadn't figured out the password. And he could tell that multiple messages had been coming in even though he couldn't access them.

He swiped across the photo of the sailboat blonde and jabbed in some random numbers, as unsuccessfully as all the others he'd tried. What he needed was a phone hacker. Unfortunately, Linc didn't happen to have such a person on his speed dial.

He left the phone where it was and went down the hall. The nursery—even full of stuff—was neater than Maddie's bedroom. He picked up one of the sleepers that were folded on top of the changing table. The elf-looking one. It was so tiny.

He'd gotten over Jax and Dana. As much as he ever would, anyway. But this—

He crumpled the sleeper in his fist.

He heard a wail from downstairs and dropped it, striding out into the hall. From the head of the stairs, he watched Maddie juggle the baby and the diaper bag and the house key as she entered the house.

She was home.

The relief was almost more than he could stand.

He closed his hand tightly over the newel post. "Where the hell have you been all day?" *Good one, Linc. Just piss her off right from the start.*

Her head jerked back as she looked up the staircase, her dark hair gleaming beneath the chandelier. "We spent the day with Ali." Her voice was cool as she unwrapped the blanket around Layla and shrugged out of her coat. "Where the hell have *you* been all day?"

"Same place I've been all week. Keeping my father from selling Swift Oil out from under us all."

Layla was still crying, but Maddie went stock-still, looking up at him. "Are you serious?"

He unlocked his grip and started down the stairs. "Is she hungry or something?"

"Since she's always hungry, I'm guessing yes." Maddie dumped her coat on the bottom stair alongside the diaper bag. "Unfortunately, I didn't plan for her to go through as many bottles as she did today. Either that, or Ali was drinking formula behind my back." She headed into the kitchen, stopping short when she spotted the high chair that had been delivered that day. "Linc." She looked over her shoulder as he followed her. "How much more stuff are you planning to buy for her?"

"As much as she needs."

"Then I guess you better not let Swift Oil get sold out from under you." She sidestepped the high chair that he'd positioned near the island and carried the baby into the pantry. She came out a second later with the can of powdered formula.

He took it from her. "I'll do it."

Her lashes swept down, but not soon enough to hide the surprise in her eyes. While he quickly grabbed a clean bottle and started filling it, she tried distracting Layla with the usual wooden spoon, but the baby wasn't having any of it. The only thing that quieted her was the bottle when he finally handed it to Maddie.

She slid onto one of the barstools and held the baby on her lap to feed her. "So how serious is this thing with your father? Really."

"Couple hundred million dollars' worth of serious." Linc grimaced. "I'm buying him out."

She looked shocked. "Just like that." She snapped her fingers.

"It's a little more complicated than that, but essentially. Money's what matters to my father, so money's what he'll get."

"And Jax? Doesn't he have any say?"

"If he were here in the first place, it wouldn't even be necessary. I wouldn't have to sell off some of my own holdings just to keep the entire damned company safe."

"My brain doesn't even understand numbers that high," she murmured. "I don't know why I keep forgetting that you're rich."

"Not as rich as I was when I woke up this morning. And fortunately, my lawyers do understand."

She was silent for a moment, looking down at Layla. She tenderly smoothed the baby's hair that looked blonder than ever against the dark red sweater Maddie wore. Then she seemed to take a deep breath. "Justin called me when we were on our way back here," she said quickly. "Your DNA profile is finished."

His muscles tightened. "And?"

"And nothing. Layla's test isn't complete yet."

He almost wished she hadn't told him. His stomach burned and he grabbed the milk from the fridge.

"He said he'd let me know the second they're able to compare them."

"Before the hearing on Tuesday?"

She was chewing her lip. "I don't know. Maybe."

He swore under his breath. "Give me lawyers and my old man any day of the week." He flipped the cap off the glass milk bottle and drank straight from it. When he finally capped it again, Maddie was watching him.

Her eyes were dark. "If you have an ulcer, you shouldn't have been drinking whiskey last night."

"I don't have an ulcer." He grimaced. "I *did*, but it's healed."

She raised an eyebrow, looking pointedly at the milk.

"Call it prevention." He shoved the bottle back into

the fridge. "We need to take her to the parade," he said abruptly.

Her mouth rounded slightly. "It's already started. That's why it took me so long to get here. Trying to navigate around all the closed-off streets."

"I still want her to see it."

"She's only three—" Maddie shrugged. "Okay." She slid off the barstool. "Bring the formula. Just in case."

He grabbed the canister and the only clean bottle sitting in the rack and shoved them into the diaper bag.

"Where are we going to watch from? The stroller's in my trunk." She wrapped Layla into a tiny white coat.

He hadn't even known they made coats for babies her size.

"She seems to prefer the carrier, though." Maddie was still talking as she maneuvered her arms into her own coat while still holding the bundled baby and the bottle. "Can't say I blame her. Body contact and all. She shouldn't really know that she was left the way she was, but who is to say for sure?" She flipped her hair out from the collar of her coat and glanced up at Linc.

Everything about her seemed to still, except for those deep, expressive eyes. "What?"

He stepped closer. Leaned down and kissed her.

She gave a startled jerk, followed immediately by the heady softening of her lips. Followed just as immediately by her hand on his chest, shoving him away.

Then she scrambled from him for good measure, clutching the baby against her. Even Layla was giving him a wide-eyed look, momentarily disinterested in the bottle that Maddie had also seemed to forget. "What on earth are you thinking?"

That she was right. A marriage of convenience had been a stupid idea. "That you should marry me before

Tuesday. Then when we get to court next week, it'll be a done deal."

She turned away from him, giving the bottle once more to the baby. "You're out of your tree."

"We both want Layla."

"Linc—"

"And I want you."

She froze. "You're only saying that because of the situation."

"The situation being that you turn me on the same way you always have?"

She huffed. Her cheeks flushed. "Cut it out. You're just panicking."

"Over…?"

"You know. The DNA test being done. The hearing getting closer. The—"

"—fact that you were gone the entire day and I wasn't sure you'd come back?"

She blinked. Layla blinked.

Then Maddie cleared her throat. "As long as the judge lets me keep Layla, I'm not going anywhere," she said huskily. "Just, um, just stop proposing."

"Or what?"

Her lips compressed. Her eyes were suddenly filled with ire. "Or I might accept just to spite you. And *then* where would we be?"

In bed, he thought immediately.

Fortunately, he managed to have the good sense not to say it.

Chapter Twelve

"What do you think?"

Maddie stared up at the enormous tree. "I think it's probably illegal to cut down a tree like this."

Linc's smile flashed. "Not if I own the land it's on."

It was Sunday morning and they were standing in the middle of nowhere. All because Maddie had evidently lost her mind where Linc was concerned.

It wasn't even the proposals, which she resolutely refused to take seriously. Yes, she'd lost all hope of objectivity where Layla and Linc were concerned. But she hadn't lost every shred of her common sense. And common sense dictated there were solutions to be found that didn't involve saying vows that weren't true.

No, it wasn't the proposals.

It wasn't even the kiss that had rocked her back on her heels despite its brevity.

It was the parade.

And the fact that Linc had found a spot, right on the curb in front of the Swift Oil office, where they'd sat and watched all of the cars and trucks and even people, wrapped in Christmas lights, progress along the street while Christmas carols played from loudspeakers, sometimes warring with the high school band and the choral groups who passed.

It was the fact that he'd plucked Layla out of Maddie's arms and held her up so she could see over the kids sitting on the ground in front of them.

It was the fact that he'd finally, *finally*, had a smile on his face.

The kind of smile that he used to have.

The kind of smile that he was giving her now.

He had mirrored sunglasses on his face and a chainsaw in his gloved hand and he used it to point at the tree again. "Well?"

She glanced back at the truck. Layla was in her car seat, safely strapped inside. She'd fallen asleep before they'd even gotten outside of town. She hadn't stirred a muscle since.

Maddie waved her arm and tried to pretend she didn't feel all warm and gooey inside every time she looked his way. "This isn't an oil field." There hadn't been a single pump jack or derrick in miles. The snowy hillside where he'd driven them was more suited to a ski run. Their only stop on the hour-long drive had been at a dinky café also in the middle of nowhere. But the delicious coffee and breakfast sandwiches explained the surprising number of vehicles that had been parked outside of it. "How do I trust that you actually own it?"

He made a point of patting the pockets of his down jacket. "Sorry. I must have left the deed in my other coat." He extended one long arm. "This is the same hillside where my grandmother always got her tree. *Her* tree. Because Gus planted all of these firs for her about a million years ago. So, yes or no?"

"If I say no, you're going to drag us around looking at every tree here, aren't you."

He considered it. "Maybe."

Maddie couldn't help but laugh. If anyone had told her even twenty-four hours ago that they'd be standing together this way, knee-deep in snow, she'd have said that *they* were the ones who'd lost their minds.

But it was just her.

Mindless Maddie.

"How long has it been since you've had a Christmas tree?"

"I don't know. Long time. Before college. You gonna keep asking questions or pick a tree?"

"Pick," she said, nodding toward the tree in question. "It's perfect."

He started toward it. "Get back in the truck." He braced the back of the saw against his leg and gave a pull on the start cord. The chainsaw whirred to life with a low rumble.

Then he hit the throttle a few times, and it growled louder.

It was stupid. But she felt a visceral jolt deep inside her when he easily swung the heavy-duty saw around to the base of the tree.

It didn't take him long. It was over almost as quickly as it began. The chainsaw buzzed, chips of bark flew, and a moment later, Linc was pushing the tree away from him. It fell, almost in slow motion, its deep bluish green branches sending up a cloud of snow when it hit the ground.

He killed the chainsaw, then leaned down and

grabbed the base of the tree and started dragging it back toward her.

All manly, manly man.

God help her.

"Told you to get in the truck," he said when he neared.

"You should know by now that I don't always listen well." It was better to stay active than stand there drooling, so she lowered the tailgate herself and moved around the tall tree to help him lift it into the bed. She wasn't much help. She barely grabbed a few branches before he'd shoved the tree into the bed. Since it had to be at least twelve feet tall, it stuck out well beyond the tailgate.

"Close the gate when I lift it, would you?"

She scrambled under the tree, squinting against the heady scent.

"You're not going to end up with another rash, I hope." He lifted the tree.

She nimbly closed the gate and popped back out from beneath the tree. "Never have before." She brushed a few needles out of her hair. "It's the artificial stuff that got me. Ali's been on a tear about the fire hazards of real trees or we'd have had one ourselves."

"Yeah, well, this thing is so fresh, it'll be good until February." He unwound a bundle of rope and tossed it over the tree. She grabbed the end and went up on her toes to reach inside the bed, her gloved fingers searching. His boots crunched on the snow as he came around to her side. He gave her a surprised look when he realized she'd already looped the rope through the tie-down.

"Come on," she said. "Just because we were girls didn't mean my dad made us sit in the truck staying all pretty and clean every time we went out for firewood and stuff."

He smiled faintly and threw the rope back across the tree, then headed around to the far side of the truck. "No cutting your own Christmas trees?"

"Always picked them from one of the lots in town." She caught the rope again when it headed her way. "My mother always opts for the scraggliest one—you know the one. The Charlie Brown tree. 'Cause she figures it needs more love. My dad always likes the fattest." She closed her eyes, feeling along the inside of the truck bed for the next tie-down. Linc had a fancy bed liner, so it wasn't quite what she was used to. "Which tree did we always end up with?" Her fingertip finally found the notch and she quickly slithered the long rope through it. "The scraggly one. Because my father has never been able to say no to my mom. They're still besotted with each other. It was embarrassing when we were kids."

"And now?"

She tossed the rope over the tree, missing by a long shot. But he still managed to snag the rope and pull it across. "Now?" It was what she wanted. What they all wanted. "Catching your parents making out?" she said with a tart laugh. "Still embarrassing."

He sent the rope back her way. "Better than finding them making out with other people." His voice was dry.

"Well, that's true."

Between the two of them, they quickly had the tree secured beneath the crisscrossing rope. The branches would still blow a lot when they got back on the highway—no way to prevent it—but the tree was definitely not going anywhere they didn't want it to go.

Then Linc stored the chainsaw in the bed, too, and they got back inside the truck.

Layla had slept the entire while.

"Sure," Maddie murmured as she leaned over the back of her seat to adjust the blanket over the baby. "You can't sleep three hours straight at night, but when it's daylight?" She lightly brushed the red cap on Layla's head and then pushed herself back into her own seat. She felt a little breathless and she loosened her coat and pulled off her gloves before fastening her seatbelt.

Linc was just sitting there, watching her.

"Don't tell me you're out of gas," she warned. But of course, she knew they weren't. The truck had been running the entire while they'd been messing with the tree.

"I should have hired you some help with Layla."

She gaped at him, then shook her head, trying not to feel as flustered as he made her. "I *am* the help, remember?" She gestured at the windshield. "Come on. Get moving. There's a tree yet to be decorated."

He put the truck in gear and slowly turned until he was lined up once more with the tracks they'd made in the snow on their way there. "There's nothing wrong with my memory and you cleared me up once on that point. You're not a babysitter."

"Yeah, well, that's when I thought the reason you called me was to get Layla off your hands." Which seemed a lot longer ago than it really had been.

She realized she was staring at his hands. He'd taken off his gloves, too. His fingers were lightly wrapped around the steering wheel.

"So." She swallowed, looking away. "I hope you kept your grandmother's tree ornaments. Otherwise we'll be stringing a lot of popcorn to get that sucker covered."

"Should be in the attic. I didn't get rid of anything of hers. Just moved a few things around to make room for some new."

Of course he hadn't. "New like your den."

"Home office. Master bedroom. Much as I appreciate my grandmother's antiques, I draw the line at the dinky beds."

Red flashing lights of danger there. Maddie did not need to be thinking about his bedroom. Much less his bed.

So, of course, she did. His room was at the very end of the hall. She'd learned that much over the past week. It was several doors down from hers.

Seven doors, to be exact.

She chewed the inside of her cheek, blindly studying the landscape outside her window.

"Marry me and you could make whatever changes you wanted. Even choose a scraggly tree next year."

She shot him a look.

He shrugged, looking anything but innocent. "Just sayin'."

She exhaled noisily and looked out the side window again.

And she absolutely did *not* feel a smile tugging at her lips.

Four hours later, the tree was standing tall and stately next to the staircase.

Linc had dragged two boxes of ornaments down from the attic and a ladder up from the basement.

It was obvious at first glance the ornament boxes hadn't been opened in quite some time. Probably not since his grandmother died.

She'd vowed right then and there to make certain every single item got placed on the tree. Even the popsicle-stick ones that were in major danger of falling apart as soon as she touched them.

She was wearing Layla in the fabric carrier. At Linc's

request, she'd made another batch of homemade brownies. She'd added hot chocolate to the menu. And Christmas music.

With the snowflakes blowing around outside the windows, they probably looked like a very normal family enjoying the holiday season.

But they weren't normal.

And they weren't a family.

And it was more than a little worrisome that she had to keep reminding herself of that fact.

"Here." She reached into the box and pulled out a wooden nutcracker. The paint on it was faded. Layla reached for it, but Maddie avoided the little grasping hands, giving it to Linc where he stood on the ladder. "Only thing that's left in the box is the star." She bent down and retrieved it, too, pulling the silver and white tree topper carefully from its protective nest of shredded paper. Layla grabbed at it and promptly started crying when Maddie held it out of her reach. "Sorry, baby." She brushed her lips against Layla's cheek. "This one's not for you, either."

"Should have got some rattles for her to hang," Linc said, stepping down the ladder. "Here, give her to me."

Maddie stared. Then she hurriedly set down the star next to their cocoa mugs and unzipped the pack, working Layla out of it.

The baby kicked, almost squirming out of Maddie's hands, but she held fast until Linc took her.

Layla looked as surprised as Maddie felt when he lifted the baby up to look into her face.

She kicked a few more times.

She stopped crying.

Then she gave him a few gurgling sounds that

quickly developed into her distinctive chortle that charmed Maddie every single time she heard it.

He wasn't immune, either. She could tell by the way he grinned.

He adjusted his hold on the infant, tucking her against his chest, and stepped up the ladder with her. "Hand me the star."

Maddie sucked in her lip. One part of her wanted to warn him to be careful on the ladder with the baby.

The other part wanted to savor the moment forever.

She handed him the star.

He went up two more rungs.

She quickly dragged her phone out of her pocket and snapped a picture of him as he reached up to put the star in place on top of the tree.

"How's it look?"

She swallowed the knot in her throat and slid her phone away before he could see. The star was listing slightly to one side. Layla was grabbing for the nearest thing, which happened to be Linc's shirt collar. "It's perfect," she said huskily.

He came down the ladder and looked up to survey his handiwork. "You need glasses."

She laughed softly, shaking her head. She handed him a brownie. "Don't argue. I said it was perfect."

Then he smiled, too. "Okay. It's perfect." He wolfed the brownie in two bites and dropped his arm over her shoulders as he looked again at the tree. "My grandmother would have liked it," he said after a moment.

Her chest tightened. "Yeah." It was all she could manage. She shifted, enough for the casual arm around her shoulders to fall away. She could breathe easier, but did she really want to? "I, uh, I should probably fix us something more substantial to eat than brownies."

He took the last one from the plate and grabbed her wrist, looking at her watch. "A little early for dinner, isn't it?"

She retrieved her tingling arm and needlessly adjusted her watchband. "Not when there's an infant in the house who needs bathing and rocking before she'll even entertain the idea of sleep."

He considered that. "I don't usually eat much here."

"I noticed. Aside from baby formula, your pantry was mostly shelf-paper and saltines."

"So how'd you make the brownies?"

"Wiggling my nose? We shopped, obviously." She picked up the plate and the mugs and carried them into the kitchen, leaving him still holding Layla.

"You shouldn't have done that." He'd followed her.

"Well. It's done. You have peanut butter on your pantry shelf now." She turned on the faucet to rinse out the mugs. "Live with it."

"I'll take you out to dinner."

She nearly dropped the crockery in the sink. "That's not necessary."

"Not for you, maybe. But how do I know you can cook? Brownies aside—"

"Oh, nice! Just for that, you deserve to buy me dinner. An expensive one." She shut off the water and flicked her wet fingers at him. Layla laughed and bumped her head against Linc's chin. "Layla agrees."

"Expensive restaurant." He narrowed his eyes in exaggerated thought. "In Braden."

"Okay. So maybe not expensive. But not takeout." She slid Layla out of his hold. "We want proper sit-down with table service. Isn't that right, Layla?"

The baby batted her blue eyes and gave her gummy smile.

Then, because it was feeling much, much too homey standing in his kitchen together, Maddie forced herself to move away.

"Where are you going now?"

She gave him a quick grin that hopefully masked her odd breathlessness. "Young ladies of a certain age need to dress properly for every occasion. Particularly those of the three-ish month range who have a drawer full of pretty things with their price tags still on."

"So much for the proper dress," Linc said a few hours later when he came into the nursery to find Layla in the middle of a diaper change. He made a face and took a step back toward the doorway. "What's *in* that stuff she drinks?"

Maddie chuckled and finished wiping Layla's tiny little butt. "Wonderful nourishment. And trust me. This is better than it'll be when she starts eating pizza like what we just had." She twisted up the soiled diaper and wipes and nudged her toe against the diaper pail. The lid popped up and she dropped it inside. She left the lid to close automatically and picked up the naked baby.

"You don't put 'em out in the garbage?"

What happened to the manly manly-man? "You are *such* a priss," she accused on a laugh as she went into the bathroom. "You bought the diaper pail!"

"Terry—"

"Yeah, yeah. Your receptionist and gatekeeper. I know." She leaned over and turned on the water and while it warmed, grabbed the usual stack of towels. "Just warning you now that you'd better put Terry on a budget where choosing stuff for Layla is concerned, or one day you'll have a very spoiled little girl on your hands." She went down on her knees alongside the tub and tucked a towel between Layla's rear and her jeans. Just in case.

He'd moved to the doorway. He was standing on the threshold, his boots close, but not crossing it. "Got enough towels there?" His voice was dry.

"Probably not." She flipped the stopper and made a production of adjusting the water temperature. "You going to stand there and watch, or help?" Then she tucked her tongue between her teeth, reminding herself that Rome hadn't been built in a day. The Christmas tree? The noisy pizza joint with Layla banging the table and spilling his beer?

Miracles had already happened. It was greedy— foolish—of her to want more.

His boot slowly moved forward. "We should be doing this in my bathroom," he murmured when he crouched down beside her. "Lot more room there." His shoulder bumped hers. "Now what?"

Maddie quickly shut off the water, hoping he wouldn't notice her shaking hands. "Make sure the water isn't too hot for her."

"How am I supposed to know what's too hot for her?"

"Oh, for heaven's sake." She grabbed his hand and splashed it into the water. "Is it too hot for you?"

His gaze slid over her and she nearly stopped breathing. Beneath the warm water, his palm rested against hers. "Feeling pretty hot to me."

Her mouth opened. But no words came. She quickly pulled her hand away from his and lifted Layla into the tub. Even before her toes made contact with the water, she started kicking and squealing. By the time she was sitting in the few inches, she'd churned up her usual miniature tidal wave.

"Holy—" Linc sat back when a cascade of water splashed up the side of the tub, right into his face.

Maddie laughed. "I guess that ought to cool Uncle Linc off, right, Layla?" She grabbed the small, soft washcloth and dunked it in the tub, shooting Linc a look. "Now you see why we need all the towels."

"What if she turns onto her stomach," Linc whispered, leaning over the crib as he lowered the baby onto the mattress. "That's supposed to be bad, right? Sleeping on their stomach?"

"She won't turn over," Maddie assured him.

They'd survived the bath. Another bottle. Another diaper.

"How do you know?"

"Because she hasn't learned how to, yet." She picked up the baby monitor and took his arm, pulling him away from the crib.

"Well, when's she going to learn?" He followed her into the hall.

"Sooner than you'll be ready for."

"It's two freaking o'clock." He threw himself down on the bed beside her.

Maddie shook her head, not wanting to lift her cheek from the pillow. But she peeled her eyes open enough to see him sprawled beside her. Jeans. No shirt. Arm tossed across his eyes. "You have a bed of your own. One that's not dinky."

"Too far," he muttered. He was holding the baby monitor in his hand. "How long's she going to sleep this time?"

She closed her eyes again. "Not long enough," she whispered.

* * *

"S'not my turn, babe," Linc murmured. He rolled over, essentially pushing her out of her own bed. The monitor was on the floor. No need for it when they could both hear Layla crying, plain as 5:00 a.m.

Maddie dragged herself out of bed, nearly tripping over the boots on the floor. His? Hers? Who could tell?

Another diaper.

Another bottle.

"Your turn next time," she whispered, crawling back into bed.

He grunted. His arm hooked over her waist and he buried his nose in her neck.

She should have noticed more, but her eyes were already closing.

The sun was warm through the window.

Maddie sighed luxuriously. Stretched her legs.

It wasn't the sun that was warm.

She opened her eyes. Felt the heavy arm around her.

She leaned forward carefully, remembering that the monitor was on the floor.

His thigh pushed against hers. "She's asleep. Miraculously." The monitor dropped from his other hand onto the mattress near her nose. "Be still."

When everything inside her was skittering around like oil in a hot skillet? "It's Monday. Don't you have to go to work?"

"Boss's privilege." His arm tightened. "Told you to be still."

As if. She tried to remember when he'd come in to lie on her bed. "Linc—"

He exhaled and grabbed her hands, rolling over her.

"I warned you. Morning breath coming in." His head lowered over hers.

There was no morning breath.

Only a long, slow, lazy kiss that made her dissolve.

"I shouldn't do this," she whispered when his hands slid beneath her sweater.

He didn't stop. "But I should." He pulled the sweater over her head. His intense eyes slid over like a warm caress.

"I don't, uh, don't know if it's ethical—" It was an excuse. Anything to stem the churning need that rose inside her as surely as Layla's bathwater flooded the floor every single time. "I'm Layla's care—" His mouth cut off her words.

She couldn't help the sound that rose in her throat when his hands slid away from hers, but only to make her jeans slide away, too.

"If you wake up Layla," he murmured against her throat, "I'm going to have to get rough here."

She shuddered, running her greedy fingers over his hot chest. If he stopped, she was going to get positively crazy. "I'm quaking in my boots," she managed almost soundlessly.

"You're not wearing any." He proved it by kissing his way down her thigh to her knee.

Neither was he, she realized dimly.

And then his kiss started upward again.

And then she simply quaked.

Chapter Thirteen

"Get your coat."

Maddie paused and looked down at the sink full of suds where she was washing their lunch dishes. "Um... can we finish here?" She rinsed the plate and held it toward him.

His eyes glinted and he dropped a kiss on her shoulder, ignoring the plate that he'd claimed he would dry. "I do like the way we finish."

She flushed. Not even the fact that Layla was strapped to the front of her kept warm, slippery heat from filling her. "You said you'd dry," she reminded him.

He grabbed the plate and gave it a cursory rub with the dishtowel. "It's dry. And next time use the dishwasher. That's what it's for." He took the sponge out of her hand and pulled her out of the kitchen.

She couldn't help laughing. "Linc!"

He brushed her lips with his, then ducked his head and brushed a kiss over Layla's nose. "Now go and get your coat."

"Why?"

His teeth flashed. "You'll see." He bolted up the stairs, taking them two and three at a time.

Maddie looked at Layla. "Who is that pod person who's taken over Uncle Linc? Hmm?"

Layla kicked and chortled. She grabbed Maddie's hair and gave a merry yank.

"Yeah, I like him, too," Maddie admitted quietly.

She more than liked him. She was stick stupid head over her heels for the man.

"You getting your coat?" Linc yelled from upstairs.

"Yes," she yelled back. They were hanging in the foyer. She tucked Layla into hers first, then strapped her into the fabric carrier before pulling on her own coat. She couldn't fasten the buttons, but with their combined body heat, she wasn't concerned. Then she covered the baby's head with Vivian's cap and hoped that it would stay there for more than a few minutes.

Maddie heard him on the stairs and turned to look.

And she was afraid that her heart would just crack right then and there.

Because he was carrying an old-fashioned wooden sled.

When he reached her, he leaned it against the door long enough to pull on his own coat. "It was in the attic, too." He picked it up again and opened the door. "Be lucky if it even glides. Runners haven't been waxed in God knows how long. But I figure it's worth a try."

She swallowed past the knot in her throat and followed him out onto the wide porch, down the brick steps and out onto the lawn where he dropped the sled in the snow. There was a short length of rope tied to the pointed front end. Probably the same rope that had been there when they were children. And it had been old, even then.

He stuck his boot down on the wood slats, experimentally pushing the sled back and forth. "Better than I expected."

She hugged her arms around Layla. She was kicking even more excitedly, as if she knew something fun awaited. Or maybe she was just keeping tempo with the chugging of Maddie's racing heart.

"Come on." He took the rope and gestured to the sled. "The chariot awaits."

Everything inside her wanted to get on that sled. But she hesitated. "I don't know. Layla—"

"I can't fit a car seat on the thing," he said dryly. "I'm just going to pull you around the yard, not hook you up to the back of the truck."

She crunched through the snow, waddling a little to keep her balance.

"You look like you're about twenty months pregnant with her strapped to the front of you like she is."

"Lovely." She knew her cheeks were red and blamed it on the cold. She was on the pill. But just the word "pregnant" made her thoughts zip where they had no business zipping.

She awkwardly straddled the sleigh and managed to sit down on it without falling on her butt. She adjusted Layla a little and crossed her legs atop the sled. "I don't remember this thing being quite so narrow."

He laughed softly. "You're still pretty damn cute on it, though." He grabbed the rope and started walking. "Hold on."

"To what?" She gasped as the sled jerked forward. "Layla or the sled?"

"Both." He walked a little faster. The runners began moving a little more smoothly. "I don't remember this thing being quite so heavy."

She scooped up a handful of snow and pelted the back of his head.

He jerked as it hit and looked back at her. He brushed snow out of his hair, his hazel eyes crinkling at the corners. "Good thing you've got Layla protecting you."

"Yeah, I'm really worried."

His expression turned downright wicked. "Quaking in your boots?"

She opened her mouth, but had no retort. Probably because all of her senses were swirling around in memories from that morning when they'd made love.

Then Layla squealed, kicking her feet, and Linc laughed again. He grabbed fresh hold of the rope and started running, dragging the sled and her heart merrily along.

They made it twice up and down the long, sloping yard and almost all the way out to the iron gate and back before Linc finally called it quits.

He pulled the sleigh up to the front of the house and dropped right onto his back in the snow. "That," he puffed, "is work."

Maddie unfolded her legs, groaning at how stiff they felt. "Nobody said you had to pull us for *miles*." Holding one arm around Layla, she managed to slide off the sled until she was on her back in the snow, too. She automatically pulled Layla's hat more firmly down over her ears. The afternoon sky was turning pale overhead. Clouds were starting to form. "But thank you."

She reached out her gloved hand until it bumped Linc. "That was—" *perfect* "—a lot of fun."

He bumped her back. "Thank you."

Her vision blurred and she blinked hard, willing it to clear.

But then his hand moved away and he sat up.

Only then did she realize a car was heading up the long driveway. She didn't even think a thing about it as she sat up, too, and watched it approach. Cold was seeping through her jeans by the time it reached the wide circle in front of the house and parked.

Then she scrambled to her feet when she recognized her cousin climbing from the vehicle.

"What's Justin doing here?" Linc stood also.

She swallowed. Her mouth had gone dry. She wrapped one arm around Layla, and reached for him with her other. "He must have the DNA comparison." She couldn't imagine any other reason why he would have made the drive to Braden.

Linc exhaled an oath. His hand tightened around hers, almost crushing her fingers. "He's not smiling."

She felt an abrupt urge to turn. To take Layla and just keep running.

But she didn't. She watched Justin head up the first set of shallow brick steps. Then the second. Until finally he stopped in front of them.

And she knew. Just from the solemn expression in his eyes.

"They're not a match," she said huskily.

Justin looked at Linc. "I'm sorry." He was holding an envelope in his hand. "I figured you'd want to know as soon as possible, but I couldn't make myself tell you over the phone. The woman at your office said you hadn't come in." He extended the envelope. "I know it's not what you were expecting. This is a copy of the report I've transmitted to the court."

Linc slowly released Maddie's hand before taking it. "This is a mistake."

"We ran them twice," Justin said. "I checked them personally. Even if Jax were here to compare—" He broke off, shaking his head. "I could cite all the technical jargon I explain in the report, but there is no way Layla is your brother's child, Linc. Not unless you and Jax have different biological fathers." He waited a beat. As if he hoped to hear it was possible. But Linc didn't even flinch. "You should have a certain percentage of half-identical DNA," he continued. "And you don't. It's not even close. I'm sorry."

Linc slowly sank down on the porch step. He stared at the unopened envelope in his hand. The hollow expression in his eyes was more than Maddie could bear.

Justin lightly touched Maddie's elbow. Sympathy was clear in his face. Then he turned and headed back to his car.

She watched him go through a glaze of tears.

Linc still hadn't moved, even when Justin's car was no longer in sight.

She sat next to him, pressing her cheek against Layla's head. She'd fallen asleep. At least she had no clue of the blow.

Maddie slid her hand over Linc's shoulder. "Linc. What Justin said. About you and Jax having different fathers—"

He finally stirred. "We don't." His voice came from somewhere very deep. "Out of all our parents' sins, that isn't one of them."

She chewed the inside of her cheek, wishing that such questions never needed to be asked. But his parents' infidelities were common knowledge. "How do you know for certain?"

"Ernestine," he said heavily. "She didn't like us hearing rumors. She made sure she knew who we were. Her grandsons."

"I'm sorry," she whispered.

"You warned me. I didn't listen." His voice went even lower. Rawer. "You need to leave me alone now, Maddie."

Her tears spilled over. She wiped them away and leaned toward him, pressing her mouth to his temple before she stood.

Then she carried the baby inside the house. Up the stairs past the Christmas tree. Beyond the tilted star. Into the nursery.

She carefully unwound herself from her coat and the multistrapped carrier, finally unveiling the baby. She didn't put Layla in the crib, though. She just sat down in the upholstered chair and held her close.

Because now there really was no guarantee how much longer she'd be able to hold her at all.

And without Layla, there would also be no reason for Maddie to stay.

"Take it all." Linc stood in the doorway of the nursery.

They'd just come from court.

Judge Stokes had been sympathetic. But inflexible.

They knew even less about Layla than they thought. If her mother—or father, whoever he might be—didn't step forward within the next ninety days, Layla would be eligible for adoption.

And the list of families waiting for a baby just like her was about a mile and a half long.

Even if Maddie and Linc got their names on the list, there were dozens ahead of them. The fact that they'd been caring for Layla for the past week and a half counted for nothing.

"The Perezes are a good couple." Her composure was tenuous as she packed Layla's clothes into a box.

Ray had taken Layla from them at the courthouse. Maddie had feared that Linc was going to physically assault her boss when he'd done so. But she knew that Ray was truly no happier about the result than she was. He'd even told her she could come back from vacation. He'd assign her as Layla's caseworker.

It was small comfort when she wanted to be so much more.

"They h-have two children of their own. Shelley— Mrs. Perez—used to be a nurse. Now, she's a stay-at-home mom. Steven is a school counselor. I've worked with them for…for years—" Her voice broke and she cleared her throat. "They're good fosters. They'll take excellent care of her." But she knew from experience how much space the Perezes had in their four-bedroom house. "They don't have room for any of this, though." She slowly closed the flaps of the box. "Except clothes and diapers—" Her voice broke again.

Linc crossed the room and pulled her against him. "I could still be a foster parent. Get qualified. If you married me, we'd be almost as good as the Perezes."

She buried her face against his chest. She couldn't bear his offer of marriage. "They won't be keeping her, either. Not once she's available for adoption."

His arms tightened. "There's still an investigation about who she is." His voice was rough. "Who left her. No matter what your cousin said about the profile, Jax is involved somehow. Layla's mother wouldn't have left her here with that note. If they'd just agree to hack his damn phone, there are messages. Phone calls. Something that would have to help."

"Jax isn't under suspicion for any wrongdoing. There's no presumption he's her father. He wasn't even here when she was left. The phone is a dead issue." She was simply repeating what the prosecutor had said. Because he, too, had been at the hearing.

Just one big, very unhappy family.

"I need to get Layla's things over to her." She swiped her face and pushed away from him. Her throat ached. Her heart ached. She looked up at him. "Are you going to be okay?"

His jaw tightened. "Are you?"

She swiped her cheek again. She picked up the box. "This is my job."

"It's more than your job. It's been more than your job from the second you asked your brother to call the judge."

"And look what good it's done."

He'd opened his heart to a baby girl, only to lose her.

"I'll pick up my things later."

"Terry can take care of it."

She felt like the hole inside her couldn't yawn any wider.

Without Layla, what purpose did she have there?

Humiliation at seventeen was nothing compared to heartbreak at thirty.

"Fine," she whispered. She carried the box past him. "Goodbye, Linc."

"What's going on? Somebody die?"

Linc looked up from the bottle of whiskey sitting in front of him. He blinked past the sandpaper in his eyes when the chandelier came on, dousing the gloomy living room in painful light. "Jax?"

His brother dropped his duffel bag on the floor, giving the Christmas tree a surprised look as he walked past it. "What're you sitting in the dark for?" He strolled closer and picked up the near-empty bottle. "Thought you gave that stuff up after Gram died."

Linc shot off his chair, grabbing his brother by his jacket. "Where the *hell* have you been?"

"Christ, Linc! What's—"

Linc shoved him. Hard. It was either that, or punch the hell out of him.

Jax landed in the leather chair behind him with a *whoosh*. He swore loudly and started to pop back up.

Linc lifted a warning hand. "Do. Not. Move."

Jax warily spread his palms in surrender and sat back in the chair. "How much *have* you had to drink?"

"Not anywhere near enough." Not enough to get Maddie's face out of his head. It had been four days since she'd carried that box out of his home and turned the place back into just a house. "You should have told me about Layla."

Jax's eyes narrowed. Unlike Linc's, they were blue. Very blue against his tanned face. "Layla." He waited a beat. "Afraid you'll have to be a little more specific."

Linc yanked the copy of the note he'd made out of his pocket. The edges where he'd folded it were creased and creased again from the number of times he'd studied it. He tossed it at his brother's head. "Layla."

"Eat some prunes, brother." Jax unfolded the note, but the words on it clearly made no impression. "So I ask again, who is Layla?"

Linc's ears buzzed. Maybe he was just going to have

a stroke. He'd leave Swift Oil to his brother, who'd either run it into the ground or not.

He rubbed his eyes with his palms, then dropped his hands. "Where have you been?"

Jax looked away. "Turks and Caicos."

"With Dana?"

His brother hesitated.

"She's going to ruin you one day," Linc said, sighing.

"Like she ruined you?"

"She's not the one who ruined me," he countered. "You should have just told me you were going. Or at least taken your damn phone." He picked up the note. "Someone left this for you."

"Who?"

"If I knew," Linc said through his teeth, "I wouldn't have cared where you were. Or how long you'd be."

"Man, you have lost your nut." Jax looked over at the tree. "What's with the whole merry, merry thing, anyway?"

"You'd lose your nut, too, if someone left a baby on your doorstep with just a *note* attached!"

Jax gaped. "What are you talking about?"

"Layla," Linc said. "The infant who was dumped on our doorstep two weeks ago. With that note to *Jaxie* attached!"

His brother shot out of his chair, finally looking alarmed. "Well, she wasn't *mine*."

"I know that. Now." Linc sat, exhausted. It was his turn to watch his brother pace around the room for a while. "The DNA they did on us proved that."

"So what happened to the kid?"

"That *kid* has a name. Layla."

"Fine. What happened to *Layla*?"

He rubbed at the pain in his chest. It was worse than the ulcer had ever been. "She's gone."

"Gone." His brother turned pale. "Dead?"

"No!"

"Jesus Christ, Linc." Jax sat down, too. "Stop freaking me out!"

"She's with a foster family. And since you're not her father, we don't know *who* she is."

"Or where she belongs, I'm guessing," Jax murmured slowly.

"I know where she belongs." Linc closed his eyes and leaned his head back. Maddie's face swam behind his lids. Maddie laughing. Maddie crying. Maddie watching him through her lashes while she pulled him into her—

"Look, Linc." Jax picked up the copy of the note. "It's taken me more than twelve hours to get home. And following you is more than I can deal with. Why don't you start from the beginning."

So Linc did.

When he was finished, Jax silently reached for the bottle of whiskey. He didn't bother with a glass, just took a shot straight from the bottle. "Damn."

"All we have is that note."

His brother spread it over his thigh. "'Jaxie, please take care of Layla for me.'" The toe of his hiking boot bounced. "Jaxie. Nobody calls me that. 'Cept—" He made a face.

Linc almost grabbed Jax by the throat again. *"Except?"*

"Hold on. It'll come to me. She had a stripper name." Jax tapped his fingers against his forehead. Then he stopped and looked at Linc. "Miranda," he said. "Daisy Miranda. Waitressed for me," he frowned again, "for

a few months. Over a year ago. She wasn't pregnant.
Never said it, anyway. And damn sure didn't look it.
But she did call me Jaxie."

Linc stood and pulled his brother out of his chair.
"Come on."

"Where?"

"Magic Jax. You keep records of your employees,
don't you?"

"Since my business partner frowns on it if I don't—"
Jax rolled his eyes when Linc glared. "Yes, I keep records."

"Then we're going to get every piece of information
you've got about Daisy Miranda and give it to Maddie.
She'll know what to do with it."

"And have Daisy arrested for abandoning her kid?"

"Maybe. But at least Layla can't get adopted by
somebody else before they have a chance to even find
her real mother."

"Yeah, but why Maddie?"

Linc glared.

His brother lifted his hands. "Dude. Relax. It's like
that, is it?"

"Yeah." He grabbed his coat and yanked open the
door. "It's like that."

"What d'you know." Jax followed him out into the
evening. "She always was a sweetheart."

Linc stopped in his tracks. "If you so much as look
at her, I'll—"

Jax lifted his hands. "Not ever. Not again."

Linc unlocked his jaw. Dana was one thing. Maddie another. And he didn't want to have to kill his own
brother.

"Just gotta say," Jax grinned a little crookedly. "It is
good to know you've still got a heart."

Chapter Fourteen

"I don't think I've seen a longer face in all of my life." Vivian, dressed in shimmering silver, held a glass of amber liquid out to Maddie.

Maddie had no more interest in alcohol than she did in being at her grandmother's fancy Christmas party. But she tucked her phone behind her and took the glass anyway. One sip and her throat was on fire. It might have felt a little less potent if she'd spent more time eating something of substance versus pointlessly staring at the photo she'd taken of Linc and Layla. "I didn't think anyone would notice I slipped out. I certainly don't want to take you away from your own party."

She was sitting in Vivian's sunroom. *Conservatory*, as her grandmother insisted on calling it. Whatever. It was a window-lined room filled with exotic plants that had no business whatsoever flourishing in the middle of a Wyoming winter. But thanks to her grandmother's fancy lighting and the air she probably had bottled and flown in from the tropics, they did. And the silent plants were better companions than the guests who were filling the two-story atrium at the center of Vivian's enormous house.

If Maddie could have blocked out the sounds of the Christmas music being played by a trio that her eccentric grandmother had hired out of Phoenix, of all places, she'd have been even happier in her misery.

"I notice lots of things," Vivian said. "And since it *is* my party, I get to do as I please." She sipped at the other glass she'd been carrying as she arranged herself on one of the padded metal settees that dotted the conservatory. "Not that I need a party to do as I please," she added wryly.

Maddie smiled, as Vivian clearly meant her to do. She took another sip of the burning whiskey.

It made her think of Linc.

Putting down the glass wouldn't matter, though.

Not when everything made her think of Linc.

"I had an interesting lunch the other day," Vivian said. "With Horvald Stokes."

Maddie quickly set down the glass before she dropped it. "What? Why?"

"I wanted to see if he had a price."

"Vivian!" Maddie shoved out of her chair, nearly tripping over the long blue dress that she'd borrowed from Hayley. She'd heard time and again from her dad about his mother's manipulative nature, but had never seen it in action. "You can't be serious."

"Calm down." Her grandmother picked up Maddie's glass and handed it to her once more.

"I won't calm down." Agitated, she snatched the glass and tossed back the contents, then had to lean over as she coughed through the pain of it. "What… possessed…you?" Her stomach churned.

Vivian leisurely sat back against the settee. "He doesn't," she said. "Have a price, that is. I quite liked that about him, actually."

"Judge Stokes is happily married, Vivian. Don't be looking for a fifth husband there."

Her grandmother chuckled softly. "I have no desire for a fifth. I'm quite content knowing I had the best in Arthur. And very aware that he could have done so much better than me." She sobered. "Sadly, I can't help you or your Lincoln where the baby is concerned. But I wanted to."

Maddie's eyes stung. "He's not my Lincoln. And Layla—"

"Isn't anyone's." Vivian sighed. "Heartbreaking, really."

Maddie pinched the bridge of her nose. "I'm really not up to doing this," she whispered.

"Your mother seems to think you're in love with him."

The musical trio was singing "Have Yourself a Merry Little Christmas." The same song that had been playing when she and Layla had visited Linc at his office. Her chest ached even more. "It doesn't matter."

Vivian tsked. "Of course it matters."

"He doesn't love *me*, Vivian. He only proposed because—"

"Proposed!" Vivian sat forward, like a cat pouncing.

"Don't get excited. It was only because he thought it would improve his chances of keeping Layla. I promise you, I set him straight." She was nauseated just thinking about it. Or maybe it was the whiskey on an empty stomach.

"Did you now."

"What's that supposed to mean?"

"I once thought I set Arthur straight. He brought me around to his thinking, of course. But I wish that I'd never wasted all that time that we could have spent together before he did. We had little enough of it together in the end."

"This is not the same situation, Vivian. I turned him down." Four times. Four times, she'd turned him down. "Linc's not the kind of man to get over that."

"Of course not, dear. No doubt, he is the most unforgiving soul there ever was." She held out her hand. "Help me up. I'm neglecting my other guests."

Maddie quickly took her arm and helped her rise, even though she had the strong sense that Vivian needed no assistance whatsoever. "He's not unforgiving," she muttered.

"Whatever you say, dear." Vivian patted her cheek. "When you're tired of drinking among the palms, come back out and join us."

Then she gathered her shimmering dress and swept out of the room.

Maddie exhaled. She had nothing left to drink among the palms. She followed her grandmother.

The tree in the center of the atrium was taller than the one she and Linc had cut. More slender and more perfectly manicured.

She stopped in front of it, looking up at all the crystal and gold. But in her mind, she was seeing one with faded nutcrackers and a lopsided star.

"You were right. It's an art piece."

Maddie jerked, whirling around. "Linc." He was looking very un-Linc-like. His eyes were bloodshot.

His hair fell over the lines in his forehead. His jeans looked ancient and his shirt was wrinkled.

And he still was the best sight in the room.

"Does Vivian know you're here?"

"Yeah. I saw her a few minutes ago. Didn't seem to mind me crashing too much."

Behind him, she saw her grandmother smiling as she crossed the room. "I'll bet she didn't." She crossed her arms over the front of her low-cut dress that she didn't fill out anywhere as well as Hayley and turned to face the tree again. "What are you doing here?"

"Jax is back."

Her jaw loosened. She dropped her arms and turned toward him. The lights around them danced dizzily. "What?"

"He knows who wrote the note."

It was as though his voice was suddenly coming through a tunnel. She blinked. "Layla's note." Of course he meant Layla's note. What other note was there?

His hands closed around her shoulders. "Are you all right? You look like you're—"

"—*fine*," she cut him off, shrugging away from his touch. She bumped the tree behind her, and crystal and gold shimmered and tinkled. "I am...*fu-hine*."

And to prove it, her eyes rolled and she pitched forward, straight into his arms.

"Well." Linc sat on the edge of the couch where he'd deposited her. "I guess we know who gets to be the fireworks at your grandmother's party this year." He handed her a glass. "Water."

Maddie peered at him. Her mouth felt like cotton. She took the water and drained it. She didn't recognize the room. Nor could she hear the Christmas trio anymore. Between knocking into the tree and realizing he was carrying her into this room, everything was blank. "Please tell me I didn't yack on Vivian's marble floor or something."

"It was a pretty straightforward passing out, actually." His fingers grazed her hand and he stood. "I'll be back in a minute." He walked over to the door and she could hear him talking to someone, though his voice was too low to tell what he said.

She pressed her arm over her eyes. "Top of your game, Maude," she murmured.

After a moment, he returned and sat back down on the edge of the couch, his hip crowding her thighs. "Nice dress."

She self-consciously tugged the bodice. "It's Hayley's. No time to alter it. Who was at the door?"

"Your mom. She knows you're okay."

Maddie could only imagine.

Mrs. Lincoln Swift.

She struggled awkwardly to sit. Considering her long skirt was caught under him, it was an effort in futility. She gave up and stared at him. "You said Jax is back. He knows who wrote the note."

"A cocktail waitress. Worked for him for a short time over a year ago. Daisy Miranda."

The name meant nothing to her. "Layla Miranda," she murmured. She suddenly pushed at him again. "Let me up. I need to get in touch with Ray. And Judge Stokes. And the Prosecutor's Office."

His hands pushed her back down. "All of that is being done. Ali. Greer. Archer. They're all doing their part."

She subsided. "This is good news, Linc, but—"

"I know. It doesn't mean anything changes where Layla and you and I are concerned."

Her eyes stung. "I wish I could have made every-thing work out. For everyone."

"You can't fix everything."

"If there's a chance of locating Daisy, Judge Stokes will hold off placing her for adoption as long as he can. Which means she'll need more long-term foster care than we planned. And it's not unheard of for people to end up adopting a child they've fostered. Stokes has never approved it, but. I… I can at least help you get qualified as a foster parent. Prove to Judge Stokes that you are the best one for Layla even if you aren't mar-ried. I mean, it's an old-fashioned notion and it's high time he—"

He pressed his hand over her lips.

"—started realizing it," she mumbled, too far gone to stop.

"You can't fix everything," he repeated softly.

"I know, but—"

"But you can fix me."

She stared at him above his big, warm hand.

"I know I'm nowhere near good enough for you, Maddie Templeton. But I'll do my damnedest to try. Just say you'll marry me." He cautiously pulled his hand away.

Her heart charged inside her chest. "Layla—"

"This isn't about Layla. I want her in our life. And we'll figure out how to make that happen. But this is about *me*. And *you*. And the fact that my house hasn't been the same since the day you left it."

"You don't love me," she whispered. "You can't pos-sibly."

His eyebrows lifted. "Because I don't have parents who're still besotted with each other to have shown me how?"

"*No!* You're so much better than that. You're good and you care so *much* about doing what's right—"

He covered her mouth again. But this time, with just his thumb. "—and I love you." His thumb glided along her lip, then made way for his kiss. "Just tell me there's a chance you could love me back," he whispered. "And I'll be happy to break Gus's record every day of the week until you say yes."

She stared up at him, her eyes searching. She wanted so desperately to believe. "I loved you when I was seventeen." She shakily touched his cheek, brushed his tumbled hair back from his eyes. "I never knew how much I could love you now."

"What are you saying?"

It was the hope that got her. It lit his hazel eyes. It heated her through to her soul. She didn't need to be at the top of her game with him.

She just needed to be. With him.

"I'm saying five times is enough, Lincoln Swift." She lifted her mouth to his. "I'm saying yes."

Maddie stole a glance over her shoulder before leaning her head closer to Linc. "Stop fidgeting," she whispered.

He stretched his arm along the crowded church pew behind her and leaned his head closer to hers. "This is the longest Christmas Eve service in the history of time."

She bit her lip, trying not to smile. It was true. The church service—dominated by the children's pageant—had been dragging on longer than usual. Which was good, because Ray had promised to get there before it ended.

She slid her fingers between Linc's. "Just imagine Layla singing in a children's choir like this one day."

He made a low sound and shifted again. "Swift Oil's gonna donate padded seats," he whispered.

She ducked her chin, muffling her quick laugh and stole another look toward the back of the church.

Still no Ray.

"Hey." Ali sat forward from her spot on the pew behind them, and stuck her head between theirs. "Quiet down. Mayor's giving you guys the stink eye."

Maddie's shoulders shook. "Shh."

Grinning wickedly, and satisfied with her results, Ali sat back. They were all there. Ali. Greer. Her parents. Even Hayley and Seth.

Linc's hand went from the pew to Maddie's shoulder. "She's right," he murmured against her cheek. "Big-time stink eye. I always knew it was more interesting sitting over here with your family."

She closed her eyes and prayed that they wouldn't be struck with lightning for not showing the proper reverence while three toddler-size Wise Men tripped over their robes as they made their way to the manger.

"Let's go to Vegas," he whispered. "We can be married by morning."

Her lips parted. For a moment, she forgot all about her boss as she looked at Linc. "Now?"

"Unless you want the whole hometown wedding thing."

A wedding there meant time wasted through the holiday, waiting for a marriage license. Time that could be spent together. As his wife. Right now. Or at least as soon as he could get them to Las Vegas.

Considering he had resources upon resources, she wasn't too concerned on that front.

"Mrs. Lincoln Swift," Maddie murmured. She pressed her lips to his. "All I want is you." There was no doubt. No hesitation at all. "But maybe we should at least wait until the service is over."

This time, Meredith leaned forward. "Shh." But her eyes were sparkling.

And Linc wasn't the least bit cowed. "Let's do it now." Holding her hand, he stood.

Following seemed simpler than arguing. At least right there in the middle of the kids breaking into another Christmas carol. She felt certain it was their twentieth. Murmuring apologies as she went, she slowly followed him out of the crowded pew, Linc's hand in one hand, her coat in the other. Once they were free of the bodies, though, she didn't even care that they'd become the focus of the congregation as they hurried out.

Because Judge Stokes and his wife were hurrying in. And he gave Maddie a benevolent smile as they slipped into the standing-room only space at the rear of the church.

She relaxed a little. If Stokes was there, she knew Ray would soon follow.

Snow was drifting from the sky when they slipped out the church doors. Linc helped her on with her coat and kept hold of the collar. "I love you, Maddie."

Her heart skittered. She reached up and brushed a snowflake from his hair. "I love you, too. But before we go to Vegas, there's something I need to tell you. Something that just came up today, actually."

He hooked his hands behind her back. "There's nothing you can tell me that's going to slow us down or keep us going to from Vegas. I want you *all* to myself."

Delight shivered through her. If she hadn't spotted

her boss just then, she might well have forgotten everything except Linc. "No sharing?"

"*No* sharing."

She reached up and brushed her lips against his. "You might want to rethink that." She pushed his shoulder until he turned enough to see Ray.

Heading toward them. Obviously carrying something.

Some*one*.

She felt Linc go still. His hand tightened on hers. "What's going on?"

"Shelley Perez's sister went into premature labor this afternoon." She bit her lip. "She needed to leave town to be with her. And, well—"

Ray stopped in front of them, looking typically out of breath. "Figured I'd get here before this, but it took a while for Steven to get Layla's clothes together." He grinned and handed over the baby. She was dressed in her tiny white coat, a familiar red cap covering her head.

Even though she'd been expecting the baby, tears still blurred Maddie's vision as she clasped Layla to her chest. The baby smacked her chin and chortled.

"I don't understand." Linc's voice was gruff. His hand shook as he covered Maddie's.

She met his gaze. "With Shelley Perez out of town indefinitely because of her sister, her husband can't handle their kids and an infant all on his own. Which means Layla needs new foster care."

"And now there's some information about her mother to actually investigate," Ray inserted. "Which is why, a few minutes ago, Stokes agreed to name you both joint custodians until we can get more answers."

"*Both* of us!" Maddie hadn't expected that. "He's never done anything like that before!"

Ray winked. "Even judges get a little Christmas spirit." He patted the baby's arm. "I'll get her stuff from my car." He walked away.

"I can't believe this," Linc said. "You *knew* this was happening?"

"Not about the joint custodianship, but yes." She smiled tremulously. "It's not permanent, but it's something."

"It's everything." Linc's arms surrounded them both. "And *you* are amazing."

She lifted Layla higher. "Say Merry Christmas to Uncle Linc, baby."

Layla kicked and chortled. She reached for Linc's face. He caught her tiny mittened hand and kissed it. Then he kissed Maddie. And the sweetness that slid through her veins was going to last a lifetime.

"This changes things about Vegas." His voice was husky. "We'll get a license when the holidays are over. Get married at the courthouse."

"We could do that," she allowed. "But you know, we *do* have a church and a judge right here who's evidently in the holiday spirit…"

Linc threw back his head and laughed. Then he grabbed Maddie's hand and tugged her back toward the church.

* * * * *

Phoebe was still awake, nestled in his arms, gazing upward as if trying to make sense of this man who was holding her.

This man sitting beside Sunny.

They were sitting at the end of the pew, in case Phoebe decided to roar and they had to take her out.

Anyone looking at her and at Max might think…

Don't go there, Sunny thought. This was a fantasy. There'd never been time or space for her to think of a love life.

She gazed down at her hands, at the lines and calluses formed by years of hard work, at the absence of rings. She stretched them out and suddenly, astonishingly, Max's fingers were closing over hers.

'Good hands,' he said in an undervoice. 'Honourable hands.'

She should… She didn't know what she should do. Had he known what she was thinking? How many hands had this man seen that looked like hers? *None*.

She should tug her hand back and the contact would be over. That was the sensible course, the only course, but she couldn't quite manage it. His clasp was warm and strong. Good.

Fantasy enveloped her again for a moment, insidious in its sweetness. To keep sitting here, to feel the peace of this moment, this place, this man…

THE BILLIONAIRE'S CHRISTMAS BABY

BY
MARION LENNOX

First Published in Great Britain 2017
By Mills & Boon, an imprint of HarperCollins*Publishers*
1 London Bridge Street, London, SE1 9GF

© 2017 Marion Lennox

ISBN: 978-0-263-92353-7

23-1217

MIX
Paper from
responsible sources
FSC™ C007454

Printed and bound in Spain
by CPI, Barcelona

Marion Lennox has written more than one hundred romances, and is published in over a hundred countries and thirty languages. Her multiple awards include the prestigious RITA® Award (twice), and the *RT Book Reviews* Career Achievement Award for 'a body of work which makes us laugh and teaches us about love'. Marion adores her family, her kayak, her dog— and lying on the beach with a book someone else has written. Heaven!

CHAPTER ONE

SHE'D FORGOTTEN GRAN'S cherry liqueur chocolates.

No!

Sunny Raye abandoned her scrubbing and gave in to the horror of her memory lapse. The discount store near home brought in mountains of chocolates for Christmas. They were cheap and delicious, but they'd be sold out by now.

It was ten at night and she was bone-weary. She'd agreed to work overtime because she needed the pay—Christmas was expensive—but all she wanted now was her bed. Tomorrow was Christmas Eve and she was rostered to work again from eight to five. Where could she find time to buy Gran's chocolates, and how much would she need to spend?

Aaagh!

'How long does it take to scrub one floor?'

Uh-oh.

The stain on the tiles was hard against the bathroom door. She hadn't been able to shut it, which meant she was in full view of the guest sitting at the desk. He was annoyed? The feeling was mutual. This was a job for Maintenance, not for a scrubbing brush.

But Sunny's job was to make the guest feel that this was a scrubbed stain rather than a missed-by-Housekeeping stain. *Keep him happy at all costs*—that had been the order. When Max Grayland was in town the hotel fell over itself to make sure all was right with his world. Heads would roll over this stain, but it wouldn't be her head.

Enough. She dried the floor with care, then rose. Oh, her knees hurt, but perky must be maintained.

'I'm so sorry, sir,' she told him brightly, as if this was the start of her shift rather than two hours after she was supposed to be gone. 'It appears to be a bleach stain, possibly from hair dye. It should have been noticed and I apologise that it wasn't. I can arrange for the tile to be replaced now, if you like.'

Ross in Maintenance would kill her, but she had to offer.

'However, it'll involve noise and you may wish us to leave it until morning,' she added. 'Meanwhile, I can assure you it's clean and totally hygienic.'

'Leave it then.' Max Grayland pushed the documents he'd been working on aside and rose, and she sensed he was almost as weary as she was. With reason? She knew he'd flown in from New York this morning, but Max Grayland crossed the globe at will. Surely travelling in first class luxury prevented jet lag?

How would she know? Sunny had never flown in her life.

But he did look tired. Rumpled.

He was a financial whiz, she'd been told, a man in his mid-thirties, at the top of his game. The media described him as a legal eagle, and that was what he looked like. He was tall, dark and imposing, with deep, hooded eyes and a body that seemed toned to the point of impossible.

He was still wearing the clothes he'd worn at check-in but he'd ditched his jacket, unbuttoned the top of his shirt and rolled his sleeves. His after-five shadow looked like after five from the night before.

What was a man like this doing looking exhausted? Didn't he have minions to jump to his every whim?

He stalked over and stared at the stain as if it personally offended him, but she had a feeling he was seeing far more than the stain. He raked his dark hair and his look of exhaustion deepened.

'Leave it,' he growled again. 'Thanks for your help.'

That was something at least. Most of the guests who stayed in the penthouse didn't bother to say thank you.

'I'm sorry I can't do more.' She edged past him, which was a bit problematic. She was carrying a mop and bucket and she had to edge sideways. She didn't edge far enough and her body brushed his.

She smelled the faint scent of aftershave, something incredibly masculine, nice...

Sexy.

Good one, Sunny, she thought. This morning her hair had been tied into a neat knot, but the knot had loosened hours ago and she hadn't had time to redo it. After a day's hard physical work in the hotel's often overheated rooms, her curls were limp and plastered against her face. Her uniform was stained. She knew she smelled of cleaning products—and she was suddenly acutely aware that the guy she was brushing past was a hunk.

A billionaire hunk.

Get a grip.

'Goodnight, sir,' she said primly and headed for the door. For some reason she wanted to scuttle. What was he doing, unsettling her like this?

Cherry liqueur chocolates, she told herself firmly. *Focus on imperatives.*

But a rap at the door made her pause.

Her training told her to melt into the background, which was impossible when she was in his room, carrying an armload of cleaning gear.

'What the...?' Behind her, Max Grayland growled his displeasure. 'I don't need anyone else fussing over this. Tell your people to leave it.'

He was assuming it'd be the manager, coming to grovel his apologies. She hadn't reported that she couldn't fix the stain, though. Brent wouldn't be here yet.

But access to the penthouse suite floor was security locked. Stray visitors didn't make it up here.

'You're not expecting anyone, sir?'

'I'm not,' he snapped. 'Tell them to go away.' And he re-treated behind his desk.

There was nothing for it. She put down her mop and bucket, pushed her stray curls back behind her ears—*gee, that'd make a difference*—and opened the door.

And almost fainted.

She knew the woman in front of her. Of course she did—this was a face that was emblazoned on billboards, on buses, on perfume advertisements nationwide. Exotic and glamorous, Isabelle Steinway's pouty face was her fortune. She was famous for...well, for being famous. Her fame had just started to fade when news of her pregnancy had hit the tabloids, and for the last few months the media had been going nuts. There'd been gossip galore, fed by Isabelle's publicity machine—a secret father, the body beautiful doing all the 'right things' and selling those 'right things' as exclusives...

And then nothing. For the last few weeks Isabelle had inexplicably gone to ground. There'd been a publicity statement that she wished for privacy for the birth, which was a huge ask for the public to believe.

But she was here now, glamorous as ever, in a tight-fitting frock that made a mockery of the fact that she must have just given birth.

A night porter was standing behind her, looking anxious. Nigel must have been badgered into allowing her up here, Sunny thought, but who could blame him? The media reported that what Isabelle wanted, Isabelle got, and one pimply-faced teenage porter wouldn't be enough to stand in her way. Nigel looked terrified. And deeply unhappy.

He was pushing a pram and the pram was wailing.

But Isabelle was ignoring the pram. The moment Sunny opened the door, she swept in, brushing her aside as if she was nothing. As indeed she should be. She should disappear, but Nigel was blocking her way. He'd pushed the pram into the doorway, stopping her leaving, and his gaze was that of a rabbit caught in headlights.

They were both stuck.

She might as well turn and watch the tableau in front of her.

The penthouse had been decorated for Christmas. A massive tree sparkled behind them. There were tasteful bud lights hanging from the windows, and through those windows the lights of Sydney Harbour glittered like a fairy tale.

The two centrepieces in this tableau were also like something out of a fairy tale. Yes, Max looked exhausted, but this man would look good after a week in the bush fighting to survive. The warrior image suited him—business clothes seemed almost inappropriate.

And Isabelle? She was wearing a silver-sequined frock that would have cost Sunny a year's wages or more. How had she got into it so soon after giving birth? There must be a whalebone corset somewhere under there, Sunny thought. Her blonde hair was shoulder-length, every curl exquisitely positioned. Her crimson mouth was painted into a heart shape. Everything about her seemed perfect.

Except the pram behind her. The wail coming from its depths was growing increasingly desperate.

But Isabelle seemed oblivious to the wail. She was focusing on Max, her glower designed to skewer at twenty paces.

'She's yours,' she spat and Sunny watched Max react with blank incredulity.

'I beg your pardon?'

'Do you think I want her?' Isabelle's voice was vituperative. 'I never wanted her in the first place. Your father... "Have a baby and I'll marry you," he said. "You'll be taken care of for life. You'll never have to work again."' Her voice was a mock imitation, a vicious recount of words obviously said long ago. 'And now...your father's will... Yeah, he changed it, like he promised he would. His whole fortune for this kid, held in trust by me until the age of twenty-one. But he never said anything to me about a son! I would have aborted. No, I'd have never got pregnant in the first place. So now he's dead and the will says everything goes to his youngest son. But there's only one son, and that's you. You get it all, and my lawyer says I'll even have to file a claim for this one's maintenance. Do you think I slept with a seventy-eight-year-old egomaniac and carried his kid for maintenance?'

Her voice ended on a screech. She sounded out of control, Sunny thought—there was real suffering under there. Real betrayal.

She looked again at Max and saw blank amazement.

'I have no idea what you're talking about,' he managed.

'So welcome to the real world,' Isabelle snapped, fighting to get her voice back to a reasonable level—which was tricky seeing she was talking over a baby's screams. 'She was born last week. Two days after your father's heart attack. You can do a paternity test if you like—I don't care. She's your father's. Her papers are with her. Everything's in the pram. Her name's Phoebe because Phoebe's the midwife who delivered her and when I said I didn't care she sounded shocked so I said I'd call her after her. But now... if you think I'll sit at your father's funeral like a grieving widow you have another think coming. My lawyers will be contacting you for compensation.'

'Isabelle...' Max sounded gobsmacked. 'I'm so sorry...'

'I don't want your sympathy,' Isabelle hissed. 'Your father lied through his teeth to persuade me to have this kid and I might have known... But it's over. There's a house party up north starting tomorrow, with people who really matter. I have no intention of taking that...' she gestured at the howling pram '...with me. You inherited everything your father possessed, so she's yours.'

'You're planning to abandon your baby?' Max's voice was

filled with shock, but also the beginnings of anger. 'Yours and my father's baby?'

'Of course I'm abandoning it. It was a business contract and he broke it.'

'So he planned a son—why? To keep me from inheriting?'

'If he'd told me that I might have even done something,' Isabelle snapped. 'For the amount of money he promised me, I could have fixed it. Sex selection's illegal in this country but he had enough money to pay for me to go abroad. But the stupid old fool didn't even have the sense to be upfront.'

'You know he had a brain tumour. He died of a heart attack but he had cancer. You know he wasn't thinking straight.'

'I don't know anything and I care less,' Isabelle snapped. 'All I know is that I'm leaving. My lawyers will be in touch.' She whirled back to the door, blocked now by the goggling Nigel and the pram. 'Get out of my way.'

Nigel, shocked beyond belief, edged the pram aside so Isabelle could shove her way past. She stalked the four steps to the elevator and hit the button.

The elevator slid open as if it had been waiting.

'Isabelle!' Max strode forward, but the terrified Nigel had swung the pram back into the doorway and bolted, straight through the fire door.

The pram held Max back for precious moments.

The elevator doors slid closed and the fire door slammed.

Isabelle and Nigel were gone.

CHAPTER TWO

THE FIRE DOOR looked very, very appealing.

Cleaning staff were supposed to be invisible.

'Enter discreetly. If guests are present, act as if you're a shadow. Listen to nothing and if there's the slightest sense of unease disappear and go back later. If there's a problem call Housekeeping and have a guest relations manager handle it.'

That had been the mantra drilled into her two years ago when she'd taken this job and Sunny liked it that way. There was too much drama and worry in her personal life to want any more at work.

So, like Nigel, she should bolt for the fire door. Except that would mean pushing past Max, pushing past the pram, possibly even dripping her mop on both.

He'd have to move. He'd have to tug the pram inside, so she could edge out.

Meanwhile, she tried melting against the wall, acting like part of the plaster, hoping he wouldn't notice her.

Though there was a sneaky little voice that was thinking, *Whoa, did I really see what I just saw?* Where was a camera when she needed it? The media would go nuts over what had just happened.

Right. And she'd lose her job and she wouldn't get one again in the service industry and what else was she trained for? She'd left school at fifteen and there'd only been sporadic attendance before then. She was fit for nothing except blending into the wall, which she'd done before and she had every intention of doing now.

Max didn't seem to notice her. Why would he? He'd just been handed a bombshell.

He walked cautiously forward and peered into the pram. The wails increased to the point of desperation and the look on Max's face matched exactly.

She expected him to back away in alarm. Instead he leaned over and scooped a white bundle into his arms. The wails didn't cease. He stood, looking down into the crumpled face of a newborn, and something in his own face twisted.

The pram was still blocking her path but with the baby out of it she could pull it to one side. She could leave.

She edged forward and Max turned as if he suddenly realised he had company.

'You…'

She was still standing with her mop and bucket. Her cleaner's uniform was damp down the front. Her curls were escaping from her regulation knot. She looked nothing like the image of immaculate efficiency the hotel insisted she maintain. Brent would have kittens if he could see her now, she thought, but there was nothing she could do about it.

'Yes, sir.'

'Do you know anything about babies?'

There was a loaded question. The answer was more than she wanted to think about, but she wasn't going there.

'If you need help, you might ring Housekeeping,' she suggested, clutching her mop and bucket like a shield and lance. 'Or I can ask them to send someone up.' She listened to the wails and softened just a little. 'She sounds like she needs feeding,' she suggested. 'You might check the pram for formula, or Housekeeping could provide some. Goodnight, sir…' And she edged forward.

She didn't make it two steps. He was in front of her, blocking her way.

'You're not going anywhere,' he growled. 'Take her.'

'I'm the cleaner.' She wasn't putting her mop and bucket down for the world.

'Until I find someone else, you're here to help. You stay until I get Housekeeping up here. Put that gear down and take her.'

'Sir, she's your baby...'

'*She is not my baby.*'

It was a deep, guttural snap that shocked them both. It appeared to shock even the baby. There was a moment's stunned silence while all of them, baby included, took a breath and reloaded.

Max recovered first. Maybe he had the most to lose. He strode to the door, slammed it shut, pushed the pram in front of it and then walked straight to her. He held the bundle out, pressing it against her.

She could hold her mop and bucket with all the dignity she could muster, or she could take this bundle of misery, a crumpled newborn.

Did she have a choice? *What's new?* she thought bitterly. *When there's a mess, hand it to Sunny.*

She set the cleaning aids aside and took the bundle. As if on cue, it—she—started wailing again.

'I'll ring Housekeeping,' Max snapped. 'Stop her crying.'

Stop her crying. Right. In what universe did this man live? A universe where babies had off switches?

But as he stalked to the phone she relented and peered into the pram.

There was a bag tucked in the side. She investigated with hope.

A folder with documents. A tin of formula. A couple of bottles. Two diapers.

Okay, this baby's mother wasn't completely heartless. Or...she was pretty heartless, but Sunny had coped with worse.

She sighed and headed for the penthouse's kitchenette.

She'd seen Max make himself a hot drink a few minutes ago. Blessedly, he'd overfilled the kettle, so she had boiled water. She balanced baby in one hand, scoop and bottle in the other, made it up, then ran cold water in the sink to immerse the base of the bottle to cool it.

The wailing continued but she could hear Max in the background on the phone. 'What do you mean, no one? I want a babysitter. Now. Find someone. An outside agency. I don't care. Just do it.'

A babysitter at ten o'clock, the night before Christmas Eve? Christmas was on a Sunday this year, which meant today was Friday. The whole world—except the likes of hotel cleaners—would have started Christmas holidays today. Celebrations would be almost universal and every babysitting service would be stretched to the limit.

Good luck, she thought drily, but then she looked down into the baby's face. Phoebe was tiny, her face creased in distress, her rosebud mouth working frantically. How long since she'd been fed?

This little one's mother had handed her over without a backward glance. This man didn't want her.

There were echoes of Sunny's background all over the place here, and she didn't like it one bit.

She needed to leave.

She could feel sogginess under her hand. And the baby… smelled?

'Get someone up here. Get me the manager.' Max was barking into the phone, but she tuned it out. How long since this little one had been changed?

A tentative examination made her shudder. *Ugh*. She gave up on the thought of a simple change and headed for the bathroom. She stripped off all the baby's clothes, then used the washbasin to clean her. The wailing was starting to sound exhausted, but the baby had enough strength to flail her legs in objection to the warm water.

But Sunny was an old hand. Washing was brisk and efficient. She had a replacement nappy but no change of clothes. No matter—she was warmed and dry. Sunny wrapped her expertly in one of the hotel's fluffy towels, carried her back to the living room, checked the bottle, settled down on the settee—had she ever sat on anything so luxurious in her life?—and popped one teat into one desperate mouth.

Then finally the world settled. The silence was almost overwhelming.

Even Sunny was tempted to smile.

Such little things. A clean bottom. A feed. *Deal with the basics and worry about tomorrow tomorrow.* That had been Sunny's mantra all her life and it served her still.

But now she had time to think.

Next on her list was getting out of here.

She glanced across at Max, still barking orders into the phone. He looked like a man at the peak of his powers, a business magnate accustomed to ordering minions at will. He was trying to summon minions now.

But there weren't many Australian minions who'd drop everything at this hour to be at his beck and call.

It's not my problem, she told herself and turned her attention back to the bundle in her arms.

She was a real newborn. A week old at most, Sunny thought, suddenly remembering Tom. Sunny had been nine years old when Tom was born. She remembered weeks where she couldn't go to school, where she'd struggled with a colicky newborn, where she'd felt more trapped than she ever wanted to feel again.

But she wasn't trapped now. This little one had a family and that family wasn't her. What was she—half-sister to the man on the phone? She even looked like him, Sunny thought. Same dark hair. Same skin tone—she looked as if she'd spent some of her time in utero under a sun lamp.

Did she have the same nose? It was difficult to say, she decided. It was a cute nose.

She was a cute baby. Wrapped in her white towel, she looked very new, and totally defenceless. She was still sucking her bottle but desperation had faded and tiredness was starting to take over. Sunny could feel the little body relax, drifting towards sleep.

Great. She could pop her back into the pram and leave.

'She's going to sleep?'

The deep voice, the hand on her shoulder made her start with shock. She hadn't heard him leave the desk and walk over to her.

He was standing behind her, staring down at the baby.

'She was well overdue for a feed,' she managed. Why had he put his hand on her shoulder? To hold her down? To keep her here?

Or maybe he simply wanted contact, reassurance that he wasn't alone.

He was alone, she thought. She was leaving.

'Can I ask you to keep quiet about what's happened?' he asked.

'Sorry?' Her mind had been heading in all sorts of directions, one of them being the way she was reacting to this man's touch. How inappropriate was that? Somehow she managed to focus.

'I work on the staff here,' she managed. 'I signed a confidentiality agreement.'

'And you'll keep it? The media will pay for a story like this. If they make you an offer... I'll meet it.'

'I said I signed a confidentiality agreement,' she retorted, flushing. 'You think I'd break it for money?'

'I have no idea what you'd do.' He lifted a corner of the towel so he could see her name, embroidered discreetly under the hotel logo on her uniform. 'Sunny Raye. What sort of name is that?'

'Mine.' She was starting to feel a bit glowery.

'I'm sorry. I didn't mean to be personal.'

'That's good. There's no need to be personal. I'm a cleaner and I need to go back to work.'

The bottle was finished and laid aside. Phoebe's eyes were closed. Her tiny rosebud mouth was still making involuntary twitches, as if the bottle was still there.

She was beautiful, Sunny thought, but then she'd always been a sucker for a baby. A sucker for being needed?

Of course. Wasn't that the story of her whole life?

'I'll pop her back in the pram,' she suggested. She wanted to rise but the hand was still on her shoulder. The grip tightened.

Uh-oh. It *was* pressure.

'You can't leave.'

Watch me, she thought. And then she thought of the discreet little disc attached at her waist, like an extra button on her uniform. A security disc.

Even at exclusive hotels—and this was surely the most exclusive in Sydney—incidents happened. Guests drank too much. They were away from home. The normal rules often didn't seem to apply.

Female staff were taught how to back away fast from situations, but as a last resort there was the disc. Three pushes and she'd have security guards here in moments.

Protecting her from this man?

He wasn't harassing her for himself, though. He needed her for his baby.

Right, and she had chocolate cherry liqueurs to find and sleep to have and gifts to wrap before she returned here for her Christmas Eve shift tomorrow. *Harden up, girl*, she told herself. *Even use the security disc if you must. You're a cleaner. This is not your business.*

She rose, despite the pressure of his hand. He released her—with real reluctance, it seemed—and stood back.

'She's fed and changed, sir,' she told him, facing him head-on. 'I'll pop her back into the pram if you like, but I need to go. Though…' A sudden pang of conscience made her add, 'I'll clean the bathroom before I go.'

'You just cleaned the bathroom.'

'Yes, sir,' she said woodenly and he frowned and opened the bathroom door. And recoiled.

'My giddy aunt…'

'Yes, sir,' she said primly. She used his distraction to slip her sleeping bundle back in the pram. The pram was a mess too, filled with forms, baby clutter, a stupid elephant mobile strung across the top. But this wasn't her concern either. She pulled out the loose stuff and laid it on the floor. Already his swish suite was starting to look as if a bomb had hit it, but this guy should have a few hours' peace to sort things out. 'Would you like me to clean?' she asked primly.

'Of course.'

'There will be a charge,' she said. 'The stain on the tiles was our responsibility, but extra cleaning for normal hotel use incurs an out-of-hours service fee.'

'You're charging me for cleaning?' He sounded incredulous.

'I'm sorry, sir.' She glanced at her watch. She'd been here for almost an hour and it'd go on the hotel's time sheets. If she wanted to be paid for overtime, she had to report it. And he had to pay.

'That's unreasonable.'

She was overtired. She was at the end of a stupidly long shift. She'd had enough.

'Unreasonable for me to be paid for scrubbing? Really?' So much for being a shadow. She let her glower have full sway. 'I know, I'm just a money-hungry grub.' Grub was the truth. She felt filthy. 'But your decision shouldn't be my business. I've done what I was sent to do, and more. Ring Housekeeping if you want the bathroom cleaned, and discuss charges with them. My shift is finished.' And she took a deep breath and strode to the door, prepared to depart with as much dignity as she could muster.

She swung the door open, and Brent was there.

Brent. Assistant hotel manager. Guy on the way up. Obviously here to appease.

He looked at her and grub didn't begin to describe the look he gave her. Okay, she was filthy. She'd been down on her knees scrubbing. She'd just tended one distressed baby. The wet splotches on her uniform—*you try bathing a baby in a bathroom sink*—could have been anything. Maybe they were 'anything'. Maybe she smelled as well. Who knew? Who cared? She was over this.

'What seems to be the problem, Miss Raye?' Brent said, silky-smooth, and she thought, *I am in so much trouble*. Cleaning staff should never, ever be noticed, much less by the assistant manager of the entire hotel.

'Sir, I was sent up to clean a stain in Mr Grayland's bathroom.' She hauled back on her temper, doing her best to make herself sound subservient. Yes, she'd let her anger hold sway for a moment but she needed this job. She needed to retreat fast. 'I've done my best with the tiles but the stain needs Maintenance. I was about to report it, but before I could leave Mr Grayland requested urgent assistance with his baby.'

'It's not my baby!'

She ignored the savage growl from behind. She was too busy salvaging her career to care.

'I'll talk to you later,' Brent told her, in the tone used the world over to convey menace to underlings when on the surface all had to be rosy. 'Wait for me before you leave.' And he turned to Max and put on his full managerial, ingratiating smile. 'Now, sir…'

She was free. She'd have to wait in the change room for Brent to tell her what he thought of her but at least she was out of here. She grabbed her trusty mop and bucket and headed for the fire stairs. No elevator was going to be fast enough.

'Stop her.'

'Sir?' Brent sounded confused. Sunny had almost reached the stairs. Almost gone...

'If you're here to tell me there's no babysitting service available, I want this woman to stay,' Max snapped. 'And I'm prepared to pay whatever it takes to keep her.'

Brent hadn't got where he was by being thick. Or slow. He'd got it in one. Her desperation to leave. Max's desperation to have her stay. Without seeming to move, Brent was suddenly, seamlessly between Sunny and her precious stairwell.

Yikes.

'Put your equipment down,' he told her and once again she got that look of disdain. Brent was immaculate, smoothly urbane, doing what the guest needed. That he had to put himself so close to an actual cleaner was obviously distasteful in the extreme—that he had to talk to her was worse.

But he was blocking her path and he was making it clear she had no option. She put her mop and bucket down again but she wasn't buying into whatever was happening. She put her hands behind her back, looked at the floor and waited. A good little cleaning lady...

'Sir...' With Sunny trapped, Brent turned back to Max. 'We apologise but there is no babysitting service available. If you'd booked your baby in earlier...'

'I didn't have a baby earlier,' Max snapped. 'And I told you before—she's not my baby.'

'She's his sister,' Sunny muttered because she'd just spent twenty minutes cleaning and feeding a little girl and it suddenly seemed important—no, imperative—that someone laid claim to her. But as she said it, memories surfaced.

A social worker, taking Chloe from her arms. '*You can't take care of her, sweetheart.*'

And Sunny yelling back with all the might of her small self. '*But she's my sister!*'

Those memories weren't appropriate now, but they were strong enough to make her lift her gaze to Max and look defiant. But his anger blazed back at her.

'I asked you to keep quiet about what's just happened,' he snapped.

Right. She went back to staring at the floor, but not before she'd seen the stab of shock as she'd said the word *sister*. Not before she'd seen him glance back at the pram with a look that was suddenly uncertain.

Up until now his reaction had been one of shock and anger. Something had messed with his world and he needed to put it right. But now…his face suddenly showed a new emotion.

Sister…

What sort of family did this man have? Obviously there'd been friction between father and son. Where was the rest of his family?

Why did the word *sister* register with such shock?

But Brent was forging on, trying to make sense of what was happening. Focusing on the near target.

'Mr Grayland had to ask you to be quiet?' he demanded.

'He's talking of my confidentiality agreement,' she told him, still staring at the floor. 'He doesn't wish me to talk of what's happened outside this room.'

'Or inside either,' Max snapped and amazingly Brent came to her defence.

'Miss Raye is required to report anything that happens in this hotel to me. But of course the confidentiality agreement extends to me as well. I'd like Miss Raye to leave. She has work to be getting on with, and as a cleaner she can hardly be of any use to you.'

'But you don't have a babysitter for me.'

'No, sir.'

'And Miss Raye knows how to care for babies.'

Brent sent her an uncertain glance. He wasn't sure where to go with this. 'Is this true, Miss Raye?'

'Please…' She needed to get out of here. She spoke directly to her boss. 'I'm at the end of a double shift. If you'll excuse me…'

'But you do know about babies?'

Did she know about babies? It was practically the only thing she did know. But now wasn't the time for hollow laughter. *Be invisible. Disappear.*

'She does,' Max said, suddenly softening. 'She washed her and fed her.'

'Miss Raye?' Brent reacted with shock. 'That's not in your list of duties. Our insurance doesn't cover…'

'Damn your insurance.' Max's anger flared again, but once again he turned to Sunny. Who was still desperately looking at the floor. 'Miss Raye, you obviously know how to care for a baby. She's sleeping now. You're at the end of a double shift? You must be tired.' He gazed around the suite and she could almost see cogs whirring. 'This living room has a massive settee. Your manager… Mr…' He looked in query at Brent.

'Cottee,' Brent told him smoothly. 'Brent Cottee.'

'Thank you. Mr Cottee can no doubt send up nightwear, toothbrush, anything you need to stay the night. My bedroom has an en suite bathroom so you can be separate. Mr Cottee, I'm prepared to pay full babysitting services for the night, doubled, plus the same amount to Miss Raye personally.' He looked uncertainly back at the pram but forged on, plan in place. 'This could suit.'

'Suit who?' Sunny muttered.

'Suit me,' Max said smoothly. This obviously wasn't a

man who let objections trouble his path. 'I can't believe money wouldn't be useful at this time of the year.'

Was he kidding? Of course it would. It'd be glorious.

And the alternative? By the time she got home it'd be midnight and she was due to start work again at eight. Gran and Pa wouldn't even realise she hadn't come home.

'The insurance...' Brent bleated but it was a weak bleat. He looked almost hopeful.

'I'll sign a waiver,' Max told him. 'Miss Raye might not have childcare credentials but I've seen enough to know I want her.'

'You're on duty again tomorrow?' Brent demanded.

'Yes, sir, at eight.'

He nodded. 'Then it seems satisfactory.' The fact that she'd just done a double shift, that she could well be up all night with a newborn and she had to work tomorrow seemed to worry neither of them. But then she thought... double money. A double shift today, payment for a double shift tonight and then tomorrow's shift... She could almost pay for Tom's tooth to be capped with that. Tom was working all summer to pay his uni fees but the money wouldn't stretch to dentistry.

And baby Phoebe was asleep. With luck, it'd be just a couple of quick feeds during the night.

So... She had her back to the wall but she also had Max Grayland at her mercy.

She could try.

So she tilted her chin and met his gaze square-on.

'I agree,' she told him. 'On one more condition.'

'Which is?'

'I need the biggest, fanciest box of cherry liqueur chocolates that money can buy, gift-wrapped and delivered here before I leave work tomorrow. If you can find me those, we have a deal.'

'You're kidding,' Max said, astounded.

'Miss Raye...' A hissed warning from Brent.

But she ignored him. Tomorrow night would be crazy. Christmas Eve would be in full swing before she got home. She'd have cooking, gift-wrapping, hugging, greeting, chaos... And Gran was expecting her chocolates.

'That or nothing,' she told him and Max met her look. A muscle twitched at the side of his mouth. For a moment she even saw a twinkle. Laughter?

'They're that important?'

'That or nothing,' she repeated and the twitch turned into a smile.

It transformed his face. She'd thought he seemed harsh, autocratic, bleak, but suddenly he was laughing at her... no, with her, she thought, because his smile seemed almost kind. His gaze was still on hers, holding her, blocking out the rest of the world.

Oh, my... It was enough to take a girl's breath away.

Actually, it had taken her breath away. She needed to find herself a nice, quiet place and remember how to get it back.

But Max had moved on. He turned to Brent. 'Mr Cottee? Cherry liqueur chocolates?'

'I'm sure Miss Raye doesn't mean it,' Brent said.

Sunny opened her mouth to retort but she didn't need to. Max got in before her.

'Miss Raye doesn't have to explain,' Max said smoothly. 'It's me who requires it. The biggest, fanciest box of cherry liqueur chocolates money can buy, delivered to this suite before Miss Raye finishes work tomorrow.'

At least this was easy. This hotel seemingly had links to every service industry in town. The cost would be high but Brent knew enough not to quibble. 'Yes, sir. We can do that.'

'And a qualified child carer to take over from Miss Raye in the morning.'

'Yes, sir,' Brent said and maybe Max heard the uncertainty in Brent's voice or maybe he didn't. Sunny did, but she wasn't saying anything. Tomorrow's worries were for Max, not for her.

'Then that's settled,' Max said smoothly. He glanced at his watch. 'I have a conference call coming in from New York in five minutes. I'll work from my bedroom. Miss Raye, you can use the separate bathroom out here, the kitchenette and anything you need from room service. Mr Cottee will no doubt organise it. I'll see you in the morning.'

So that was it. A child, dumped…

No.

'Say goodnight to her,' she managed.

'What?'

'You heard. Say goodnight to your sister.'

'She's asleep.'

'Yes, and you're family. Who knows what she can hear or not hear, but it seems to me you're all the family she's got. Say goodnight to her.'

'Miss Raye…' Brent sounded outraged but she was past caring. Once again she met Max's gaze full-on, defiant, and memories were all around.

Her childish voice from the past. *'She's your baby. You should feed her…'* And her mother slapping her hard and slamming the door as she left.

This man wasn't in a position to slap her. She could still walk away. This was her only chance—maybe baby Phoebe's only chance—to find herself someone who cared.

And once again something twisted on Max Grayland's face. He gave her a look she didn't understand, then wheeled and walked back to the pram.

'Goodnight,' he muttered.

'Properly,' she hissed. 'Touch her. Say it properly.'

'Miss Raye!' Brent was practically exploding but she wasn't backing down.

'Do it.'

And Max sent her a look that was almost afraid. There

was a long silence. He knew what she was demanding, she thought, and he was afraid of it.

But finally he turned back to the pram. He gazed down for a long moment at the sleeping baby—a newborn, who was his half-sister.

And his expression changed yet again. He put a finger down and stroked the tiny face, a feather touch, a blessing.

'Goodnight,' he said again and then looked back at Sunny. 'Satisfied?'

'That'll do for now,' she said smugly and smiled.

The look he sent her was pure bafflement. But then his phone rang. He snagged it from his pocket, glanced at the screen and swore. 'My conference call…'

'We'll take care of everything, sir,' Brent said smoothly. 'Take your call. Goodnight.'

'Thank you,' he said formally and, with a last uncertain glance at Sunny, he turned, walked into his grand bedroom and closed the door behind him.

CHAPTER THREE

WHAT HAD WOKEN HIM? Probably nothing, he conceded. His body was still on New York time, even if in reality his body was lying in a king-sized bed in a suite overlooking Sydney Harbour.

Four a.m.

Today was the day he'd bury his father.

Nothing less important than this would have dragged him half a world from New York for Christmas. His usual method of coping with the festive season was to have his housekeeper fill his apartment with food, set himself up with the company's financial statements and use the break to conduct an overall assessment. It was a satisfying process, even if it meant a nasty shock for the occasional employee returning to work in the New Year.

But now... His mobile laptop didn't allow him to access the innermost secrets of the Grayland Corporation. Too risky. He'd brought some work but it wouldn't take all his concentration—and he needed his concentration to be taken.

His father's funeral...

And a baby sister?

What had the old man been thinking?

He knew his father's illness had made him confused over the last year. There'd never been any love lost between them at the best of times, but Colin Grayland had been proud of his company and fiercely patriarchal. There'd never been any hint that he'd disinherit Max, but that had been mainly through lack of choice, and for the last twelve months the old man had been obsessively secretive.

Max had learned of Isabelle's existence two days ago. As

sole heir, the lawyers had transferred his father's personal banking details to him before he'd left New York. A quick perusal had shown a massive payment to Isabelle almost a year ago. Then another seven months back—was that when Isabelle had her pregnancy confirmed?—and then regular deposits until the last few days of the old man's life.

He'd assumed Isabelle had been his father's mistress but the amounts had been staggering, and now he knew why.

Colin Grayland had paid for a baby. A son, if Isabelle was to be believed, though he must have been too confused to think of the ramifications, or the possibility, of a daughter.

And now he was landed with a baby. His sister?

The thought was doing his head in. He had no idea how to face it.

Lawyers? Surely it was illegal to dump a baby. Isabelle would have to take the baby back.

But she didn't want her.

So adoption? For a baby who was…his sister?

He couldn't think straight. He needed a drink, badly.

Was he kidding? It was four in the morning.

Yeah, but it was midday in New York. He travelled often and his rule for coping with jet lag was not to convert to local time unless he was staying for more than a few days. So his body was telling him he'd stayed up late and now he'd overslept. It was thus time for lunch and a man could have a whisky with lunch.

He wouldn't mind a sandwich either. Room service was his go-to option in such circumstances but he couldn't wake the pair in the next room.

He didn't want to think about the pair in the next room.

But the next room also held the minibar. A packet of crisps and a whisky would set him up to sit and write the final version of what he had to say at his father's funeral.

He definitely needed a whisky to write what had to be said.

If you can't say anything nice, don't say anything at all.

That had been a mantra drummed into him by some long ago nanny, and it normally held true, but a huge section of Australia's business community would turn out. They'd be expecting praise for a man who'd made his money sucking the resources of a country dry.

He did need a whisky, but that'd involved the minibar. Which involved walking into the next room.

They were in the next room. Sleeping.

Or…had something woken him? Maybe they were awake and he was wasting time, hanging out for a snack. Besides, he was paying her.

Do it.

The minibar was by the door through to the elevators. Moonlight from the open drapes showed the way.

He moved soundlessly across the room.

And stopped.

A sliver of moonlight was casting a beam of light across the settee.

The woman—Sunny Raye, her name tag had said—was sleeping. The settee had been made up as a bed, loaded with the hotel's luxury sheets and duvet and pillows.

They weren't being appreciated.

The pillows were on the floor. The duvet had been discarded as well, so her bedding consisted of an under-sheet and an open weave cotton blanket pulled to her waist.

Having discarded the pillows, she was using her arm to support her head. That'd give her a crick neck or a stiff shoulder in the morning, he thought, but he was distracted.

She was wearing an oversized golfing T-shirt with the hotel's logo emblazoned on the chest. Her curls, caught up in a knot when he'd last seen her, were now splayed over the white sheet. Brown with a hint of copper. Shoulder-length. Tangled.

Nice.

Earlier he'd thought she was in her thirties. Her face had

worn the look he often saw on hotel staff at the lower end of the pay scale—pale from not enough sunlight, weary, worn from hard physical work.

Now, though, he revised his age guess downward. She looked younger, peaceful in sleep, even vulnerable?

And then a faint stir in the crook of her arm had him focusing to her far side.

The baby was asleep beside her.

In what universe…? Even he knew this!

'What do you think you're doing?' The exclamation was out before he could stop himself. She jerked awake, staring up, as if unsure where she was, what she was doing, what he was.

She looked terrified.

He took a couple of fast steps back to give her space. He didn't apologise, though. He might have scared her but he was paying for childcare. He wanted childcare—not a baby suffocated in sleep.

'She shouldn't be sleeping with you,' he said, louder than he should because there were suddenly emotions everywhere. He shouldn't care. Or should he care? Of course he should because this baby was his sister, but that was something he didn't have head space to think about. The idea, though, made him angrier. 'I know little about babies but even I know it's dangerous to sleep in the same bed,' he snapped. 'Surely you know it too.'

He saw the confusion of sleep disappear, incredulity take its place. She pushed herself up on her elbow, making a futile effort to push her tumbling curls from her eyes. The baby slept on beside her, neatly swaddled, lying on her back, eyes blissfully closed.

'You want an apology?' she demanded and an anger that matched his was in her voice. 'It's not going to happen. I'm a cleaner, not a nanny.'

'I'm paying you to care for her.'

'Which I'm doing to the best of my ability. Sack me if you don't like it. Look after your baby yourself.'

'I might have to if you won't.'

And the anger in her face turned to full scale fury. All traces of sleep were gone. 'Might?' she demanded. '*Might?* How much danger would she have to be in before you showed you care enough to do that?' She rose to face him. She was wearing T-shirt and knickers but nothing else. Her legs were long and thin and her bare feet on the plush carpet made her seem strangely vulnerable. His impression of her age did another descent. 'You want me to leave?'

'I want you to do what you're being paid for.'

'Believe it or not, I am.' She glared her fury. 'Your sister's sleeping on a firm settee that has no cracks in the cushioning and a sloping back that's too firm to smother her. See the lovely soft settee cushions? They're over there. See my pillows and my nice fluffy duvet? They're over there too. So I'm sleeping on a rock-hard settee with no cushions and no duvet.'

'Because...'

'Because the moron who set up Phoebe's pram filled it with a feather mattress, which is far more dangerous to a newborn than how I've arranged things. The mattress is stuck in the pram. Did you notice? Of course not. But I did when I checked her before I went to sleep. Some idiot's screwed in an elephant mobile—for a newborn!—and they've caught the fabric of the mattress. I'd need to rip the mattress to get it out and feathers would go everywhere and you'd probably make me pay for it. Housekeeping's up to their ears in work and it would've taken them an hour to get me a cot, even if there was one available, which I doubt. I didn't fancy putting her to sleep on the floor and by the time I'd figured all that out I was tired and over it so she slept with me. She's been as safe as I could make her. But take over, by all means. I've a crick in my arm like you wouldn't believe. It's been over four hours since she fed so she's likely to wake up any minute but she has formula and the instructions are on the tin. Forget the money. I couldn't give a toss. I'm leaving.'

There was a stunned silence. He stared at the settee, bereft of anything soft. He looked at the still miraculously sleeping Phoebe.

He looked at the furious, tired, overworked woman in front of him and he felt a sweep of shame.

He was way out of his comfort zone and he knew enough to realise he had to back off.

'I apologise.'

'Of course you do. You've given me a lecture. Now you're expecting to go back to your nice comfy bed and leave me holding the baby. I don't think so.' She was a ball of fury, standing in her bare feet in the near-dark, venting her fury. Righteous fury.

'I could double the chocolates,' he said, feeling helpless.

'You think you can buy me with chocolates?'

'I thought I already had.'

'Get stuffed,' she told him and flicked on the table lamp and started searching among the discarded bedding for her uniform.

And, as if on cue, the baby woke.

Phoebe. His sister.

She didn't cry but he was attuned to her, and the moment her eyes flickered open he noticed.

She was so tiny. So fragile. She was swaddled in a soft wrap, all white. Her hair was black. Her eyes were dark too.

She looked nothing like Isabelle.

She was all his father.

She was all…him?

Dear heaven…

'The formula's on the sink,' Sunny said, sulkily now, as

if she thought she was misbehaving. 'Make sure the bottle's clean and the water's been boiled.'

'I can't.'

'You don't know what you can do until you have to. Believe me, I know.' She snagged her uniform from the floor and headed for the bathroom. 'She's all yours.'

And, as if the idea terrified her, Phoebe opened her mouth and started to wail.

'Well,' Sunny said, over her shoulder. 'Pick her up.'

'I can't.'

'Don't be ridiculous.' She reached the bathroom and closed the door firmly behind her.

Help...

The baby's wails escalated, from sad bleats to a full-throated roar in seconds. How could such a beautiful, perfect wee thing turn into an angry, red-faced ball of desperation?

Was it the thought of being left with him? He knew nothing of babies. Zip.

This was his sister. Half-sister, he reminded himself, but it didn't help.

The bathroom door was still firmly closed.

Somehow he'd sacked his babysitter for no reason.

How could he have thought she'd been unsafe? Sunny had her as safe as she could make her. She'd checked her before she'd gone to sleep. She'd noticed the too-soft mattress.

He hadn't.

Tentatively he lifted the wailing bundle into his arms. Even the movement seemed to soothe her, and her sobs eased. Did she sense then how close she was to being abandoned?

The bathroom door opened again. Sunny stood there, still rumpled by sleep, but back in her stained uniform, her sensible shoes, her workday gear.

'Where will you go?' he asked, because he couldn't think of anything else to say.

'Home.'

'Where's home?'

'Out west. Because there's no public transport at four a.m. it's an hour's bike ride but that's none of your business. I have no idea why I'm telling you.'

'Stay.'

'In your dreams.'

'Sunny, I'm sorry,' he said and he was. Deeply sorry. He looked at her tilted chin, her weary pride, her humiliation, and he felt a shame so deep it threatened to overwhelm him. That she was tired and overworked he had no doubt. Hotel cleaners were a race apart from the likes of him. They were shadows in the background of his world.

This one was suddenly front and centre.

And then he had a thought. A bad one.

'You know about babies.' The words were suddenly hard to form. 'Are you...? Do you...?'

She got it before he could find the words. 'You mean do I have my own baby strapped to my bike, waiting for me to finish my shift? Or left in a kitchen drawer with a bottle of formula laced with gin?' She gave a snort of mirthless laughter. 'Hardly. But I've raised four, or maybe I should say I've been there for them while they raised themselves. They're grown up now, almost independent, apart from Tom's teeth. But that's my problem and you have your own. Goodnight and good luck.' She headed for the door.

But he was before her, striding forward with a speed born of desperation. Putting his body between her and the door. But her words were still hanging in the air even as he prevented her leaving.

Four? He thought of how old she was, and how young she must have started, and he thought of a world that was as removed from his as another planet.

And she got that too. She gave a sardonic grin. 'Yep, I started mothering when I was five, with four babies by the time I was nine. Life got busy for a while, and I admit I even co-slept. Not just with one baby—sometimes all five of us were in the same bed. But, hey, they're all healthy and your Phoebe's still alive so maybe I'm not such a failure. Now, if you'd let me leave…'

He didn't understand but now wasn't the time to ask questions. 'Please,' he said, doing his best to sound humble. 'Stay.'

'You can cope.'

'I probably can,' he admitted. 'If you refuse then I'll pay for a taxi to take you home and to bring you back tomorrow.' He hesitated. 'But, to be honest, it's Phoebe who needs you. She shouldn't be left with someone so inept.'

She hesitated, obviously torn between sense and pride. It was four in the morning. Even in a taxi it'd take time for her to get home, he thought. She was weary and she had to be back here again in a few hours.

Logic should win, but he could also sense something else, an anger that didn't stem from what had just happened.

He was replaying things she'd said. *'How much danger would she have to be in before you showed you care?'* She thought he didn't care and she was right. He had nothing invested in this baby. Tomorrow he'd see lawyers, come to some arrangement, pay whatever it took to reunite her with her mother.

Except…she looked like him. And this woman was looking at him with judgement.

'I'll do it on one condition,' she said.

'I've already said more chocolates. And I'll double your pay.'

'Gran's got the appetite of a bird. One box is fine, and I'm not taking any more of your money.'

'Then what?'

'I'll stay on condition you change her and feed her now,' she told him. 'I'll watch but you do it.'

'I need to write the eulogy for my father's funeral.' He said it harshly but he couldn't hide the note of panic. 'That's why I'm awake.'

'Oh, that's hard,' she said, her voice softening. 'I'm sorry about your dad.' But then her chin tilted again. 'But your dad's dead and this little one's not, and it seems to me that someone's got to go into bat for her. So you change her and feed her and then you can do what you like. I'll go back to caring. My way. But it's that or nothing, Mr Grayland.'

She met his gaze full-on, anger still brimming. She was flushed, indignant, defiant, and suddenly he thought... *She's beautiful.*

Which was an entirely inappropriate thing to think and, as if she agreed with him, baby Phoebe opened her mouth and wailed again.

'Fine,' he said helplessly. 'Show me how.'

'It'd be my pleasure,' she said and grinned and went to fetch a diaper.

She could have insisted that he take the baby back to his bedroom to feed her, but Max's tension was tangible. She could almost reach out and touch it. According to the media, this man was one of the most powerful businessmen in the world, but right now he was simply a guy who'd been thrust a baby he didn't know what to do with.

And didn't she know what that felt like?

So she helped prepare the bottle, showed him the skin test for heat and agreed there should be some scientific way— there probably was but who had time to search for a thermometer at four in the morning? She watched as he did the diaper change, blessing herself that she'd asked the hotel shop to send up extras. It took him three tries to get it right without messing with the adhesive tapes.

Then she retreated to her settee and gave herself the luxury of leaning on pillows, while Max sat at the desk by the window and fed his little sister.

When she'd fed her last time it had been a desperate feed, a baby over-tired and over-hungry, relieved beyond measure that here was the milk she needed. She'd sucked with desperation.

This time, though, things had settled. Phoebe was warm and dry, and the bottle was being offered almost as soon as she'd let the world know she needed it. She seemed content to suck lazily, gazing upward at the world, at the man who was holding her.

They hadn't turned on the main light. Sunny was watching by moonlight, seeing the tension slowly evaporate as Max realised he was doing things right. As Phoebe realised things were okay in her world.

It wouldn't always be as easy as this, Sunny thought. What did this man have in store for him? Colic? Inexplicable crying jags? Teething? All the complications that went with babies. Would he cope with them?

Of course he wouldn't. The thought was laughable. He'd been so desperate for help that he'd employed her, a cleaner. He'd employ someone more suitable the moment he could.

Still, she had to cut him some slack. He'd come to Australia for his father's funeral. All the world knew that. Colin Grayland had been a colossus of the Australian mining scene. His son had taken over the less controversial part of a financial empire that was generations old. He must have kept his head down, because she knew little about him. He'd been an occasional guest in this hotel. There was always a buzz when he visited, but it was mostly among the female staff because a billionaire who looked so gorgeous...well, why wouldn't there be a buzz? And there was also a buzz because his visits usually coincided with his father storming into the hotel, usually shouting.

Here in Australia, Colin Grayland had seemed to court

controversy. He'd ripped into open cut mining, overriding environmental protections, refusing to restore land after it had been sucked of anything of any value. He had such power, such resources, that even legal channels seemed powerless to stop him.

His son, however, seemed to disagree with much of what the old man had done. The media gossip of clashes between the two was legion.

'So what will you say about your father tomorrow?' she asked into the silence and thought, *Whoa, did I just ask that?* Cleaner asking tycoon what his eulogy would be? But the man had said he'd woken to write the eulogy. Maybe she could be helpful.

She tucked her arms around her knees, looked interested and prepared to be helpful.

'I don't know,' Max said shortly.

'You don't know.' Phoebe was steadily sucking. The near dark lent a weird kind of intimacy to the setting. It was like a pyjama party, Sunny thought. But different. She watched him for a while, his big hands cradling his little sister, the bottle being slowly but steadily sucked. Okay, not a pyjama party, she conceded. Like...like...

Like two parents. Like the dad taking his share.

What did she know of either? Pyjama parties? Not in her world. And parents sharing?

Ha.

But now wasn't the time for going there; indeed she hardly ever did. Now was the time to focus on the man before her and his immediate problems.

Actually, his immediate problem was sorted for now. But his dad... She'd read the newspapers. The funeral would be huge. Every cashed-up developer, every politician on the make, even the Honourables would be there, because even with the old man gone the Grayland influence was huge.

And this man was doing the eulogy. In less than seven hours.

'I'd be so scared I'd be running a mile,' she told him. 'But then public speaking's not my thing. Are you thinking you'll wing it?'

'What, decide what I'll say in front of the microphone?'

'The way you're going, you'll need to.'

'Says the woman who won't give me time to think, who won't feed my baby.'

My baby. They were loaded words. She saw his shock when he realised he'd said them. She saw his horror.

'Hey, I'm happy to help with the speech,' she told him hurriedly. 'How hard can it be?'

And she watched his face and saw…what? A determination to steer the conversation away from the baby he was holding? Because he couldn't face what he was feeling? 'To say my father and I didn't get on is an understatement,' he told her. 'Look how little I knew of his personal life.'

'Because?' She said it tentatively. She had no right to ask, and no need, but he didn't have to answer if he didn't want to, and something told her that he wanted to talk. About anything but the baby.

'My parents were pretty much absent all my life,' he told her. 'I was an only child, with nannies from the start. My parents divorced when I was two and went their separate ways. I lived with whoever's current partner didn't mind a kid and a nanny tagging along, or the nanny and I had separate quarters if it didn't suit. But I was raised to take over the financial empire. It was only when I developed a mind of my own—and a social conscience—that I saw my father often. Our meetings have never been pretty. Maybe I should have walked away but I've been given enough autonomy to realise I can eventually make a difference. As he's grown older and more frail I've been able to stop the worst of his excesses. But now…to give a eulogy…'

She heard his bleakness and something inside her twisted. She thought of her own childhood, itself bleak. But she'd always had her siblings. She'd always felt part of a family.

But this was a man in charge of his destiny, as well as the destiny of the thousands of people he employed. She refused to feel sorry for him.

'Hey, reality doesn't matter at funerals,' she told him. 'No one's there for a bare-all exposé. You want my advice? Tell them a funny story to start with, a personal touch, like how he wouldn't buy you an ice cream when you were six because you hadn't saved up for it. There must have been something you can think of, something like that'll make them all laugh and put them onside with you. Then give his achievement spiel. Look him up on Mr Google. That'll list all his glories. Finally, choke up a little, say he'll be sadly missed and walk off. Job done.'

He sent her a curious look. 'You want to do it for me?'

'I would,' she told him agreeably. 'But I'm working tomorrow. Eleven o'clock will see you at the lectern, and I'll be scrubbing bathrooms.'

'You can't take the day off?'

'To give your father's eulogy? I don't think so.'

He smiled. She sensed it rather than saw it. Nice, she thought, and hugged her knees a bit more.

It really was weirdly intimate, sitting in the moonlight in her almost-PJs, talking to this…stranger.

'I'm guessing here,' he ventured, sounding cautious. 'But am I hearing the voice of experience? You've worked out a eulogy for someone you didn't like?'

That was enough to destroy any hint of intimacy. She hugged her knees a bit tighter, needing the comfort.

'I might have.'

'These kids you looked after…were they your brothers and sisters?'

'It's none of your business.'

'It's not,' he agreed. 'But you know a lot about me now. It's dark, we're both tired and this is a weird space. I wouldn't mind pretending I'm not alone in it.'

And she got it.

He was sitting in an impersonal hotel half a world away from where he lived. He was holding a baby he hadn't known existed and later that morning he'd have to stand in a vast cathedral and speak about a father it sounded as if he'd loathed.

He felt alone? He felt as if he needed some sort of reassurance that he wasn't the only one who'd ended up in a mess up to their neck?

After tomorrow she'd never see this man again. Why not give it to him?

'I gave my mother's eulogy when I was fourteen,' she said and she felt rather than saw the shock her words caused.

'At fourteen...'

'There was no one else. Mum died of an overdose after she'd alienated everyone. I never knew my father. She had me a couple of years after she'd run away from home, and then there was a gap. Who knows why? Maybe she was responsible enough to use birth control for a while, but it didn't last. The next four babies came in quick succession and for some reason she kept us. But *kept* is a loose description. We were raised...well, we weren't raised. We lurched from one crisis to the next. Finally she died. The social worker said we didn't need to go to the funeral, but they hadn't found Gran and Pa then, so there was only us. And they'd already split us up. Daisy and Sam had gone to one set of foster parents, Chloe and Tom to another. It's hard to find foster parents for a fourteen-year-old, so I was placed in a home for...troubled adolescents and I was going nuts, wanting to see them. So when the coroner released the body for burial I made a king-sized fuss and said we all had to be at the funeral. Our case worker said she had reservations but she arranged it anyway. Then I figured I had to say something the kids could remember.'

'You did?' he demanded, sounding awed.

'I did,' she said proudly. 'I made them laugh by telling them about Mum's awful cooking. I reminded them of the way she could never get her toenails perfect and the way she had funny names for all of us, even if sometimes she couldn't quite remember which one of us she was talking to. They were sort of sad stories but I made them smile. Then, when we came out, the social worker had organised morning tea. I still remember the sausage rolls! And then she sat us down, very serious, and told us they'd found Gran and Pa. Apparently, they hadn't even known we existed! Mum had robbed them blind when she was young and then, when she knew they had no more money, she cut off all contact. But they're just…wonderful. I can't tell you how wonderful. They had somewhere we could live and they loved us straight away. So then we all lived happily ever after. Isn't that nice? So it's worth thinking of something good, even if it kills you to say it.'

There was an appalled silence. It stretched on and on and she thought *uh-oh,* she shouldn't have said. Kid of a drug addict? It was a wonder he even let her near his baby.

But it seemed he wasn't thinking that. 'You make me feel ashamed,' he said at last.

'There's no need to feel ashamed,' she said with asperity. 'Unless you intend to let a fourteen-year-old girl beat you at the eulogy stakes. Let me have Phoebe. You can write your eulogy in peace.' She unhugged her knees and headed over to take the baby from him.

But he held on, just for a moment.

'Thank you,' he said simply.

'You're paying me.'

'Not enough for what you're doing tonight.'

'I don't think you realise how big a deal Gran's chocolates are,' she told him. 'For those alone I'd have written your eulogy for you. Now, off you go and write. The intro's easy. Lords, Ladies, distinguished guests, ladies and gentlemen…there's the thing half done.' And she scooped the now sleeping baby into her arms and backed away.

She needed to back away, she thought. The look on this man's face…

This was a night out of frame. The intimacy between them was something that couldn't be replicated and could never exist in the light of day.

She needed to back off fast, and she did. And he let her.

'I'll write in the bedroom,' he managed and she nodded. 'You came out for something? Or to check on me.'

'I came out for a whisky.'

'It won't help the jet lag. Or the eulogy.'

'I know that,' he told her. 'And I don't need it any more. You've given me all I need.'

'Really?'

'Really.'

She grinned. 'Hooray. Advice by Auntie Sunny. Off you go then like a good boy and get it done.'

'Yes, ma'am,' he said and cast her a look she didn't understand. A look full of questions she couldn't hope to answer.

He rose and left.

She settled Phoebe again with care, and told herself to sleep.

Sleep didn't come. For some reason the memory of that appalling time, her mother's dreadful funeral, was suddenly all around her.

She was thinking too of the grand funeral waiting for Max tomorrow, and she was thinking there were similarities.

She hugged Phoebe because she suddenly needed the comfort and she thought again of the man through the bedroom door. Who did he hug?

It wasn't any of her business, but the question stayed with her until finally sleep overcame her.

Who did Max Grayland hug?

And the answer came with certainty. It was an answer written in the harshness of his voice, in the strain in his eyes, in the way he held himself.

The answer was no one.

CHAPTER FOUR

AT SEVEN THE next morning a brisk knock signalled the arrival of a hotel maid bearing a pristine uniform for Sunny. Behind her was a dour woman in her fifties. 'I'm from the hotel's childcare,' she announced.

'Excellent.' Sunny had answered the door still in her T-shirt and knickers. Yes, there were bathrobes in the suite but they were in the bedroom, where Max was either asleep or still writing his eulogy. She motioned to the sleeping baby. 'She's all yours.'

'She slept on the settee?' the woman demanded, shocked.

'She slept safely.' The low growl behind her made Sunny jump. Max. 'Thanks to Miss Raye. But maybe you can organise a cot.'

'Certainly.' The woman looked at Sunny in incredulity. 'I gather this was an emergency arrangement. Most unsatisfactory. However, you can now return to your duties.'

'Thank you,' Sunny said simply and grabbed her new uniform and headed for the bathroom.

'Miss Raye?' Max said.

'Yes?' She was desperate to disappear. The maid, the babysitter and Max were all looking at her. She was wearing a T-shirt and knickers and nothing else. Her tangled curls were flying every which way. She needed Superman's telephone booth, she thought grimly, one that showered her, cleaned her teeth, fixed her hair into a decent knot and dressed her in an instant. But instead she was forced to turn and face Max—who was wearing one of the gorgeous hotel bathrobes.

She glowered. She couldn't help herself.

'What's wrong?' he asked, looking bemused.

'What do you think is wrong? I need your bathrobe.'

And the toe-rag grinned. Grinned! 'Now? Shall I take it off?'

Oh, for heaven's sake. She could only imagine what he was wearing underneath—or not. 'Don't be ridiculous. If you'll excuse me…'

'Sunny…'

'Yes?'

'Come back before you finish tonight and collect your chocolates.'

'Can you arrange for them to be delivered to the staff quarters?'

'I need to ensure they're satisfactory. So here?'

'Fine,' she said, goaded, desperate to be away.

'And Sunny?'

'Yes?' They were all looking at her. She felt like a bug under a microscope. Helpless.

'Thank you,' he said.

He smiled. Oh, he shouldn't do that. That smile…

'Think nothing of it,' she said, trying not to sound grumpy. And…breathless in the face of that smile.

'And Sunny?'

'Yes.'

'I mean it,' he said, and then, before she knew what he was about, before she could even guess what he intended, he crossed the room, he placed a finger under her chin, he tilted her chin—and he kissed her.

It was a feather kiss. A trace of a kiss. It hit her forehead, not her lips. There was no reason at all for it to take her breath away, for her to stand stock-still as if she'd been seared.

Already he'd stepped back. He put his hands on her arms as if to steady her—why would he think she needed steadying?—and he was back to smiling at her. Quizzically. Almost mockingly.

'Your work was above and beyond the call of duty,' he said, his tone softening. 'Where's the form I need to fill in to give this staff member five stars? Or more.'

'Miss Raye!' It was the babysitter, appalled. 'Get your uniform on. You know the rules about fraternising with the guests. This will be reported...'

'It will be reported,' Max said, his gaze not moving from Sunny's face. 'Like the dispatches from Waterloo. Victory with all honour. Service like no other. Thank you, Sunny.'

'I'll... I'll see you this afternoon,' she managed, clutching her clean uniform as if it were armour. 'I... Will that be all, sir?'

'Thank you, yes.'

Excellent. Or was it? She had no idea.

But her time here was over and she fled.

Give his achievement spiel. Choke up a little, say he'll be sadly missed and walk off. Job done.

He followed Sunny's advice pretty much all the way, though he couldn't quite manage the choking up part.

But he got away with it. The post-funeral luncheon, organised by his father's ex-secretary, was truly sumptuous and as he moved among the assembled dignitaries he received approving nods and handshakes from all sides.

'Well done, boy. We look forward to seeing you move into your father's footsteps. Business as usual, hey?'

In your dreams, he thought, but now wasn't the time to say it. Half these people were about to get a rude shock when their cosy business deals were turned on their heads.

That should be giving him satisfaction. And the death of his father should be making him emotional too. It had, a little, when he'd stood in front of the congregation and thought of the things most men could say of their fathers. That they'd been loved. That they'd be remembered with affection.

It was hard to feel affection for someone he'd known

only through business dealings, who he knew had scorned his ideas—and who'd paid to have someone bear a child to supplant him as heir.

And that was where his attention was as he mingled with the crowd, as he responded as expected, as he murmured pleasantries.

He was thinking of a baby called Phoebe.

And a woman called Sunny?

Why Sunny? Sunny was surely irrelevant, a hotel cleaner hired for the night. From now on he'd have proper, qualified staff.

To look after a child he didn't want?

A child no one wanted?

She was already messing with his plans. He'd intended to be on tonight's plane, back to New York. But walking away from his…walking away was impossible, and there was no way he could get paperwork in place fast enough to take her with him.

Even if he wanted to.

Did he have a choice?

And then he was thinking of Sunny again, of her fierceness, her courage, her care.

Sunny would expect him to care.

'Well done, lad.' It was one of his father's cronies, a financier with a finger seemingly in every crooked pie in the land. He'd had a beer or six and now walked up and clapped Max on the shoulder. It was as much as Max could do not to flinch. 'We'll be seeing you in Australia most of the time now, I imagine. This is where you can make the most money. Your father saw it. Any advice I can give you, feel free to ask. You're staying on for Christmas, I expect?'

And there was only one answer to that. He didn't even know where Isabelle was and he was the executor of his father's estate. One baby was therefore his priority. He was stuck.

He needed help.

Once more he thought of Sunny, in her absurd night-wear, her tangle of curls, with her smudged dark eyes and that glimmer of defiance against the world.

She was a hotel cleaner. She had no qualifications to take care of a baby, even if he wanted her to.

He'd seen the hotel manager this morning and made it clear that not only did he need to extend his booking, he wanted paid professional childcare, possibly until New Year. By which time he'd have it sorted. Surely?

'Yes, sir, I'm staying for Christmas,' he managed and the man clapped his shoulder again and gave him a beery grin.

'Well, Merry Christmas,' he boomed. 'May Santa be good to you.'

Just like he always was, Max thought wryly, and moved on to the next polite inanity.

If she didn't really need the chocolates she wouldn't be here. But they were Gran's treat, treasured from time immemorial. Or from that first Christmas when, as a frightened, defensive fourteen-year-old, Gran and Pa had suddenly appeared, mi-raculously wanting to help. And love. She'd had no money but the guy at the local discount sweets shop had watched her looking at the gaudily wrapped boxes and told her if she was prepared to spend a few hours breaking down cardboard boxes out the back she could have the box of her choice.

Gran had opened them on Christmas morning and cried. 'I would have cried even if they weren't my favourite,' she'd sobbed. 'Oh, Sunny…'

That memory still caused her to blink back tears, and it had her heading up towards the penthouse suite for the last time. She'd ditched her uniform. She was back in her all-weather jeans and T-shirt. Her bike was waiting. Christmas was waiting.

She knocked on the door and hoped this could be fast. It

was after five already. The kids would be arriving at Gran and Pa's before she got there and she had so much to do.

There were voices coming from inside, male voices, raised, polite but urgent.

'I'm sorry, sir, but some things are impossible.'

'You're telling me there's no babysitter in this entire country?'

'There may well be babysitters, but we can't find anyone. The lady who worked for you today has finished her shift and left the hotel. All the agencies are closed. Most have been closed from midday and won't open again until next Tuesday. None of our staff are prepared to take the extra shifts at this short notice, and who can blame them? They all have their Christmases organised.'

'You're saying I'm stuck in a hotel for the next two days with *this*?'

For *this* was screaming her head off again, and the word caught Sunny as nothing else could. There was a part of Sunny that wanted to turn and flee. But...*this*?

She knocked harder and then almost fell inside as the door was wrenched open.

'You,' Max snapped and his tone was close to one of loathing.

Sunny was used to anger in every shape and form. She'd learned the best way to deal with it was to retreat, to make yourself invisible, but if you couldn't do that then stand up to the toe-rag. She'd even kicked one of her mother's boyfriends once. She had a scar under her hairline to prove it but she didn't regret it one bit.

She faced him head-on. *This.* The word was still reverberating.

'I've come for my chocolates,' she said and his anger was put on hold as he realised who it was.

'I'm sorry. Of course.'

And she should butt out—but she couldn't. 'Don't apologise to me,' she snapped. 'Apologise to your sister. Calling her *this*…'

'You heard.'

'I imagine half the hotel heard.'

'Miss Raye!'

Finally she had time to take in the other person in the room. The hotel manager. The head honcho himself. This man had eyes in the back of his head. She was wearing her staff lanyard but even without it he'd have known her name. This man had the reputation of knowing what went on in the hotel before it happened. His voice now held reproof, quiet but chilling. 'What are you doing here?'

'I'm collecting something that's mine,' she muttered. She needed to calm down. She valued this job.

'I have it.' Max snagged a box from the sideboard—and what a box! It was enormous, exquisitely wrapped in gold, with crimson bows that must be worth what she usually paid for the whole box. He handed it over and managed a smile. 'I'm sorry. There was no reason to snap at you. I am indeed grateful.'

'And your sister's not *this*.'

'I beg your pardon.'

'Don't say sorry to me. She's Phoebe. Not *this*.'

'No,' he said, chastised. 'I beg her pardon too.'

'She sounds like she needs a feed.'

'She's just had one. I have no idea what to do.'

'Miss Raye…' It was the manager again, smooth as silk. 'I hear you did an emergency stint as babysitter last night.' His eyes were calmly assessing. She could almost see the cogs turning. How to keep this most valuable client happy? He turned again to Max. 'Sir, Miss Raye doesn't have childcare qualifications but she's cared for your sister already. If you found her satisfactory… Miss Raye, if we offered double pay rates, and Mr Grayland, if it's satisfactory to you… Miss Raye, would you be prepared to stay on over Christmas?'

Oh, for heaven's sake...

She stood, clutching her chocolates, staring at the men before her.

To miss Christmas... Who were they kidding?

'No,' she said blankly. 'My family's waiting.'

'You're not married, Miss Raye.' The manager was stating a fact, not asking a question.

And that took her breath away. How much did the manager know about her? She'd been vetted when she'd taken the job at this prestigious hotel but this was ridiculous.

'I can't see that makes any difference,' she said stiffly. 'I need to go.'

'But Mr Grayland's stranded in an unknown country, staying in a hotel for Christmas with a baby he didn't know existed until yesterday.' The manager's voice was urbane, persuasive, doing what he did best. 'You must see how hard that will be for him.'

'I imagine it will be,' she muttered and clung to her chocolates. And to her Christmas. 'But it's...'

'None of your business,' Max broke in. 'But if there's anything that could persuade you... I'll double what the hotel will pay you. Multiply it by ten if you like.'

Multiply by ten... There were dollar signs in neon flashing in her head. If it wasn't Christmas...

But it was Christmas. Gran and Pa were waiting. She had no choice.

But other factors were starting to niggle now. Behind Max, she could see tiny Phoebe lying in her too-big cot. She'd pushed herself out of her swaddle and was waving her tiny hands in desperation. Her face was red with screaming.

She was so tiny. She needed to be hugged, cradled, told all was right with her world. Despite herself, Sunny's heart twisted.

But to forgo Christmas? *No way.*

'I can't,' she told him, still hugging her chocolates. But

then she met Max's gaze. This man was in charge of his world but he looked…desperate. The pressure in her head was suddenly overwhelming.

And she made a decision. What she was about to say was ridiculous, crazy, but the sight of those tiny waving arms, that red, desperate face was doing something to her she didn't understand and the words were out practically before she knew she'd utter them.

'Here's my only suggestion,' she told them. 'If you really do want my help… My Gran and Pa live in a big old house in the outer suburbs. It's nothing fancy; in fact it's pretty much falling down. They were caretakers for years and the owner left them lifetime occupancy. It might be dilapidated but it's huge. Daisy and Sam don't live there any more; they live with their partners. Tom and Chloe live in university colleges—blessedly they both have scholarships—so they're home over the summer break, but there's still plenty of room. So no, Mr Grayland, I won't spend Christmas here with you, but if you're desperate, if you truly think you can't manage Phoebe alone, then you're welcome to join us until you can make other arrangements. I'll check with Gran and Pa but I'm sure they'll say yes. They've welcomed waifs and strays before and they've never said no. So, Mr Grayland, that's my only offer. You can stay here and take care of Phoebe yourself, you can make other arrangements or you can come home with me. Take it or leave it.'

Max Grayland was a man accustomed to control. Complete control. He'd been that way almost since birth. Absent parents, a succession of nannies, a succession of strange apartments, homes, hotels and then boarding schools, had seen him develop a shell that was pretty near impermeable. He lived a self-contained, independent life where everything was ordered. He had the means, the staff and the will to ensure all stayed that way.

This woman—this cleaning lady—was asking if he'd step into a world he knew nothing of and wished to know less. A dilapidated house somewhere in the suburbs. Her grandparents and whoever and whatever else might be there.

He was being classified as…a waif or stray?

He was in his pristine hotel penthouse. He had room service at his beck and call. He had his bed, his desk, his work.

But he had a baby who was red in the face from screaming. The childminder had finished her shift at four. She'd fed her, put her into her cot and left her asleep. He'd thought he could cope.

Phoebe had been screaming now for an hour. She wouldn't take another bottle. She'd arched back in his arms, seemingly desperate, and he didn't have one clue what to do about it.

He stood staring at the woman in the doorway, with her bland offer of help. It was ridiculous. There had to be other options.

'Could you take Phoebe home with you?' he asked and her eyes widened in incredulity. And anger.

'Are you kidding? What do you know about me?'

'I assume the hotel will vouch for you.'

'I was hired as a cleaner, not a childcare professional. Would you really do that? Hand your baby over to a stranger?'

'I've watched you care for her. You're good.'

'And how do you know I don't come from a house full of drunken louts and rotting garbage?'

'Miss Raye!' The manager sounded appalled, but Sunny wasn't focused on the manager.

'I don't,' Max said stiffly.

'Is that why you won't come yourself? But you'll send your sister?'

'I…okay. Bad idea,' he managed. 'I hadn't thought it through.'

'Obviously. The offer was both of you or nothing. You

seem to be all this little one has, and I'm not interfering in that for the world.'

'What, you're forcing us to bond?'

'I'm not forcing you to do anything. I'm going home.'

And Max Grayland's world suddenly moved to full-blown panic.

She was leaving. The hotel manager would walk out too. He'd be left…not with *this*. With his sister.

You seem to be all this little one has.

Sunny's words resonated in his head. So did the screams behind him. Or were they sobs? Phoebe had been crying for so long she was sounding exhausted. He'd walked the floor with her, tried to feed her again—for heaven's sake, he'd even tried rocking and singing. The next few days stretched ahead, frightening with their lack of help.

What were his options?

Option one: stay here and hope the screams settled, hope he'd be able to feed her, calm her, keep her alive until Tuesday. The prospect had him terrified.

Option two: take her to the nearest hospital. Say her mother had dumped her and he couldn't cope. The authorities would surely step in, hand her to a professional whose job it was to care for abandoned children.

Abandoned.

Sunny was watching him. He could read the condemnation in her eyes. She knew what he was thinking? *What the…?*

So…option three. Throw himself into the unknown. Go with the hotel cleaner to a Christmas with people he'd never met, to an environment he had no idea of. To lose control.

But he was out of control now, and Sunny was watching.

And he thought suddenly of the slivers he knew of this woman's background. Abandonment had been in this girl's past too, he thought. She knew it and somehow he knew she was expecting the same for Phoebe.

So now, seeing the condemnation on her face—or was it resignation?—he had no choice.

'Can you stop her screaming?' he asked. 'For now? While I think?'

She gave him a hard, assessing look and then she sighed. Laying her precious chocolates on the hall table, she walked to the cot, adjusted the swaddle and lifted Phoebe into her arms. Tucking the baby's head under her chin, she cradled her so she was almost moulded against her. Then she rocked, rubbing her back, crooning a faint tune barely audible to the men watching.

The sobs were still there, but Sunny seemed oblivious. She crooned and rubbed and rocked and crooned and rubbed...

And then Phoebe belched. It was a belch to make a grown man proud. It was a belch that stunned both watching men.

The baby's eyes widened as if she'd shocked herself that she could possibly make such a noise.

And then her eyelids drooped, her tiny head curved into Sunny's soft neck—and she was asleep.

'I'm thinking your childminder was in a hurry when she fed her,' Sunny said as the silence stretched on and the two men watched the magic in amazement. 'A too fast bottle, no burping and the crying will have made things worse. She should be right now.'

'Until when?' Max demanded, incredulous at this small display of magic.

'I have no idea,' Sunny said truthfully. 'Shall I put her back in the cot?'

Max Grayland was known throughout the finance world for his intelligence, his instant assessment of risk, his capacity to make fast decisions that almost always turned out right.

He was so far out of his comfort zone that he felt as if he were drowning, but he was facing three options. The first was to keep this baby and have her wake again the moment Sunny left. The second was to abandon her to social services… Yeah, he could. After all, what did she have to do with him? A token blood relationship?

But Sunny was looking at him, waiting for an answer, and he could read exactly what she thought of him.

So what? She was a hotel cleaner.

She was a hotel cleaner holding a baby who looked exactly like the photographs he'd seen of himself as a newborn.

She was a feisty, warm woman, with skill and humour, and she'd offered him a place at her Christmas table.

So…

So Max Grayland made his decision. He shook his head and moved to stand between Sunny and the cot.

'Let's not put her down,' he told her. 'If I could accept your offer…if it's still on the table…?'

Sunny looked at him, wary now. 'I guess.'

'I'll pay for my accommodation,' he told her. 'Hotel rates.'

'Wait until you see the accommodation before you say that.' And was that laughter behind her eyes?

No matter. Decision made, he was moving on. He turned back to the hotel manager. 'Could you hold this room for me? I'll return on Tuesday and I'll need professional full-time childcare. I'm not sure how long for—I imagine the legalities will take time to work through. Meanwhile, could you arrange a limousine to take me, Miss Raye and…and Phoebe to wherever Miss Raye directs? With baby supplies?'

'You're really going with her?' the manager demanded, stunned.

'Do I have a choice?' Max said drily. 'I appear to have none, and Miss Raye, believe it or not, I'm grateful.'

CHAPTER FIVE

MAX HAD RESERVATIONS before he arrived at the house. When the hotel limousine pulled into the driveway of Sunny's grandparents' home he very nearly demanded the driver pull out again.

This was like something out of a Gothic novel—in an Australian setting. All it needed was a Halloween moon and a couple of witches hovering overhead on broomsticks to make the picture complete.

It was a ramshackle, tumbledown mansion, or maybe not a mansion, just a house that had been extended upward and outward at random, that had had balconies and turrets added as an afterthought, and had been almost swallowed by the mass of bushland growing right up to the rickety verandas.

It was a wilderness in the middle of suburbia, a house set on a huge block that had been allowed to grow wild.

'Don't tell me,' Sunny said, seeing his look as he unfolded his long frame from the car and looked disbelievingly at what was before him. 'The letter box could do with a splash of paint.'

And he couldn't suppress it. He chuckled and Sunny grinned back at him.

'Yep. Awful. But it's home. Gran and Pa have been caretakers here for fifty years. Miss Murchison passed away almost twenty years ago and left them life tenancy. It's a double-edged sword. It's been fabulous to live in but there's no money to maintain it. I do my best but...'

'You...?'

'Gran and Pa are getting on now and the kids are all busy.

So, as I said, the letter box needs painting. Ignore it though and come inside. I texted Gran and she's expecting us.'

And, as if on cue, the front door swung wide. A stout little lady peered out at them and then waved wildly. 'Come on in,' she called, beaming. 'Everyone's here for dinner. Bring the man in, Sunny, and let's meet this baby.'

After that, it turned into a confused mass of faces, noise, laughter. Max struggled to get names. There were Sunny's brothers and sisters, Daisy, Sam, Chloe and a gap-toothed Tom. There were assorted boyfriends and girlfriends and a few general hangers-on. More importantly, there were Ruby and John, Sunny's grandparents. Ruby seemed cheerful, bustling, full of Christmas energy, but it was obvious John wasn't well. Frail and wizened, he sat in state at the head of the dining table. His seat was a wheelchair. He welcomed Max with quiet dignity and apologised for not rising, but he beamed on the noisy proceedings with pride.

And Sunny was everywhere. She showed Max to a room close to the kitchen. 'It's officially the sunroom now, but Daisy used to sleep here and it still has a bed. It's close to the kitchen so we can hear Phoebe.' She sorted the borrowed baby gear and then scooped Phoebe back from Ruby, who'd been cooing over her, and settled her into her new bed. She set up the baby monitor. She then towed the almost speechless Max back to the dining room, demanded the crowd make room, wedged him between Daisy and Tom and then bustled on.

Dinner was a barbecue of sorts. Tom and Sam were officially in charge but were distracted so a stream of blackened sausages were making their unsteady way to the table. No one worried. There were mounds of fresh bread, vast bowls of simple salads, huge bowls of strawberries—'Picked this morning,' Daisy announced proudly—an ocean of cream and a myriad of assorted treats each guest had brought to contribute.

Sunny was busy around the table, making sure plates were filled, reloading empty bowls, refilling glasses, nagging the boys to check the sausages—the standard of cooking did seem to have improved since she'd arrived—and gently chiding her grandfather to eat. All unobtrusively. The family hardly seemed to notice. Ruby seemed to have relaxed the moment Sunny arrived. It was obvious the responsibility for making things work pretty much devolved onto Sunny.

And Max thought of the last thirty-six hours. He thought of Sunny as he'd first seen her, on her knees scrubbing his bathroom floor. A double shift. How many floors had she scrubbed in the last two days? And last night... She'd been up and down to Phoebe. She'd slept on a hard settee with no pillows. She'd woken to another shift of cleaning today.

She was cheerful, happy, laughing and her gaze was everywhere. She was worrying about her Grandpa. She was making sure the myriad guests—including him—felt welcome.

He looked closer and saw shadows under her eyes and wondered if they were always there.

All her siblings seemed much younger than she was. He wondered if they noticed the shadows.

There was little he could do about it. He was wedged between Tom and Daisy. Once they realised he was American they launched into basketball talk. He knew enough to keep his end up, and the rest of the table joined in. As the strawberries were finished he was challenged to throw some hoops, which was the signal for everyone to head outside.

'I'll open Phoebe's window so she can be heard outside but I'll hear her from the kitchen,' Sunny told him.

'She's my responsibility.' He was so at sea here.

'So as soon as she wakes she's over to you, but meanwhile you've been challenged.'

'You're not coming outside yourself?'

'Are you kidding? I have a turkey to stuff, gifts to wrap...'

'I could help.'

'No need. Off you go, kids, and enjoy yourselves.'

So that was how she saw him? One of the kids? One of her responsibilities? But he had little choice but to be ushered outside.

Out the back was the remains of an ancient tennis court. Long ago someone had attached hoops to trees growing at either end. The ground was pitted with tree roots, but that didn't stop a long and very rowdy game being played between makeshift teams.

Max had gym shoes—when did he ever travel without them?—and tossing a basketball was one of his life skills. It was a skill that he'd practised as a teenager with little else to fill his time. He'd never played competitively but the gym had him toned.

'Yay, Max,' was the call as the game was declared over. Thirty-seven to twenty-nine, and twelve of the thirty-seven goals had been his.

And suddenly he was thinking of what he could be doing tonight. Back in New York he'd be well into the company accounts by now. And if he'd been alone at the hotel with Phoebe… *Whoa*, that didn't bear thinking of.

He'd buried his father this morning and the death was still a heavy weight. It'd probably take years to come to terms with his relationship with the old man. Added to that, he was still shocked to the core by Phoebe's arrival, but tonight had given him time out.

He wondered if Sunny knew it. If she knew she'd given him a gift.

The kids were dispersing. Boyfriends and girlfriends were leaving, Daisy and Sam with them. 'But we'll be back tomorrow,' they called and whooped their way out onto the road to collect their myriad cars and head home. Chloe and Tom headed to their rooms to sleep or do last-minute wrapping. Sunny had appeared momentarily halfway through the game to help Ruby take John to bed, so they were gone too.

Sunny.

He headed to the kitchen and found her sitting by the kitchen range, feeding Phoebe.

The sight of her was almost a physical jolt.

She hadn't had time to change since she'd arrived home. She was still in the jeans and T-shirt she'd put on before she left the hotel.

That she'd been cooking was obvious. A mountainous turkey was under a mesh cover on the bench, stuffed and trussed, ready to go into the oven in the morning. A load of fresh baked mince pies sat on cooling trays and another tray of pastry cases was waiting to be filled.

She had bowls out on the table. A whisk. Eggs. Cream. Brandy.

She'd obviously been interrupted mid-bake by Phoebe's need for a feed. She had smudges of flour on her face. Her curls had flour in as well, and her clothes...

'Yeah, I'm a messy cook,' she said and grinned at him and that jolt turned into something he had no hope of identifying. She looked...

Nope. He had no descriptor. He only knew that the sight of her, flour-coated, no make-up, shadowed, holding his baby sister, smiling up at him—it did something to him that he'd never felt before.

'You won,' she said, still smiling, and he thought yeah, he'd won and he hadn't even heard Phoebe. He'd been out there competing for inconsequential hoops while Sunny had taken over everything else.

He glanced through to the dining room, which two hours ago had been sketchily cleared. It was now transformed, covered with a faded lace tablecloth, glassware, cutlery, bonbons, a tangle of crimson bottle brush acting as a Christmas centrepiece...

She must have done this too.

'It gets a bit busy in the morning,' she told him, following his gaze. 'Gran loves us all to go to church so I like to get ahead. The basketball kept them all outside and gave me space. Thank you.'

She was thanking him?

He was feeling about two inches high. That she'd done all this—and now fed his…fed Phoebe.

'I should have heard her,' he said weakly and there was that smile again. It really was an extraordinary smile. There were dimples right where dimples should be. A smudge of flour lay on the right dimple and he could just…

Or not. Did he want to be tossed out into the snow for Christmas? Or into whatever Australians decreed was their outdoor norm at this time of year?

'It's a lovely warm night so you'd be fine if we threw you out,' she said, still smiling. 'But it's not hot, hooray. I can eat loads more when it's not hot.'

What the…? Had she guessed what he was *thinking*?

Was she fey?

'And you couldn't have heard her because she didn't cry,' she continued, as if she hadn't just poleaxed him. 'I checked and she was snuffling, so I thought I'd get in first. Much better to feed her before she gets distressed, don't you think?'

'I…yes.' He didn't have a clue. 'Could I take her?' he asked weakly. 'I should feed her. You obviously have things to do.'

'Well, I do,' she agreed and that smile appeared again, but it was a weary smile. 'I should say yes. You two need to bond. But you know what? I'm sitting down and I haven't sat down for a while. How about you make the brandy sauce while I supervise?'

'Me?' he said, stunned. 'Cook…?'

'Under direction,' she said severely. 'You needn't think I'm leaving something so vital to a novice.'

'But…'

'But what?'

He looked at the way her arms cradled the baby. He looked at her stained clothes. He looked at the shadows under her eyes, at the straggles of curls wisping across her forehead and he knew the weariness he'd heard in her voice was bone-deep. How much did this woman have to cope with, and how much more had he added to it by agreeing to come here?

For the first time he thought of this Christmas from her perspective, not his. The young adults around her were in the oblivious land of adolescence. Her Gran, cheerful but frail herself, seemed fully occupied in caring for her John. He'd seen Sunny helping there too, her assistance almost inconspicuous, but obviously needed.

This ancient tumbledown house…this tangled garden… It felt good, it felt a home, but how much of that was due to one slip of a girl? A woman, he reminded himself, because Sunny was every inch a woman. A woman who was asking him to make brandy sauce, under her direction, while she cared for his child.

His child.

It…*she*…wasn't his, he told himself but the thought slammed back in response. If she wasn't his then whose was she? Would she be put up for adoption? For some reason every instinct rebelled.

His father's estate would surely provide for her—legally, it must. As his father's executor he'd need to set up a base, employ a nanny, make sure she was provided with all material necessities until she came of age.

He looked again at Sunny. She was smiling down into Phoebe's little face, tender, caring.

Where would he find a nanny like this? His experience with nannies had been bleak, moved from parent to parent, from place to place. Time after time he remembered… 'Get over it, Max, she's only a nanny. We'll find someone else at the next place. Oh, for heaven's sake, boy, stop snivelling. You don't cry over a hired hand.'

To be raised by...hired hands?

Phoebe was facing the same path.

'So will you be making the brandy sauce or not?' Sunny asked mildly and he forced his mind away from a future that suddenly seemed inordinately bleak and focused on the here and now. He needed to help this woman who'd pulled him out of short-term trouble, at some cost to herself.

'I can try,' he said bravely and she grinned.

'What a hero. You know how to separate eggs?'

'I...no.'

'Then you're about to learn. We keep chooks so we have plenty. What a good thing! Okay, Mr Grayland, pinny on.'

'Pinny?'

'That's a very nice shirt,' she told him. 'To say nothing of the fact that you're still wearing your suit pants. They wouldn't go well with brandy sauce. Pinnies are behind the pantry door. The pink one's mine but there's one behind it the boys use for barbecuing. It says "The Man, The Myth, The Legend". See if you can prove it right.'

It took him five shots before he got an egg separated without contaminating the white with broken yolk.

'That's okay. I'll sieve the shell out and use them to make quiche on Boxing Day,' Sunny said serenely.

'So what happens if yolk gets into the white?'

'The white doesn't fluff. How can you make brandy sauce without fluff?'

For heaven's sake... He thought briefly of the massive financial decisions waiting for him in his briefcase, and here he was, worrying about fluff.

But it seemed important, mostly because Sunny was waiting for him to succeed. He was being measured by fluff.

He cracked the next egg and managed to get the yolk in one container and the white in the bowl.

Yay for him.

'Don't crack the next egg over the same bowl,' Sunny told him. 'Use a mug and tip the white in the bowl when you succeed. You don't want to contaminate what you've done.'

There was a comparison he could make—isolating financial deals so success or failure didn't drag others down.

Not so different really. Their worlds.

He glanced at the flour-smudged Sunny, holding the now sleeping baby, and he thought, *Who am I kidding?*

He messed another egg. Badly.

'Concentrate,' Sunny said severely. 'Brandy sauce is important.'

It was. Mostly because he could block out tomorrow and the day after that and all the days following while he focused on whipping egg white and creaming yolks and sugar and whipping cream and then adding brandy bit by bit. '*We wouldn't want to overdo it and make it curdle, but there's nothing worse than a not-very-brandyish brandy sauce.*'

He finished. Sunny ordered that he pour two small glasses—just to test. He tested and it was magnificent.

Phoebe slept. Outside the wind was stirring the massive eucalypts around the house, and a kookaburra was making a late-night complaint.

How far was he from New York? This was another universe.

Sunny was smiling into the sleeping face of baby Phoebe, her face gentler, younger, almost free.

Two different universes... They'd collided and what on earth was he going to do about it?

Sunny's room was just down the hall from the room Max and Phoebe were sharing. She heard Phoebe wake at two and was out in the kitchen preparing the bottle before Max emerged.

He had no hotel dressing gown here. He was wearing boxers and nothing else. The sight took her aback. He stood, looking half asleep, in the doorway, blinking in the harsh kitchen light.

He was carrying Phoebe.

Almost naked man, holding baby. *It's a cliché*, Sunny told herself. *It's a set-up designed to slam under every female's defences and I'm no exception.*

'Take her back to the bedroom,' she managed. 'I'll bring the bottle.'

'I'll feed her here…'

'Feed her in the half dark. She needs to start delineating night and day as soon as possible. Go on, get her out of the light.'

'Yes, ma'am,' he said in a strange voice but he left. Two minutes later she knocked and entered his bedroom. He was perched on the windowsill. The window was open and the room was moonlit. The silhouette of man and baby framed by the window took her breath away all over again.

'I could have made it myself,' Max told her as she struggled with composure and managed to hand over the bottle.

'You'd have coped in the hotel.'

'I'd have been terrified. Thank you, Sunny. I will make this up to you.'

'It's okay,' she told him in a voice that was none too steady. She needed to back out fast. What was it with this guy? He was so far out of her league he might as well exist on another planet. What was it about the gentleness in his voice that made something inside her twist? Something that had never twisted before…

It's because it's never had time to twist, she told herself, struggling to think practically. Here she was, almost thirty, and she'd never had a proper boyfriend. She'd never had time. Shift work, massive pressures at home, the fact that she'd had practically no schooling and what man would be interested in a woman who hadn't even passed Year Eight...?

'Are you okay?' Max asked, still gentle, and she backed off with a start.

'I...yes. Thank you.'

'It's I who need to thank you.'

'Then you're welcome. Don't forget to burp her. And if she doesn't finish the bottle don't reheat it next time she's hungry. She needs sterilised bottles and newly made formula.'

'Yes, ma'am.'

'And you're right with the nappy?'

'Nappy?'

'Diaper.'

'I am.' He sounded smug. 'I changed her before I came out to the kitchen. Nothing to it.'

'By which you mean it was only wet.'

And he chuckled. He'd popped the teat into his little sister's mouth. Phoebe accepted the teat with eagerness, and started suckling.

This man...this baby...this chuckle...

'I guess I did mean that,' he told her. 'But I'm sure I'll cope when the time comes.' And then he gazed down at the baby in his arms and seemed to change his mind. 'No,' he said. 'I'm not sure I'll cope. I hope I don't need to.'

'You mean you don't want her?' It was none of her business. She should retreat but there was something about this man... Something about this night that made her probe.

'I hope Isabelle will change her mind.'

'I do too,' Sunny admitted. 'But I doubt she will.'

'Why?'

'Because she insisted a porter push the pram. Because she didn't once falter. Because she didn't even look into the pram as she left.'

And Max looked at her for a long, long moment.

She should have dressed, she decided, feeling totally discomfited. She was wearing a shabby nightgown and an even shabbier cardigan. She felt like someone's poor relation.

She needed to back away, but…

'Is that how your mother treated you?' he asked gently. 'Did your mother not look at you, or at your brothers and sisters? Was it you who did all the looking, Sunny Raye?'

She couldn't answer. What sort of question was that, to be asked by a stranger?

'I don't… I have to go now,' she managed at last, suddenly feeling close to tears. Why? What earthly reason did she have to cry? It was just…this man got to her.

No. It was the situation. One more baby left to fend for herself.

'Don't get up the next time she wakes,' Max told her, even more gently, obviously deciding she wouldn't or couldn't answer. 'I'll call you if I need you but I'm sure I can manage. You need sleep.'

'I…yes.' There seemed nothing else to say. 'You could have managed at the hotel.'

'But I didn't have to and I'll be grateful for ever. And Sunny… I pay my debts.'

'There's no debt to pay,' she whispered and her emotions were suddenly too much.

She wasn't emotional—she wasn't. She was pragmatic. Dependable. Unflappable. That was how she'd survived this long and that was how she needed to survive now.

'Indeed there is.' And Max was smiling at her in such a way she didn't feel the least bit pragmatic, dependable or unflappable. 'Oh, and Sunny…'

'Yes?' She was almost out of the door.

'Merry Christmas,' he told her softly and she stood for a long moment and looked back at him.

'I… Merry Christmas,' she said at last, and bolted.

Phoebe was fast asleep before her bottle was finished but Max had learned his lesson. He set her on his shoulder as he'd seen Sunny do. He walked her back and forth across the room, rubbing her little back with care, and was rewarded by a satisfactory belch. It wasn't nearly as impressive as the one he'd heard back at the hotel but then, Phoebe hadn't begun to be upset yet.

He set her back into her borrowed cot and stood watching her sleep.

He knew nothing about babies. He'd never thought of having a child of his own.

Or maybe he had, but the idea was vague. Some time in the future he might be a parent but the concept was nebulous because the practicalities seemed overwhelming.

He'd need to find a woman he wanted to spend the rest of his life with, which seemed pretty much impossible. He liked his life as a loner. He could do as he pleased, answer to no one, care for no one. And no one would care for him. The thought of someone caring was a bridge too far. He'd let her down or she'd let him down.

He remembered time after time with the nannies. Always leaving.

And then there was the pup given to him when he was eight years old, the dog which for some reason even now seemed the biggest grief of all. But he wasn't going there. All he knew was that attachment hurt. He didn't need it and he didn't want it.

So…marriage without attachment? As if that would happen.

This nebulous partner would no doubt want to share his bed and he'd had enough affairs to realise women didn't like men who worked late, slept briefly and then listened to the world's financial affairs instead of sleeping. He'd head to his desk to check something and they'd wake and want bed talk. But his head would be doing business deals in Switzerland and something would go wrong and he'd need to be on the next plane. He'd leave with apologies but usually all he'd feel was relief.

Which brought him back to one sleeping baby.

If Sunny was right and Isabelle really didn't care, then he was her only family.

The thought was terrifying.

Could he turn his back?

Adoption? There were surely plenty of good, kind people who were desperate to give a baby a home.

But how could he know who to choose? How could he be sure he was doing the right thing?

And...she was his sister.

Half-sister, he told himself fiercely. He *could* walk away.

As someone had walked away from Sunny Raye.

Why could he not stop thinking of her? She was a hotel cleaner who'd helped him out. Nothing more.

She was a woman who took on the world. He didn't need to be told how much caring for this extended family cost her. He'd watched as her grandparents and her siblings deferred to her, depended on her, loved her.

Where was the room for Sunny Raye in all this? He'd heard the family chatter over the dinner table, of outside lives, of jobs, of studies, of interests. Even John and Ruby had been talking of the cricket, looking forward to the Boxing Day test, remembering past matches and knowing they could settle in front of the telly while Sunny... Sunny went back to scrubbing floors at the hotel.

It wasn't any of his business, he told himself. He'd pay her well for helping out this Christmas and that would help her financial situation. He needed to focus on Phoebe.

Phoebe.

It might be ridiculous to care about such a scrap of a thing after one day but he did and he wasn't about to let her go for adoption. Which meant he had to get the paperwork in order.

He needed to find Isabelle and get her permission to take Phoebe from the country. He needed to…adopt her himself?

There was a bag of worms. What would he do with her?

He'd do what his parents had done. He'd find a nanny. He wouldn't move as his parents had moved. He could find a nanny who was likely to stay.

But that'd take time. Even finding Isabelle would take time. The hotel childminder came to mind. He hadn't warmed to the woman. She'd done her job punctiliously but she hadn't cared.

Not like Sunny cared.

And then his mind stopped.

Sunny.

He was seeing her now as he'd first seen her, a cleaning woman on her knees, her uniform stained, her hands worn by years of hard work, scrubbing a stain from the bathroom floor. How many bathroom floors had she scrubbed? And was she due to return to her scrubbing the day after Christmas? He'd seen how she'd responded to the offer of double pay and now he'd seen her home he knew why. Of course she'd be back at work.

But she was good with Phoebe. Awesome.

Did she have a passport?

No matter. Technicalities were what he was good at.

But he'd seen how much the old couple depended on her. Her whole family…

So put your ducks in a row first, he told himself and then he decided he'd tell Phoebe his idea.

'I'll try,' he told his little sister. 'I suspect it can't be permanent but if Sunny will help… Do you agree? Yes? Then let's go for it.'

CHAPTER SIX

CHRISTMAS MORNING. Sunny woke at six and allowed herself a couple of moments of doing nothing at all.

She couldn't hear Phoebe. Max had coped by himself, then. Good.

Except she wouldn't think of him. She had these few precious minutes before the demands of Christmas took over. Tomorrow she'd be heading back to work. Life would start again.

Life. She put her hands behind her head and let herself drift to where she went so often. She tried not to, but as she saw each of her siblings follow their dreams it was hard to avoid.

What if...?

What if she'd had a decent education? What if she didn't have family obligations that took every cent and every moment? What if she wasn't almost thirty and her hands looked like she was seventy and her hair didn't need a cut and she could afford...?

A spa. There was a spectacular spa in the hotel. She saw patrons coming and going, pink and scrubbed, eyes glazed from pampering, from soothing music, from gentle hands...

She knew some of the masseurs. They looked a little like she did. They were the pamperers, not the pamperees. Just like she was.

But, just for this moment, she let herself lie under the covers and dream that her life could include a spa or two. Or that she could have the life she'd managed to give her siblings. Education. Boyfriends and girlfriends. Fun.

Um, not. Get over it, Sunny, she told herself. *You've done great. You never thought you'd get this far and it's Christmas morning, so get out of bed and do the vegetables before you need to help shower Pa. Before Max needs you to help with Phoebe.*

Max… Phoebe… Okay, she had to think of him a little and why did that worry her? What was it about the man and his baby that had her so unsettled? He was simply a hotel guest she was being kind to.

Except he was gorgeous.

He represented everything she didn't have, she thought, but then she thought it was more than that. His smile… His chuckle… The way he looked at Phoebe.

He could have taken the baby straight to the nearest welfare service, or he could have let the media know and the ensuing storm might have ensured Isabelle would take the baby back. Publicity was Isabelle's reason for existing. She could see Isabelle facing the press, woebegone, all innocence.

I just needed my beautiful daughter's family to acknowledge her existence. She's part of the Grayland dynasty and she's been ignored…

Okay, she didn't know if that was how it would have played out but Max hadn't risked it. He'd accepted responsibility, even though it meant… Christmas with her?

What a sacrifice. Christmas with the cleaning lady.

She found herself smiling. This was fantasy, being landed with a billionaire. For two days.

Okay, one day because she'd be back at work tomorrow. Max would stay on for the extra day, she guessed, because there was no babysitting service at the hotel until after Boxing Day. But Gran could give advice while she was at work and Chloe and Tom didn't start back at their holiday jobs until the day after Boxing Day either. They could look after one little baby. They could even have fun.

And there was that worm again, that niggle of jealousy she spent her life suppressing. Whenever something nice happened she had to work. Or do something else. Nice things happened to other people.

Like Max staying an extra day? Was that nice?

There was a thought that wasn't worth exploring. He was a guy she was being kind to. He was part of her working life.

Speaking of which, she had to get those veggies done. She had a decent veggie garden out the back and she'd been threatening death to anyone who touched a pea for the last week. Therefore they were ripe for picking. She'd left it until this morning so they'd be at their peak.

So get up and pick peas and stop thinking about Max, she told herself fiercely, and threw back the covers and headed for the shower.

Merry Christmas.

Phoebe woke early but Max was already awake. As she started to stir he dressed fast, then headed for the kitchen. He made her bottle quietly so as not to disturb the sleeping house and by the time she opened her mouth to wail he was ready to scoop her up and give her what she needed.

Success!

He sat on the windowsill while he fed her, so he saw Chloe heading off for a run. He had them sorted by now. Chloe was the fourth of the siblings, studying fashion design. She'd been on the opposing basketball team last night, a ball of vibrant energy, and it didn't surprise him to see her running into the dawn. Half an hour later he watched her return, check her time then start to do a wind-down on the back lawn.

Phoebe was still awake, lying sleepily in his arms. He carried his bundle out to meet her.

'Hey, Chloe!'

'Hey,' she said cheerily. 'How's the rug rat?'

'Fed and sleepy. Can I talk to you?'

'Sure.'

Fifteen minutes later they were still sitting on the back step when Sunny emerged. She was wearing old jeans and a stained T-shirt, carrying a colander. She looked like she meant business.

She stopped dead when she saw them.

'Hey.' Chloe jumped up and greeted her big sister with a hug. 'Happy Christmas. It's going to be a gorgeous day. Max and I have been busy making plans.'

'What plans?'

'That'd be telling. Christmas is all about surprises and I'm loving this one. Meanwhile, I promised Kim and Sarah I'd Skype them. They're in London—it's still Christmas Eve over there and I need to catch them before they go clubbing. See you soon.'

She disappeared and Max watched Sunny's face as she watched her go. It was a mixture of pride and resignation—mostly pride, though. He looked again at the colander, at Sunny's working clothes, and he thought, *Does anyone in this family notice?* Last night they'd all played basketball and Sunny had cooked. Now Chloe was Skyping her club-bing friends while Sunny worked again.

'Colander?' he queried but Sunny was stooping to check Phoebe. Making sure he'd kept her alive during the night?

'Great,' she said softly, touching a tiny, sleepy cheek. 'Well done, you.'

And what was in those few words to make his chest swell? He'd kept Phoebe alive overnight without waking Sunny. What a hero!

'I'm glad we didn't need to wake you,' he managed.

'Me too. I was tired.'

You're still tired, he thought, looking at the shadows under her eyes, but somehow he knew those shadows were permanent.

'Colander?' he said again.

'Peas.'

'Peas. Right.'

'In the veggie garden. You want to see?'

'Okay.' He rose and carried the sleepy baby in his arms, following her around to the back of the house.

He hadn't seen this last night. It was a vegetable garden of magnificent proportions. Tomatoes, beans, peas, corn, lettuces, berries—rows of carefully tended crops in all different stages of growth.

Sunny headed for the peas and started picking. With Phoebe in his arms he couldn't help. He watched for a while, stunned at the scale of the garden. 'Who cares for all this?'

'Pa started it decades back,' she told him, picking with the speed of long practice. 'He set it up and loved it. He can't do so much now, though.'

'So it's down to you.'

'The kids don't have time. Every now and then I bully them to do some weeding or digging, but they have their own lives. You have no idea how much money it saves us, though. Daisy and Sam raid it every time they come home too, so it helps them.'

'They're not self-sufficient?'

'Almost.' He could hear the pride of a parent in her voice. 'Daisy finished physiotherapy last November. She starts her first job this week. She and her boyfriend have just set up a flat together. He's as broke as she is, though, so it's been a struggle. Sam's just finished an IT degree and he's been offered a post-grad scholarship. He's living in at the uni, tutoring to pay expenses. He works in a call centre a couple of nights a week too, so he's almost off my hands. Chloe and Tom…they have a way to go but the end's in sight.'

'And you?'

'Me?'

'What's the end in sight for you?'

'To see them all safe.' She said it solidly, definitely. 'When Mum died and they were all sent to foster homes…

you have no idea how terrified I was. I made a vow then and I've kept it.' She caught herself, no doubt hearing the grim determination behind her words, and looked up and gave him a shamefaced grin. 'That sounds like it's been all me and it hasn't. Gran and Pa have been awesome.'

'But what happens after they're safe?' Max asked. 'What happens to Sunny?'

She shook her head. 'Who knows? I haven't been brave enough to look that far ahead.'

'I think you're brave enough to do anything.'

Her colander was full. How fast was she? She took a moment out, split a pod open and ate some peas, then split another and offered it to him. 'Sometimes I am,' she agreed. 'I applied to the best hotel in Sydney for a cleaning job and I can't tell you how much courage that took. The interview made me quake in my boots but I got it. Regular hours. Union negotiated wages. Meal breaks. I'd been doing casual house cleaning until then and the change was heaven. Taste?'

He tasted a freshly opened pea, standing in the garden in the small hours of Christmas morning. There were birds everywhere, raucous in the trees above their heads. Sunny had netted the most vulnerable of the crops but he had a feeling they were being watched, in the hope the netting could be breached.

He didn't blame the birds. This pea was worth fighting for. He glanced across at the splashes of crimson under the netting and Sunny saw where he was looking and grinned.

'The strawberries have had a week's embargo until yesterday too,' she told him. 'These are for tonight's pavlovas, which reminds me, I need to get the pavs into the oven before I need it for the turkey. Can you manage to take the peas inside while I do the watering and let the chooks out? I need to get on.'

Of course she did. He carried Phoebe and the peas back

up to the veranda and then stood and watched as Sunny headed down the path towards the hen house.

It'd take more than Chloe, he thought. Tom too? And support from Daisy and Sam.

He needed to knock on a few bedroom doors, he decided, and he needed to do it fast.

Church. Sunny still had nightmares of the year her mother had died, the year the world had seemed irredeemably shattered and her siblings had been cast into the separate paths of foster care. But then the social workers had found Gran and Pa, and miraculously they'd been enfolded with love. That Christmas, for the first time, Gran and Pa had played Santa Claus and there'd been a gift for Sunny.

She'd stood in church that first Christmas morning and she'd held Gran's hand and she'd wept. For some reason, every Christmas since then she'd felt the same way.

Everyone she cared about was with her now. The kids knew how important this was, to her and to Gran and Pa. Pa sat at the end of the pew in his wheelchair. Would he be here next Christmas? The thought made her cringe but she put it away.

She was here to count her blessings, as she did every Christmas.

The only problem was, this Christmas she had a distraction—a large one—sitting beside her.

For, as the family had readied for church, Gran had rounded on Max. 'We've ordered the maxi-taxi to take us. That gives us room for John's wheelchair so there's room for you and for Phoebe.'

'Phoebe might cry,' Max had protested and it was true. She'd been fed again but she was restless.

'And if the lot of us can't dandle one baby between us there's something wrong,' Pa had declared, so now Phoebe was still awake, nestled in his arms but seemingly content, gazing upward as if trying to make sense of this man who was holding her.

This man sitting beside Sunny.

They were sitting at the end of the pew, in case Phoebe decided to roar and they had to take her out. The kids were on the far side of Sunny. Gran and Pa were in the pew in front so his wheelchair could sit in the aisle.

Gran and Pa, holding hands.

Sunny and Max and baby Phoebe.

Family.

Anyone looking at her and Max might think…might think…

Don't go there, Sunny thought, as the Christmas sermon stretched on, but how could she not? Fantasy?

But this was a fantasy. There'd never been time or space for her to think of a love life and, besides, who'd want her?

She gazed down at her hands, at the lines and calluses formed by years of hard manual work, at the cracked, blunt nails, at the absence of rings. She stretched them out for just a moment and suddenly, astonishingly, Max's fingers were closing over hers.

'Good hands,' he said in a low voice. 'Honourable hands.'

She should pull away. She should…

Okay, she didn't know what she should do. Had he known what she was thinking? How many hands had this man seen that looked like hers? None. She knew it.

She should tug her hand back from his and the contact would be over. That would be the sensible course, the only course, but she couldn't quite manage it. His clasp was warm and strong. Good.

Fantasy enveloped her again for a moment, insidious in its sweetness. To keep sitting here, to feel the peace of this moment, this place, this man…

The organ murmured and then soared into the introduction of *Silent Night*.

It needed only this, she thought wildly. Her favourite

carol. Her entire family safe and happy. A billionaire to-die-for. A perfect baby…

And then the perfect baby opened her mouth and squawked, and Tom on the other side of her noticed where her hand was and dug her hard in the ribs. He grinned and waggled his eyebrows. The congregation was rising to its feet and starting to sing.

And Sunny tugged her hand from Max. She took the wailing Phoebe from him and propped her on her shoulder and rubbed her back. Phoebe subsided. Sunny looked firmly down at the printed words Tom was holding for her—she needed something to look at rather than Max—and she started to sing too.

She'd had moments like this before, she told herself. Moments of fantasy. But they were just that—fantasy. She was indeed blessed with her family, so what was she doing dreaming of more?

And then she realised why Phoebe hadn't been sleeping and what was behind the wail.

'Phew…' Tom gasped and Sunny winced.

'I'll take her,' Max said and for a moment she almost let him. But the fantasy had her unsettled. She needed to ground herself fast and what better way than a nappy change?

'I've agreed to take on responsibilities today,' she whispered. 'If I were you I'd soak it up because after Christmas she's all yours.'

Max didn't sing. Instead he stood and listened as the music swelled around him. He watched Sunny's family; they hadn't realised Sunny had slipped out. Like last night playing basketball… Sunny was out of sight, in the background, working to make them happy.

She deserved his Christmas gift.

Would she accept?

He could only hope.

* * *

Max might be pretty much a hermit where Christmas was concerned but he wasn't completely isolated. He usually emerged from his self-inflicted solitude for Christmas dinner, sharing it with like-minded souls in the restaurant near his apartment. The menu was always stunning, oysters maybe, caviar, turkey with truffle stuffing, an elegant modern take on plum pudding... The wines would be breathtakingly excellent. There'd be exquisite Swiss truffles with coffee, with cognac and the finest of Cuban cigars for those inclined.

This Christmas dinner was about as far from that as it was possible to be. There was no entrée—just a turkey so big it took two of the boys to carry it to the table. Sausage and herb stuffing, mounds of potato mash, a vast jug of gravy, and bowls of vegetables and salads. There was no elegance—it was a cheerful free-for-all.

Max found he wasn't missing his oysters and trufflestuffing one bit.

Then there was the pudding and there was no modern take here. 'I've handed the recipe to Sunny now and she's done us proud,' Ruby told him, beaming. 'You're the guest; you light it.' So with the family watching—with a certain amount of anxiety—he followed Ruby's instructions, heating the brandy and then flaming the pudding. They'd pulled the blinds closed and the flames lit the room.

Then the pudding was taken firmly from him—apparently he might be trusted to light it but only Ruby was going to serve. 'Cream, ice cream or brandy sauce?' Ruby asked but the question was met with howls of derision.

'He may live half a world away but the man's not stupid,' Sunny declared. 'Give him all three.'

So he had all three and came back for more. And Sunny grinned at him as she watched him pour more of the truly wonderful brandy sauce and he thought...

Um...not. Was the brandy sauce going to his head? There was no reason his thoughts were suddenly wandering in impossible directions.

'And now's the best part.' It was Tom, the youngest. 'Presents! Where's Phoebe? She has to be included.'

Phoebe was in the next room, sleeping soundly, but her presence was deemed essential. Sunny brought her in as they headed to the living room—and the Christmas tree. She handed the baby over to Max and he sat and held her as the family swapped gifts.

These weren't big gifts. His cherry liqueur chocolates were the largest offering of all, greeted with stunned delight from Ruby and hoots of laughter from everyone else.

'She always hides them in her knicker drawer,' Sunny told him. 'We've given her a conundrum. The box is too big.'

'The knickers will have to go,' Ruby declared, clutching her precious box. 'And now here's something for you and Phoebe.'

For him… He accepted a parcel wrapped in brown paper and tied with an obviously recycled crimson ribbon.

Things were getting a bit much. He wasn't used to this kind of personal. To say he was out of his comfort zone would be putting it mildly.

'Open it,' Sunny told him and somehow he balanced a sleeping Phoebe while he unfastened the wrapping.

It was a sock. An old sock, by the look of things, black, with a toe that was almost worn through, but it had been transformed.

It had embroidered eyes, nose and a wide crimson smile. Great bushy eyebrows were made with brown wool, as was its hair. The two toe ends had been tied to make waggly ears.

'Sunny made all the kids a Mr Sock when they were little and we decided Phoebe needed one too,' Ruby told him. 'You can use him to tell her stories. Starting now. Kids are never too young to hear stories.'

And he glanced at Sunny and caught such an expression...

A glimmer of tears?

But the room was suddenly full of laughing conflict.

'My Mr Sock is bigger,' Tom said proudly.

'Yeah, but my Mr Sock's pink.' Daisy gave him a shove. 'Much better.'

'You've all kept your Mr Socks?'

'Why wouldn't we?' Sam demanded. 'Is that the end of the gifts? I hear shortbread calling.'

'There's something more,' Max said. He was still watching Sunny. She was on the floor, surrounded by a sea of wrapping paper, misty-eyed, and he thought she looked...

Yeah, he didn't understand that either. Why the sight of her should do that twisting thing...

'I have a gift for Sunny,' he said and got nods of conspiratorial pleasure from everyone except Sunny, who looked confused.

'I don't need...'

'No,' he said softly. 'But you deserve. You might not wish to accept it, though. Try it and see.' And he took a folded slip of paper from his back pocket and handed it over.

She flicked it open and read it—and looked even more confused.

'It's...an airline ticket. Sydney to New York.' She read the detail, looking increasingly bewildered. 'First class. And there's no date.' She stared up at him. 'Max, I can't take this. I can't...'

'You can,' he said gently. 'But, before you accept or decline, you need to know there's a catch. It's not a freebie.'

'I don't understand.'

'I need a childminder.' And then, as she opened her mouth to tell him all the reasons that was a crazy idea, he held up his hand. 'Give me a moment. Let me explain.'

What he really wanted was space, privacy to explain his

carefully thought-out plan, but in this weird old house, surrounded by family and all the trappings of Christmas—and knowing his idea would never get off the ground without the enthusiasm of everyone—he needed to say it now.

'You're not a childminder.' In truth, he wasn't sure what she was—she'd stopped seeming like a cleaner and he didn't have a job description to replace it with. 'But you work for the most prestigious hotel in Sydney. Ruby says you value your job and wouldn't want to lose it. So this morning I rang the manager. He was able to make an executive decision—and that decision is to grant you leave without pay for the next few weeks. I'll make a donation to compensate them for the loss of someone who must surely rate as one of their best employees.'

She was staring at him as if he'd grown two heads. 'You rang the manager? About me?'

'I told him he has gold. I told him you're astoundingly undervalued.'

'No!' She sounded panicked. 'That's my job. You can't...'

'Sunny, hear me out.' His gaze met hers and held. He was willing reassurance into his gaze, confidence, trustworthiness—everything he most needed her to see. 'Sunny, firstly I have not jeopardised your job in any way. That's a promise. However, I have a proposition, and all I've done is make it possible for you to accept if you wish. Sunny, I'm intending to take Phoebe back to the States as soon as possible. There are bureaucratic issues but if Isabelle's still insistent that she doesn't want her then I can pull a legal team together and make things happen fast. So, for the next week or so, I'd ask that I base myself here. Ruby and John have already said we're welcome. Then...' he hesitated, because this was the biggie '...then I'd ask that you travel back to New York with me. I'd ask that you stay for a month. Help me settle her into a routine. And help me employ a nanny.'

'Hey, that's all work,' Tom said, as Sunny stared at him

as if he'd lost his mind. 'Full-time childcare doesn't sound like fun. We thought…'

'That the deal was better than that?' Max nodded. 'I hope it is.' Still Max was watching Sunny. 'I have a large apartment overlooking Central Park. I also have a housekeeper. Eliza will cook and clean and I'm sure she'll also take care of Phoebe for a few hours each day. Sunny, you'll have time off to explore New York. You'll also have an open-ended credit card, to see shows, museums, to shop…'

'You're giving her an open-ended credit card to shop?' Chloe squeaked, full of little-sister glee. 'Sunny, you could…'

'Shop for Sunny,' Max said firmly, grinning as he saw where Chloe's mind was headed. 'Any size fifteen basketball boots or clubbing heels meant for…oh, maybe a fashion student won't get past my eagle-eyed inspection.' And then he looked at Sunny and he glanced again at Phoebe's Mr Sock. 'But it won't be very eagle-eyed. Sunny, I want you to have fun and I know gifts would give you pleasure.'

But Sunny was still looking thunderstruck. 'Max, I can't. You know I can't. This is…'

'A cruel offer if I didn't mean it,' he agreed. 'But I do mean it. My housekeeper's part-time. She can take care of Phoebe a little but not for full days. I need to get back to work and Phoebe needs a constant until I can find her a nanny. I have no idea what to look for in a good nanny but I suspect you do. And, before you hit me with all the other reasons you can't come, your grandparents and brothers and sisters and I have been talking.'

'What, all of you?'

'Serially, not in a bunch,' Tom said gleefully. 'Wait till you hear, Sun.'

'It's awesome,' Chloe added but he shook his head to silence both of them. Once again he wished he could take her somewhere private. The look on her face was worrying him. She looked…terrified.

'It's okay,' he said gently. 'No one's bullying you. But your grandparents tell me January is holiday month in Australia. The universities are closed, which means Chloe and Tom are staying here. That means they can help your grandparents at night. But they also have holiday jobs. Tom's pulling beer at the local pub and Chloe's working retail at the Christmas sales. They tell me they need the jobs for the family to survive, but I've offered them alternatives. The plan is for them to quit and stay here.'

'And help Gran take care of Pa, and work in the garden and even paint the letter box,' Chloe announced. 'Though why the letter box seems important...' She grinned, shrugged and continued. 'No matter. We'll be doing everything you usually do, Sunny, only more because it'll be our full-time job, and the truly amazing thing is that Max will pay. He's offered what we were getting as a holiday job plus fifty per cent. Fifty per cent! Oh, plus the work on Tom's teeth. He must really want you, Sunny. He must think you're as awesome as we do.'

'But I'm not awesome,' Sunny said in a small voice. 'I'm...' She faltered and shook her head. 'New York...' She said it as if it was outer space.

'Will you come?'

'You'd spend all that money on me?' She glanced at Tom then, at the gap where he'd fallen skateboarding and broken a tooth. 'On us?'

'I'm rich in my own right,' he said gently. 'But my father was obscenely rich and I'll use his money if it'll make you feel better. This is about Phoebe. His daughter deserves the best care money can buy.'

'I'm not even trained.'

'I can't believe you can say that. Your family seems to think you almost single-handedly raised them. You coped on your own for years, and if that's not training in childcare I don't know what is.'

'You can get the best…'

'I know the best when I see it. You're the best.'

She stared at him and then stared wildly at Ruby. 'Gran…'

And Gran grinned. 'My mother used to tell me never to look a gift horse in the mouth and if Max isn't a gift horse I don't know what is. Just say yes.'

'A gift horse…' She practically choked.

'Exactly.' Ruby beamed. 'And Max promised that your ticket's open-ended so you can come home any time you need.' She was suddenly stern. 'So if this apartment isn't big enough to be separate and if you feel you're being pushed… to do anything you're not happy with…'

'She means if he pushes you to be his mistress,' Tom said, leering evilly, and Daisy kicked him.

'She mightn't mind being his mistress,' Chloe added and moved out of the range of Daisy's feet fast.

But Sunny wasn't noticing. To say she looked stunned would be an understatement.

'So agree,' Ruby said, beaming. 'And then we can all take a nice nap and then get on with filling the pavlovas for tea.'

'I can't…'

'You can't take it all in,' Max said swiftly. The last thing he wanted was a panicked no. 'Think about it and we'll talk later. Then you can tell me your qualms and I can tell you the ways I've solved them.'

'What a hero,' Daisy said and grinned and the whole family was grinning—apart from Sunny.

'I'm not a hero,' Max said. 'I'm an ordinary guy who needs help.'

'An ordinary billionaire with a baby,' Chloe added. 'Go for it, our Sunny. You might just have a ball.'

CHAPTER SEVEN

CHRISTMAS TEA. Leftovers and pavlova. It was her favourite meal of the year, Sunny thought, but this year she hardly tasted it.

As the tea things were cleared, yet another basketball session was mooted. Once again Sunny stayed on the sidelines. In truth she'd never learned to toss a hoop—she'd never seemed to have time—but she loved watching them.

But now she was watching Max have fun with her family. She was watching the kids fall under his spell and she thought, *That's what it is. A spell.*

He had her mesmerised and it scared her. His proposition scared her.

When she heard Phoebe fussing again it was almost a relief. She slipped away from the game, gathered the baby in her arms and carried her out onto the path leading up to the hills beyond.

This was a suburban setting but bushland had been preserved. There were parrots in the flowering gums that lined the streets, squawking a cacophony that was almost a part of her. The houses were all set well back, with trees between street and house. Discreet Christmas tableaux decorated the yards but the streets were deserted. The tableaux seemed almost out of place now that Christmas was done.

But was Christmas done? She walked and crooned as Phoebe fussed and she thought about Max's extraordinary gift. She really thought about it.

What she needed to do, she decided, was to take Max out of the equation. Because her first thought as she'd opened the envelope and seen the tickets was… *He wants to take me to New York.*

Which was a dumb thing to think. He wanted to hand Phoebe over and for some reason he'd decided he could trust her.

He had the money to pay whatever it took. So why not go? New York…

She'd never been on an aeroplane. She'd never even managed to get interstate.

This was a once-in-a-lifetime chance.

So take it.

It scared her.

Why? She'd faced down many things in her life—her mother's drunken rages, desertion, loss, far too much responsibility. She'd coped with everything and she hadn't flinched. She prided herself on her strength. Indeed, sometimes it was the only thing she had to cling to.

So why was she scared?

She knew why. It was because of her initial reaction to those tickets. Because she'd suddenly thought, *He wants me.* The thought had been fleeting, short-lived, ridiculous, but it had her deeply unsettled.

She thought of Tom's youthful teasing. *Mistress*…

What would it be like to be whisked off by a man like Max, ensconced in luxury, cosseted, cared for, indulged…

And held…

There was the crux of the matter. The sweet but poisonous hub.

To be held by such a man. To feel her body sink into his. To be cherished…

'Oh, for heaven's sake, go buy yourself a romance novel,' she muttered. 'Meanwhile, think of this proposition sensibly. It's a business proposal. There's nothing personal about it.'

Phoebe had settled. She was sleeping, a tiny warm being cradled against her breast. That was a siren song too. Babies…

Stop it, stop it, stop it. She gave herself a hard mental shake and turned her feet to home.

And Max was striding towards her in the dusk.

Max.

'Stop it,' she muttered again, because her heart was starting to race and it had no business racing. She had to be sensible.

'I'm heading home,' she managed. 'There was no need…'

'There was a need.' He smiled and, oh, that smile…

Stop it!

'You should have told me,' he said reprovingly. 'She's my responsibility. You agreed to help me, not take over entirely.'

'I needed a walk to clear my head.'

'While you think about New York?'

'I can't think about New York. The idea's crazy. We've given you two days board and lodging. You don't need to repay us with the world.'

'Like with like,' he told her. 'You made Phoebe's Mr Sock.'

'Yes, but…'

'And it took you, what, an hour? Plus the thought that went into it beforehand. Tomorrow I'll ring up my father's favoured lawyer. He's a Queen's Counsel. Have you any idea how much such a man demands as an hourly rate?'

'What's that got to do with me?' She tried to walk past him but he put his hand on her arm and stopped her.

'Sunny, value yourself,' he said urgently. 'Give yourself a treat. Believe me when I tell you it'll cost me so little I won't notice.'

And she gazed up at him and realised it really did mean nothing. Handing over first class air tickets, a credit card with no limit, a month in New York for a cleaning lady…

Her thoughts were racing.

Nothing.

Phoebe stirred in her arms and she thought of how easily

had Max accepted her. There'd been initial panic but now...
He was doing the right thing. He'd take his half-sister back
to New York. He'd take Sunny with him to make the tran-
sition as easy as possible. Then he'd install a nanny and life
would resume its rightful pattern.

He'd be nice to his little sister, she decided, because she'd
figured that was what Max was. Nice. Honourable even.
He'd do the right thing.

But this man's reputation had come before him. He was
an international businessman with fingers in a thousand financial pies. Max had kept below the radar of most of the
gossip columnists but the fact that the hotel management
bowed and scraped told its own story, and there was enough
interest in him to know he was solitary. Aloof.

So yes, he'd care for Phoebe—but would he notice?
Would he still walk alone?

She glanced down at Phoebe, at this tiny face still wrinkled from birth. She thought of Phoebe's appalling mother.

And then she thought of her own family, her brothers and
sisters, and the fight she'd had to keep them close.

Who would love Phoebe?

Who would fight for Phoebe?

And suddenly the money didn't make sense, the first
class flights, the month in New York, the limitless credit
card. What made sense was this little life she was holding.

He was still holding her arm. Pressuring her?

Two could play at that game. She tilted her chin and met
his gaze full-on.

'Okay,' she said. 'I accept. On one condition.'

'Which is?' He sounded bemused, as well he might. How
many women in her place would have imposed a condition?
But this was her only chance.

No, it was Phoebe's only chance.

'I'll do it if you take the month off.'

His brows snapped together. 'Sorry?'

'The month I'm there. Yes, I'll come and yes, I'll care for Phoebe. But this housekeeper you say will babysit while I spend your credit card… Does she like babies? Is she kind?'

'I have no idea,' he said honestly. 'But if that doesn't work we can hire…'

'We can't hire,' she said flatly. 'That's the condition. That I come and help, but for the next month her main carer is you. I understand you'll need to do some work but there are home computers and telephones and I'll be in the background. As far as I can see, you're the only person who can possibly learn to love her, so that's what I'm demanding. That you care. I won't stand back and watch as you hand responsibility over to people you hire, at least not until you've figured whether you can love her or not. So there's my line in the sand. We both care for your baby for a month or I don't come. Take it or leave it, Max Grayland, but that's my final word.'

There was a long silence. A very long silence.

Max's hand was still on her arm. They seemed linked in a way she didn't understand, but she needed to focus.

What sort of idiot imposed conditions when faced with such an incredible offer? Max's face said it all. He looked stunned. Incredulous. Was there also the beginnings of anger?

'You think I won't look after her?' he demanded at last and she shook her head.

'You've just proved that you'll look after her with every cent your fortune can provide. But will you love her?'

'She's nothing to do with me,' he snapped. 'She's my father's child.' And yet he paused as if he realised what he'd said. *My father's child.* Family?

'She's a person,' Sunny said, knowing what was at stake here. 'If you intend taking responsibility for her, then surely your life should change. You think you can buy her care?

From the sound of things, that's what happened to you. Is that what you want for Phoebe?'

'What happened to me has nothing to do with anything.' It was practically an explosion.

'Doesn't it? Did you have Christmases like we have? How many people would you break your heart over, Max Grayland? I watched you as you struggled to think of your dad's eulogy and I thought I've never seen someone so alone in my life. Is that what you want for Phoebe?'

'No. But I can't take a month off.'

'Really? How many new parents don't take any time off to learn to love their little one? You've just had a new baby. You need to accept it.'

'She's not my baby. And this is…'

'None of my business,' she retorted. 'No, it's not.' She took a deep breath and stepped back from his touch, from his anger, from his pressure. And then she made a decision.

She stepped forward again and, before he knew what she intended, she'd folded Phoebe into his arms. She simply pressed the baby to his chest, waited until his arms closed involuntarily on the sleeping bundle, and then she stepped back.

'If she's not your baby then you need to accept it now,' she told him. 'Buying me won't help you, and it won't help Phoebe. Thank you for the gift, but you need to face it. It was a cop-out for you, and for Phoebe's sake I can't let you take it. The kids will be disappointed. Gran and Pa will be disappointed too, because they'd love to see me travel, but that's the problem with surprise gifts. They have consequences and I can't let those consequences get in the way of Phoebe's care. Take Phoebe back to the house now, Max. I'll be home soon. I just need to walk off a bit of steam.'

She cast him one last look. She saw anger, confusion,

shock, but there was nothing she could do about it. Before he could respond she turned away and started walking.

Fast.

For a long moment he didn't move.

He felt as if he was stranded, stuck in time, standing in the dark in a strange country, with a sleeping baby in his arms. He had no idea where Sunny had gone. He couldn't go after her. He had no choice but to turn and walk back to the house.

It was almost surreal, walking under the trees where the nesting parrots stirred and twittered as he passed, where the only lights were those of the muted Christmas decorations in the front yards, where echoes of Christmas music wafted from households readying for bed, readying to farewell Christmas for another year.

Phoebe stayed sleeping in his arms, a warm, fed bundle, nestled against his chest.

You think you can buy her care? Is that what you want for Phoebe?

Sunny's words echoed in his head. He thought of the Christmases he'd had as a child—fantastic, extravagant parties where he was expected to behave, be silent, be grateful and be a charming child for his parents' guests. For there were always guests. They were people he didn't know, the children of his parents' latest lover, business acquaintances, a gathering of society's finest, all trying their darnedest to impress.

He thought of the gifts he'd been given, motorised toy cars—a toy Lamborghini, for heaven's sake—an exquisitely carved rocking horse, designer clothes, vouchers for exclusive stores, sound systems to take his breath away.

And then there'd been the pup.

He'd been eight years old, flown as an unaccompanied minor from the US to England, from boarding school and his father's apartment on the odd weekend to the English country house of his mother's latest lover. Who had a title his mother lusted after. Who welcomed him with affable friendliness. Who bred Border collies.

He could still feel the shock, the joy and the wonder of that Christmas morning. A tiny bundle of black and white fur, moist, licking, wriggling with excitement, with a huge crimson bow around her neck.

'Of course you can keep her. Happy Christmas, darling.'

And he'd fallen completely, besottedly in love.

He'd had her for two months. He'd called her Lassie—how naff was that? but she was the best Christmas gift ever. She'd played with him, exploring the strange farm he'd ended up on. She'd rolled in sheep dung or whatever else disgusting they could find on their adventures. She'd crawled all over him, slept with him, loved him back, a warm, fun bundle of pup he'd thought was his for ever.

But that was the last time he'd ever let himself love. As his mother's relationship folded, as the pretence of happy families disappeared as it always did, he was sent back to his father. That last awful morning…his mother had wrenched the pup from his arms and slapped him when he'd tried to grab her back.

He still couldn't come to terms with the pain of that moment.

He'd do better with Phoebe, he thought. Maybe she could even have a dog? But as he looked down into her sleeping face Sunny's words kept echoing.

You think you can buy her care?

He did think that. This baby had been thrust on him and he had no intention of changing his life. She'd have to fit around the edges.

And, as if on cue, Phoebe opened her eyes and gazed up at him.

Okay, he'd care, he conceded.

But enough to take a month out of his life?

It was more than that, though.

Could he care enough to let himself fall for this tiny creature? Enough to truly acknowledge she was his sister?

There'd been judgement in Sunny's tone and maybe he deserved it. If Phoebe was adopted, if he decided he couldn't care and Isabelle wouldn't, then one of hundreds of couples desperate to have a baby would welcome her with joy. He knew that. They'd certainly take time out of their lives to learn to love her.

They'd open their hearts…

And that was the crux. Opening his heart…

He didn't know how to any more. He was a loner. The lessons learned from his childhood were soul-deep.

So put her up for adoption.

But he gazed down into her face and Sunny's words kept playing and replaying. And then he thought of Sunny's Mr Sock.

'She'd care,' he told Phoebe. And then he added a rider. 'Maybe she can teach me how.'

A month. A month with Phoebe and Sunny.

He thought of the business negotiations waiting for him to deal with as soon as he got back to the States. He thought of complication after complication.

He looked down at Phoebe again and then he thought of Sunny, venting her frustration by walking too fast into the night. He thought of her last night, weary beyond belief, staying up even later to make a Mr Sock.

'Maybe she can teach me,' he said again to Phoebe. But there was something there that…scared him?

Was it Sunny herself? Sunny, with her huge heart. Sunny, with a background so much harder than his, a cleaning lady who sweated blood to love her family.

She deserved her time in New York. She deserved what he could give her.

'So I need to agree to her terms,' he told Phoebe and he

thought suddenly of a month in New York with no business. And Sunny.

Surely the sky wouldn't fall on his head if he had a break. But then… Sunny?

The sky was suddenly threatening and he wasn't sure why.

The way he felt…

You can cut that out, he told himself fiercely as he turned and headed for home. *It's all very well to let yourself fall for a baby. But Sunny?*

Her life was as far from his as it was possible to get.

A month, he told himself. A month and then his life would get back to what it should be.

She walked for an hour, trying to figure what she was doing rejecting such an amazing offer—and also trying to suppress her anger that he'd put such a deal in front of her, a temptation she could almost taste.

She remembered all that time ago, a social worker taking her aside. *'You're a clever girl, Sunny, and the responsibilities you're facing are too much. We'll take you all into care. You can go to school, do what normal kids do, look after Sunny for a change.'*

The social workers had been called in because her mother had been arrested for being drunk and disorderly. They'd found Sunny trying to cope and had been horrified.

Overwhelmed, Sunny had felt herself tempted. To walk away… To have time for Sunny…

It had been a siren song but she'd looked at her brothers and sisters and known there was only one path to tread. She'd reacted with anger; she'd insisted they were all safe and that this episode with her mother had been a one-off. She'd had no choice.

As there was no choice now, but this time it was about

Phoebe. 'And she's just as important as Daisy and Sam and Chloe and Tom,' she muttered.

But he'd just employ someone else. Why shouldn't it be her?

'Because I won't watch while he pays me to keep her.' She hiked some more, stomping out her anger.

But she had to go home. With Max's preposterous suggestion off the table she needed to go to work tomorrow. It was almost midnight. She needed to sleep.

As if that was going to happen. But she turned and made her reluctant way home, trying not to think of New York. Trying not to think of Phoebe.

Trying not to think of Max.

She turned into the driveway and Max was sitting on the veranda steps. Waiting.

'Hi.'

For some reason she wanted to turn and run but she forced herself to keep walking. His greeting was low and gravelly. The rest of the house must be asleep—the house was in darkness. The window behind him into the room he shared with Phoebe was open but there was silence there as well. He'd have put her down and come outside—to wait for her?

'Hi,' she managed and headed for the steps. She needed to brush past fast. 'G...goodnight. I need to go to bed.'

'I need you to come to New York.'

'I already told you...' She was halfway up the stairs, trying to brush past him fast.

'Of your conditions. I accept.'

She stopped dead. Her world seemed to wobble and she had to put out a hand on the balustrade to steady herself.

'Really?' she managed.

'Really. And Sunny, I'm sorry.'

'For...for what?'

'For not getting it.' He edged aside. 'Will you sit down?'

'I need...'

'To listen. Oh, and I have the brandy sauce.'

'You...what?'

'Ruby was up making herself a cup of tea and eating a mince pie when I got home. She diluted some of the brandy sauce into a jug, with orders to give you some. And she told me to tell you to quit it with the qualms, take my offer and run.'

She smiled, despite her...qualms. 'That sounds like Gran.'

He poured two glasses and held one out. 'Sit,' he told her.

She should... She should...

She sat.

'So, about this offer,' Max said. 'It's still open. A month in New York, all expenses paid; the only catch is now you'll need to put up with me a bit more than you expected.'

Yeah, that'd be a disaster, she thought, but she didn't say it. How inappropriate was that?

'So you'll take a month off work?' she managed. She needed to get this clear. She needed to get a lot of things clear.

'Mostly.' He gave a rueful smile. 'There'll be things I need to attend to. Dad's death has left loose ends that need to be tied but, as you say, I have a computer and a phone. Everything that can be put off will be put off.'

'For Phoebe.'

'For Phoebe.' He handed her the glass and clinked his. 'So is this to shared childminding?'

'I... I guess.' She was too hornswoggled to make much sense. She tipped the glass...and practically choked. 'What the...?'

He drank too, and grinned. 'I guess she diluted it with more brandy, huh?'

'My grandmother...' She glowered and he grinned and it broke the tension.

'She's awesome.'

'She is,' Sunny agreed. This was a safe topic at least. 'I don't know that I can leave her.'

'If there weren't others to care I'd say not. But you know you can.'

'If anything happened to Pa…'

'I'd have you on the next plane. But Daisy tells me it's not likely.'

'Did she tell you about his heart?'

'He has a new stent. It seems to be working. Daisy says there are no promises but he's better now than he has been. She also says this might be your only window before…before something does happen.'

'A window…'

'A window to do something different, something that might even be fun. Something for Sunny. Your whole family wants this for you, Sunny. So just say yes.'

'My whole family and you.'

'That's right.'

'Why?' She took another sip of her brandy sauce and then carefully set it down. Who knew what strength it was, and she needed every bit of concentration she could muster. 'New York will be full of extraordinary childminders, nannies, the works. Americans don't take January off. You could employ someone in a flash.'

'And I'm good at employing people,' he agreed. 'I could find someone highly skilled, great work ethic, honest, capable, efficient. But I'm not sure if that's what Phoebe needs. I run a huge corporation, Sunny, and I've learned others have the skills I don't. Hiring nannies… I don't have the first clue. All I know is that I want someone like you. I know you can't take the job permanently, but if you give me a month we can find someone together.'

How did she answer that?

So why not?

Max was throwing money at her problems. Chloe and

Tom were more than capable of taking care of Gran and Pa, and they'd love the chance to stay here rather than take the menial holiday jobs they had to do to survive. Gran and Pa would love their company, love the extra attention. Daisy and Sam would be in the background, ready to help.

Max had somehow wangled her leave without pay. She could return in a month and walk back into her job.

So why not?

Because…because…

He was too close.

And there was the reason in a nutshell. She was sitting beside him in the dark. The step wasn't wide enough to allow any distance. His body was brushing against hers.

She could feel his heat. She could sense his strength.

It made her feel…frightened?

Not exactly. It was a sensation she had no way of describing.

Oh, for heaven's sake… She was quibbling and why? She knew this man was honourable—the fact that he'd come here with his baby rather than taking Phoebe to the nearest welfare worker told her that. His name was known the world over. If there was any of…what Gran would call 'funny business'…she could have his name plastered over every tabloid in the Western world.

'You can trust me,' he said and infuriatingly there was laughter behind his words. How did he know? 'Huge apartment,' he continued. 'Master bedroom one end. Guest suite at the other with about an acre of living room in between.'

'It sounds…lonely,' she managed.

'Lonely's the way I like it. But with Phoebe… I guess I need to change. I'm depending on you to teach me.'

'Lonely's never been a problem for me,' she managed. 'Sometimes I…'

'Wouldn't mind a taste? This is your chance. I promise I'll do as much of the caring as I can. You'll have time to yourself. Real time. I'm guessing for you that could be worth gold.'

'I…yes.' But she wasn't sure.

'So you'll come?'

She looked at him in the moonlight, a big, solitary man she knew nothing of apart from his reputation as one of the world's most ruthless businessmen.

But she did know him better than that, she thought. She'd watched the way he held Phoebe. She'd seen the pain as he'd fought for something to say at his father's funeral. She'd watched him lose himself in the kids' silly basketball match and she'd listened to him talk to Pa. Pa was a bit forgetful, a bit inclined to tell the same stories over and over, but Max had listened with courtesy and interest. He'd made Pa smile.

And what he was offering…

Just say yes.

'Yes,' she said and it felt as if she'd just jumped off a very high cliff.

What had she done?

But Max was setting his glass down and turning to face her. He took her hands in his and it felt right. It felt…as if the world was slowing down to let something important happen. Something out of her control?

'Thank you,' he said and she found her breathing wasn't quite happening. But who needed to breathe when the world was tipping on its axis?

What was in that brandy sauce?

'I think…' How to get her voice above a whisper? 'I think it's the wrong way around. It's me who should be thanking you. This is…an extraordinary offer.'

'You deserve it. You're an extraordinary woman.'

'I'm a cleaning lady.'

'And so much more. Don't you dare devalue yourself. Has anyone ever told you how beautiful you are?'

She practically laughed. Beautiful? With her worn hands,

her hair she cut herself, her faded clothes… He had to be mocking.

But his eyes weren't mocking. His eyes said he spoke the truth and for one glorious moment she let herself believe. For this wasn't her. This was some other woman, sitting in the moonlight with the most beautiful man…

This was a tableau, make-believe, magic.

But she couldn't make it stop, and why would she? For he was drawing her gently to him. No pressure. She could pull away at any moment. She could…

She couldn't, for he'd released one of her hands, and with his free hand he was tilting her chin. He was cupping her face. He was tilting her mouth to his.

And kissing…

She'd been kissed before—of course she had. She knew how kissing could feel.

Only it wasn't like this.

It was as if her body simply fused. His hands caught her waist and he tugged her close. The moment their mouths met… The sensations… The heat, the strength, the feel of him… The taste… The sheer masculine scent…

The rasp of after-five shadow. The strength of his jawline. The tenderness with strength and urgency behind it.

She was sinking into him, melting, aching to be a part of something she had no hope of understanding. Did she whimper? She hoped not but she might have. She'd never felt like this. She was sitting on her grandparents' front step and yet she felt a world away, transported into another life. A life where there was just Max and Sunny.

Fantasy.

And with that thought reality came slamming in, like a wash of ice water. What was she doing? She, Sunny, was sitting on the porch kissing a billionaire, a man who'd just employed her, a man who was about to be her boss.

And Chloe's words were suddenly right there. '*She mightn't mind being his mistress.*'

What sort of dangerous game was this?

Somehow she managed to tug away. She was released in an instant. She sat staring at him and thought... *He looks almost as stunned as me.*

'No,' she stammered.

'No?'

'I...you're employing me. This is...you have no right.'

'I don't.' But he sounded regretful.

'It won't work if you...if you take liberties.'

And the ready laughter flashed back. 'Liberties? If I'm not mistaken, you were kissing back.'

She couldn't deny it. Nor did she want to, but some things had to be set straight.

'Enough.' She rose and brushed her hands on her jeans as if wiping away a stain. 'That was an aberration.'

'There's a big word.'

A big word. Whoa?

And reality slammed right back, as it always did. She was the dumb one, the kid who'd hardly been to school, the one who'd been lucky to get a job as a hotel cleaner. What right did she have to use big words?

What right did she have to kiss this guy and, if she did, what would he expect in return?

'Yeah, I must have read it on the back of a cornflakes packet,' she muttered. 'Aberration. Deviation from the norm. Beware, there's the odd cornflake in here that might not meet expectations. Just like me saying aberration.'

'I'm sorry.' He got her anger. 'Sunny, I didn't mean...' He started to rise but she backed away.

'I accept your offer of a job,' she told him. 'My family's right; it's an awesome offer too good to refuse. And I'll do my best. I'll care for Phoebe as I'd care for my own family, but that's all I'm committing to. I'm staff, Max Grayland, the hired help, so don't you dare try anything on with me.'

'I wouldn't…'

'You just did.'

'Wasn't it consensual?'

'There's another big word,' she snapped. 'That's beside the point. I'm the hired help, got it? Stay clear of me, Max Grayland. I'll work for you, I'll care for Phoebe and I'll probably enjoy it, but if you touch me again I'll tell you where you can put your consensual. Now, goodnight. Christmas is over and I'm done. Oh, and I'll do Phoebe's next feed. I'm paid staff, remember, and I start being treated as paid staff right now.'

Paid staff.

He'd kissed her and she didn't feel like paid staff at all.

He had no idea what she felt like. He tried to analyse it and all he could come up with was…different. The bland adjective didn't begin to describe his reaction.

No one like Sunny had ever come into his orbit. She was a hotel cleaner and yet she wasn't. Or she was, but she was so much more. He was seeing beneath the outer layer but there were more layers concealing what lay underneath, complexities he had no way of knowing.

Did he want to know?

He didn't. Of course he didn't, because he had no wish to become involved.

Forty-eight hours ago a baby had been thrust into his life, making him more involved than he'd ever wanted to be. Threatening his precious independence. And here was Sunny…threatening the same?

Except she wasn't. Sunny knew the rules.

'I'm paid staff, remember, and I start being treated as paid staff right now.'

So what was he doing, kissing her? He'd pushed hard to

get her to come to New York. It was a sensible plan to solve his problems, not a first step in making more.

Kissing her made more.

No. Feeling as he did made more. The touch of her…the taste of her lips…the warmth of her body…the twinkle, the strength, the love…

Love. There was a scary word. She had it in abundance, he thought—love to share.

He wanted it for Phoebe so he was paying for it, but he didn't want it for himself. He knew the perils of loving and he had no intention of going there. Kissing Sunny had risked his perfectly crafted plans for nothing.

'So keep your hands to yourself.' He said it out loud and then noticed the open window and wondered if Sunny was inside—if Sunny could hear.

So what? Let her think what had happened was simply a *boss makes an inappropriate move* moment. He'd apologise in the morning, trust she didn't sue for sexist harassment in the workplace and move on.

But the way the kiss had made him feel…

'Move on,' he told himself, again out loud, roughly, harshly. 'You have enough complications without that.'

'Oi!' The voice above his head startled him. It was Tom, leaning out of an upstairs window. 'Are you enjoying talking to yourself or would you like company?'

'Thanks but no.' He rose and walked down the steps so he could grin ruefully up at Tom. 'Sorry to disturb you.'

'You sure you don't want a mate to drink with?'

'Thank you but no. I'm heading to bed and I'm happy on my own.'

'People who talk to themselves aren't happy on their own,' Tom said sagely. 'Just lucky our Sunny's going back to New York with you.'

'Yes, it is,' he agreed and headed inside.

But should he have agreed? His head—and his body—
were starting to have all sorts of doubts.

Was it lucky that Sunny was coming back with him?

It was sensible, he told himself. But it also felt…

Risky.

CHAPTER EIGHT

THE FLIGHT TO New York was awesome, though it might just ruin her for flying for ever. How could she ever appreciate cattle class now? Her first ever time in an aeroplane was a first class flight, with extra seats booked for Phoebe and her baby gear.

Max Grayland was obviously a platinum flyer, privileged beyond belief. Every time he blinked—or Sunny blinked—someone was there to help. Who knew what the flight attendants thought of her, but not by a twitch of their perfectly groomed faces did they show how out of place her faded jeans and discount store jacket looked in this place.

For the most part Max stayed engrossed in his work. It was urgent stuff, she gathered, by the way his fingers flew over the keyboard and by the amount of paperwork littered around his seat. But he was taking her stipulation seriously. When Phoebe was awake he'd leave his work and take the baby from her. He'd dandle her and smile and play, and Sunny watched him and thought she was almost redundant.

Except…she was included too. They had four seats, two pairs across the aisle from each other. When Phoebe was awake Max moved to the seat next to hers. He chatted to his little sister, he told her all the treats that were in store for her in New York, but he included Sunny in the conversation.

'It'll be cold,' he told his little sister. 'Really cold. That's the first thing we need to do, get you some warm baby clothes. And Sunny too. A decent down jacket, I think, and some fur-lined boots so you two can explore together.'

'I can…' Sunny started but she knew she couldn't. She

didn't have the wherewithal to buy her own down jacket and she'd have no clue as to where to buy a cheap one.

'You probably could,' Max agreed gravely, giving her her dignity. 'But it would be my privilege to buy them for you. Besides, girls like shopping and it'll be fun watching you two hit the stores.'

'Fun?' She didn't believe him.

'Okay, I have no idea if it'll be fun,' he admitted. 'But grant me the privilege of finding out.'

And then they were landing. A chauffeur met them and a limousine took them straight to Max's apartment. She had a brief impression of a vast park on one side of the street, with old stone buildings on the other, solid and imposing. Then they were ushered inside and Sunny could barely take in such luxury. A housekeeper with a smiley face and a head full of tight white curls greeted them with pleasure.

'Supper or bed?' Max asked Sunny, and the care and empathy in his smile was almost her undoing. For despite the luxury, despite the attention—or maybe because of it, because it had left her in a limbo of tension as she'd tried to figure what her role was—she was exhausted.

'I…just a cup of tea and bed,' she told him. 'But I'll settle Phoebe…'

'How about a toasted cheese sandwich and cocoa in bed?' Max asked. 'Eliza and I can look after Phoebe, can't we, Eliza?'

And Eliza was nodding and smiling, scooping Phoebe out of her carry capsule and cradling her with care. Making Phoebe even less sure of her role.

'We certainly can. I'll show you to your bedroom, Miss Raye. May I suggest a bath—a nice long soak—and then supper and bed?' And she smiled at Max and she smiled down at Phoebe. 'Oh, Mr Grayland, this is going to be fun.'

So she lay in a king-sized tub with bubbles up to her neck and tried to figure what was going on. She was ensconced in luxury and Max Grayland had a housekeeper who looked like everyone's favourite granny.

How could she be needed? Phoebe was just one little girl...

Who was wailing. Maybe she'd been in the bath a tad long. Maybe she'd almost snoozed. She dried fast and wrapped a bathrobe round her—hey, Max had those fancy hotel-type robes, only better. She wrapped her wet hair in one of his gorgeous towels and padded out to see.

Max was pacing the floor with Phoebe, encouraging her to take the bottle. Phoebe, however, was having none of it.

For a moment she stood in the doorway and watched him. The living room was enormous, with vast plate glass windows showing the skyline of practically all of Manhattan. The room itself was amazing, luxury meshed with indescribable comfort. It was a living room with a kitchen/dining area. There were vast planked benches, a polished wood floor with tapestry rugs, sofas and chairs you'd just want to sink into, a planked table that matched the benches with twelve leather chairs, a fireplace with a crackling fire augmenting the obviously very efficient central heating...

And a man who couldn't handle a baby.

'Drink it, sweetheart.' He was almost pleading. 'We need to show Sunny we can cope.'

His hair was ruffled, his shirt was half out and he looked...baffled? He was a man in unfamiliar territory. But he lived here, she reminded herself before taking pity on him.

'Do you need help?'

His expression of almost pathetic gratitude made her laugh. 'Yes. Please.'

'Hey, it's not that bad.'

'She says it is.'

'Where's Eliza?'

'She finished at seven. She comes in for an hour in the

morning and then for a couple of hours in the evening. She makes me supper and leaves it in the warming drawer. Which reminds me, your toasted cheese sandwich is in the oven.'

'I'll have it later.' She scooped Phoebe out of Max's arms and cradled her against her breast, gently rocking. 'Hey, sweetheart. Hey, little one.'

Max proffered the bottle but she shook her head. 'She won't take it like this. I need to calm her down first.' She kept on rocking and crooning while she looked out of the window at the truly amazing view and thought that this man had everything...

Everything? A housekeeper who leaves his supper in the warming drawer?

'Eliza seems lovely,' she said, while Phoebe hiccupped life's tragedies into her shoulder. 'Surely she could help you look after Phoebe.'

'I wouldn't know.'

'How do you mean? She seems caring.'

'I've only met her twice.' Max sounded almost goaded. 'I met her when I hired her and gave her the key to the apartment. Her references were great, her cooking's excellent and she cleans efficiently. That's hardly enough of a reference to leave Phoebe with her, even if I knew she had time to spare. I know nothing about her personal life.'

'But if you did?' Privately she felt okay that he had qualms. He wouldn't leave Phoebe with just anyone, but instinct told her Eliza was solid. 'You could check her out and I could go home now.'

'Do you want to?'

Well, there was a question.

She'd seen the bed she'd be sleeping in. It was the king of plush, luxurious beyond measure. Outside the windows of this magnificent apartment stretched all of Manhattan. Of course she didn't want to go home.

But it was more than that.

Max was standing by the window, seemingly as exhausted as she was, and suddenly she thought... *He seems alone.*

It was a weird thing to think. This man had the world at his feet. The Grayland Corporation employed thousands worldwide. He could snap his fingers and have a dozen employees here to take care of Phoebe right now.

But... His housekeeper came in while he was at work, made him dinner and left it in the warming drawer and he didn't know her. This place was designer perfect but, glancing around, she saw no signs of personality. There were no photographs, no silly souvenirs or fridge magnets. She thought of the jumble of detritus in her grandparents' house and she thought...

Maybe she *was* lucky?

The thought came from out of left field, so unexpected that it almost blindsided her. For the past few years—okay, maybe for all her life—she'd existed by doing what came next. The arrival of her grandparents on the scene had seemed a miracle. The worst of the threats had disappeared and she'd been loved and protected ever since. But it hadn't stopped the grind of daily life. Ruby and John were living in a tumbledown home they didn't own. They had life tenure so they couldn't sell it, and there was no way they could afford to rent a home that'd be big enough for all of them. Their daughter had robbed them blind and put them deep in debt during her early drug-taking years and they had no money, so Sunny was forced to keep on working, putting one foot in front of the other as she did what she'd sworn to do. She'd get her siblings an education. She'd see them safe.

But she'd missed out herself. Apart from the blessings of having Gran and Pa on the scene, she'd never once thought she was lucky.

But now, standing in this grand apartment, looking at

this man standing solitary against windows overlooking the world, she thought maybe she was.

And she thought…a month. Maybe in a month she could show him…fun. In her arms she held the embryo of a family. Max's family. With luck Phoebe could grow to be a bouncy, happy toddler, a cheerful little girl, a child who'd greet her big brother with joy when he got home every night. He could be a big brother who'd collect her from school, who'd attend interminable school concerts, who'd commiserate over broken love affairs and bad hairstyles.

He didn't have a clue, she thought, and she had a month to teach him.

Phoebe had settled to the stage where her sobs were simply hiccups of exhaustion. Sunny sank onto one of the massive down-filled armchairs and held her hand out for the bottle. Max handed it to her and then perched on the chair's wide arm and watched while Phoebe fed.

'You make it seem easy.'

'I make it seem like I've done this before.'

'For all your siblings?'

'As far as I remember. I was only five when Daisy was born so Mum must have been around, but I still remember making bottles in the middle of the night.'

'Hell, Sunny…'

'I loved them,' she said simply. 'It's easy when you love. I learned that early.' She smiled down into Phoebe's face, now tightly screwed up in concentration as she sucked. 'I'd take Daisy into bed with me and cuddle her and we'd go back to sleep together. She was better than a doll.'

And it was *much* better than being alone. She remembered that too, the sound of the door slamming as her mother left for the night, and the warmth of the baby in her arms. She'd been something to hold onto.

What did Max hold onto?

He was right by her. His hip was brushing against her arm. She could…

She couldn't.

'So what shall we do tomorrow?' she asked, forcing a brightness she didn't feel.

'Sleep?'

'Will you sleep?'

'Probably not. I'm used to crossing time zones. But I'll work from home while you catch up on Zs. I won't wake you unless I need you.'

'Wake me anyway. I'm only here for a month and I don't want to miss a minute. Besides, two people giving cuddles are much better than one.'

There was a moment's silence. He was looking down at her and the feeling was…weird? She glanced up at him and then looked away.

She didn't understand what was happening. She'd never felt like this and it frightened her, but the look on his face said he was almost as confounded as she was.

'Let's take tomorrow as it comes,' he said. 'It's Saturday. Eliza won't be here so I may well need you.'

'I hope you do.' But then she thought should she have said that?

She was in unknown territory and she didn't have a clue where to take it.

Take it to bed, she thought. Bed was good. Time out, in her gorgeous bedroom.

Phoebe had finished her bottle. She hoisted her onto her shoulder and rubbed her back and was rewarded with a satisfactory burp. 'You have somewhere for this little one to sleep?'

'I had Eliza organise it.' He rose and she followed, carrying the sleeping Phoebe. He opened the bedroom door next to hers and it was all she could do not to gasp.

Okay, she did gasp. It was an ode to pink and silver, a

baby's nursery like no other. The wallpaper was embossed with pink and silver elephants. Pink curtains covered the windows and lush pink carpet covered the floor. A magnificent cot stood at one end, white and silver with pink bedding. There was a pram that looked like something Mary Poppins would push, a true English perambulator. A baby bath on a stand. A myriad of beautiful mobiles hanging from the ceiling. An open wardrobe full of pink.

'What…how did this happen?' she gasped.

'My staff had notice. You can buy anything with money.'

She stared around her in astonishment while Max lifted the sleeping Phoebe from her arms and laid her in her cot.

'See? No cushions and a nice firm mattress,' he told her. 'But a buffer to stop her hitting the sides. My instructions were explicit.'

'Good for you,' she managed as Phoebe stirred and snuffled and then settled to serious sleep. 'But there's no adjoining door into my room. I won't hear her in the night.'

'That's what this is for.' He held up a state-of-the-art baby monitor. 'But the receiver's in my room. I'm taking this seriously.'

'I…good.'

She had no cause for complaint.

But then as she gazed around the magnificent nursery she found herself thinking of the one-bedroom apartment she'd been raised in, the jumble of kids and noise and chaos, the ancient cane bassinet used by successive babies until they were big enough to join the tangle of kids in the shared bed.

And she looked at Phoebe in her magnificent crib and she looked at the vast room and the state-of-the-art baby monitor, and she looked again at Max, who thought he had it all under control.

But his expression said he wasn't sure. His expression said maybe he had as many doubts as she did—but now wasn't the time for voicing them.

'Goodnight, then,' she told him, and almost before she knew what she intended, she crossed the room and stood on tiptoe and kissed him lightly on the cheek. It was a feather-touch, a brush of friendship. 'You've done good, Max Grayland. Good luck with your baby monitor.'

She was gone, deviating back to the kitchen to grab her sandwich and a glass of milk—a girl had to be practical—then heading to her room and shutting the door behind her.

And there was no reason in the world why Max Grayland stood in the baby's darkened room with his hand to his cheek.

No reason at all.

CHAPTER NINE

TRUE TO HIS WORD, Max kept the baby monitor. On Sunny's first morning in New York she slept until ten, which was almost unheard-of for her. She yelped when she saw the time and bounced out of bed, to find Max at his desk at the far end of the massive living room with Phoebe in her perambulator beside him.

'We took a few rounds of the apartment,' he told her with evident pride. 'She likes the perambulator. She got a bit scratchy for a while and we were worried we'd wake you but it didn't reach full-throated roar. We decided she was just bored. So we went up and down in the elevator a few times and I explained its workings. She was most interested and now she's gone to sleep to dream of counterweights and pulleys. Her eyes glazed over a bit when I started on elevator algorithms but she's young. She'll get it in time.'

'She…you talked elevator algorithms…?'

'She's smart.' Max's voice held all the pride of a new dad. 'She'll have it nailed by this time next week.'

'Of course she will.' She was having trouble keeping her voice steady.

'Breakfast? I'm up for a second. Waffles? We have a waffle maker and Eliza's made up a batter. Eggs? Bacon? Maple syrup? You name it.' And then he looked at her more closely. 'And then back to bed, I think. The weather's filthy, wind blowing straight from the Arctic. Phoebe and I are doing fine.'

'I can't… I'm here to work.'

'You're here as backup,' he said, seriously now. 'That was the deal. And Sunny, you can't tell me you don't need a break. The alcove over there is my library. We have movies to stream, newspapers, video games... There's a lap pool in the basement and a gym. Anything you want...'

'I didn't come for a holiday.'

'No,' he agreed. 'You came to give me the courage to do what I'm doing, and you're succeeding.' He was smiling, his eyes kind but also...searching? As if he could see the bone-deep weariness that had been with her almost since she was born. 'So while you're succeeding, how about looking after Sunny for a change?' He rose. 'Okay, you're about to see a sight that's not been seen by many. Max Grayland cooking.'

'Can you?'

'I think so,' he said and grinned. 'Eliza's left me instructions. How hard can one waffle be?'

The waffle was excellent but it was hard to concentrate. Sunny ate in silence. She drank juice and coffee. She looked out of the windows at the vision of a rain-soaked Central Park. She tried not to look at Max.

How could she stay here for four weeks...so close...when he just had to smile...?

But as she finished her coffee he excused himself and headed back to his desk, and Phoebe.

'If you'll pardon us, we have work to do,' he told Sunny. 'Bed again? Or whatever you like. Your choice.'

Sunny glanced at the gleaming dishwasher and thought she didn't even have to wash a mug. She had time to herself... The sensation was so extraordinary she felt as if she were floating.

She wouldn't mind...just sitting and watching Max with Phoebe.

He was back at his desk, sorting papers but glancing occasionally at the sleeping baby by his side. He looked tense, but he was trying. He was taking this seriously.

He wanted a little sister?

The vision of Phoebe's over-the-top nursery was suddenly front and centre and she didn't need to be told that this was how Max had been raised. A loner. A guy who didn't do family.

But he was trying and she'd been sent back to bed.

As if she could sleep. *Ha!* But to go back to bed...to have nothing to do...

She edged towards the library and Max cast her a glance of approval. 'Anything you like...'

Anything she liked. There was a concept that had the power to disconcert her all by itself. But she checked the books and saw what was there and almost forgot Max and Phoebe.

Five minutes later she was scuttling back to her bedroom, clutching an armload of tomes.

A whole day. Books. Warmth. Bed...

And Max Grayland sitting in the room next door, gently rocking his baby sister.

They spent the weekend ensconced in their cocoon while Max figured Phoebe out and Sunny tried to figure herself out. There were times when Phoebe's needs required her attention but Max was trying manfully to cope by himself. His phone was never silent but when Phoebe needed his attention he switched it off. Sunny was starting to feel seriously impressed.

This man had been thrown a baby out of left field and he was doing his best. Sure, there were times when Phoebe screamed and nothing he could do seemed to placate her. That was what babies did and all she could do was reassure him.

'A doctor once told me being a paediatrician's like being a vet,' she told him at two a.m. on the Monday morning when they were taking turns walking the circuit of the living room. 'Babies and dogs…you know when they're miserable but they can't tell you what's wrong.'

'So what's wrong?'

'Who knows?' She adjusted the screaming baby on her shoulder. 'She's not hungry. She's clean and dry and warm. Maybe her tummy's taking time to adjust to formula. Maybe she doesn't like your colour scheme. Maybe she's just figuring how her lungs work.'

'Or maybe she's ill.'

'Maybe she is,' Sunny told him. 'But if you take her to Emergency and tell them she's been screaming for less than an hour they'll grin and say *Welcome to the world of babies*. Chances are the moment you're admitted to see the doctor she'll go to sleep.'

'So I ignore screaming.'

'You cuddle screaming. It's the quiet stuff that's scary.'

'The quiet stuff?' They were talking over Phoebe's sobs and Phoebe's sobs were doing something to him. Making him feel helpless? Making him feel he could never cope alone.

'That's when the doctors jump,' Sunny told him. 'A limp baby who's off her food and doesn't have the energy to cry is a scary thing.'

'Is that what you had to cope with?' If he was frightened of being alone…how much worse would it have been for Sunny?

'I learned the difference. I took Tom to the hospital one night when he wouldn't stop crying but he was fine and next thing I knew we had a bevy of social workers breathing down our necks. They didn't like the idea of a ten-year-old presenting with a sick baby. Mum nearly killed me.'

'But she didn't take him herself?'

'She wasn't home. Hey, I think your sister's asleep. Finally. You want me to take her in with me? Not in my bed,' she said hastily. 'In the pram beside me.'

'What's wrong with her room?'

'It's lonely. Maybe that's why she's crying. Who'd want to be alone?'

And he looked at her oddly.

This was a weird intimacy.

Max was looking absurdly good for a guy woken in the middle of the night, but maybe having a gorgeous haircut, after-five shadow that looked downright sexy and pretty decent blue and white striped pyjamas did that for a guy. Whereas she was wearing a bad haircut and an oversized nightie she'd bought in an op shop two years ago.

'Have you ever been alone?' he asked.

She tilted her head and looked at him, considering. The question, the way he made her feel, the way she was feeling—strangely aware of his vulnerability—made her answer with honesty.

'Alone? Hardly ever,' she told him. 'I'd imagine that's your specialty. But lonely…that night when I was scared for Tom, and all the other nights…you'd better believe it. But since Gran and Pa gave us a home I've pretty much forgotten what lonely feels like and I never want to go back there. So will you let her sleep with me? I swear she won't miss her pink palace.'

'She can sleep with me if you think she needs company.' He was watching her as if he couldn't figure her out. 'Though it'll take some getting used to—not being alone.'

'There are advantages,' she said, forcing herself to sound brisk. Employee chatting to employer. In her nightgown. 'Here's hoping she doesn't snore. I'll head back to bed then. Alone. I kind of like it.'

'Sunny…'

'Mmm?'

'What would you like to do tomorrow? The forecast is reasonable. We could pack Phoebe up and…perambulate. First stop is to buy you a decent jacket and shoes. Next…

The Statue of Liberty? The Empire State Building? You name it. Let's go sightseeing.'

'You don't need to work?'

'We made a deal. I'm sticking to it. Besides,' he admitted, 'it might be fun.'

'I bet you've already seen the Statue of Liberty.'

'I have,' he agreed. 'But she's worth a second look.'

'Or a thousandth?'

'Sunny…whatever you want.'

She hesitated. *What she really wanted…*

She thought back to the pile of books she'd been reading and thought, *Why not say it?*

'How about City Hall Station?'

'City Hall Station?' he said blankly. 'What the…?'

'You have influence, right?'

'I…yes.'

'I hoped you might. You'd need to pull a few strings to get us down there but they say there are guides who can organise it. Do you know what I'm talking of?'

'I have no idea.'

'It's not used. I've just been reading about it. It was opened in 1904, deep in the belly of New York's subway system. Apparently it's a beautiful, untouched station that hardly anyone seems to know about. The architecture's amazing. Apart from the skill of the engineering, it has the most gorgeous tiled arches, untouched brass fixtures that take your breath away and magnificent skylights running across the entire curve of the station.'

'Why isn't it used?' he said faintly.

'It was gorgeous but stupid. The engineers got everything right, apart from the biggie. Train carriages are long, neat rectangles, but the tracks at the platform are so curved they couldn't stop the train without leaving a gap between the doors and the platform. Crazy, huh? It was used for a while with restrictions and then closed in 1945. I'd love to see it.'

'But...why?'

And he had her on her hobby horse. Despite the hour, despite the weirdness of the setting, she told him. 'I love tunnels,' she confessed. 'There was an opening to a drain near us when I was a kid and I used to go exploring. The authorities have wised up to risks now and there are protective barriers in place. There aren't many opportunities to go underground, but then...'

'You went down drains?' he said faintly. 'On your own?'

And she hesitated but then decided. Why not tell him?

'It was my retreat,' she confessed. 'How corny's that? I was always sensible—watchful for weather even when I was very small. But I remember...early on, one of Mum's boyfriends hit me and I ran away. I found the drain, the opening to the tunnel and I sat in it for hours, far in, where no one could find me but I could still see the arch of the opening. Maybe I should have been frightened but the dim light, the silence, the huge, solid stones around me... somehow they made me feel safe. By the time I came out again I felt...stronger.'

'Sunny!'

'Dumb, isn't it,' she said sheepishly. 'It makes no sense but there it is. And it's stayed. Tunnels. I love 'em. The skill in making them... Can you imagine digging underground, then building vast stone arches so they met at the top, strong enough to handle the load of a city, cars, people, buildings, even trains?' She shook her head. 'If I had more education I'd have done engineering and learned how to dig them. I even tried to get a job on a construction crew when I was fifteen, but apparently teenage girls aren't what they want around hard hats and diggers. But I read about them and now... The City Hall station... I bet you could get me down there.'

'Maybe,' he said cautiously. 'If I chose...'

'So will you choose?'

'Phoebe...'

'It's not dangerous. If we're buying me a coat we could also buy a baby cocoon. Then Phoebe can see City Hall Station too. I bet that's why she's been crying. I was telling her about it this afternoon and she thought she'd miss out. But wouldn't that be a cool thing to do?'

'I…very cool.' Wandering through unused underground subway stations instead of doing the work that was piling up…

But Sunny was looking at him with eyes that were bright with excitement. She'd woken at two in the morning to help him with a screaming baby. She was wearing a nightgown that was too big, faded, frayed around the hem. Her hair was tousled, she was wearing no make-up, there was a smattering of freckles on the bridge of her nose…

He had the strongest desire to kiss…

Um…not. She was holding his baby.

Not his baby.

His world was feeling more and more lopsided.

'Do you still want to dig tunnels?' he asked faintly and she grinned.

'I've let that go,' she said with regret. 'I imagine tunnelling would require years of hands-on experience and it's too late for that now.' She took a deep breath. 'But I would so love to study architecture. And I will.'

She suddenly seemed to have stars in her eyes, a kid thinking of Christmas. *It's a dream*, he told himself, and he shouldn't mess with dreams. 'That's um…great,' he said weakly. 'Good for you.'

Her twinkle didn't fade but her look became speculative. 'You think I'm nuts.'

'I think…it'll be hard.'

'But not impossible.'

'I guess… What age did you leave school?'

'I hardly went to school, but that doesn't mean I don't know stuff. I pushed every one of my siblings through years of homework. Calculus? Geography? Try me. But universities need proof, so that's what I'm doing. Slowly and online but I'm four university entrance units down. After another two I can apply. The course will take me years because I'll still need to work but by the time I'm forty I might just be there. A fully-fledged architect. How cool would that be?'

'Very cool,' he managed, stunned. He shook his head. 'How many things in your life are cool?'

'Lots. And yours?'

'I…maybe.' But he'd never looked at life with the zest and enthusiasm this woman had. She was blowing him away.

'Bed,' she said now, with the same enthusiasm. 'We have a big day tomorrow and Phoebe might wake up again.'

'She might but she can sleep in my room while she decides.'

She'd taken Phoebe off her shoulder and was cradling her against her breast. Phoebe's face had relaxed in sleep. The screaming jag was done. Sunny was smiling down at her, as peaceful as the baby herself.

He came close to take her, and then paused. Caught by the night. The quiet. The total silence.

This woman who'd been through so much, who'd faced the world with such bravery, who had so much to give…

This woman was beautiful.

She looked up at him, questioning, wondering why he was hesitating. Her face was tilted…

She seemed infinitely precious, infinitely fragile.

He shouldn't. She was alone in his apartment. She was his employee. She was totally vulnerable…

'If you want to kiss me then kiss me,' she said, and suddenly she was grinning.

'What?'

'Have I misread the signs?'

'No.' He was smiling too. 'You haven't. But Sunny… Back in Australia…'

'I know. I stopped you because it seemed scary. You're my employer and there seemed all sorts of minefields. So maybe there are but right now… You know, right now I'm over being sensible. It felt good then and somehow I suspect it might feel even better now.' And then, as she looked at his face, the hint of mischief returned. 'Oh, for heaven's sake, Max Grayland, just kiss me.'

And what was a man to do? He chuckled. And then he kissed her.

The first time Max had kissed her, two weeks ago now, she'd felt as if her world had changed, and, to be honest, there'd been a voice inside her all this time demanding she try again. Was that first reaction her imagination?

It wasn't.

It was as if her breathing had been taken over by another. More, it was as if her body had been taken over. She was no longer Sunny.

Somehow, two parts of a whole, a being she hadn't known existed, had been miraculously brought together and joined. Every piece fitted into place and now its heat was soldering them together in some way that could never be undone.

Weird? Fanciful? She didn't care. All she cared about was that she was in his arms. Phoebe was tucked between them, warm and safe, both of their bodies curved to protect her, and that was weird too. It was as if Phoebe was part of them. A bonding that couldn't be undone?

But these feelings were subliminal, a wash of sensation, a wave of intuition that told her she was right out of her comfort zone but somehow the zone she was in seemed…right?

A woman could die in this kiss.

And, yes, it was nuts to be kissing this man. It was crazy to be standing in the window of his beautiful apartment overlooking all of Manhattan. It was a dream, one she surely had to wake from.

But waking was no part of her plans. He was kissing her with heat, with passion and with desire, and she had no option but to kiss him back. To do anything else would be to deny a part of her she hadn't known existed.

This was a fairy tale, she thought, in the tiny part of her mind that was available for thought. Cinders with her prince. The thought almost made her laugh, and if she wasn't being kissed maybe she would have, but the thought of not being kissed was unbearable.

So shut up, she told her consciousness. *Just kiss.*
Let yourself dissolve...

And she didn't have to say it. She just did.

His strong hands were cupping her chin, holding her, lifting so his mouth could merge with hers. Her mouth was opening to welcome him.

Fire meeting fire. Strength meeting strength.

Home.

For that was what this felt like. It was a wash of sensation so intense if felt as if this man, this baby, this moment was where she was meant to be for ever.

She was kissing back with an intensity that matched his. She was still cradling the baby—both of them were—and the feel of this warm, tiny bundle between them only heightened the sensation of earthquake within.

She was someone else. A woman free to love.

To be loved by Max?

Max.

Her body ached to be closer. She wanted to mould to him, to sink into him, to surrender to what she had never known she craved until this moment. If Phoebe wasn't in her arms she'd hold him tight but it didn't matter. How much closer could she be than she was right now? This was...perfect.

Scary?

No. Perfect. Right.

The night, the moment, the wash of light from the view

outside, everything seemed to be dissolving. His mouth and hers formed a link fused by fire. His hands had dropped now to the small of her back, moulding her against him, but pulling her so Phoebe had the perfect cocoon.

Delicious, delectable, dangerous...

Max.

A man who was holding her with passion. Whose mouth turned her to fire. Whose eyes caressed her, loved her, told her anything was possible...

A hotel cleaner and a billionaire?

It didn't matter. It couldn't matter.

But then Phoebe stirred between them, a tiny movement, a mewed whimper, and she knew it did. Was it her consciousness that had disturbed the baby? Was Phoebe reminding her reality was right here, waiting to take hold and shake her back to where she belonged?

Which wasn't here. She'd wanted this but she had to stop. Surely she did.

Someone had to see sense and in the end it was Phoebe.

Phoebe's whimpering was telling them this moment was mad.

Phoebe whimpered and reality flooded back—and also sense.

More than anything else in the world, he wanted to pick this woman up and carry her into his bedroom. He wanted to lay her down on the welcoming covers of his king-sized bed and take this to its inevitable conclusion. For that was what it felt like. Inevitable. That his body could love her and she could love him...

But, no matter what was between them, she was here at his behest, paid to take care of his sister, paid to be alone with him. And she was alone. She had no one on this side of the world. Even though her body had moulded to his, even though she'd welcomed his kiss, had kissed him back with an intensity that matched his, a part of him was achingly aware of her vulnerability.

And...his?

If he gave himself to Sunny...

The thought was blindsiding him.

He'd had women before, of course he had, and some of those relationships had been long-standing. But every one of them had been superficial. Demanding nothing of each other but mutual enjoyment, the convenience of having a partner, decent sex. He'd been prepared to lay his cards on the table early but mostly he hadn't needed to. The women he dated were from his social milieu, out for a good time, as protective of their personal space as he was.

But Sunny... She'd want more, he thought, with insight that came from nowhere but he knew had to be the truth. She had none of the social gloss, the layers of armour, the self-sufficiency he sought in his women. She was a woman who loved, freely and without thought of self.

She could love him—but if she did she'd expect him to love her back and he didn't know how. And did he want that?

His life was organised. His childhood had taught him that independence was the only way to go. Attachment left him gutted.

And now he'd been landed with a baby. That, in itself, was huge. He'd probably end up attached; he could sense that. That scared him enough.

He looked down at the doubts in Sunny's face and he thought Phoebe was enough. To have two people dependent on him for their happiness...

He couldn't do it. He had to draw the curtain on this now.

But Sunny already had. He didn't know what she could read in his face but her face reflected...dismay? As if she'd overstepped some boundary she'd set herself and it scared her as much as it scared him.

'Wow,' she breathed, taking a step back. 'I...you pack quite a punch.'

'I'm sorry.'

And amazingly the twinkle flashed back. 'You're sorry for packing a punch?'

'I shouldn't have kissed you.'

'Why not?'

'You're my employee.' It was a lame statement and it made the twinkle disappear.

'So I am,' she said and cocked her head so she was surveying him with eyes that saw too much. 'But we're not talking of a fumble under the stairs with the kitchen maid here.'

'I wouldn't...'

'Is that how you see me? The kitchen maid?'

'Of course not.' But he didn't know where to take it.

She did, though. She gazed at him for a long minute and then gave a brisk nod. 'Okay. Don't worry. The kitchen maid isn't getting ideas. She knows you won't jump her, and in turn she won't jump you. Your boundaries are safe, and in truth they're very wise. There's a mountain between us, Max Grayland, and no one's about to knock it down because of lust.' She turned and laid Phoebe gently back into her perambulator, kissing her softly on the cheek as she tucked her in.

'Goodnight, little one,' she whispered, speaking a bit too fast. Breathlessly? 'You go and sleep by your big brother. He'll love you in the end, I know he will. He has a huge heart. He just...he just needs to figure out how big.'

And with that enigmatic statement she disappeared.

She almost ran.

Phoebe slept on. He should wheel her back to his room. Instead he stood staring at the door that led to where Sunny was...sleeping?

Could she sleep after that kiss?

Had it hit her as it'd hit him?

It didn't matter, he told himself harshly. It was just a kiss.

But it was more. What she'd just said...

How did she know him? How did she see what he was most afraid of?

He had no idea.

It must be an illusion, for how could she know when he scarcely had it figured himself?

'Go to bed,' he told himself out loud. 'Forget it. And leave her be. She's here to help for four weeks and that's it. Keep it friendly, keep it formal and keep it distant.'

And as if in protest Phoebe stirred and whimpered.

He rocked the pram for a little, then wheeled her through to his room, parking it beside his bed, then lay in his too-big bed and listened to her resettling, the faint snuffles of a baby totally dependent on him.

Phoebe needed loving, he thought. But then he thought Phoebe needed Sunny's kind of loving. Not his.

And then he thought...

No. The idea was crazy. The idea was impossible.

He put it aside decisively and attempted to sleep.

He couldn't. The idea was still with him and it wouldn't let him rest.

It was an amazing idea. Crazy? Possibly. Probably.

'It's too soon to even think about it,' he muttered into his pillow. 'Give it time. Meanwhile, friendly, formal and distant. She needs to trust.'

And so did he, he thought, and that was a bigger ask.

Four weeks...

Maybe?

CHAPTER TEN

THE EXPEDITION TO City Hall Station took some organising. Clothes were the first thing. Both Sunny and Phoebe needed fitting out to face New York's winter. 'I can go with them,' Eliza said, but Max had his word to stick to and he did. Thus, armed with baby advice from Eliza and advice from his secretary—bemused by her boss's absence and his requests for help on women's fashion—they spent a day shopping. And doing a little exploring as well.

'I know you've seen a thousand pictures of our lady but you need to see her in person,' Max growled and the three of them took a chartered boat and sailed the harbour.

It was a practice run to see how Phoebe took to exploring and the answer was very well. Warmly ensconced in a padded carry cocoon, she allowed herself to be carried at will. She woke to feed and be cuddled and then went back to sleep again.

So Sunny was free to enjoy the day and she did enjoy it. She was dressed in the most beautiful jacket she'd ever owned, plus warm pants and sheepskin-lined boots. She was sitting in the back of a luxurious cruiser, watching the sights of New York's harbour, with Max beside her giving an intelligent and sometimes fun commentary. How could she not enjoy herself?

How could she not let herself be drawn into the illusion that there was more…?

That this man beside her was making her laugh because he cared?

That was crazy. He was being nice. He'd kissed her the

night before because…well, he was a man and she was a woman and she'd practically asked for it.

He'd pulled away the moment she'd stiffened.

He was an honourable man.

She tried—hard—to stop thinking of Max the man and concentrate instead on his commentary. It containted gems that had her fascinated. Did she know that Albert Einstein's eyeballs were stored in a safe deposit box in the city? That there were tiny shrimp called copepods in Manhattan's drinking water? Or once upon a time there'd been a pneumatic mail tube system dug about four feet underground, capable of moving over ninety thousand letters a day around the whole island? 'I wish I could show you,' Max said sadly. 'But some fool seems to have dug it up.' He looked so despondent she almost giggled—okay, she did giggle—and then she thought, *Wow*, she, Sunny Raye, was being given a personalised tour of Manhattan by Max Grayland.

'Did you know all this or did you research it for the day?' she asked and he grinned.

'I asked my secretary for a list of New York's oddest. She now thinks I've lost my mind.'

And that did her head in too. She was in some sort of dream, she decided, as she gazed up at the truly magnificent Statue of Liberty. Max was right—it was far better than in the pictures.

So was Max Grayland. He had Phoebe strapped against his chest. He was smiling at her, watching her enjoy herself, wanting her to enjoy herself. She knew from his phone calls—he kept it on silent, simply glancing at the screen now and then to ensure the sky hadn't fallen—that the sky *could* almost fall at his behest and yet, not only was he sticking by his word to care for Phoebe, he was making every effort he could to ensure Sunny was having fun.

It was a dream. Australia was half a world away. She,

Sunny, was having fun with a guy who, quite simply, made her toes curl.

'You're blushing,' Max said, on a note of discovery. 'What is it about our lady that makes you blush?' He glanced up at the enormous statue looming above their heads. 'As far as I can see, she's very respectably dressed.'

'I'm not blushing. I'm just…flushed.'

'Coat too hot?' he asked solicitously and, yeah, it was a lot too hot but it wasn't the coat and there wasn't a thing she could do about it.

'What…what next?' she managed.

'Empire State Building?' he queried. 'And then maybe it's time to go home.'

Home. There was another loaded word.

What was it about that statement that made her want to blush all over again?

They kept their hands off each other that night—with difficulty. *Ten out of ten*, Sunny told herself as she snuggled under her gorgeous bedclothes. She wasn't really tired but there was no way she was watching Max give Phoebe her last feed.

She had to keep her distance. Employer/employee. That was their relationship and it had to stay that way.

Except…the way he looked at her… She couldn't figure it out. It was as if he didn't understand what she was. As if he was trying to figure some puzzle that wouldn't come right. She almost asked, but whenever he caught her looking at him he'd smile and it'd make something twist inside her and she backed off in fright.

He didn't understand?

Neither did she, and it was starting to seriously scare her.

The next day they did City Hall Station.

There were tour groups that came down here—she'd read

about them. Tour groups, however, were not for Max Grayland. He'd contacted a Professor of Urban Studies, Francis, a guy who'd apparently gone to university with Max, a friend who seemed to have the keys to practically all of Manhattan's underground and who professed it would be his pleasure to take them down.

'What would you like to know?' Francis asked Sunny as they trod the great underground cavern. Max stood back with Phoebe strapped to his chest and appeared to enjoy it as Sunny learned more than she'd believed possible about New York's network of rail tunnels. Past, present, future. Francis knew the entire history, everything she could possibly want to know. She drank it in, and for a while she even forgot Max was watching.

'You need someone with architecture knowledge as well,' Francis told her. He turned back to Max. 'Max, you know Tom Clifford? Anything you want to know about historical tunnelling, he's your man, and I believe he'll be in town this weekend. How about you and Sunny come to dinner? Tom and Sunny can go hammer and tongs and the rest of us can learn and enjoy.'

'I don't…we don't go out,' Sunny said, too fast. Oh, for heaven's sake, as if she was part of Max Grayland's social life… 'Phoebe…'

'Hmm, yeah.' Francis smiled benignly at the sleeping bundle on Max's chest. 'My wife and I have three rug rats. They do cramp your style. But surely you have a nanny.'

'I'm the nanny,' Sunny managed.

'She's not.' Max had hardly spoken but he intervened now, putting a hand on Sunny's shoulder. And why the touch should go through her…

She was wearing three layers of padding to protect her from the creeping cold associated with being so far underground. There was no way she should feel it.

She felt it as if his fingers were on her naked skin.

She shuddered, and Max felt it.

'Time to go up,' he decreed. 'No, Sunny's not a nanny; she's a friend helping out until I find one. But dinner sounds a great idea. At my place. Francis, you and your wife? Tom and his partner? Anyone else who'd enjoy the conversation?'

'Mary Rutherford's into the history of the rail network. She's great company. I could persuade her.'

'Max…' Sunny said, feeling desperate. 'I can't…'

'Hey, there's nothing to this,' Max reassured her. 'This is Manhattan. There's a whole world of caterers out there. I'll have my secretary organise it. All you need to do, Sunny, is sit back and enjoy it.'

'That's not what I'm here for.'

'Yes, it is,' he told her and he smiled, and such a smile… It was all she could do not to gasp. But the smile had been fleeting and he'd turned back to Francis. 'So… Saturday? Anyone else you can think of who Sunny might enjoy grilling? I might need to do some pre-dinner research to keep up.'

And it was done.

Saturday night. Sunny had thrown every objection she could think of at him and he'd overruled them all.

The final one had been dress and that was the biggest hurdle. He and Phoebe had escorted her to the salon his secretary had told him of and she'd looked at the prices and almost had kittens.

'No way,' she'd declared, walking straight out. 'With that sort of money I could buy a new wheelchair for Pa. Not a dress for a night.'

'I'll pay for a wheelchair anyway,' he growled and she looked at him as if he'd lost his mind.

'You're my boss, not my sugar daddy. But, seeing you've organised this dinner…' He'd given her a credit card as promised and now she took it from her purse and looked at it doubtfully. 'You're sure I can use this?'

'Absolutely. It's part of the deal.'

'You've already bought me cold weather gear. But now…
if I can take a couple of hours off…'

'Of course.'

'I promise I won't abuse it.'

'I'd enjoy watching you abuse it.'

'The coat was bad enough,' she retorted. 'Having you
watch while I try on slinky gowns…'

'I'd definitely enjoy it.'

She'd grinned, but it was a grin that put him in his place.
It said sexy banter was just that, banter, and he needed to
shut up.

So he shut up and hoped she'd choose something that
wouldn't make her feel like a poor relation when she met
for dinner with people he knew had style and impeccable
taste and confidence.

But when she emerged from her room on Saturday night
she took his breath away.

She was wearing a dress of silver-grey lace, a frock that
would have been equally at home in a nineteen-twenties
drawing room as it was here. It was a simple tube, scoop-
necked, reaching to just above her knees. The tube consisted
entirely of circles of fringing, soft, silky and delicate, and
it shimmered as she moved, so even though the dress itself
seemed shapeless, somehow it accentuated every one of her
delicious curves.

She was wearing silver court shoes with kitten heels. A
single rope of some kind of white shell that shimmered like
pearls. Tiny matched earrings.

Her hair had been let loose. It was tucked behind her
ears but cascaded to her shoulders in a mass of shiny curls.

Her make-up was simple—a touch of lipstick, a brush of
blush to accentuate her beautiful cheekbones.

She looked so lovely she took his breath away.

'How…how is it?' she asked a little self-consciously and he didn't answer for a moment. He couldn't.

But she looked worried. 'I found it in a vintage shop in Soho and it was a bit battered,' she told him. 'I had to sew a lot of the lace back on but I love it. It's not too much for to-night? They won't think I'm doing a fancy dress?'

'They will *not* think you're doing a fancy dress,' he breathed and then the doorbell pealed and it was the cater-ers and waiting staff he'd hired for the occasion, and it was just as well because if they hadn't arrived then, who knew what would have happened?

All Max knew was that he felt as if he'd just been punched. Hard. Or was that the wrong word? Wrong metaphor—punched?

Knocked sideways.

He wanted to lock the door, lock the world out and spend the night alone with this woman. He wanted to touch her bare shoulders, draw her to him, feel the soft silk mould to his body.

And the idea that had been an embryo just days ago was growing. It was starting to become…something that seemed a consummation devoutly to be wished?

If he could pull it off…

But he needed to keep his hands off her now. He needed not to scare her, to keep things businesslike, to let her see how they could make things work.

But meanwhile the caterers were heading for the kitchen and Sunny was looking doubtful, as if she really imagined her appearance might be inappropriate. Which was so far from the truth…

'You look beautiful,' he told her and he thought of the minuscule amount he'd seen when he'd checked his credit card details after her shopping expedition. He'd come close to demanding to see what she'd bought so he could march her out to buy something more suitable—but no money in the world could make her look more beautiful than she did right now. 'You're perfect,' he added and she blushed and the temptation to kiss her was so great...

'Thank you,' she said simply. 'I'll check on Phoebe before the guests arrive.'

'I can do that.'

'That's what I'm here for,' she said, almost sternly. 'You're being incredibly generous but I'm not about to forget my role.' The doorbell pealed again and she nodded, affirming the truth for herself. 'Go and greet your guests, Max,' she told him. 'I'll meet you in the dining room, as long as Phoebe doesn't need me.'

Phoebe was sound asleep. The baby monitor was routed to the dining room. There was nothing for Sunny to do but return.

She didn't for a while, though. She stood and gazed down at the sleeping baby. She thought of Max greeting guests, in his jet-black Italian suit with crisp white shirt, his silk tie, a billionaire at the top of his game. And she thought of the way he'd looked at her.

I need to be so careful. She almost whispered it aloud but the intercom was on and she wasn't so far gone to forget where she was.

Or who she was.

I'm here to do a job, she told herself as she listened to the sound of arriving guests, of Max meeting them with the ease of long-standing friendship or, in the case of those he hadn't met, with the assurance of his place in the world.

I'm a hotel cleaner, she told herself. *Remember it. Max has invited these people to meet you. Which is very good of him. If I ever get to study architecture they might... I might...*

But the impossibility of *might* was enough to bring her to her senses. She knew why she was here and she knew what she was going home to.

It's just a dinner, she told herself. *With a boss who's being charming to an employee. So the boss kissed the chambermaid? That's the way things have been since time immemorial. Get over it, Sunny. Move on.*

The voices from the dining room seemed relaxed. There was laughter, banter, ease of social standing.

So stay in the background like a good little employee, she told herself. *Know your place. Okay, Sunny Raye, big breath. You can do this.*

But heaven only knew the courage it took to walk through that door.

For the first part of the dinner Sunny seemed deliberately retiring. The talk was general as his guests got to know each other, friendly and unthreatening. Sunny was asked about her home in Australia, her thoughts on New York, but mostly she was left alone. She seemed to want it that way.

After the main course Phoebe woke and Sunny excused herself. Through the intercom they heard Sunny's soft crooning as Phoebe fed and then settled.

'She's some lady.' His friend, Francis, had listened to her in the tunnel and had been impressed. Now he was eyeing Max with speculation. Max tried for a non-committal shrug but Francis had known him for a long time. Maybe he saw… what he was thinking?

And when Sunny returned it was Francis who deliberately brought Sunny into the conversation. He led the discussion to the tunnels underpinning Manhattan, and from there to the history of tunnelling, to the architecture involved, to the engineering that formed the foundations for almost every city in the world.

Who'd have thought tunnels could be so fascinating? Max thought. Maybe they weren't, but he was fascinated with Sunny's response.

They were talking of the Lincoln Tunnel, built in the

nineteen-thirties to carry traffic under the Hudson. 'There may be problems in the future,' Francis was saying and Sunny nodded. Her decision to stay in the background faltered in the face of Francis's determination to have her join in.

'Battery Park City,' she murmured and Francis eyed her cautiously.

'You know the problems?'

'I guess…' She seemed almost embarrassed.

'I don't know of any problems,' Max said and she cast him a look that was almost resentful. She'd asked questions as they'd talked and they'd been intelligent but she'd been backward in contributing. He thought that it had been like that at Christmas, probably for most of her life. Sunny's siblings were deemed the 'intelligent' ones, the ones with the education. Sunny stayed in the background and listened.

But she was caught now, by Francis's interest and by Max's direct probe. He watched her hesitate, almost as if she was afraid to reveal what she knew. But the interest around her was friendly. She'd had a couple of glasses of wine.

He almost saw her give a mental shrug.

'The Hudson River's main current has always been close to the edge of Lower Manhattan,' she told him. 'As far as I understand, building Battery Park City has rerouted it. The current's now closer to the river centre and it's washing away much of the soil on the walls and ceiling of the tunnel. It means they're a lot more susceptible to shifting and cracking. It's a huge problem the world over—a demonstration of why city planners need to take a broader view. When the initial rail tunnels were built there was an overview of every surface and underground construction. Now…it's like a rabbit warren as each developer fights for space.' She eyed him speculatively, almost challengingly. 'The Grayland Corporation has fingers in Battery Park projects, I believe. And you're not aware of it?'

She arched an eyebrow, gently quizzing, and beside her Francis gave a snort of laughter. 'Well, well. A lady with an overview of the entire Grayland Corporation—in your own home. You're in trouble, Max.'

This was his father's legacy. He'd already taken steps to counter such problems in the future, so now he could grin and hold up his hands in surrender. He could defend his company's structural sensitivities and move on.

The moment passed but the conversation had changed. Sunny was now a respected participant.

She was no longer the nanny. Not even close. As they talked of the difficulties of maintaining past tunnels and building new ones, as they discussed soil density and rock formation and river flow, as they talked of population growth and the need to accommodate more, she held her own and pushed further.

She hadn't learned all this in the last few days, he thought, stunned. How much had she stored in that head of hers while she'd scrubbed floors?

He found himself resenting it when others spoke. All he wanted was to listen, sit back and watch. She was smart, funny, quick. She was warm, loyal, loving.

She was perfect.

She was a woman he'd never thought he'd meet.

A woman he'd be proud to call his...wife?

He sat as the conversation washed around him and let the concept drift.

Three weeks ago he'd been single, schooled in independence by a cold, isolated upbringing. That had been okay. Independence had its own rewards.

But Phoebe's arrival had changed that. He'd had a choice: adopt the child and rear her with love, or walk away. He hadn't been able to walk, and his precious independence was shattered.

But then came Sunny. This woman was a life-saver. She'd

rescued him from a situation that did his head in. She'd shown him how to love, what warmth was, what commitment was, and he wanted it. He wanted it for Phoebe and now...as he watched her he thought he wanted it for himself.

And the thought was there, a selfish niggle but one that stayed reassuringly in place. With Sunny here as his wife, as Phoebe's...mom...he could go back to the life he knew. His commitment to his financial empire could stay unchanged. He'd not have the emotional burden of thinking Phoebe was home with a paid nanny. He wouldn't have to check and check again, or go through the emotional turmoil he remembered as a child when a beloved nanny left.

And when he did come home...this place would be different. Sunny would be here as she was now, smart, feisty, welcoming. They could still hire a nanny, but part-time. Sunny could study her beloved architecture but that'd be in college hours. When he got home she'd be here.

Family. Ready-built.

And it'd be great for her. The change to her life would be amazing. No more scrubbing... He could help her family back home...

The concept got better and better, and Francis glanced across the table at him and raised his brows.

'You're looking smug.'

'Smug?' *Uh-oh.* He schooled his expression with haste. There were things he needed to put in place before he could afford to look smug. Like asking her.

But how could she say no? He knew she was as attracted to him as he was to her. He could feel it. They'd lived together for weeks now, first at her grandparents' house and then here. He could feel the frisson of sexual tug that happened whenever they came close.

'I like it when a plan comes together,' he admitted to Francis. 'Like this dinner. You guys seem to be hitting it off.'

'I'm taking Sunny for a tour of a couple of our old rail

tunnels the general public don't know about,' Francis told him. 'We'll organise it as soon as she has a day off.'

'A day off?'

'Isn't Sunny working as your nanny?'

'Sunny's not a nanny,' he growled, almost roughly. 'Sunny's my...godsend. Sunny's my friend.'

She didn't feel like a friend.

The dinner over, guests and caterers departed, Max did a fast check on his emails and went to find Sunny. She was watching a sleeping Phoebe.

She'd kicked off her shoes. She was still wearing her beautiful dress. Her curls were soft and shining. He stood at the door and watched her in the dim light, bent almost protectively over the cot.

They'd moved the cot into his room now. The room was massive. A vast bed. A cot with a sleeping baby. Moonlight playing in the window and a beautiful woman standing guard.

He walked slowly forward and placed his hands on her waist. He felt her stiffen but only for a moment. He felt the instant she decided to relax, the moment her body leaned back into his, the instant her loveliness curved against his chest.

'It was a great night,' he said softly and he couldn't help himself; he buried his face into her curls and kissed her.

'It was.' But was she trembling?

He turned her to face him. She looked troubled. Doubtful. Scared?

'Sunny, I won't...if you don't want this...'

'That's just the problem,' she whispered. 'I know it's dumb. I know it's unwise, but oh, Max, I do want this.'

'Then as one consenting adult to another...' He cupped her chin and kissed her lips, a kiss so tender it almost blew him away. He didn't know he could kiss like this. He didn't know he could care. 'Sunny, as one consenting adult to another, would you do me the very great honour of coming to my bed?'

She drew back a little, watching him in the moonlight, her face still troubled.

'Because?'

'Because I want you,' he said honestly because there was no room for anything but honesty between them right now. 'But Sunny, it's more. I think… I think I'm starting to love you.'

'Well, how about that?' Her voice was a breathless whisper. 'How about that for a miracle, Max Grayland? Because… because I think I'm starting to love you, too.'

CHAPTER ELEVEN

WHAT FOLLOWED WAS two weeks of time out of frame. Two weeks of fantasy.

For two weeks they were a make-believe family. Max seemed to drop almost everything and devote himself to her and to Phoebe.

With Phoebe strapped securely against Max's chest, they explored New York in winter.

Every morning when she woke Sunny was presented with a list of things he thought might be fun. Museums. Art galleries. A flea market. A New Year firecracker ceremony. A winter jazz festival. A snow carnival with ice carving. They were hers to choose, but Max put himself behind every one of them with enthusiasm and enjoyment.

They'd even ended up at a knitting festival where he'd tried his hand, then bought wool and declared his intention of knitting Phoebe a scarf. She'd watched him that night, laboriously casting on and dropping stitches while they waited up for Phoebe's last feed. In helpless laughter, with the wool a tangled knot, they'd made a mutual decision that knitting wasn't their forte.

She'd watched him carefully untangle the knot. She'd thought of the business empire this man controlled and her sense of fantasy had deepened.

But how could she care that it was fantasy? She was so in love.

For every night he took her to his bed and she fell deeper and deeper…

Max Grayland. A fantasy?

Her love.

How could she leave? She knew she must, but she wouldn't—she couldn't think of it yet.

A week before she was due to leave she woke in his arms and her sense of peace and contentment was all-enveloping. Fantasy seemed real and she let herself believe. How could she not? The morning light started to filter though the half-closed curtains. She was warm, she was sated—she was sleeping in the arms of the man she loved.

She'd never thought this could happen to her and, miraculously, it seemed to be returned. The way Max held her…the way he looked at her, laughed with her, loved her…

Her body seemed his and vice versa. From the moment he'd lifted her joyously and carried her to his bed it seemed as if this was her place. This was where she'd been meant to be all her life.

How could this be fantasy?

And yet it was. She knew that. Her life was half a world away, and yet who was thinking forward? Not her. She couldn't bear to. Only here and now mattered.

Phoebe lay sleeping in her crib on the far side of the room, a contented cherub who had no idea she'd been abandoned. Who acted as if she'd been loved all her life.

So what of the future?

Forget the future, Sunny told herself. For now she was milking this moment for everything it was worth, taking Max's love and savouring it because…because…

There was no *because*. There was no need to worry about the future. It was all *now*.

Her face was resting on Max's chest. It should be an uncomfortable sleeping position but Max's arms held her, supported her, cradled her body against him as if she were the most precious thing…

What it was to be precious in this man's eyes…

'Awake already?' he whispered, his voice teasing, and

she knew his eyes would already be glinting with laughter. In these last weeks there'd been so much…joy.

Joy to last a lifetime.

Do not think forward.

'I'm dozing,' she whispered back. 'Don't move. I think I'm in heaven.'

'Really?'

'Okay, I know I'm in heaven.'

'Me too,' he whispered but he did move and it was entirely appropriate that he did because heaven just got better.

Love… She let it take her where it would. Her surrender—and his—was complete.

When finally they surfaced the sun was streaming in. It was a stunningly perfect winter's day. Phoebe was still sleeping but soon she'd stir. Their day would begin.

Seven days to go…

The last weeks had been…heaven. Sure, they'd had a tiny baby to care for but somehow she'd fitted right into their plans—right into their hearts?

'I'd like to walk all the way around Central Park today,' she ventured. There'd been so many things she'd seen, but the weather hadn't permitted a full circuit.

'Can we do that tomorrow? The forecast is for this weather to hold.' He was holding her close, hugging her as if she belonged. Skin against skin… It was the most erotic sensation in the world. 'Sunny…my secretary's lined up nanny interviews this afternoon. I'd like you to sit in.'

'Of course.' That was what she was here for after all, but the thought was an intrusion, an acknowledgment that what was happening now was a dream. Time out of frame. A nanny would take over. Max would return to his high-pressure world.

She'd go…home.

'But first…' He kissed her gently on the lips, a feather touch, a touch of such intimacy she could weep. 'If it's okay... I've organised time out, something just for us. Eliza's coming in to look after Phoebe. The nanny appointments are scheduled from three and after, so we'll have time together.'

'You've planned this.'

'I have.' Once more he kissed her. 'Sunny, I need this day to be even more special than it is already.'

And then he gathered her even closer, the kiss became deeper, the need became more urgent...and there was no room for questions. There was room only for each other.

He wouldn't tell her where they were going. 'Wear what you wore underground,' he said and he dressed that way as well, in a cool leather jacket, casual pants, a cashmere scarf that made him look...

Okay, she shouldn't think of how he looked.

His car—with chauffeur—dropped them at the Rockefeller Center.

'How are you on ice?' he asked as he led her through the complex and she stopped so fast the couple walking behind them almost bumped into them.

'Ice?'

'I thought we might skate.'

'You're kidding.'

'This is the coolest ice rink in the world.'

'And I don't skate. I've never seen ice bigger than little cubes you put in drinks.'

'You don't rollerblade? Ski?'

She didn't move, all the memories of her rubbish childhood flooding back. Watching other kids skateboard and rollerblade. Listening to kids telling tales of how their parents had taken them to the admittedly sparse Australian ski fields. Saving so she could buy roller skates for her siblings.

Not for her.

'No,' she said shortly. And then she thought that was no

reason to spoil what for him seemed a very exciting plan. 'But it'll be fun to watch you.'

'I have no intention of letting you watch,' he told her and there was that smile again. 'I pretty much guessed you'd have no experience. I was just checking. Will you trust me? This'll be fun.'

Really? Fun for who?

But Max wasn't listening to her protests. He led her on until the vast ice rink stretched before them. It wasn't crowded—apparently Tuesday morning wasn't the time for most people to skate—but there were enough skaters flying around the rink, spinning, doing figures of eight, totally at ease with their environment, for her doubts to consolidate into one great wall of objection.

'I can't.'

'But I can,' he said gently and then he asked again. 'Trust me?'

Oh, for heaven's sake... She'd break a leg. She'd have her fingers sliced off. She'd be carried home in a box...

'I won't let that happen,' he said and she almost glared. How dare this man see what she was thinking? Was she so transparent?

'Trust me,' he said for the third time, and she gazed into his face. She thought of the warmth, the heat, the strength of this body she was starting to know and love so much and there was only one answer.

But first a quibble. 'My pet goldfish...' she murmured.

'What?'

'I need a pen and paper to write an advanced directive. If I die Daisy will want her, because she's the responsible one, but she won't talk to her and Flippy likes to chat. Flippy goes to Sam.'

'You're planning on writing a will—right here and now?'

'I want it legal,' she told him. 'A paper napkin will do and a couple of random skaters for witnesses.'

'Okay,' he said faintly. 'But then you'll skate?'

'You swear I'll come out in one piece?'

'I swear.'

'I hold you to your promise but you never know. Flippy gets catered for first.'

So minutes later…skates on, standing—shakily—at the edge of the gorgeous rink, looking at skilled skaters using every inch of the ice, looking at the magnificent golden statue at the end of the rink, seeing the myriad sightseers watching the skaters…

She was ready?

She was so unready it was ridiculous.

'Max…'

'Trust me,' he said for the fourth time and his arm came around her waist, strong and sure. 'Relax and let me guide you. Come on, Sunny, let's fly.' And that's exactly what happened. Somehow, some way, she was out on the ice, flying over its surface, held tightly against Max… She was… skating.

She was really skating!

Or… not. If he was a matador, she was the cape, but in his skilled hands she moved as if she was born on the rink.

This man was seriously good. He skated as if it was a part of him—and she was another part. Or maybe not a part. Maybe she'd melted into him, been absorbed, just… Sunny and Max.

For the first few seconds she fought to relax, she had to school herself to trust him, but as she felt his skill, as she felt his strength and certainty, she found herself relaxing. More. Enjoying.

Loving?

For that was what this was. It was subjugation of her body to his but in a way that could only bring joy. She could think of nothing but this moment. There was no future, no past, simply this man spinning her around, moving her with a deftness that made her feel...

Like Torvill and Dean? The image of the world-famous Olympians sprang to mind and she almost choked on laughter. If she simply let Max do what he willed...

'What's funny?' he asked into her hair as they spun seamlessly together and she smiled back. Her body was moulded to his. If he let her go she'd be a puddle on the ice in seconds, but he wouldn't let her go. She knew it. She knew this man.

'I'm thinking Olympics R Us,' she managed and he chuckled and held her tighter.

'It's the together,' he told her. 'Together we can do anything we like. The world is ours, Sunny Raye. Let's just enjoy it.'

And she did.

Could he do this? Take this one last step?

As he held her and skated, he felt his world almost dissolve in love and laughter and desire. But it didn't quite dissolve. There remained a part of him that was almost separate, watching from above, seeing what he was doing and testing it for sense.

The sensible part of him, the part that had formed from childhood, turning finally and harshly into a dark, aloof entity the day they'd wrenched a pup from him and told him to grow up, that part said it was risky.

Could he do this? Could he love this woman and keep himself safe?

There were so many positives. Sunny would gain so much. Phoebe would grow up without that dark fear he had. And he...

He'd have Sunny beside him, curled against him in the dark, trusting, loving...

He could love her. He could keep her safe. They could be a family.

The two sides of him had warred since he'd met her, but now, holding her close as they spun, as she laughed and held him, as he felt her warmth, her trust...

He could love her. He would. The two sides of him could find some way of moving forward.

Some things were worth the risk.

She was so exhausted she could hardly speak. She was so in love...

When even Max was breathless, he led her from the rink, helped her remove her skates and took her to a tiny café high up, overlooking the rink, seemingly overlooking the whole of Manhattan.

They ate pancakes, piled high with creamed butter and maple syrup, with vast bowls of strawberries on the side. They drank coffee like Sunny had never tasted before. Nothing had ever tasted like this before. The world seemed to have changed. It was no longer her world. It was a fantasy.

And then, as the waiter cleared their dishes, as they were left in their private space, Max leaned over and took her hand.

And then, just as she thought the fantasy couldn't get any better, he opened his other hand.

A box.

Crimson velvet.

Tiny.

He flicked it open and he smiled into her eyes with such tenderness she forgot to breathe. How could she breathe? Did she need to when this was a fairy tale?

But he was speaking. Somehow she had to pretend it was real.

Somehow she had to catch her breath.

'Sunny Raye,' he said, softly but surely. 'I can't think of a better time or a better place. I've fallen deeply in love with you, so deeply that I never want to let you go. So there's only one question to ask. Will you do me the very great honour of becoming my wife?'

My wife...

A ring...

She felt as if she'd been shifted into a parallel universe.

He was handing her a ring.

How could she get her voice to work?

What was she supposed to say? Was she supposed to pretend this fairy tale was real?

Yes! Every single fibre of her being screamed it. She wanted the fairy tale. She gazed down at the perfect diamond set in white gold, and the compulsion to slip it on her finger was so great it was like a physical force.

To marry this man she loved... To love Max Grayland for ever...

But in the end it was the skating that made her hesitate. It was the skating that made her look up into Max's eyes, to see the love, but also something else.

And some survival instinct played back his words.

I never want to let you go.

The skating... He'd held her close. She'd been safe and she'd had fun but he'd been totally in control.

This was his world.

I never want to let you go.

So instead of looking mistily into his eyes and whispering what her heart most wanted—*Yes!*—she found another part of her answering. A part she didn't want to acknowledge, but there seemed no choice.

'How...how would that work?' She could barely get the words out. 'Max...how could marriage to me possibly work?'

'Brilliantly.' He was still holding her hand. The ring still lay on its bed of velvet, a siren song. It would be so easy to slip it on.

'But…how?'

'I have it planned. That's why I needed to talk to you before we interview the nannies this afternoon. I thought I'd need a full-time nanny but…'

'But you'll marry me instead?'

'That's not the way I'd ever intend it,' he said, suddenly harsh, in a voice that said he spoke absolute truth. 'I don't need to marry you to provide a nanny for Phoebe. I hope you know me better than that.'

'Then…'

'But we'll still need one.' His hold on her hand tightened.

She looked into his face and she thought, *He has this all figured.* She'd come in on this late. He had his plans in place.

'You want to study architecture,' he told her. 'That can be arranged.'

'I don't have schooling…'

'You'd pass every entrance test they could ever devise and I can pull strings. I can get you in. You can do it part-time if you like—that'd give you time to catch up on gaps you might have—or full-time if you want. That's why we need to think about what we need the nanny for. I need to go back to work and give it my total commitment. I'll cut back a bit—of course—but I can't be depended on to be here for Phoebe. But you'd be here for her. The nanny would do the hard yards but she'd have you to love. And when I come home…we'll be a family.'

'When you come home…'

'I'll do the best I can,' he told her. 'But my job's huge. But Sunny, think. Us. Family. No more cleaning. No more scrubbing your hands raw and worrying about money. I can take care of your grandparents…'

'Now that's something I don't understand.' And suddenly something inside her was growing angry. She hardly understood but the world was starting to look…a little bit red? 'How can you do that? Chloe and Tom are due to go back to university at the end of summer. They lead their own lives. Are you intending to keep paying them to stay on with Gran and Pa?'

'I can afford a carer—a good one. You can fly home and do the interviewing if you like. In fact you'd probably like to marry from there. I can take a little more time off if you need my help. We can take Phoebe with us, take the time to set things up to make them safe.'

'By employing strangers.' Her voice sounded hollow.

The ring was still on the table. The joy she'd felt on seeing it had disappeared completely. It seemed to be mocking her.

Why? Why couldn't she just say yes? She could fall into his arms. She could live in his beautiful apartment for ever. She could love a little girl she… Well, to be honest, she already did love.

She could love a man she already did love.

'Sunny…' The hold on her hand was compelling. 'You've put yourself last almost from the time of your birth. You've done everything for your family that you possibly could. It's time to let me help.'

'By employing strangers.'

'By letting me make them safe. By giving you the chance to stop being a martyr.'

'Is that what you think I am—a martyr?'

'Yes,' he said gently. 'You've done it for love but you're a martyr nevertheless. I love you for it but I won't let you continue. It's Sunny's time.'

'I don't think…' She was struggling to get her mind to work. 'Max, I don't think doing anything for love can possibly be martyrdom. It's just what you do.'

'And you have done it. But it's done. Dusted. It's time for you to stop being needed.'

'So if I lived with you… I wouldn't be needed.'

'You'd be loved—of course you'd be loved. But I wouldn't let Phoebe's needs stand in the way of your ambitions. We'll employ the right nanny so you can be as involved as you want.'

'But I wasn't talking about Phoebe.' Still her voice sounded hollow. Dull. She knew it but there wasn't a thing she could do about it. 'I was talking about you. Would you need me, Max?'

'I want you.'

'That's not the same.'

'Haven't you had enough of being needed?'

'Yes. No!' She was so confused. The tenderness, the romance of the moment was gone.

'Sunny, not everyone needs like your family does.'

'You don't need anyone?'

'I've worked on that. Needing causes pain and I won't go there. But Sunny, loving you…it'd bring joy…'

'In the time we had available. The time between your business commitments. These weeks…they've been a time out for you, but you want to go back.'

'I have to go back.'

'To your business.'

'It's what I am.'

'And there's the difference.' She was struggling to speak, struggling to get the words out. 'My work isn't what I am.'

'Because you're a cleaner.'

'That's insulting. As if what I do isn't important…'

'How can it be?'

'Because it's just work? And yours is different?' She rose, pushing her chair back so fast it almost fell. The knot of anger inside her couldn't be contained. But was it anger?

It was desolation. It was a sinking sense of certainty. It was the knowledge that the ring lying on the table could never be hers.

She took a deep breath and struggled to stay calm. To be still. To say it like it was.

'What's important is family,' she told him. 'I understand…

you've never had that so you don't know. You've made your-self believe that independence is the most important thing, but believe me...' She closed her eyes. 'The day after Mum died... When the social workers came and took the kids to foster homes... They told me they'd be safe and cared for and that was the most important thing, but I was fourteen years old and I knew it wasn't. Even at fourteen I knew that love was bigger, and I knew I'd give up everything to get it right. Tell me, Max, what will you do if—when—Phoebe needs you? Will you drop anything and go to her? Or will you send a nanny?'

'If she really needs...'

'Define *needs*,' she said harshly. 'Does she have to fall under a bus for that need to kick in? What if she just needs a cuddle? Or someone to read to her every night?'

'If it's minor...' He was hopelessly out of his depth and she knew it. He didn't understand, and it was useless try-ing to change it.

The situation was impossible. The whole thing was im-possible.

She reached down and flipped the top of the crimson box closed. It closed with a snap that seemed to resound through the restaurant.

Dream over.

'It can't work,' she said dully. 'This time...for me it's been magic. A dream. But that's all it can be, a dream. I wish for Phoebe's sake—and, okay, for ours—that I could say yes but I'd be giving up too much. Gran and Pa need me. Daisy and Sam and Chloe and Tom are part of what I am. They're my family. Yes, they can put too many demands on me, and yes, sometimes I resent it, but love goes both ways. I need them as much as they need me. Living with you... Loving a man who gives and gives and never acknowledges that need is a part of loving too...' She shook her head. 'Okay, I'm not making sense. I can see that you don't understand and I can't help. But please…accept it's over. Let's go interview these nannies because we need one soon. I'm going home, Max. I'm going back to where I belong.'

There was no way to dissuade her.

They worked their way through the list of nannies. Sunny was a great interviewer. She asked questions he would never have thought of.

How are you at cuddles? What's your favourite kids' storybook? What would you do if the kindergarten teacher phoned and said Phoebe's just bitten someone? How do you feel about puppies? What do you feel is the most important part of your job?

The one who stood out was Karen, a single mum with a toddler of her own, Harry.

'How do you feel about living in if you get the job?' Sunny asked and Max pretty much froze. To have two kids…

But Karen was warm and caring, and as she left Sunny turned to him and said, 'She's perfect.'

And he knew she was. He'd been around Sunny long enough now to know what perfect was.

Only Sunny was more perfect.

'And she can start now,' Sunny said in satisfaction. 'Which means I can go home.'

'I don't want you to go home.'

'That's where I'm needed,' she told him and before he could say anything more she'd backed away and headed to the sanctuary of her own room.

A room she hadn't used for two weeks because she'd slept with him.

Her rejection had him stunned. What was between them was so right. She was everything he'd ever wanted in a woman. Their bodies meshed. Her intelligence blew him away. Her warmth and humour reached parts of him he hadn't known existed.

He could offer her so much and yet her rejection of his offer had been instantaneous.

She'd said no and she meant it. She was going home and he had no way of stopping her.

Except by changing.

But how could she expect him to change when he didn't have a clue what she was on about?

He was gutted but he was also…angry? To throw away what he was offering…

Don't think about it, he told himself. *It's her choice. Head into the study, draw up a contract for the new nanny and then get on with your life.*

Move on alone, as you always have. You should know by now that it's the only way.

And, as if on cue, while Sunny lay sleepless, staring at the ceiling, her cell phone rang.

Chloe.

'Sunny, Pa's had another stroke. Not…not fatal, we think. We hope. We're not even sure how bad it is but…we thought you'd want to know.'

'Oh, Chloe…' Sunny heard sobs suppressed behind her sister's voice. They matched the sobs she'd been trying to suppress herself.

'I'll come home,' she said.

'I don't think… I wish I could say…'

'Don't say anything at all,' Sunny told her. 'I'm coming.'

She disconnected. Then she headed for the bathroom and washed her face.

The light showed under Max's door. She knocked and asked for his help.

At eight the next morning the jet took off, heading for Australia.

The dream was over. She was on her way home.

CHAPTER TWELVE

It was a huge day in the life of Phoebe Raye Grayland.

And of Max.

The adoption had taken almost a year to organise but this afternoon Max had stood in front of a judge with Phoebe in his arms. He'd promised to provide her with a loving home, for ever and ever.

He'd expected it to be a formality, a simple signing of documents. Instead, as the attorney had asked him to confirm before the judge his intention to love her and care for her, he'd felt something shift inside him. Something huge.

And then the judge had taken Phoebe from him and dandled her, and told Max how lucky he was. He'd let Phoebe have the gavel and Phoebe had banged it with gusto.

The documents were signed and sealed. Phoebe was his.

Family.

The feeling was almost overwhelming.

He should send the picture of Phoebe and the gavel to Sunny.

Would she like it that he'd added her name to Phoebe's?

He'd taken the full day off to mark the occasion. Karen and her Harry were out Christmas shopping.

Max was pushing a dozy Phoebe in her stroller, feeling… discombobulated. As if he wasn't sure how to feel.

Manhattan looked like one blazing Christmas tree, albeit an oddly shaped one. Cold had descended in earnest. There were flurries of snow in the air. Phoebe was currently wearing the cutest little Christmas hat, half beanie, half muffler.

Eliza had bought it for her. Karen had decreed it was the cutest thing and Phoebe loved its furriness. A week ago he'd arrived home to find both women clucking over his half-sister, and Phoebe grinning toothily at both of them. She'd pretty much worn it night and day since.

He'd done okay by her. She was loved.

So now she was his. *His.*

For some reason he couldn't go home. He needed this time, pushing his little sister through the throng of Christmas shoppers. To look at the shops. To lose himself...

To think of Christmas.

To think of what was happening back in Australia?

Except he shouldn't be wondering. He knew. Once a week he had an email from Sunny, outlining how things were. Her grandfather had pulled up after the stroke, weakened but still essentially okay. The new gardener he'd insisted on paying for was doing magnificently and the house repairs were very much appreciated. How was Phoebe doing?

They were grateful emails. She was embarrassed that he was doing so much, though there was so much he'd like to do that she wouldn't permit. He was permitted to help Gran and Pa, but not her. Nothing personal.

Her emails were thus filled with gratitude, plus concern and care for a child she'd learned to love.

They contained nothing to admit she might love him.

He wrote back in the same style. They'd become... friends?

At his insistence she told him the basics. She was back at the hotel, working, but she'd been promoted. She was now a team leader, so scrubbing floors was no longer part of her usual duties. She only scrubbed occasionally, in a crisis.

She was doing another subject at night school.

She was still bicycling to work, caring for her grandparents, worrying about her siblings.

Preparing for Christmas.

He'd ordered a hamper to be sent. It was filled with the most indulgent delicacies money could buy. He'd topped it with another truly extravagant box of cherry liqueur chocolates and he'd sent it in plenty of time to reach them.

Except as soon as he'd sent it he'd had doubts. Was part of Gran's pleasure in receiving the sweets the fact that Sunny gave them to her? Had Sunny already bought a cheaper version?

He was second-guessing himself and that was pretty much how he was these days. In unfamiliar territory.

In his business world he was crisp, incisive, authoritarian. His father's legacy of dubious business dealings was over. The Grayland financial empire was going from strength to strength. In the financial world, Max Grayland was a man in charge.

But he came home at night and Phoebe reached her little arms up to be cuddled and doubts crept in. He held her close, he snuggled her warm little person, he admired the new skills she'd learned that day and he wanted…someone to share.

Karen and Eliza were great but…

But yesterday Phoebe had pushed herself to a wobbly standing position. Today he'd formally adopted her. Both were huge milestones in the life of Phoebe.

And he'd wanted…he'd ached for Sunny to be there. To share it with him.

He'd taken today off but last night he'd reached home at eight, and he'd had ten minutes admiring Phoebe's new standing skill before she'd slept.

Sunny would have expected—needed—him to be home before that because Sunny needed a family. She hadn't emailed him yet this week and he guessed it was because she was caught up with Christmas preparations. He thought of the vast Christmas table at her grandparents' house, of the preparation, of the work she'd be doing to make this Christmas wonderful.

And he had to fight back a longing so powerful it made him stop dead in the street.

A Christmas tree bumped into him and apologies were everywhere. The tree—Mum and Dad under it, three kids trailing behind—went on its way and he watched its going.

Christmas trees were being half towed, half carried along the snow-covered streets, lugged by laughing friends, mums and dads, grandpas, tribes of kids. Young women breezed past him in bright, happy groups, laden with Christmas shopping. An elderly lady slipped on the icy pavement and her husband fell to his knees to help her. They were surrounded in an instant by a crowd of people aching to assist. The lady rose shakily to her feet, smiling her thanks. The old man put his arm around her and ushered her into the warmth of a nearby café.

He was lonely.

The thought almost blindsided him. He, Max Grayland, who'd carefully built his life so he needed no one, was lonely.

How could he be lonely? He had this new person in his life, a beautiful little girl he'd grown to love. Back home he had Eliza, and Karen and her little Harry, increasingly belonging, increasingly filling the apartment with charm and laughter.

At work there were people everywhere.

He was surrounded, so how could he be lonely?

They'd been walking past shop windows full of brightly lit Christmas tableaux. Phoebe had been fascinated but was now drifting to contented sleep. He needed to get her home. And there was another jolt. *Home.*

How come, filled with all these people, his apartment didn't feel like home?

It must be Christmas, he decided savagely. He hated this time of year. It did his head in. And this year, once again he couldn't hide away with his accounts and a formal dinner with his friends.

Karen and Eliza would both be spending the day with their families.

It'd be just him and Phoebe.

Oh, for heaven's sake. He was getting maudlin. What was different? He could still bring in his accounts and work when Phoebe slept. And when she was awake…they could have fun.

They'd have more fun if Sunny was here.

His phone pinged in his jacket pocket and he almost lunged to reach it. He'd set his emails to silent. They were a huge constant in his life, almost overwhelming, but there was one email address he'd given priority to, and set up an alert.

Sunny.

And the words on the screen were heart-wrenching.

Hi Max

Sorry for the silence. I had to make a decision whether to tell you and decided not to. We didn't want you making some heroic effort to come for something that really affected only our family. But I need to let you know now.

Pa died a week ago last Sunday, suddenly, in his sleep, from a massive stroke. He'd had a lovely afternoon in the garden you've helped make so beautiful. All of us had been here for one of Gran's roasts, which he presided over. He didn't eat much but he seemed happy and contented as Gran and I helped him to bed. He made one of his awful puns that made us giggle, then hugged us goodnight and went to sleep. And didn't wake.

So his passing was as good as it could be. That doesn't mean we're not all gutted, but we know to count our blessings.

We had his funeral in the little church you came to with us, the church he and Gran have attended all their lives. It was lovely. Now it's hard to believe it's over but we're trying to pick up the pieces. All our care has to be for Gran.

She'd been needed so much for so long and suddenly she's lost. We're caring for her as best we can but her grief…

I don't know how to help her and it's doing my head in.

Enough, though. You don't need to worry, we'll get through this.

Your hamper arrived yesterday. It has pride of place under the Christmas tree but we're not opening it until Christmas morning. Though I'll admit I had a peek and saw the cherry liqueurs. Thank you. That's one thing I can now remember that I can forget.

We hope you and Phoebe have a lovely Christmas Day. I suspect all the kids will text you after they open the hamper, but I thought I should give you this heads-up first.

Christmas will be strange but it'll still happen.

Love you

Sunny

He didn't move. He couldn't. Shoppers, Christmas trees, bundles of gifts on legs, had to detour around the man standing in the middle of the pavement staring at his phone.

John was dead and he hadn't known.

Sunny would be gutted.

But more… His thoughts didn't stay with Sunny. They moved tangentially to Ruby, to the lovely old lady who'd taken in her five grandchildren and loved them so fiercely. And to the rest of Sunny's family. He imagined them at the funeral, young men and women fiercely protecting their gran. Gutted with grief. Loving…

He should have been there.

Home.

Why did the word slam back and stay? Why was it so powerful it didn't let him move?

He crouched down, almost involuntarily, and gathered Phoebe up into his arms. She was almost asleep, but happy to be hugged. She nuzzled into his neck, warm and secure.

Loved.

Sunny had given him this.

Home.

The tableau in the store behind him changed its tune from a corny rendition of *Jingle Bells* to a softer, lovelier melody.

Silent Night.

Sleep in heavenly peace…

That was what Phoebe was doing, he thought as her warm little body curved into his. Sleeping in peace.

Knowing she was loved.

And across the world… Sunny would be sleeping alone because he, Max Grayland, thought independence was everything.

He thought again of that front row pew at the funeral. Of grief. Loss went with love, he thought. That was why he'd held himself so tight, so rigid, so aloof. To deny himself something he wanted to be a part of so much it was a physical pain.

Sunny…

He was walking. He was moving automatically back towards the apartment, pushing the stroller with one hand, cradling Phoebe with the other, because there was no way he was putting her down.

He needed her.

And there was another flash of insight so great it almost blindsided him. He'd taken on Phoebe's care because she needed him but now…

He needed her.

He could never go back to what he had been. His defences had been breached and he didn't want them.

And his feet kept moving. He knew what he wanted and he was a man on his way to get it.

He had four days before Christmas. No. Three days, he reminded himself because Australia was almost a day ahead.

There was so much to organise…but if there was one thing Max Grayland was good at it was organising.

There was so much to hope for…and that was one thing he wasn't good at. Max Grayland liked certainty. He liked his world being ordered. He liked…

No. He didn't like any more, he reminded himself. He loved and that was a whole new ball game.

It meant that life as he knew it was about to turn upside down.

CHAPTER THIRTEEN

IT WAS PUTTING one foot in front of the other. Going through the motions. Getting through it.

They'd discussed—briefly—going out for Christmas dinner. Taking a picnic to the park. Booking into a restaurant. Anything to take the focus off the empty chair, the empty space, the emptiness of grief. But in the end Gran needed the quietness of this place, time with her family. So the kids were all here.

Sam was manfully carving the roast, trying to pretend it was no big deal to be doing what Pa had done for years. Gran was pretending to eat. They were pretending to laugh at the dumb jokes in the bonbons. They were wearing silly party hats, thinking of stories to fill the silence. Anything…

Sunny was trying not to watch Gran. She was trying not to cry.

And there was a part of her that was trying not to think of last Christmas. Trying not to wonder what Max was doing. Trying not to think of Max and Phoebe sharing Christmas on the other side of the world.

I could have made it better for them, a little voice kept saying in the back of her head, but she only had to look at Gran to know she was right to be here.

'What goes ninety-nine thump, ninety-nine thump, ninety-nine thump?' Daisy demanded, her grin as natural as she could make it.

And they answered in chorus, 'A centipede with a wooden leg.' They'd heard this joke for years and suddenly…it made things better. A little. That they could shout the answer, that they'd shared this joke for so many Christmases.

That they were family.

Except Max wasn't here.

He wasn't family, Sunny told herself fiercely. He wasn't.

And then the doorbell rang.

'It's the timer for the pudding,' Daisy said—how could it be anything else but the cooking timer?—and Sunny's heart rate settled. It had lurched...

But then... No. She knew the sound of the timer.

She knew the sound of the doorbell.

And so did Gran. She half rose and Tom glanced at her and then at Sunny and headed for the door.

And Sunny tried hard to stay where she was. It was a crazy thought—what she'd just thought. It couldn't be.

But...

'It's Phoebe!' Tom's shout echoed through the house, from top to bottom. 'Hey, it's Phoebe and she's *growed*! Wow, she's growed! Phoebe, what have they been feeding you? Hey, gorgeous, come to Uncle Tom. And Max. Is that you under that baby stuff? Come on out. Come on in.'

And Sunny's heart forgot to race.

Sunny's heart almost stopped altogether.

There was nothing like a baby to cheer Christmas. Gran hugged Phoebe like a lifeline. Phoebe cooed and chuckled and banged a spoon on whatever Gran was eating. Gran ended up covered with soggy pudding and totally distracted and...almost happy.

Time out from grief...

'Thank you for the chocolates, young man,' she told Max. 'They're almost as good as the ones Sunny used to buy.'

The family hooted with laughter, and Sunny grinned and tried not to feel...as if she had no idea how she was feeling.

Max ate as if he hadn't eaten for a year. The kids told him the joke about the centipede and couldn't believe he'd never heard it. He talked and laughed as if he belonged.

And Sunny tried to eat, tried not to gaze at him, tried to smile, tried to figure how to get her thoughts back into some sort of order.

'I had to come,' Max had said simply as he'd arrived. He'd hugged Gran and then he'd walked around the table to where Sunny sat, feeling frozen. He'd touched her hair, a feather touch, that was all, and then he'd sat where Sam had set a fast place. But that touch…

With dinner done, the house settled for the afternoon. Phoebe napped in a makeshift cot upstairs next to Gran's bed because that was where Gran wanted her. Gran slept too, probably the first peaceful sleep she'd fallen into since Pa had died. The dishes were done. Christmas afternoon stretched as it always did, sated, sleepy, as if Christmas was over, but this time, for Sunny, it felt…it was as if the gifts hadn't been opened yet?

'So…basketball?' Tom demanded but Max shook his head.

'I need to talk to Sunny.'

And the way he said it…

The look on the kids' combined faces was priceless. They fell over themselves to gear up and get out to the hoops without looking at their sister.

They disappeared as Sunny and Max walked out of the front door, through the now beautifully kept front garden and along the lanes they'd walked twelve months ago today.

Why was he here? So much had changed, Sunny thought, yet so much stayed the same.

Her life was here, she reminded herself. If possible, she was needed even more.

'I've missed you,' Max said, and her heart seemed to clench. She couldn't handle more pressure. She loved this man. She also loved the little girl currently sleeping beside Gran but it couldn't be allowed to matter.

Her place was here.

No. Not here. Not right here. She was walking beside Max, and she thought that this was where she didn't need to be.

Oh, but she wanted...

'I haven't come to put more pressure on you,' he said. They were walking side by side, close but not as close as lovers. Close enough for friends?

That was what they were, she reminded herself. Friends who emailed once a week. Friends who'd almost been something more.

He was still talking, softly, almost to himself. 'I'd like to say I don't need you,' he said into the stillness. Their feet seemed to be walking automatically. He wasn't looking at her but at the path ahead, as if what he was saying wasn't monumentally important. 'I'd like to say everything I'm about to offer you is for you, Sunny, and has nothing to do with me. I'd like to be that selfless but I can't do it.'

'I don't... I don't understand.'

He paused then and took her hand, twisting her to face him. 'Sunny... Let me say what I've been thinking. And I've been thinking...what I offered you back in Manhattan was monumentally selfish. It was all about me. It was an offer that gave me a wife, a lover, a mother for Phoebe, a partner I could admire and love for the rest of my life. But it was all on my terms. You left and I tried to understand, but I couldn't get it. I didn't see how I could change my life for a life on your terms.'

'But...'

'No, let me finish. Sunny, three days ago I was standing in a Manhattan street watching families prepare for Christmas and your email came through. John was dead. And I stood there like I was frozen and all I could think of was that I wanted to be in that front pew at your grandfather's funeral. I wanted to be with you. But it was more than that. It was huge. I wanted to have the right to hug your gran, to hug the kids. I know this sounds dumb, maybe still even selfish, but I wanted to have the right to grieve like you were all grieving.'

He hesitated then, as if he was waiting for her to comment but she couldn't say a word. The whole world seemed to be holding its breath. Waiting for…what?

The warmth of the day was eased by the shade of the massive gum trees overhead. There were bird calls, muted but lovely, and the smell of eucalypt was everywhere. These were the sounds and smell of an Australian Christmas—but right now who was thinking of Christmas?

'Do you know what I finally figured?' Max asked at last. 'I wanted the right to be gutted.'

She stared at him, confused. 'Okay,' she confessed. 'I don't get it.'

'So I'll try and explain.' He took both her hands in his. His gaze met hers and held and her heart twisted before he even began to speak. Or maybe it didn't twist. Maybe it simply stilled. Hoped…

'Sunny, I'm the son of parents who never gave a toss,' he told her. 'I was important only because I was the heir. I was raised by a succession of nannies but even they were impermanent because I was moving all the time. My parents moved from one country to another, from one partner to another, and I was simply the kid who had to be fitted in with whoever's life I didn't complicate too much at the time. And whenever I started to love a nanny, or be fond of a step-parent, or love a puppy given to me on a whim…there was a Christmas gift that broke my heart…well, life simply moved on and what I loved was left behind.'

'Oh, Max…'

'Yeah, tough,' he said and managed a lopsided smile. 'It was nowhere near as tough as you had it, Sunny, but you know what? I came out of my childhood with an armour so thick I thought it couldn't be pierced. You, though…you

never did armour. You never could. You love and you love
and that's your thing. That's who you are, Sunny. And me...
it's taken a woman like you to pierce the armour I've built.
You showed me almost instantly the kind of life Phoebe
would have if I didn't love her. I've learned—sort of—but
it's taken me a year to realise...if I'm learning to fight to
keep Phoebe from that kind of isolation, maybe... I should
fight for me too.'

'But...how?' The world had stilled. The world held its
breath.

'By learning to be family?' His words were tentative.
'I've adopted Phoebe now—did you know? She now shares
part of your name. Phoebe Raye Grayland. I called her that
because you seem part of us, but...we need more.'

'We...we had this conversation back in Manhattan.'

'Yeah, but then I didn't get it.' He dropped her hands and
drew her in by the waist so she was curved against him. 'Back
then I thought...you and me and Phoebe would be enough.
And I could do it part-time. I could pay people to fill the
gaps. So that's what I tried. Even this Christmas when I did
my Christmas planning I decided I could play with Phoebe
in the morning and work on business imperatives—get back
to my real life—while she slept. And then your email arrived
and suddenly my life seemed...the wrong way up. And I
thought...where is my real life? It's not in the gaps of time
where Phoebe sleeps. It's not even in Manhattan. Sunny, I
need it to be with you.'

'But it won't work.' She was close to tears, immeasurably
distressed. It'd be so easy to sink into this man's arms, to
say yes, to love him for ever. But the thought of that huge,
designer furnished apartment in Manhattan, the thought of
staff to care for Phoebe so the baby wouldn't interfere with
their lives, the thought of Max being gone six days out of
seven, and on the end of his phone the rest of the time—it
was like a cold, blank wall. She'd seen how much of an ef-

fort it had cost him to step away for those weeks. She'd heard the promises he'd made to callers…

'I'll be back on deck at the end of the month. Let's keep everything on hold…'

'Your life's on hold now?' she asked, forcing herself to ask, knowing it had to be said. 'You've taken time off to come over and ask me again?'

'You think this is the same?' His hold on her tightened as if he was fearful she might disappear. 'Sunny, I've had an epiphany.'

'That sounds…painful?'

He grinned but his smile was uncertain. 'It was,' he told her. 'I had it when your email came through, right there on the streets of Manhattan, and it almost knocked me sideways. I was bumped by about six Christmas trees while I was coming to terms with it. And maybe those trees bumped some sense into my thick head. Sunny, what if we make it all about you? What if…instead of asking you to be part of my life, if I ask to be part of your life?'

She was struggling here. Really struggling. *Keep it light,* she told herself desperately. *Do not allow yourself to hope…*

'What? Share my mop?' she managed. 'I'm not sure the hotel approves of job-sharing.'

'Are you so attached to your mop you wouldn't hand it in if a better offer came your way?'

'It's…it's a very good mop.' This was dumb but it was all she could come up with. 'It's industrial strength with a nice blue handle.'

'I've seen it.'

'No, you haven't. My job's been upgraded. I only mop in an emergency now and they've issued me a new one. Didn't you even notice my last mop was ancient?'

'No.' His smile was tender. 'How could I? I was too busy noticing you.'

'Compliments won't get you mop sharing.' This was ridiculous, but that was how this conversation felt. Ridiculous.

But Max's words didn't sound ridiculous at all.

'Okay, here's the thing,' he told her tenderly, lovingly. 'Three days ago I stood on a Manhattan street and watched families. All sorts of families. Friends, kids, grandparents, lovers. I watched love of all sorts, people getting ready for Christmas. Messy Christmases. Christmases in all sorts of circumstances. And even though I'd just adopted Phoebe it didn't seem the same. But I stood there and thought of you as a kid making sock puppets for your family. I thought of you fighting for your siblings, putting them first. When I proposed eleven months ago that's what I thought I was buying. I wanted that kind of commitment, Sunny. I wanted it for me and for Phoebe. But what I didn't see until now was that…it has to come from me. I got it wrong. Sunny, I want to be allowed to fight for you. More… I want to be allowed to need you, as the kids, as your gran needs you. But I want the rest too. I want you to need me. I love you, Sunny, and I need us to be a family. I want to be a part of your family, and I'll do…whatever it takes.'

'You…you already…you've said…'

'That I'll send you to university. That I'll pay for nannies, housekeepers. That I'll pay for your family here to be looked after. Yes, I said all that, and you know what? It cost me nothing. Because there was no me in the equation. Sunny, now I'm asking you to marry me, and in return… whatever you want…'

'I don't have a price.' It was a snap; frustration, fear, everything she had was in that word. Did he not get it?

'I'm not talking price,' he said, evenly now as if he finally understood what she was saying. 'I'm talking me. My commitment to your life. My love. Sunny, how would you feel if I moved here? If we did this big old house up so it'll last another hundred years…?'

'It's not ours,' she whispered, trying fiercely to be practical. 'It's a life tenancy until Gran dies.'

'Then we find the person who eventually inherits and make them an offer they can't refuse—we can do that.'

'You can't move here. Your life's in Manhattan.'

'My apartment's in Manhattan. My life's all over the world. Do you know how much time I spend in the air? But that can stop. It will stop.'

'It's what you are.'

'It's what I've been raised to be. It's not what I want to be for the rest of my life. My company's full of extraordinary talent. With my father gone, I can run things the way I want. I can control things here as well as in Manhattan. And I hear there are very good architecture courses in Australia.'

'Max, I don't want a nanny!'

'You won't need one. Phoebe's not your responsibility. She's mine.'

'But I love her.' The words were out before she could stop them and Max's expression changed.

'Of course you do. That's your specialty and that's pretty much what I expected you to say. Which is part of what I've figured. That loving me shouldn't mean loving anyone else any less. Take me as an example if you like. Twelve months ago I didn't love anyone. Now… I love Phoebe. The pain when I knew Pa was dead was like a kick in the guts. I care for your Gran and for Daisy and Sam and Chloe and Tom. And there's more. Twelve months ago I hardly knew my housekeeper and now…not only do I know about every one of her grandchildren, she even carted me out so Phoebe and I could help her choose gifts. And Karen, our nanny… She and her little boy… They've learned to love Phoebe and in turn they've twisted their way into my heart too. I think… if you do agree to my proposal…that I'll leave them in my apartment in caretaker mode. With Eliza, too. Karen dreams of being a potter. With Eliza's help to care for Harry, she could do that.'

'You'd let…you'd have them stay in that apartment…?'

'It'd still be there, then,' he said. 'A base when we…if we wanted to visit New York. Because there might be times…'

'Max…'

'Because I would be busy,' he said, with the air of someone putting all their cards on the table and the consequences would have to play out. 'Sunny, I can't let go of the corporation. It's too big, too important; it has the power to affect too many lives.'

'And you care about it.' Her vision was starting to blur. She never wept but her cheeks were wet now. 'You want it to make a difference.'

'I do,' he admitted. 'Dad did so much damage but he's left me in a position where not only can I right the damage, I can move the company forward to do great things. But…' He took a deep breath. 'Sunny, I used to think I could do it on my own but I can't. I know that now. Sure, I can do a little, but with you beside me, with my family around me, with love… Sunny, we could conquer the world.'

'The world…'

'Why not? But you… When it comes to the world or you… Sunny, you'll always come first. You always will. So how about it, my love? Will you trust me enough to put your hand in mine? To take me on? To haul me back when I get out of line, when I stop remembering what's important?'

And then he paused and the pause stretched out. He was looking down into her eyes and she was trying her hardest to meet his gaze but tears were tracking down her face. She couldn't stop them. She needed a tissue but her hands were in his and there was no way she was letting go.

And then he kissed her, gently, on each cheek, kissing away her tears.

'Sunny,' he said gently, softly, lovingly. 'Will you teach me to love? Will you let me into your heart?'

And there was only one answer. Of course there was.

Together they could take on the world?

There was no need for that, she thought mistily. Who needed the world?

Max was here. Max loved her.

'You're already there,' she whispered back. 'Oh, Max... oh, my love, you can share my mop any time you want.'

Was Christmas the time for a wedding?

Yes, it was. It hadn't seemed right to hold it straight after they'd lost Pa. It had seemed somehow fitting that they waited for a full year. In truth they might have waited longer—they were so close, so truly family there seemed little need for a formal wedding and Gran's grief needed time to play out. But finally Gran decided to shed her grief enough to move on. On a warm spring day, while Sunny and Max were helping Phoebe plant strawberries—with mixed results—she came to find them.

Fixing Max with a gimlet eye, she made her demand. 'Well, young man. When are you going to make an honest woman out of my granddaughter?'

'Sunny's been wearing my engagement ring for ten months,' Max said, grinning and tugging Sunny to stand beside him. 'She's had my heart for much longer. I believe we're waiting for you to say the word.'

'Because?'

'Because we want you to be happy at our wedding,' Max said simply. 'Sunny won't have it any other way, and neither will I. If you feel you can cope with a celebration...'

'I knew it.' Ruby smiled mistily at both of them. 'I was just lying down on my bed thinking bridal and I thought... I bet they're waiting for me. And then I thought Pa would have my hide if I don't say something. So how about Christmas Eve? All the kids will be home. What a truly splendid time that'd be.'

So here he was, in the little church he'd first attended two days after he'd met Sunny. He'd expected this to be a small affair but Gran was having none of it and she'd bulldozed Sunny and Max along with her.

'All your friends from the hotel, Sunny—I know you haven't worked there for almost a year but they were nice to you. And Max, your friends from New York and those nice ladies who look after your apartment…'

'It's too far to expect anyone to come,' Max told her. 'And Karen and Eliza can't…' And then he stopped because he thought… Why not use a fraction of what his company earned to bring Eliza and Karen and Harry, Karen's little son, here? They'd been part of the first year of Phoebe's life and somehow they were no longer employees. They were friends.

On this day there were so many people here that he once would have called acquaintances but with Sunny by his side he somehow now called friends.

And Max was aware of them, and glad of them, but right now, as the music soared to announce the arrival of his bride, he had no room for anything but Sunny.

First came the ring-bearers, two tots, Karen's four-year-old Harry leading two-year-old Phoebe, both intent, serious, knowing the importance of the job in hand. Or Harry did. Phoebe simply thought that if Harry was carrying a cushion with a ring, then she would too.

Then came the bridesmaids, Daisy and Chloe, because how could they not be bridesmaids? Sam and Tom were standing beside him as groomsmen, because that seemed right too.

Then came Ruby, dressed in royal purple. The maids wore pink, but: 'Purple's such a stately colour and if I can't feel

stately today I never can,' Ruby had decreed. She was ma-
tron of honour, for how could she be anything else?

'You don't want to give me away?' Sunny had asked and
Ruby had chuckled.

'My love, you've stood on your own two feet since the
day you were born. You're giving your heart and you're
taking one in return and you can do that all on your own.'

And she surely could.

And now she was at the doorway, starting her walk down
the aisle towards him.

Max thought briefly of the great churches of Manhattan,
of the world. He thought briefly of the photographs of his
parents' wedding, a society wedding like no other.

This was right though. This was…real.

Outside, a cacophony of grass parrots was competing
with Handel for sound honours. The church was surrounded
by a sea of bcrimson bottlebrush. It was Christmas but more.
The whole country seemed festive, as if this was truly something to celebrate.

And it was. For Sunny was walking towards him, ethe-
real in her loveliness. Her gown had been her grandmother's,
cream silk with a high mandarin collar, tiny pearl buttons,
a tight fitted bodice and a skirt that seemed to almost float.
She'd left her curls hanging free but her sisters had threaded
tiny rosebuds through. She trod steadily down the aisle,
purposeful as ever, and he thought he'd never seen anyone
so lovely.

He couldn't take his eyes from her. She smiled and smiled
and as she reached him, as her gaze met his, as her hand
slid into his palm, he felt as if he'd been granted the world.

'Want to see my bouquet?' she whispered and it brought
him up with a jolt. *What?*

He hauled his eyes from hers to the flowers she was carrying, a magnificent arrangement of crimson bottlebrush, white
gypsophila—baby's breath—and four perfect frangipani…

And tucked inside was a tiny bottle, label up.

Stain remover?

'I figure I met you trying to remove a stain,' she whispered, smiling and smiling. 'And I didn't succeed on one spot, but you know what? We've cleaned up so much more. Loneliness, distrust, distance… So I thought…maybe we should go into this prepared. Stain remover out front. Just in case.'

And he grinned. His gorgeous, wonderful Sunny. It was a wonder she wasn't carrying her mop.

'Great idea,' he whispered. 'But I can't see the need. I pretty much see our future as stain-free. You want to give the vicar a say and get ourselves married? Put our trust in love?'

'Yes,' she said and beamed and, even though it was out of order to do it right then, she stood on tiptoes and kissed him. 'Yes, I do, Max Grayland. You and me and stain remover… We can take on the world.'

'Let's start with each other.'

'Let's,' she said and he kissed her back.

The music ceased. Even the parrots in the trees outside seemed to hush.

Christmas…the time of miracles.

Maybe this was a small miracle in the scheme of things but right now it felt huge. It was huge.

It was one marriage between two people who truly loved so, without further ado, Sunny Raye and Max Grayland turned together to become one.

* * * * *

WE'RE HAVING A
MAKEOVER...

We'll still be bringing you the very
best in romance from authors you
love…all with a fabulous new look!

Look out for our stylish new logo, too

MILLS & BOON

COMING JANUARY 2018

MILLS & BOON®

Cherish™

EXPERIENCE THE ULTIMATE RUSH OF FALLING IN LOVE

A sneak peek at next month's titles...

In stores from 14th December 2017:

- **The Italian Billionaire's New Year Bride** – Scarlet Wilson *and* **Her Soldier of Fortune** – Michelle Major
- **The Prince's Fake Fiancée** – Leah Ashton *and* **The Arizona Lawman** – Stella Bagwell

In stores from 28th December 2017:

- **Tempted by Her Greek Tycoon** – Katrina Cudmore *and* **Just What the Cowboy Needed** – Teresa Southwick
- **United by Their Royal Baby** – Therese Beharrie *and* **Claiming the Captain's Baby** – Rochelle Alers

---

Just can't wait?
Buy our books online before they hit the shops!
www.millsandboon.co.uk

Also available as eBooks.

MILLS & BOON®

EXCLUSIVE EXTRACT

Snowed in together on New Year's Eve, their attraction explodes…! Leaving Italian billionaire Matteo Bianchi to wonder if he could finally open his heart and make Phoebe Gates his bride.

Read on for a sneak preview of
**THE ITALIAN BILLIONAIRE'S
NEW YEAR BRIDE**

He could still taste her, and he'd never felt so hungry for more. Every part of his body urged him to continue.

But he took a deep breath and rested his forehead against hers, his hand still tangled in her hair. Phoebe's breathing was labored and heavy, just like his. But she didn't push for anything else. She seemed happy to take a moment too. Her chest was rising and falling in his eye line as they stayed for a few minutes with their heads together.

Everything felt too new. Too raw. Did he even know what he was doing here?

"Happy New Year," he said softly. "At least I'm guessing that's why we can still hear fireworks."

"There are fireworks outside? I thought they were inside." Her sparkling dark eyes met his gaze and she smiled. "Wow," she said huskily.

He let out a laugh. "Wow," he repeated.

Her hand was hesitant, reaching up, then stopping, then

reaching up again. She finally rested it against his chest, the fingertips pausing on one of the buttons of his shirt.

His mind was willing her to unfasten it. But she just let it sit there. The warmth of her fingertips permeating through his designer shirt. He could sense she wanted to say something, and it made him want to stumble and fill the silence.

For the first time in his life, Matteo Bianchi was out of his depth. It was a completely alien feeling for him. In matters of the opposite sex he was always in charge, always the one to initiate things, or, more likely, finish them. He'd never been unsure of himself, never uncomfortable.

But from the minute he'd met this woman with a warm smile and thoughtful heart, he just hadn't known how to deal with her. She had a way of looking at him as he answered a question that let him know his blasé, offhand remarks didn't wash with her. She didn't push. She didn't need to. He was quite sure that, if she wanted to, Phoebe Gates would take no prisoners. But the overwhelming aura from Phoebe was one of warmth, of kindness and sincerity. And it was making his heart beat quicker every minute.

Don't miss
THE ITALIAN BILLIONAIRE'S
NEW YEAR BRIDE
by Scarlet Wilson

Available January 2018

www.millsandboon.co.uk